THE RUNNERS REVELATION

Book One of The Runners series

Matthew Normand

Matthew Normand

Raw Fiction Publication

Raw Fiction Publication
writingrawfiction@gmail.com
www.writingrawfiction.com

Published in the United States by Raw Fiction Publication.

Normand, Matthew
The Runners Revelation / Matthew Normand. – First Raw Fiction Edition – (The
    Runners series ; 1)
ISBN: 979-8-9879497-1-9 / 1. Imaginary wars and battles – Fiction. 2. Voyages and
    travels – Fiction. I. Title.

For you, the seventh Runner.

THE RUNNERS
REVELATION

Man is not defined with what he has but with what he sacrifices.
-Barloc

Prologue

After Simul, the Guardian of the Temple of Death, defeated the being known as the Walker, the Temple came to a decision. Despite his knowledge and prowess, Simul could not extinguish the life force of the Walker, only contain it. As such, three gemstones of ruby, diamond, and citrine were crafted alongside a sword scholars at the Nexlor named *Azrael*. They were the final legacy of a conflict that left the nation of Pactus in a state of utter despair and desolation, a land now called the Void.

These artifacts, despite containing the essence of the Walker, could not remain together. After experiencing retaliation from the Scar, Simul decided to depart from his diseased home of Pactus to dispense of what remained.

He crossed the ravaged lands of the Void, through the Forest of the Received, and into Etherine where its meadows emptied into the bosom of Admah, one of the four large and expansive Nomases. This was where he scattered the gems and sword, across plains and mountains and seas, to depths and heights and nations where the astray and bold alike could not reach them. This was Simul's last great achievement. He died shortly thereafter. His journal and, thus, his legacy were buried in time.

Many of old have searched for the gems, forgetting from where they originated. Many know naught of *Azrael*; after two hundred years, like the Giants of Es'tal'mis or the settlers from the First Landing, the sword's tale became hearsay. Although it still bears the scars from the Fall of Pactus, the lands of Admah have swallowed the gems within its belly. The remnants of the Walker sleep undisturbed.

None would bring them together again.

None would reunite the gems with *Azrael*.

None except for one.

One who would bring about decimation alike to that of the Walker.

Chry's Inception

I

The farmhouse was near a wind-weathered road, its trail meager with travelers ever since the Temple of Health incident. The rosewood roof of the home was limp with a pride ruined by decades of sun, and its bent frame tossed a long shadow over the face of the Wastelands. The dead skies above were desiccated of clouds, and dead lands were sweltered by illusions of oases.

Creatures unlucky enough to live in the Wastelands were at least smart enough to stay beneath ground. Dry-Mouth Cobras killed one another quickly then dragged the corpses down below the hardpan where their young hungered for a meal. Desert beetles soaked in the dawn, their bumpy shells sweating with dew before retreating, not to be seen again until the first signs of dusk.

Chry was not so fortunate. He did not have the luxury of burying his head beneath the hardpan and forgetting that he lived here. At sixteen years reckon, he alone was obliged to protect his farmhouse and grandmother against the hardships of the Wastelands. His crops needed constant maintenance. A single plot of maize sprouted near the farmhouse, a few knuckles into its growth. Their stocks were limp, their leaves thirsty, the soil drier than what he would have liked.

You'd like to get away from here. That's *what you'd like.*

There were also fallow plots from years heretofore he hoped to cultivate in the years to come. However, hope, as with those who wandered through the Wastelands, was flimsy. One plot was difficult enough to sustain, and he could never reckon how his father and grandfather could plough and harrow land this unyielding. It was another problem his father had left him.

If it weren't for Gladion, he thought but dismissed it.

The day was at its end. He needed to finish. In truth, there was more left to do outside—there always was—but the daylight was nearly spent, and he knew grandmother was waiting for him on the porch. She always did.

Chry could not leave her alone.

This is not your choice but your obligation, his father had told him.

As the sun dipped a toe into the hardpan, Chry busied himself with the vital things: water and pigs. The well laid on the same side as the pig pen, the roof a faded auburn rosewood, added three years heretofore just before his parents died. After sending the rusted and beaten pail down and pulling a gulp of water up, he set it aside next to the slumping house and guided Mister and Missus Swiggle into their bare, tiny pens. Mister limped after a quiet Missus, his snout nudging her pulp, pinkish flesh.

With both the Swiggles and his skeletal brown gelding, Simul, safe inside their stables, Chry rounded the house where the brilliant sunset stabbed his eyes. He flinched, his vision erupting into a thousand stars, and laid a protective hand over his eyes, grunting condemnations his father would not have approved of.

Who the plos cares? He's gone. Mother's gone. All that's left is grandmother and her needs.

From a distance, he could hear the rhythmic creaking of wood.

When his eyes cleared the stars, Chry peered out onto a splintery porch. Beside the setting sun rocked his grandmother on the ruins of her rocking chair. The rocker creaked along with the boards. Any of the wood once painted white had been seared off by the glare of the sun. Only peelings remained, and these, too, would soon be flayed off by the nightly winds.

The old woman herself looked as if the hardpan had stolen her will, the sun her flesh, and the Wastelands her dearest loves. Her hair was the steel of metal and frizzled above her slumping shoulders. The spoiled spots of her scalp told the long story of time spent in the Wastelands. Sun-burned skin sagged at the cheeks, along the brow, and wrinkles crinkled beside her eyes like chicken feet. Behind him the pigs squealed with the farmhouse.

When he mounted the first step, which screamed to all of Admah that Chry had finally arrived, his grandmother rolled her head toward him. In *his* head, he heard her neck crackle and thought that the bones he'd seen while riding to Domum would sound just like that if they were alive and moving.

He should've felt pity at the thought. He *knew* he should have. He didn't.

Her crusted lips curled into a wan but warm smile.

"Suppa's ready me dear," she croaked, the words thorny inside her throat. "Come in n 'ave ya sum broth. Wouldn't want me grandson to stah-ve, now would I?"

Stepping onto the porch, pail swishing in his hand, Chry tried smiling, but it soon shriveled.

Another day of Dry-Mouth broth, he thought as if already tasting the pulpy soup slime down his throat. *Another day.*

"You don't have to worry about me so much," he said. "I'll survive."

She waved it away.

"Nunsense, leta grandma worry about 'er grandson."

She then grabbed at the armrests and pushed her fragile frame up with trembling arms. His heart screamed to help her, help her already, why wasn't he helping her. But he stood there. Waited for her to do it herself like she had wanted.

She now stood on equally trembling legs.

"It's the only thang I 'ave to do out 'ere, ye know."

Chry strained to give her another one of those smiles.

Tend to the farm, he reminded himself. *Care for grandmother. And whatever you do, don't think about your future in the Wastelands.*

5

He tried. He really, really did.

Chry opened the door hanging by a hinge—he'd have to fix that later—and led his grandmother inside.

From small steps to smaller shuffles, his grandmother guided her hand across the groaning walls. Pail in hand, Chry placed his other on her hip and watched her hands lined with every river of color between blue and purple. He didn't have to think to support her. It was ingrained into him. Taught to follow and obey, never to act. Sometimes, she'd mutter against the support, as if the decay of her mouth was full of mush, saying something about how she could "wak meself, thank ye very much." She couldn't. Both of them knew it—one careless glance would shatter her.

Gloom suffocated the narrow hall before a familiar glow saved him. Entering it brought to life an open fireplace surrounded by stone bricks. Flames whimpered beneath a black-iron kettle, too weak to cast away the shadows sleeping within the corners. From inside the kettle drifted the smell of a meaty, tender broth, relieving him of a long day out in the field.

Whatever complaints he had about the taste—and there were many—its smell was always welcoming.

An alder wood table—sun-bleached, missing a board, and brought down by Gladion, a family friend, during one of his visits—hugged the wall across from the kettle. Over it hung a slanted canvas of a young Chry smiling between his parents, edged by a gilded border faded to a bygone ocher.

His father, painted in what Aimee said was various layers of oil, was an older version of Chry: slender neck, slick black hair, a thin face, and slim lips. The only difference Chry could reckon, when looking into the polished bronze plate upstairs, was that his father wore thin-rimmed spectacles perched on the bridge of his nose. That and a stern face, asking not to be interrupted.

Ask. When did he ever ask me to do anything? It was always tell, *never* ask.

Unlike his father, though, his mother was someone whose

unbroken sentences and graceful voice he could listen to until the candle clock extinguished. Staring at the painting, he reckoned her as he always had: beautiful. Long, golden hair braided over her shoulder, a friendly smile with delicate lips, tan skin, and the deepest blue eyes he had ever seen…

Well, almost the deepest.

In the kitchen, his grandmother tried shuffling to the kettle but Chry wouldn't let her. He put a gentle hand on her shoulder to stop her.

"Sit, grandmother. I'll fetch you a bowl," Chry said as he squeezed past her. The boards squealed with each step.

"Ah," it rolled off her tongue as a bitter quiet, but Chry was beyond her grasp before she could outright refuse. "Ye work too 'ard, me dear."

Setting the pail aside and stirring the rosewood ladle in the kettle, he could feel those watery eyes judging his back. He tried not to tense. The broth simmered, the house moaned, stomachs grumbled. And still he couldn't look back at her. Wouldn't.

Eventually, there came the soft sound of feet shuffling away. He waited to hear that weak pattering of a chair being dragged across the floor before mumbling, "It doesn't bother me. None at all."

Smelling steam, Chry slopped the broth of meat and corn into bowls as appealing as their home. He took them, warm beneath his fingers, and set them on the table where his grandmother sat. Eyes downcast, he glanced at his grandmother staring into her bowl, her wrinkles never lifting from the clumpy broth.

He gave away to an imperceptible sigh.

Beside the kettle, a pewter candle holder posed as a half-beaten Dry-Mouth. He snatched the sickly wax candle within the holder and lit it with the fire beneath the kettle. *Last one we have*, he thought, *another good excuse to visit Domum again*. A flame whimpered alive as its tender glow carved his cheeks. Its wisps of smoke smelt of a woody prison.

Candle in holder, Chry filled their cups with clean water from the pail before dousing the fire. Steam hissed and billowed around the kettle and up the mud and stick chimney.

With cups on the table and the candle between them, Chry slumped into a splintery chair opposite of his grandmother. His body breathed with gratitude.

After so many tiresome tasks, he was just glad the day was done.

II

They slurped in silence.

Outside a glass window veiled in dirt was a dying dusk. Between them the candle's waxy tears pooled along a rusty bottom. Its flickering glow brought them close and embraced their worn, solemn faces, shadows quivering in a dance that reminded him of Oscar Redback when his wife, Agatha, was stabbing at him with a fiery hot poker.

I haven't seen that man get out of his rocker so fast in my life.

He could have smiled at the misfortune of the grouchy hostler. The emotion welled inside his throat but did not rise. He just looked at the shadow of his grandmother and reckoned how much more alive it was than its keeper.

She raised a spoon of broth. Her hand shook so much, droplets of broth spilled and plopped back into the bowl like rain. Another thing that was all too rare around here.

Eternity went by. Then she asked, "How's da corn dis Son?"

Chry gave his usual response as he had done every Ainason. "Plenty, like last Son."

Ah, so you blame your parents for lying, but when you do it, everyone is expected to guzzle it down like the Swiggles during morning feed. Beautiful Chry. Just beautiful.

Even though she knew it was a lie, she only nodded slightly and said nothing else as she focused on slurping her broth. He gave her a brief look before continuing to eat.

From outside, the winds rustled the cornfield, whistled through, and brought the oppressiveness of night. Its bitter, cold fingers crawled through the cracks of the home. There was the constant dripping of the candle clock and the plopping of grandmother spilling her broth. The four walls of the kitchen enclosed him. Mister and Missus Swiggle squealed. Chry tried eating quickly, his foot tapping restlessly. The impatience to go lay his head down on his straw pallet and pray for dawn to arrive compelled him further.

He slurped the dregs of his broth, but before he could leave the table, he had to tell her.

"I'm going to Domum after dawn." She didn't respond, so Chry continued. "Hoping to buy some more Edua leaves and wax. Mayhap I can barter for a bit of A Mother's Touch, too, if Eulgash is willing."

When she only nodded—trembled more like—he should've stopped, counted his blessings, tossed his bowl into the pail from the well, and scurried upstairs for the night. A nod was all he needed. Confirmation. At dawn, he'd hurry to Domum before his grandmother could think to ask anything more.

Of course, he didn't stop there.

"I also hope to visit Gladion's as well, if I have enough light to do so, that is."

His grandmother rasped a giggle his mother would've had if given another forty years. Coming from his grandmother though, it was downright horrifying.

"Tah court his daughter, eh?" She croaked a laugh leading into a fit of grating coughs. Afterward, she gathered her wrinkles into thought. "I dink her title was…" They broadened into a smile. "Aimee, wasn't it? Was dat 'er name, me dear? Do ye 'member?"

His cheeks burned metal red. It's not like she was that forgetful. Grandmother knew *exactly* who Aimee was and why he wanted to see her. She had embarrassed him heretofore by mentioning his longing for her and would continue to embarrass him until her body was carried to the Gardens. No, she hadn't lost her rattles. A lot of cobwebs in there, aye, but all there and all ready to humble him.

"I…Um…Uh…" His palms were clammy, and his eyes must've been one slap away from falling out of his skull and bouncing from their stalks. He looked down at his tan trousers, but the image wouldn't go away. "I just, uh, never-"

He couldn't take this.

He threw himself out of the chair, taking his bowl to the pail. His grandmother never stirred from the candle's comfort, laughing with a quiet croak as if this made it bearable.

He hid within the shadows, dipped a flimsy rag into a pot bloated with the Silver Oil Gladion brought last Moon, and rubbed it against the brothy bowl.

Rub, rub, clean, rub, rub, clean, rub, rub, rub...

Watery oil splashed everywhere. It was of little importance. He just prayed to Eulgash that his grandmother would decide their talk was getting dull and continue with her troubles of slurping broth from a half empty spoon.

Of course, she didn't. He was a fool to think she would. She wouldn't be his grandmother if she had.

"Me dear, ye nothin' to be ashamed abou'." She tried giggling an I'm-just-as-innocent-as-you-are giggle, but it crumbled beneath another raspy cough.

Shame waved over him. Just hearing her like this, vulnerable and fragile...It reminded him that she did not have many more Sons left. Soon, he'd take her to Domum, and the Gardeners would take her to the Gardens within the Forest where all his forefathers slept.

I wish her death would come sooner then.

He felt regret immediately thereafter. The thought had not come from his own will but from some insidious pang inside his gut. It was uncontrollable. And yet, as much as he regretted this, he would not have thought it if it didn't hold an inkling of truth.

The coughing died down to a hawking. She was like an old, skinned, and wrinkled cat coughing up a ball of hair. She leaned down and spat into a fat, iron pot by her foot. The metal tinked. He had never looked inside that pot and there was no chance he'd start now.

She cleared her throat again, looked as if she were about to spit, but then swallowed instead.

"Gladion told me abou' ye and Aimee last Moon." She continued. "Aye, when he came to play swords width ye."

Gladion. Aye. Gladion because who else could it have been besides the girl's father? A caravan? A Dry-Mouth?

"I…" He mumbled, tugged at his shirt, somehow forgetting that his hands were still soaking wet. "I…Aye…I'll try to see her."

He still wouldn't look at her. Her eroded fangs were latched onto his back. Stiff, he rubbed harder on his bowl to clean the filth he couldn't see. Every time he plunged it into the pail, the oil would splash over its rim and splatter.

More silence before she said, "Ye know, me dear, you 'ave no reason to stay 'ere. Like I've said 'eretofore, Gladion 'as offered to look afta—"

"No."

The word sliced through the gloom. His hands stopped. He stared into the sudsy oil of the pail as coils of seriousness compressed his lungs.

"We don't need him to. Like *I've* said heretofore, we're well where we are, so there's no need."

Letting the rag sink into the pail, Chry dried the rosewood bowl and his hands with another rag. His fingers were as wrinkled as the person behind him and still retained a slippery touch from the Silver Oil. He had passed the point of caring; sleep and wool clothes were waiting for him.

His grandmother, after making a noise between a disgruntled gurgle and a grunt, spoke. Her voice could have lashed at him if only years younger.

"Don't act da fool width me, Chry. Gladion comes every turn of de Moon to brin' supplies and ya've *still* been leavin' for Domum more n more. Da field look worse now den it did when ya father was tillin' it. N don't act like I can't see dat look in ya eyes. Dey are da same eyes ya father had. Once ye get dat look, ye neva return.

"N ye dink I blame ye? Neva. But Eulgash be damned if I don't say it 'ere n now: leav'. Stop ah worrin' abou' da farm. Yar young but yar ass is too scrannel to be out in da field all day. Gladion will take care ov me well width Betsy n *dat* ye know is true. N the farm? It 'as to be left sumday and dat day is dis day, I say."

He heard her wet her crusty lips, swallow, then rasp so low, he strained to hear her.

"Pray. If not for me dan for yeself, me child."

His hands were rubbing together like two Dry-Mouths anxious about who'd be tanned next. Near the end of her speech, when he reckoned his squirming hands, he stopped them.

No.

Not now.

He left the pail and stepped from the shadows. His boyish eyes were raw, uneasy... Tired. Done with talking. Everyone—from his grandmother to Gladion to Aimee on top of the Vassal's home, even to Jayce Rucker when passing his hovel—had asked when he'd be leaving this pisspot of a place. He'd heard the question so many times of late that it had grown just as tiresome as tilling the hardpan or hauling up a pail of water. He wanted to hear none of it. He already knew what was needed from him—what his father and forefathers required from him. There were no words needed to convince him otherwise. This was where he'd live. This was where he'd die. This was where he'd stay. This was his...

Home, father had said. *Protect Clostra. Protect the house. Protect the farm. This is not your choice but your obligation.*

Oh, stop lying to yourself, Chry. Your father and mother are dead, Gladion is willing, and the only reason you don't leave is because you're too...

He knelt beside her and held her hand. It was the coldness of a corpse, and he felt each band of her blood. He stared into those watery eyes. For once, Chry was decisive.

"You're wrong. I've no reason to leave...And every reason to stay."

Her mouth parted to argue but then closed. She just stared. Within her eyes, beneath a rheumy film, was an emotion he couldn't reckon.

He wanted to say he tried to understand what she felt, but in truth he didn't. He was too tired to try. His straw pallet, and Aimee the next day, was all he could think about.

"Aye, me dear," she trembled a nod. "Ye know best."

Relieved, he smiled. She smiled back.

Afterward, Chry took her bowl, corn kernels and Dry-Mouth meat bathing inside half-slurped broth, then disappeared back into the shadows.

His grandmother slumped back into her chair. It creaked as if pained by neglect. The candle's flame danced on the table next to the missing board. Soon it would stop. Soon it would extinguish. Soon there would be nothing more but darkness.

III

Chry awoke to the golden shreds of dawn, quickly ate his plain corn and Dry-Mouth porridge, flew out of the house, and tended to the crops. Like he'd been taught, he had grouped them close and used wooden stakes for those likely to lean. Luckily, none of the stalks had blown over during the night, but he'd still sometimes wake to a stalk bowing as if panting after running away from a Lanke horde.

He gathered water from the well—it took half as long as it did the day heretofore, his hands eager and swift—and watered the crops. The soil accepted greedily. Their stringy tails were still too yellow but given another two Moons, they'd be ripe enough to harvest.

Smile beaming, Chry continued on to pack the Swiggle's troughs with mush from yesterday's broth, this day's porridge, and straw. They snorted with delight. He actually chuckled a little then returned to the farmhouse.

The ball of fire was stepping onto the hardpan as Chry searched the home for what they would need: herbs, salt, cured Dry-Mouth meat, wax. Though, if he was being truthful, grandmother had been right. He didn't *need* to go to Domum; their stock of Sun-Fire's Embrace and A

Mother's Touch, corn, meat and food, Edua leaves and straw, could support them for another turn of the Moon, two if they didn't eat too much during dawn and dusk. The wax was a possible worry. They wouldn't have it for their candle clocks around the house during the night, only a fire below the kettle with sticks and steel. But they were nearing a Weary Moon when Gladion would return to bring them more supplies.

Anywise, hunger and supplies were not the things filling his thoughts.

To barter, he threw two small jars of dried corn into a patched knapsack and a handful of moxam from a drawer next to the kettle, not really counting how many there were. He'd worry about that thereafter.

Finally, he said his farewells, told his grandmother he'd be back home by dusk, saddled Simul who pawed the ground with excitement, then rode off to Domum with thoughts of Aimee on his mind.

IV

On horseback, a trip to Domum from the farmhouse usually took about four marks of a candle clock. He had traveled to Domum, by himself and with his parents, more times than there were crops in his field. Losing his bearings, like so many others had, was not a concern.

Even so, it was never pleasant riding so close to the Forest of the Lost. It seemed so... disturbing. Chry could feel, even furlongs away, its trees a thin line of innocent green, an uneasiness inside him like a handful of Desert Beetles scuttling around in his stomach. Closer, like the time when his father took him into the Gardens, and he swore he'd start hearing those little voices again, whispering their nonsense between the branches.

Another concern was the Lanke: deranged, howling savages roaming the Wastelands to raid, kill, and rape. They usually didn't travel this far East. He reckoned the Forest had something to do with that, but there was also the War down South the merchants always rambled about...Or was there still a War? Were they still fighting? Arbiter, he couldn't say for certain. Really, in the end, all he cared about was that the Lanke—with their twitches, grins, wild hair, scarred bodies, broken Low Speak, and garbs torn from dead limbs—were well away from him and his farmhouse...and that Chry never rode deep enough into the Wastelands to encounter them. If they ever *did* get close, waving their rusty weapons and howling their howls...Well, that's why he clashed swords with Gladion every Moon, right? To defend the farm. To defend his home.

Vigilance, as his father had always said, *was never to be taken for granted.*

Simul clopped along, whipping his thin mane at a fly. With his rump sore, Chry searched for a comfortable spot for his manhood on the cobra skin saddle his forefather had passed down to his father and his father to him. He couldn't find one. The stitching was frayed and loose with the leather worn white. Under the heat, the air sizzled, a bucket of sweat had painted his back, and he swore the hairs across his neck were burning like little candles. He wished he had brought his hood for shade but in his rush, he had forgotten it on the nightstand beside his pallet.

He sighed.

Thinking of his father and the Lanke had reminded him of a past memory, away from the drudgery of the present to a day beside the well with the sun falling into a late dusk. He had been eleven years reckon, five years heretofore. His father was back home teaching him how to work the rope and sheave inside the well so if he ever needed to repair it, he could. Chry, a squirt, as Gladion would say, did not remember a lick of what his father had told him but nodded whenever his father looked at his long, blank face. He found this effective.

But near the end of his father's teachings, his stern face tightened inward like he had forgotten something and then peered East to the empty flatland. Without looking, Chry asked him what was out there, what did he see, but couldn't whisper two words before his father snapped at him for silence. Chry flinched then shut his mouth, casting a

15

frighteningly childish look out at the Wastelands.

There wasn't much to see—the light behind him was dying fast and only the mists of darkness rode across the winds. Mister and Missus Swiggle snorted in their pen. The tin bucket clanged against the well's stone. He felt the wind ruffle and tug at his hair. He kicked at pebbles, glancing once, twice at his father whose face had hardened. He shivered away each time.

Before long, he noticed something out there in the gloom. Movement. The movement of bodies that might as well have been the shadowy bodies of Kemals—folk whose Halorda were said by the House of Worship to be corrupted in life and now condemned to wander across the Wastelands forevermore. Chry wasn't fooled though. Those bodies moving toward them weren't Kemals, no.

They were folk. Not one or two but many. Too many.

His father barked for him to go inside. *Now.* Chry, of course, couldn't. A scuttle of jittery beetles had infested his thoughts with what these folk could be and could only narrow it to one explanation: Lanke. The mere idea petrified him. He was eleven years reckon, and he thought himself ready, but he wasn't. At that moment, he reckoned he'd never be. Fortunately, the growl of his father diverted those fears.

There was no time for hesitation.

Nervous, Chry scurried inside, glancing over his shoulder at his father alone against the face of the unknown.

He tried peeping through the window, but it seemed like the closer the shades got, the darker the day became. Soon, he struggled to even find his father. What he hated more was that the wind would not stop screaming. Whatever words passed between his father and that horde of shades, if they had spoken at all, was snatched up by the wind and swept away to lands far from here.

But there was *something*…Or he thought it was something.

After his grandmother told him to come eat the supper she had boiled, somehow unworried by the threats he warned of, Chry sat at the kitchen table with its missing board and his family's smiles above, fingers fiddling in his lap, sulking over another bowl of Dry-Mouth broth he was not eating when he heard the screams. His grandmother hadn't noticed it, just kept slurping from her bowl. But Chry had, he *swore* he had, hadn't he? He tried listening again, really hard between the pigs squealing, the corn rustling, the backdoor knocking, and the bucket clanging, but the only screaming he heard was the wind whistling through the boards…and mayhap that's all it was…Wind.

But in his mind's eye, he kept seeing his father screaming for help and kept thinking to himself what if *he* was the one screaming and Chry was just…well, *here*, sitting and wondering if he'd heard a scream or not while his father was out there dying because Chry didn't know what to do or who to tell or if he was just hearing things again. It *could've* been the wind. It really could. But what if it wasn't? What if he was convincing himself it was when it really wasn't? Then what? What would he find if he ever got the courage to stand, walk, and take a look? What then would he see beside the well?

Oh, don't fool yourself. You know what you'd see. You'd drop the candle clock and run inside screaming, crying for grandmother to come, come, help, help, he's outside by the well, pray help him, pray.

He shouldn't have worried. Following one mark of the candle clock, Chry heard the backdoor scream open.

It was the door, that's what it was, the door was screaming, and that's what you were hearing. A door. That's all.

Moments thereafter, his father strode into the kitchen. He stomped out the dust on his pristine, black leather boots then went to the kettle. Eyes flooding with relief, Chry asked who they were, what they were doing, why they were here. The only response he received was a word.

"Lanke," his father grunted slopping broth into his bowl.

And that was that.

The next morning, he'd rushed outside to see if something, *anything*, had changed. But all he could find was a spittle of blood flicked across the side of the well and one fallen corn stalk. That was it. No bodies. No footprints or hoofmarks. No debris or iron left behind. Nothing.

His father never explained, and Chry, even though he himself had too many questions to count on his fingers alone, never asked. He'd learned long heretofore that any questioning of his father was useless; he'd have better luck catching a Dry-Mouth bare-handed.

He rubbed at his armpits where his skin was chafing. Simul bumbled along beneath him.

But...How? How did you manage to kill so many of them by yourself? I don't know how many there were, but there wasn't, like, two. More like too many. Aye, I know you had times when you've needed to protect yourself and others but how could you protect a whole farmhouse from a whole horde of Lanke?

Who were you father? Who were you really?

No longer being able to ask these questions stirred a poisonous resentment inside his belly. It wouldn't stop churning. Mayhap it'd never stop.

The sun beat at his neck. Simul panted. Chry looked ahead to where Domum would soon arise and remembered the girl who waited for him there, on a bed inside an old blacksmith's home.

He smiled. In the least, he had her to look forward to.

Simul and Chry trudged onward.

V

After what felt like forever—riding in the Wastelands always felt like that—the barren lands rewarded him with its one and only town: Domum.

What any traveler or merchant would notice first about Domum was its disrepair. Palisades, whose rosewoods were probably felled before Pactus became the Void, crawled up from the hardpan like the lower maw of a starved beast. Its stakes were scarred, cracked, and bled of its auburn hue. Behind the parapets idled guards from Etherine— three or four of them distracted with affairs other than their watch. Raising a hand to shade his eyes, Chry even noticed one sleeping with his back against the stakes. The chipped, iron head of his spear raised over the jagged walls like a hand waving for Chry to come save them.

He couldn't blame them.

Any armor they had was rust eaten—as was their Halorda, the life force of their souls—and none of them were close to the gates. Its wooden face shared in their misery. Black iron clamps clung to splinters, so loose the rivets threatened to fly off after a strong night's gale. Some were already gone, leaving behind a light shadow where the sunlight had not touched until now.

Gladion could help strengthen the gates. He has the tools and forge and everything Domum would need...Well, everything besides Vassal Renega's approval.

This was enough for the gates never to be repaired.

Closer, Chry could not see the heads of the buildings within even though the walls were not high. The only buildings outside of them were the sunken stable and the hovel behind it: a heap of wood and wattle about to drunkenly tumble onto the stables. Both were proudly owned by Oscar Redback, the same weary elder slumped in his rocking chair beneath the stable's thatched overhang like a tumble of bones wrapped in brown, sun-spotted skin. Gaps pockmarked the overhang. His rocking chair had half the armrest broken off, so his shriveled arm drooped like his pipe wiggling beneath the brim of his patchy straw hat. A wall of smoke blurred the bruises beneath his eyes—a sign that this day was not a good day to disturb him. Granted, there was never a good day for Oscar Redback. An empty Wasteland was a grand Wasteland for good ole Oscar.

Riding closer still brought on the sickly, smeared stench of the stables. Disgust twisted his stomach. It was almost as if Oscar himself was too lazy to piss in his pot so instead, he just rolled out of his chair and did his dues in one of the stalls.

How Oscar and the Domumites stomached the stench from dusk to dawn, Chry would never know.

Oscar didn't even toss him a glance when he neared; apparently, there was something out in the Wastelands more interesting to glare at. Chry slipped off his saddle and loosened its straps. Simul pawed and whinnied softly.

"That's enough riding for now," he whispered, rubbing at its dark brown mane. "I'll be back before the night."

Simul didn't believe him and kept whinnying.

He jerked the saddle off and was about to toss it aside so he could rein Simul into the stall when he stopped mid-throw. He was staring at the stalls now, blinking twice and squinting as if he were seeing the oases again.

There was something…well, odd about the stables.

At any given time there might be one, mayhap two horses lolled inside the six stalls. Even this scarcely happened. More often than naught, Chry would ride up to a stable as empty as the Wastelands itself. Domum didn't receive many visitors. Those travelers who did come through were usually merchants with their asses, mules, and occasionally oxen to carry their supplies into the Market. They didn't need Oscar's stables and Oscar didn't give a dry rattle about what they needed.

This time the stables were full. Five horses in all—a stallion, a mare, and three geldings. If a crow could believe it, there was only one stall open for his horse. Two of the beasts, the stallion and the onyx-black gelding, were staring at him intently with round, unmoving eyes. The mare and a gelding of fair, white beauty were munching on hay, and the last gelding was giving *its* dues to Oscar's stall, its messy mane the same brown which dropped from its backside.

Chry was too startled to move. That'd usually be, well, weird to say because who the plos would be startled by horses? Horses who were doing horse things like whisking tails at flies and nickering for food. Horses who were not any different from his. And yet he *was* startled. Of *course*, he was. He'd never seen so many horses in Oscar's stables heretofore…or this many horses together in one place at one time. Ever. Only ever heard about them. It was always asses and mules but never horses—these giant, massive beasts.

Reclaiming himself, Chry tugged vaguely on Simul's reins and guided him to the open stall. His eyes never left the horses. At any moment, he reckoned they would get excited and charge right through the grating. It wasn't like the wood was strong—it could barely keep the stalls upright—and if *that* happened—

Oh, that won't happen. That...It...Well, will it...?

He heard the faint voice of Gladion telling him again of how a stampede of horses—horses just like those in the stalls—had trampled one of his friends down in Etherine (Dhymes, he believed it was) and how another friend had his limbs tied to four horses and torn off. Punishment, he had said.

The blood drained from his face like a Withdraw squeezing venom out from a Dry-Mouth's sac. It didn't help that the stallion, one stall away, started whisking its tail against the stable's groaning frame, stamping at the hay, and snorting forcefully as if the sight of Chry made it sneeze in frustration.

Unwilling to peel his gaze away from the stallion, Chry asked Oscar, "Can I, um, ask why there are so many horses?"

From his chair, Oscar took a long pull from his pipe and breathed. The smoke seeped free and Oscar waited until it dissipated.

"No," he muttered. His voice was rough and harsh, butchered by age and sounding as if he had mucus stuck in his throat. "Ye can't."

Oscar, eyes lifeless like a severed head, probably thinking of how he could convince his wife to go chasing after Kemals so she could leaf him da fuck alune—his words, not Chry's—pulled again from his pipe then released. His lungs were too weak to actually blow the smoke away so it just fell from his lips, settled over his chest like a cloudy apron, then disappeared.

Uncomfortable, Chry rubbed at the back of his neck then at the front. He glanced at the stallion, then down, then back at the stallion who had calmed, then finally back at Oscar. He licked his lips, gulped once, wiped the sweat from his brow, rubbed at the back of his neck again, thought about something he couldn't really remember, then continued on.

"Shouldn't the owners have, well, I guess told you who they were or something?" he asked.

Sucking, Oscar stopped and lowered his pipe. With his neck creaking, he cast a glare at Chry that could've killed a Dry-Mouth sixteen years heretofore.

"Lookie Cry E-soul, kid, wha'eva da plos ya names is." Smoke poured from his shriveled lips like a chimney. Contemptuously, he pointed the pipe at Chry. "Ain't no damned broka, me. Dat's wat Sellas for. I 'ere for mox. Simple as dat. So pay. Or go n wast' sum oder falk's mox."

Chry blinked at Oscar. After a moment, he regarded the stallion again.

For some reason, it was staring at him. Intently. Inside those eyes Chry saw a deepness. Not a glare, he didn't think horses could glare, but he felt something that drew out an uneasiness within him. It wasn't fear or disgust either like what Gladion had talked about with the trampling horses and torn limbs. No. It was something quieter, more ominous, like a Dry-Mouth before it hissed and bit. Something inevitable. Something a straggler wouldn't notice unless they really stood here and stared into those unrelenting, beady, and bold eyes.

Whoever the owner is, may Eulgash lead me far from him.

When he didn't get a response, Oscar grumbled low like a greying ass.

"If ya goin' to stand dere like ah Sma', at least piss in me pot." Oscar joined his glare back with the Wastelands, fed his habit, then let the pipe dangle. Tired smoke trickled out. "Ya be more usefa dat way."

Chry—as curious and anxious as he was with his father and the lands beyond—looked once more at the stallion. It whisked its tail but didn't move. He thought that was enough of a sign. He appeased Oscar's demands, paid two mox upfront, tossed the saddle in with Simul, and left the old man to his peace.

VI

Domum was just as unruly and vulgar as the hearsay made it. It didn't have a rumbling stampede of horses, but it certainly had a rumbling stampede of Domumites. The first time he'd ever visited Domum by himself, an elbow had chipped his tooth and bruised his nose. The second time the crowds jostled enough that he vomited when he arrived at Gladion's and woke up the next dawn with bruised shoulders and a sore gut. Even so, this was better than being trampled…Much like Eduala Reselda had seven years heretofore: a broken, violent mess with her mother weeping over her, screaming "not 'er, not 'er, pray Eulgash, anywon bu' me las' child, noooo."

She'd been my age too. He thought, stepping away from the gate. *And now she's gone… Just one mistake.*

On this day, the entrance of Domum was rather quiet. No large crowds, only pockets coming and going. Even so, within the first few moments of arriving, he was nearly thrashed by Hal, the guard who'd let him in for apparently staring too long at his mole, watched a naked boy of around five years reckon piss on a bearded man's foot (the man swore at Eulgash then chased after the laughing boy whose nether bits swung and sprayed freely) and caught a glance of Gargen Tallow lashing his new Smar servant, one-eyed and unknown to Chry, for touching the colander.

Crowds or not, Chry did not enjoy strolling through Domum.

That's because one day I'll be the one being pissed on.

Not if you keep moving, you won't.

He obeyed this thought, down casted his gaze, and hurried down the first leg of Domum.

VII

Chry danced around two asses dropping dung mid-trot. The peasants behind the carts did not find the will to move and instead squished the remains beneath their bare feet.

Guess that's why the roads are so brown and soft.

He abandoned the thought and quickened his step with his clogs caked and back soaked. Approaching mid-day, he had to jostle through denizens congealing into waves, rewarded by the odor of stale wood, human ordure, and the heart of Domum, the Market. He was only halfway to Gladion's forge.

Great, he thought. *And I'll have to travel through the second leg too, that crowded plos.*

He groaned.

Beneath his feet, the road had pebbled from mud-like bubbles surfacing from a well of water. Soon, it shed its dirt-brown coat completely, a cobbled street parting into a broad circle with three different legs. It was the only paved road in town, swelled with a rabble of merchants battling for the mox inside his knapsack.

Along the inner edge of the road's circle were their carts crammed together like Dry-Mouths in a Pit. Mules licked at the backside of asses with one merchant, the owner of Imes's Inexpensive Goods, knuckling his ox into the herd despite the girth of his beast. With so many mules and asses neighing into the day, it was hard to hear what the merchants were yelling about. They had to know this, too. It was why they latched onto those they thought they could wring a mox out of—whether they were selling crops, skins, exotic flowers, oils, sculptures, or some other good. He'd even had one try to sell him the sweat from a famous knight of some king.

Where merchants sprouted, peasants spread. Alehouses along the outermost edge of the Market, like the Brew Beetle, attracted the local Domumites and left the space in-between trades and drinks somewhat open for Chry to stand free.

Opposite of where he stood, Eulgash's House of Worship with its formal, stern stature knelt in worship. Away from the House and to the right, gallows with two nooses and one body hanging. The decay was too far away to smell as it twisted and turned. In his thoughts, he could hear the creaking of wood and rope like skinless fingers rising from the ground to spin a toy, Vorsio. Chry shivered. It seemed Vassal Renega's harsh sentences would never stop.

Within the center, where folk barely glanced, towered the robed statue of Simul, the Guardian of the Temple of Death. Its white marble was stained and scarred black as if the cracks of the hardpan had climbed through its plinth to tug at its arms and head. Droppings from carrion crows were splattered across its robes with no hint of wash or polish. Book open in hand and four fingers short, Simul had his arms spread to embrace the denizens of Domum. They did not reciprocate. To Domumites, he was to blame for the Fall of Pactus (without good reason, Chry might add), disliked further by those like Russel Hide for apparently sending its runaways to Domum and not some other place like Etherine.

He stepped toward the statue, gaping up at Simul with broad, boyish wonder. For Chry, Simul was the only subject he had ever craved to know more about. As far as he was concerned, the hearts of those Domumites who despised Simul were hunting for folk to blame. Simul was no different. They would always blame him for Pactus, and Russel Hide would always condemn him for the runaways. In Chry's eyes, they were mistaken. Simul protected the Temple of Death and saved the lives of countless denizens while still somehow succeeding in sealing the Walker. No. That didn't just make Simul brave, it made him fearless. An immortal hero.

Chry, ever since those first days his father strode across this same Market with little Chry on his shoulders, his eyes star-stunned, even told himself that he wanted to be Simul—not to dress like him, not to live like him, not to even think like him, but to *be* him. To be a man fearless and immortal inside the hearts of many. To be an emblem of hope not just for Domum or the Wastelands but *all* of Admah. To be someone special. To be Simul.

He couldn't say for certain if he could, but he could dream that he could. That, at least, would have to do.

VIII

Gladion's forge was stowed away beneath a familiar Domum

facade. Glances at the front gave folk the feeling its rosewood build was dirtied wax melted and dried repeatedly until it was sagging and threatening to collapse. The forge itself, Betsy was its name, screamed from below. Chry gazed at the sagging home then glanced at the twin mud and stick chimneys resting against the hovel like two arms slumped over a slanted bar. They were coughing pillars of coal-black smoke.

Well, he thought. *At least some things never change.*

Chry stepped onto the porch but hesitated at the front door. It was splintery and ajar like cracked lips revealing bitter teeth.

This was nothing new. His front door was always open for anyone to walk in and greet Gladion down inside his forge or to wait on the wooden bench beside the entrance. This was… Well…Uncommon amongst Domumites. They were always barring their doors for the day and shielding their glassless windows with cloth curtains so others wouldn't go "peekin' on me damned pecka," as Jayce had told him. Gladion even had a rosewood hatch in the back leading straight into Betsy, although it had been clamped shut for Eulgash knew how long. The iron hinges were so rusty and brittle Chry had broken one off the first and only time he tried opening it. Aimee had barked with laughter that made her fall over weeping while he was stuck, sitting on his backside, gaping at this shard of rust in his hand and listening to the girl he secretly loved bray like a deranged Lanke. Worse was when Chry thought of Gladion, a Gladion he'd never seen heretofore, casting a warped and butchered shadow over him as the prelude to a rearing punishment.

That's when the tears came.

Instead of walking in, Chry knocked twice on the door. It squeaked back as if struck, then swayed on shiny iron hinges.

That's something new.

He waited until the screaming steel stopped. Around him was the silence of Domum—rumbling feet, vulgar condemnations, and the mutt Jayce hated panting at his front door. Chry raised a fist, hesitated, then knocked again, softer this time. He stepped back then took on his shoulder-slumped hunch.

This was what he always did. After years of visiting Gladion's, Chry still didn't feel right walking into someone's home uninvited. He guessed his father had something to do with that.

Teachings never die, I suppose.

Below came the clanking of stowed metals and, before long, Chry reckoned a heaviness stomping up the stairs and a patting when crossing an earthen floor. A faint shadow lumbered beyond the door.

"Chry me boi? Is dat ye?"

The question bellowed from the belly of a furnace: a blacksmith's voice. Chry remained quiet. The heavy steps approached before the new hinges squealed like newborn pigs. Gladion's massive trunk filled the frame.

Newcomers might have thought Gladion the child of an anvil and warhammer. Soot stained his plump hands and faded, cobra skin apron. Underneath, he bore a loose linen cloth the color of dry blood, now drenched in sweat and stretching against his barrel chest. Bristles of unshaven hair speckled his scalp. The scraggly beard brushing at his chest should've been the grey of steel but was instead the black of Betsy's sooty hand. Yet, Chry could never look away from his height. When he was twelve years reckon, Chry could peer over crowds with little difficulty. Now, four years thereafter, Gladion was still a head taller than him. The only features tiny on Gladion were his eyes and teeth. The eyes would've been normal on Chry or Jayce, but on, Gladion they were like little buttons pinned onto the backside of an ox.

And, of course, there was his smell. Instead of the putrid stench of Domum, Gladion smelled like any blacksmith should: burnt and smoky as if rising from a bed of ashes.

Gladion was always a welcomed change.

"Chry me boi! Wasn' expectin' ah surprise so soon!"

Gladion said this with a grin as giant as the man, revealing piss-yellow teeth whittled to their stumps. Some were chipped and cracked. Many weren't there at all.

"Uh, aye." Chry scratched the back of his skull, looking away.

"I…well…"

"Oh, stop ya blabberin'." He slapped Chry on the shoulder and nearly sent him stumbling off the porch. It was like Gladion's father the warhammer smacking the strawmen Chry. "Ya need no reason ta visit ya most beloved Domumite now do yea?"

You're right; I don't. Chry thought, almost as something resentful. Otherwise, he held his tongue and gave an uneasy smile.

Exuberant, Gladion pushed him in with one hand. "Now, stop standin' ah-round like ya sum stranga. Come in. Come in. Satch n da Rusios brought me a pig tah eat. Nevah would've thought it."

As he mentioned it, the succulent smell of almost cooked meat followed. Any worries washed from Chry.

Pig, he marveled but caught himself before he could drool. As much as his stomach begged him to devour, he was not here to eat. He was here to visit her.

With a nervous smile and nod, Chry let Gladion shove him into his hovel.

IX

Upon entering, Chry immediately hit a wall of haze and, despite that tongue-soaking scent, coughed until he teared. Gladion merely gave off a throaty laugh. With how much he worked in his forge, Chry reckoned Gladion could breathe it and be healthier than Vassal Renega.

He peered through the haze and tears. Inside was no more desirable than the outside. Raw earth packed the floor. Alder benches were scattered around a firepit in the center, their seats faded thin as if the wind had worn it down to a sliver. Along the walls were trestle tables like his at the farmhouse with the mud and stick chimneys along the outer wall. Neither opened to this room but down below. Across the enclosing space were wide stairs descending into Betsy. A spit of the promised pig roasted within the firepit.

"Take ah seat, me boy. Da benches don't bite yea. Promise yea a bushel."

Gladion, holding in a bellowing laugh, was already moving before Chry could answer, donning slim, blacksmith gloves from tools hanging upon nails. For a large man, Gladion could move surprisingly quick.

Chry shuffled his feet. Then he realized he had his sack in his hands and was clutching it to his chest like a mother with her newborn facing a pack of starving wolves.

Why does it never get easier?

"I thank you, Gladion, bu—"

"Thank ye? Boi, how many times do I needa tell ya, dere's nothin' ye needa thank me for. A've known ya far too long for dem courtesies."

Gladion rattled the hovel with his laughter as the blacksmith squatted next to the pig and prodded the coals with an iron stake hanging from the spit. The charred skin of the pig crackled. Wispy smoke from the fire hurried out of a hole from the top of the roof.

Chry chewed at his lower lip, his eyes drifting to the wall opposite the chimneys. Behind it was where Aimee slept.

After restoring the stake, Gladion slapped his hands together and headed for the chunks of wood leaning against the chimney. This was the Turkett stockpile, kept inside to keep from being stolen, even though any passerby could have walked in and taken one. There were four left. Chry's concerns were on the other side of the wall.

"But I'm sure ye ain't 'ere for pleasantries," Gladion said. "Let me cut ya ah slice ov pig. It's ahmost ready and, trufully, ya look lik Ralesh tooka bite outta ya."

If Gladion was a boisterous giant, like those Es'tal'mis giants of myth, then he was also a gentle giant.

"I thank…Uh, I just mean that I only came by to, well, pass on my greetings from grandmother." He was mumbling softer and softer as he went.

"Oh ya donts needa fladda me, son—spoutin' dis and dat about kindliness n respect." Gladion threw another chuck of wood into the firepit. The flames spat and chuckled. "If ya wanna go see Aimee n forget abou' da fadder, ya jus' has to asks. Anywise, I reckon half ov Domum knew dat sum day it was gonna happen. Me too if we're bein' honest."

There it was again. Heat at his cheeks. Not even Betsy the forge could have burned hotter.

"No, I, um, that's not…"

Taking the prod again, Gladion gave his hearty laugh but never met his eye. He flourished the stake to follow his words. The bulking boughs of his arms bulged inside his linen.

"N ya donts needa be so damned embarrass all de time, Chry me boi. Aimee n ye should've gone along ya's way ah long time heretafore." Nostalgia bore his expression. "Me daughta and me friend's son. Tell me, who else would I want width me daughta!"

Chry really, *really* hoped that wasn't a question because his lips were numb by a cold that could not possibly be there, and his fingers were, too, and his legs had sunk into the earthen floor and soon it'd be his hips and torso and head and arms and then farewell Chry me boi. The man couldn't be controlled. Next, he'd talk about opening the gorge or why his trousers were erect or why did his little boys tingle whenever he thought about the girl he loved and her golden hair and that full smile and…

He needed to run, to hide, preferably within Aimee's room.

Thankfully, it didn't last much longer.

"Anywise," Gladion continued. "If ya'd lik, I'm sure Aimee's in 'er room playin' width 'er books n 'erbs n what not. Why donts ya stop fiddlin' width ya diddle n go talk to 'er for ah mark. I'd lik ya to go around town thereafter n knowin' Aimee, she'll wanna come witch ya."

Chry was standstill, open-mouthed like the cured fish Hatchen would bring from the South.

Despite his nature, Gladion did not say a word. He prodded at tan, crispy, or collapsing wood. Sometimes, he'd bring the stake back over his lap and gaze contently into the open flame. Betsy grumbled below, neglected. After long, he started humming an upbeat, mirthful tune too fluid to be thought up now but nothing Chry had heard in Domum;

Harlequin would have played it heretofore. Chry listened before realizing that Gladion was waiting for him to go.

"I …um…Of course. I'll just…" He nodded. "Aye…"

Chry wobbled on rotten stilts around Gladion and down the hall to Aimee's door.

X

He slouched before the ashwood door.

Why are my hands shaking? Are my hands shaking? They're sweating. Ah, so clammy.

The soft pale skin of the ashwood smiled against the dying rosewood frame. The ashwood was not new. Mayhap newer than the rosewood but still scarred, splintery, and sun-faded by the harshness of the Wastelands. Where the handle should've been, there was a hole, Chry not remembering if Aimee ever had one heretofore. This was common. With all the doors back at the farmhouse, only one had a handle. Well, actually, it was a knob, brass and carved into a fowl, fastened to the door leading into his mother's room. He had not touched that knob for the last three years.

Chry stared. Through the hole hung a moth-eaten cloth no Rattle would think of wearing. First, he took a tentative, sidelong glance down the hall expecting Gladion's eyes to be wrapped around the corner. They weren't. Chry heard Betsy below whoosh alive before the tinkling of moving metal. Gladion was back at his forge.

Just knock on the fucking door already.

He closed his eyes, opened them to see no Gladion, and breathed deeply. His exhales were dry-tongued sighs.

He gave two swift knocks, planned on waiting for a response, but asked hastily, "May I, um, come in?"

A sweltering silence before he heard a dusty clap from within, what he knew to be her closing a tome.

She's always here reading, pestling, out there exploring. Really, no

31

one can stop her. Not me, not Gladion, not anyone.

He warmed to the thought of her being steps away, of her lips brushing his ear, of her hugs, of her. He clenched his stomach but that just maddened his heartbeat when he heard the whisper of her feet.

Look calm, act calm, and she'll think...

The ashwood opened. Chry stood erect.

Within revealed a room unique to Domum. Just the smell alone—a potent wash of herbs and oils—was enough to question where he was. He swore he could see their trails of purple and green wafting from her cluttered shelves: vials, steeple cups, goblets overflown with leafy stems, apothecary jars, pestle and mortar, pots, and an oblong, satchel-like object that Aimee had called a vasculum. Tomes and scrolls from the archives of the House overflowed the side tables. Both parchment and plant messed the floor.

But Aimee, she was all he could think about.

As awkward as it was to say, Chry reckoned Aimee looked much like his mother: her hair graced by golden tendrils, dainty curves sobered by rags, deceptive in its strength, and a cordial smile—not the wide, jolly grin of Gladion but the slight curve of enjoyment. He did not adore thinking about the likeness to his mother when they were together. Thankfully though, it'd always vanish beneath the details. Her smile carried full lips, curving rather than slim. Her skin—unlike Chry's family and Gladion who had the tanned skin of an unhealthy relationship with the forge—was bronze, melted and cooled within the Pool of Edo. Most of all, it was her eyes. Blue like his mother's, aye, but a deep blue he could drown in, adopted, he thought, from the seas they dreamed of visiting one day.

Aimee Turkett, the one blessing he had in the Wastelands, smiled at Chry.

"Greetings, my courageous crow."

Her light, sturdy words cupped his heart. His mouth hung open like a hollow inside a tree trunk. He was retreating into himself, numb, thinking about how absurd he must look from the eyes of Aimee.

His vision refocused as he reckoned Aimee again. Her brow had creased into a curious confusion. Had she said something? Had *he* said something? Fortunately, her confusion smoothed into a cordial smile.

"Come," she said.

Her hand, hardened and slender, slipped into his. An arrow of shock shot through him and startled him out of his daze. He gulped, noticing again that his hand was clammy.

Aimee led him around hordes of leather-backed books and tomes, those the Turketts owned having long since been burned for warmth. Gracefully, she guided him down onto her bed frame and patched pallet which was comfortable, somewhat, not really. Better than what most had.

Aimee sat beside him. To their right, a glassless window threw light down onto a side table. On top was a scroll, pinned flat with three flat stones and cowering beneath a stack of books. The writing was tiny and swirled like water, running together into a meaningless blurb. He didn't stare long. Staring for too long always made him dizzy and nauseous.

He removed his knapsack from his shoulder, somehow for his arms were as feeble as his twigs, and dropped it beside the frame's leg. He looked back at Aimee but before he could speak, she slipped her arms around one of his and rested a head on his shoulder. She did not speak. She did not explain.

Chry was not expecting this. Her warm body livened his bones to a rattle with his tongue swimming around a puddle of drool. He kept swallowing, but it wouldn't stop. Below was where his excitement had grown to a pleasantly unpleasant throb. He tried being discreet when shifting himself in his seat, but he really couldn't without disturbing her so he just stayed still and uncomfortable. Any more and he might just lose his rattles.

Eulgash pray, her touch must be what magic felt like.

Further down the road, some Domumite cursed at their child. Crows cawed on the roof.

"So, ummm, Aimee, did you, well," he scratched an invisible itch behind his head. For some reason, he thought doing this would help display the muscle of his arm, though his malnourishment displayed little and Aimee was looking downward. "Retrieve that scroll you said were going to get?"

There was a moment of pause before Aimee lifted her head and hooked the gap of her chin onto his shoulder. They were so close he could make out the brush of her freckles and the vague notion of her eyes. Her lips were enchanting.

"Hmmm," she purred. "Remind me again? I can't quite remember."

He remembered exactly: an account of the Ren'mus knights who apparently roamed around the nation of Caris'ma dressed as birds. They were trying to discover if these rumors were true.

Grinning like a Roaming Buffoon, he was about to tell yet stopped. There was something...off about Aimee. The longer he stared at her, the more distinctive her expression became: her voice was playful, but those eyes were far away with her smile forced beneath a wistful melancholy. Diving into a brooding, her presence had distanced herself a furlong. She must have felt him notice since she slipped her arms away and instead turned toward the window where the lands of Admah awaited.

Sakes, have I really been so blind that I can't even tell when my love is distressed?

Chry couldn't understand how he missed it. Despite this, he went on bumbling.

"Is everything well? We could have some pig. I haven't had any for a while, and, really, it does smell tasty."

She did not acknowledge him. She breathed nothing. He could've mistaken her for death, and Chry, her "courageous crow," couldn't handle it. Silence squirmed his fingers and backside as if a rat nosed around within. The rash beneath his armpits burned (*how the plos did I get that?*) and his brow and hands and other limbs created a moist worry.

Aimee sat still. Then she whispered so low Chry strained to hear her.

"One day, perhaps not this day but someday, do you wish to leave here?"

Chry creased his brow.

Do I want to...?

"What? I mean, what do you mean by that?"

"I mean to escape from the Rattle Trade and the Vassal and Domum. To travel South through Etherine to reach the Grey Sea. To then feel its breeze on our cheeks and sand between our toes, that which we have dreamed of and talked of for years now. To not only pretend but to *act*." Her voice bore lashes of longing—he could at least reckon that much, for what it was worth—before she slowed to take a shallow sigh. "Would you want that Chry? Do you truly want to leave like you say you do?"

His throat became a wordless well; he sent the pail further down for a trickle, but it always returned empty and dry.

This was hopeless.

When he usually visited, Aimee would talk to *him* about the experiences she had since his last visit: where she had gone, whom she had met, what labors she had seen to (at the House tending to Nomatus Cor alongside Ka'Mesa'Mala, beginning to copy Pidaculm texts onto scrolls under the eyes of the Devout, or staying with Gladion if he needed another hand around Betsy). Whatever she talked about, though, it would always end over the walls of Domum to dream of the lands she hoped to visit: to be curious, to ask questions, to wonder. Did Cadaqu really have crystal walls? Did Whitewall have white walls? Did the Grey Sea have enough water to fill the Wastelands twice over? Or was it true there were fields upon fields of Sable Agaves outside of Dhymes, as far as the Wastelands themselves?

Sure, he dreamed these dreams too, always telling Aimee about them, but Chry's greatest pleasure was listening to the smooth roll of Aimee's tongue within the safety of her home. It was calming, peaceful—well, as peaceful as Domum could be. But these strange questions? Coming from Eulgash knew where? No, they weren't peaceful; they were the Dry-Mouths that hid inside pallets at dawn and bit during the night.

"You know I do. Of course I do…" Narrowed, his throat sounded like wind through a keyhole. Why was it so difficult for him to talk about the dreams they had talked about heretofore?

Because this is serious. For whatever reason, now *it's serious.*

"It's just, well, grandmother," he started. "You understand that right? She…well, what would she do without me? I know that, um, Gladion, aye, he said he'd take care of her once heretofore but, well, it's just that, I'm her only family left since mother and father died, and I can't just leave her alone with Gladion because, well, what about the farm? I mean, what happens to the farm if I leave. That's another—"

Talking to his lap, Chry glanced up and saw a look that seared his mouth shut. Her eyes were with him now but the urgency within them was a lovely but dangerous wanting for an answer he wasn't giving. Sakes, he never realized how *demanding* they could be. Lies. He *did* know. He was just never the receiver.

Chry realized his mouth had trembled ajar but nothing was coming out. He tried gathering himself but instead, nibbled his lower lip and kneaded his fingers into his trousers. It was like his body was stuttering.

Aimee did not wait. She withdrew her stare into her lap.

Oh Eulgash, this isn't good, I should just say *something already, anything, aye, to get rid of this silence, there you go, that's a good thought, let's do that.*

Outside a door slapped open. There was the delayed thump of an uneven stride before Jayce Rucker's voice croaked at the mutt to leave, flee, get out of his ass, go open up a bitch's gorge before he "decides ta skin ya for sum mox." The mutt didn't listen; it yelped once after each warning as to challenge the human. Soon enough, there was grumbling, the same limping footfalls, then the door whining and clapping shut.

The sun dripping through the window blazed Aimee's golden hair, bronze skin, and thoughtful gaze.

"I can understand why you feel so…undecided." She continued, voice a calm breeze. "Albeit, what if we assume that you weren't restricted by your responsibilities and lineage. That the farmhouse, grandmother, and even those cute pigs of yours could be tended to by another trustworthy Larda. Then would you be willing?"

Chry almost stuttered again. He knew where this was going or at least he *thought* he knew. He could say the answer she wanted to hear, as he knew he should, but when he was meant to act and step beyond the Wastelands and into those lands infested with Dry-Mouths and Lanke and suffering and death…

He stopped, swallowed, and curved an unsure smile.

"Of course, I…"

The hands to his mind grasped a straw of wit. His grin arose. Anticipation thumped his heart mad.

"Well, only if, that is, I can have a lady as lovely as you there."

Chry, for the first time since the birth of Admah (or so it seemed), was blessed with her smile. She regarded him with interested eyes. *All* of him.

"Is that true?" She purred again.

Chry jumped out of his skin and back. This time, her coy smirk did not hold anything back. She snuck her arms around him and pressed her body onto his arm, her blond curls brushing over his shoulder. This was more than a hug. She was deliberate in her suggestion. Where the rags concealed the divinity of her figure, they failed to mask its supple flesh.

However hard he tried, he could not peel his eyes away from those wide, enticing lips. Her soft breath tickled his nose, and the dewy closeness of her skin exuded a fire's warmth.

Inside his trousers was a colt rearing to be released. The only ropes restraining it were those tied to the posts of self-restraint. Even these cracked when Aimee rested a gentle hand against his cheek. His face blazed. His mouth was dry as the bones of the Wastelands. His eyes were of youthful desire.

For as deranged as his body became, his mind was clear. He reckoned how rough her hand was on his skin—not the stone-hard yellow of Gladion's hand but the thin toughness of leather—and her smile, longing and desperate.

It's happening, he thought. *It's finally happening.*

She guided his chin toward her. His hands were pinned to the pallet but eventually pried away to reach out for her shoulders, uncertain as to where else they would hold her. The colt was bucking and kicking in those hands now, and it took every knuckle of his Halorda to rein them in.

Her lips brushed over his cheek to the corner of his lips and hesitated there. Her hand still clasped his chin too tightly before slipping down to his neck. The hairs there electrified and stood erect. Being this close brought the pleasure of her Agog Nettle scent—a kinder scent than that of the room's oily herbs—but also her hushed and desperate breaths. She wavered away the slightest so her eyes could regard him: twin sapphires coruscating beneath the stars. That look brought his hands purpose; they slid to her hips and under. The colt stampeded through his loins. He knew they could ache, but *this* felt like they were about to burst.

"Aimee," he said, feeling upon the warmth of her flushed flesh beneath his moist palms. She pressed into him, into those hands, and let out a soft moan into his ear. This was it. This was his day to become a man. "I-"

"I approve ov yar's relations." Chry and Aimee wrenched away as if whipped by rawhide. "I do but donts dink touchin' in fronts ov de fadder seems lik ah gud idea."

Aimee shot her eyes to the door, guilt paling their blue brilliance. Chry couldn't move. He was frozen shut though his skin was burning.

The laughter that followed bellowed between the boards. Chry could barely breathe. He didn't even want to turn around since he knew he was a dead man.

Dead rattles, dead rattles, swingin' from the gallows
Dead rattles, dead rattles, carried to da Gardens
Damn Garden rhymes...

Eventually, he did. The doorframe could barely contain that barrel chest and those bull arms. The hands were on triumphant hips. To the blacksmith, Aimee and Chry might as well have been Robert, Arya, and Quis'Mal'Bol stealing from Dry Trinkets again.

Gladion hitched in his chuckles. Aimee was quick to explain. Her voice swayed in confidence.

"Gladion, we-"

Gladion gave another bark of laughter.

"Ah me dear, ya dont needs ta explain any-ding ta me."

"But we-"

"No buts ah needed. I know all da excuses ya can musta n ah few more of dem yar mudda could 'ave spoken for. Swear ta Eulgash meself."

Chry's eyes explored every knuckle and crevice of Gladion besides the hollow holes of his sockets. He avoided them like Domumites do a Smar. Below him, his loins were withering; the colt (defiant moments heretofore) was now shying back into its stables with the thought of "fadder" only quickening its stride.

Gladion carried on.

"If ya can believe it, I was yar age once in me life, runnin' around da Well, mockin' dose at Ironsmelt lik we blacksmiths do, n causin' all sorts ov trouble width Ellis n Archa. Hehe, truthfully, by da age of eight, every elda knew the tree of us by name and smile."

Young Gladion—a rich mane of hair and teeth unspoiled by Domum—was not someone Chry could imagine under these circumstances.

Beneath Gladion's chuckling, Aimee withdrew. Her bosom had restrained her breathes, but a pinkish rose had blossomed across her cheeks. Eulgash, how it only made her more beautiful.

Chry couldn't be so in control at a time like this. Those chuckles were all Chry could hear.

Eulgash save me.

"Ain't nuthin' dat could've saved us dose days, ain't it so?" Gladion reminisced.

He's reading my thoughts, Chry thought under panic. *Oh Arbiter, he's reading me like Aimee reads a book.*

Gladion did hiccup a few more chuckles but then reverted to a state

Chry rarely saw.

The wrinkles of laughter disappeared into crinkles of age and tragedy: scarring around the eyes, sagging at the brow, years of costly experience rutting into deep-seated lines. His grin sobered. His Domum tan greyed like ash. In two moments, Gladion must've aged another twenty years.

Chry could not help but feel an instant pity toward the blacksmith.

"Anywise," he heaved a sigh. "I'm runnin' ah little low on sum supplies aroun' ole Betsy. Da hovel too. I'd be much obliged if ya can fetch dem from aroun' town. Not too many, I promise ya, but ya'd be doing an ole man a great kindness if ya could."

Hearing the mildness of his voice when it usually roared weighed heavily on them. Neither responded. Gladion neglected to move. Beyond the window, wings flapped beneath the cawing of a murder of crows.

Before long, Aimee whispered, "Yes, we can Gladion," but that was it. Chry's lips trembled open then back closed.

They rose and prepared to leave, Chry lagging as if all the discomfort he carried was mud he waded through. At the door, Gladion nodded slowly, as if to those whom he had lost, and returned to Betsy.

XI

What Gladion asked for wasn't demanding—the usual list of supplies. Unfortunately, since this *was* the usual run-around-town-and-do-Gladion's-bidding, the blacksmith roared from Betsy not to forget to bring Gargen—a chandler who also knew how to tan animal hide with urine—his pisspot. "We can use da coin!" He added. Chry groaned. Gladion always said that.

So it was that Chry carried the head-sized, knobby-skinned, wrought-iron pisspot to Gargen's, and so it was that Chry pretended not to hear that sullied slosh of liquid. They didn't use a pisspot back at the farmhouse—just wandered out into the Wastelands to deliver their dues. No way in plos was he going to carry a pot to Domum knowing that his grandmother had taken a squat over it and that the only thing stopping it from pouring over his thigh was the lid's badly beaten latches.

With the crowds of Domumites overwhelming the second leg, they decided to travel along the walls of the Residential District. True, the inner walls were near barren and less likely to bear the threat of flying elbows, but the scenes here were not for the kindest of souls: broken kneecaps and elbows, a dented skull, loss of limbs, sight, fingers, toes, seared ears, a smile of stitches across the throat, the palisade of Domum sun-white and splintery like chewed bones staked into the dirt, and heat burning away flesh.

He hated it all.

Here, Aimee had displayed a leather Skin—the common currency within the Rattle Trade but useless outside of the Well—and the maimed of Domum, begging from mox or even crumbs, usually huddled back beneath the warm shadow of the walls and forgot they existed. Even so, some weren't so convinced. An armless Domumite had ignored the Skin in Aimee's hand, stumbled into Chry—nearly causing him to spill the pisspot—and mumbled at his temple "Da black-eye' ring get da blu'-eye' bish," so close he could smell liquor on their breath. Then, they'd slew off him and lurch after another shadow, Chry's arm and shoulder sticky with their sweat and drink.

Really, he couldn't tell which was more uncomfortable: being jostled by a filthy, sweaty crowd, or being touched by a one-armed, erstwhile Rattle.

Eventually, they returned to the entrance of Domum and to Gargen Tallow pouring tallow into a candle clock mold. His Smar servant stood a fair distance behind him with fresh bruises and welts across their dirt-brown skin.

"Ain't no damn tanner me," Gargen spat at them when he heard why they were there. "Trad take all da dam Dry-Mouths n Gladion expects me ta tan his 'ide from sum mule's ass. If it weren't for dis Sma' massagin' me rump, I'd 'ave noticed how far Gladion's fist was up it, ya 'ear."

Regardless, Gargen gruffed and jerked his head behind him. This could have been predicted. Gladion's influence was not one to be dismissed.

After Chry gratefully delivered the pisspot, Gladion's needs dragged them down the first leg to shops like Halorda Herbs and Dry Trinkets. After each item was bought, Aimee stuffed it into her horsehide knapsack: whether it be the crude, mule leather Gargen flung at Chry, shouting for Gladion to get it himself or send his piss off to the Pools, or more herbal ingredients for Aimee's mortar and pestle. Either way, Chry didn't take much notice of what else went into that sack. Didn't really care until they were at Dry Trinkets—a decorated, mule-drawn cart on the first leg whose plump owner, flaunting her own...blessings, was a favorite among Smar men. There, Aimee bought something unknown to him. He had been...uh, well, too distracted to see, but did catch a glimpse of it before she had shoved it inside her knapsack—a lace of tiny, slivery links tailing out from her fist.

"What's that?" he heard himself ask.

She drew her hand out from the knapsack, empty, and tossed her bright, blameless eyes toward him and...and...Eulgash, what was he asking again?

Mischief curved her lips.

"Wouldn't you like to know."

He opened his mouth to say, "aye, he *would* like to know," but closed it. In the back of his thoughts, he knew better. He had waged this war many times heretofore, and at its bloody end Aimee was always the victor. She must've noticed this in his eyes because she brayed a shrill laugh, howling like a Lanke after its kill.

Arbiter, he thought but contained a hint of a smile.

When she finally calmed, she cupped the back of his arm, but all he could reckon was her smile of encouragement and the bronze glow of her dimples.

"I promise, my courageous crow, you will know soon enough."

"Oh, will I now?" he responded.

Her smile beckoned him to join before it faded into an expression of thoughtfulness. She rolled her tongue inside her mouth—something she did whenever she was in lighthearted thought—then glanced down the leg and into the crowds. Before long, a Lanke-broad grin came over her. In it, all the mischief, cheer, and boldness Chry could ever ask for.

It rattled him.

What's she-

Aimee didn't give him the chance. She snatched his hand and took off.

"Aimee, what'r—"

He was jerked off his feet. Any harder and his shoulder would've ripped from its socket.

From then on, it was a fight to regain his footing. Through stumbling and bumbling, there was the thought of *Eulgash have mercy* because Aimee, oh she was gone, yanking his arm forward whether he was upright or licking the road laid with dung.

"Aimee- I-" He gasped, tripping and avoiding another fall. "Can we stop- or just—"

She wouldn't.

They weaved through the first leg, her hair spinning behind her like loose sunlight. He couldn't predict her. Though the crowds were thin compared to the Market and second leg, she'd always jerk right, jerk left with Chry banging against a straggling cart, the coachman leaping off his rump, or shouldering into a hooded Smar returning from the Market full-handed, their mouth spouting filth dirtier than the muck across their soles. But Aimee? She never stopped. Whatever these Domumites said blended into the chaos behind. She was a carrion crow flying high towards distant lands, to leave him behind for the hardpan he would not abandon.

XII

Stumbling, he tucked the knapsack over his shoulder and thrust his legs forward. The herbal scent of Aimee purged Domum's stench, daring him to catch her. The challenge inspired a surge of- of *something* to course through his blood. His gasping slowed. Sweat stung his eye, his heel chaffed against the wood of his clogs, their hands wet and slipping, but he didn't give one dry rattle. Adventure spurred his heart and…Was he laughing? Were they *both* laughing? They were. Somehow, Chry was flying beside her and could hear her giggles turn into that uncontrollable bray of laughter.

An encouraging warmth spurred him forward. Now, despite his doubts, it was Chry who was in front, leading her, pulling her, guiding her.

"Chry, Chry," she could barely say his name between her braying and panting. "Domum isn't going anywhere!"

"That's what *I* thought," he shouted but couldn't say more for the huffing of his lungs.

He didn't stop. As far as he were concerned, Domum *was* running away from them. His legs became the weave. Mind within a dream, tearing down the hovels to construct crystal buildings high enough to touch the sun. That's what she had said about Cadaqu, right? It seemed almost impossible, but those giggles and the glint of the crystal could not lie.

"Chry"

He looked behind him.

It was Etherine and the sprawling city of Cadaqu, Aimee between its crystal spears.

Laughing.

Smiling.

Love.

"My courageous crow, oh my courageous crow, take me to Etherine my courageous crow, we can see the Grey Sea and crystal, my courageous crow, take—"

"Chry!"

If I die this day, he thought. *I will be happy. If not, let me stay here forever until our bodies lie in the Gardens beside each other, happy and—*

"Sakes Chry, STOP, *STOP!*"

There was a tug behind him, resistance, then a hand slipping between his fingers. There were words but no mind to grasp them. He was flying. *Flying.* Like one of those carrion crows he dreamed about and wished Eulgash would just let him flap his wings, caw, and soar high above Domum to beyond the—

He slammed against a wall. But only after it bounced him back and sent him tumbling did he reckon this "wall" hadn't rattled like wood, or rung like metal, but thumped like flesh.

His arm brushed against someone shouting. Then he tripped over his feet and landed hard on his backside. He was too far dazed to pinpoint pain but cried out to Eulgash with no condemnations to spare.

Aimee. Oh Eulgash, I hope she didn't hear- Ah, sakes, I need-

The taste of iron on his tongue. Head spinning. Hand caressing the whimper across his back. Moaning now, he bent his head back but above was the frizzled scene of staring at the sun for too long. He had to squint to distinguish the foggy hovels on each side, a misty sky in-between, and a shadowy figure looming.

His first thought was that it must be *Aimee, oh I thank Eulgash she's not hurt.* He thought he saw her smile, too, and must've smiled back. His hand went to rub an echoing throb along his cheek as if he could transfer the discomfort to his palm.

But when his sight straightened, the rumbling of Domum creeping back to his ear, his smile shrank. That figure. It wasn't Aimee. Aimee was *beside* the figure, and her eyes were round, pale coins of shock.

Not good.

He slid his stare back to what she was gaping at and found his eyes crawling up sun-kissed skin knuckle-by-knuckle to witness a giant the likes of which Gladion would have been dwarfed.

At first glance, he thought it *was* Gladion: an absurd height, a scruffy black beard which grew from ear to ear, and a bald head gleaming against the sun.

Unfortunately, the similarities stopped here.

This scalp was clean shaven and void of severe sunspots and dents. Its rawhide baldric crossed a bare chest and back, both robust (*Arbiter look at its* arms, *just* look *at them!*) and scarred with the many wounds of battle. Fastened to the baldric, a two-headed battleaxe peered over its bowed but beastly shoulders. Fingers as round as coins, a silver ring with some hairy animal head chewing on an obsidian ball. Around its waist, it wore a war-ruined skirt patched together by a horde of furry pelts. A black leather belt cinched the skirt.

All of its garments were bled dry by the sun, and none were furs Chry knew of. He guessed mayhap the black leather was like the boots his father had worn, but Chry did not know, he didn't know anything, nothing. This *thing* was foreign to him. The shadows of a descending day had stolen its face. He couldn't make who or what it was. A snarl, a glare, a hiss, a growl, some fangs. Impossible.

Regardless, Chry was faced with a barefaced truth about the nature of the thing in front of him. That truth rattled his bones until they were pinches of bonemeal.

It's a Lanke.

No, he thought. *It's more than a Lanke. It's the* incarnation *of a Lanke. And now it's within the walls of Domum where Lanke are forbidden and loathed and killed regardless of reason.*

And how's your reasoning going to help you now? There's one standing there like it belongs, neither dead nor chained, here to rip—

"You *Verten!*"

The growl clattered his skull. There was a collective gasp around him, but Chry couldn't reckon. He bore no knowledge of himself. That thing had overwhelmed his existence.

What's happening, what's this thing yelling at, what is it, Gladion help, pray, help me, I need help.

It would not wait for Gladion to help. A claw seized his linen-thin shirt, its palm the raw toughness of hardpan. Chry couldn't fight back. As with his mind, his muscles were numb. His back said farewell to the road as his shirt dug into his armpits like tightening twine. He tried wrapping his hands around its wrist but the grip was limp and his fingers struggled to enclose. Soon, he was hanging from the arm like tassels from a scarf.

My sword, I can grab my...

Chry stiffened. He had groped for his sheath and had come back with air. Immediately, he realized where it was; because of how uncomfortable he was on his ride to Domum, he had tied the sheath to Simul's saddle. It would be in the stalls now, lazing around when Chry needed it the most.

Oh, fuck, he thought nauseously. *This is the end. I'm dead.*

Shadows then peeled away from its face. He wished they hadn't. Whatever god the Lanke prayed to would've been proud of what it had created: cheeks and brow molded from beaten rawhide, trenches of wrinkles creased by the dead it had slaughtered, a jagged scar across its upper lip hewing its beard with the strength of its nose even though it was crooked and broken.

Yet these features fell away before its glare. Because…well…its eyes…they were silver. Two moons with black pricks in the center, fierce like silver serpents slithering from their sockets to strangle him.

As much dread as he had consumed, Chry could not prevent a bubble of awe from swelling forth.

The beast jerked him closer. Its beard reached to scratch him. Chry tried squirming away but couldn't avoid the meaty reek of its breath. A guttural growl rumbled inside its maw.

"Katarc," it muttered. Its silver serpents hissed over him. Sweat and tears stinging his eye, Chry couldn't look away. "You hit me."

He could not breathe without wheezing. His legs were flailing as if hanging from the gallows.

I can't, I can't, I can't, I can't, I can't,

"It was by…it was by…"

"Damn it! Spit it out!"

Spit sprayed his face. Chry flinched, making a childish groan that stretched into a pig's squeal.

Fear. Strangle.

47

A voice giving no slack to its one and only focus.
To kill.

XIII

"Get your filthy hands off him, you-you Rattle *fucker*!"

The hand lifting Chry stiffened. Sakes, *he* stiffened. Like a Withdraw decapitating a Dry-Mouth, the condemnation had chopped through their struggle. It muted the crowds that had gathered. But the beast, no, its glare wreathed in disbelief then contorted beneath a spiteful rage, releasing Chry to hunt for the culprit.

For the moment, the coils around his neck were loosened. Chry could actually hear himself pant now. He licked at dry lips.

*But that voice...*he thought as concern welled. *Where have I heard that voice heretofore?*

With furtive eyes, Chry searched to find the blurs around him had cleared: Smars, Domumites, and some Rattles distinguishing themselves as individuals. Each faced him—folded flesh, pockmarks, bloated noses, untidy hair—but would not near the Lanke. The visions of a brutal death had stayed them.

Sounds too—the murmur of hushed voices, the shuffling of bare feet, the quiet rustle of linen. These sounds were odd against the backdrop of Domum. The town was never a quiet one. There was always a noise to be heard: whether it be Ka'De'Coma preaching Eulgash's Judgment as a myth or shop owners under their vehement acts of persuasion. Only behind him did a baby wail.

If there was one thing Chry had learned about the fears of Domumites, it was that there were only two: the Forest and the Lanke.

Within the crowd's circle, Aimee was an unwavering force. Her sapphire eyes were defiant, fists balled into a tight squeeze, and her small bosom swelling like the bellow of a forge.

Piece by piece, Chry reckoned what Aimee had just said. His heart dropped.

48

Oh Aimee, how could you be so reckless? You should've just…well…left me.

But it was too late.

The glare of the beast snapped at Aimee. Hesitation flickered over her; she nearly stepped back, she nearly loosened her fists, she nearly softened her stance. Every lesson about the Lanke taught them to flee and hide beneath a stone. Seeing her hesitation urged Chry to protect her, but the furthest he got was to swing his legs and grunt. Its grip had not weakened.

Aimee soon collected herself and retained her defiant stance. She was not one to flee from a threat. The beast made a rumbling sound like hot iron cooled by water. Instinctively, its fingers tightened its grip though it did not pay Chry a moxam of attention.

Apparently, not many folk had ever opposed the beast its meal.

"You the boy's whore," it grunted. Then, strangely enough, Chry spotted a smirk beneath its bushy beard. "The ekah rah he leans on when his trousers are wet."

Aimee bristled, "No, but I suggest you release him before pulling that cock out of your rump."

The silver of its eyes flared. Its smirk vanished.

"Verten scum. I'll break every bone you…"

As its anger boiled, Chry's body rose.

He tried wiggling out again. As for how it went, his foot nudged its thigh, and his fingers slipped off the twisted coils of its arm. Chry whimpered as would a beaten pup.

The beast forgot he even existed.

Wish I could forget I was here—wake up in Aimee's bed sniffing herbs and watching her read. Gladion'd be down in Betsy roaring with laughter and Aimee'd be tucked safe inside my arms.

Shirt stuffed into his nose, he pressed his eyes shut and tried thinking of just that. Just as well. Unlike Aimee, he didn't have the courage to fight. He had prepared for violence with Gladion, but as his father always said, Chry was too cowardly to encounter violence. He never said it openly, but it was always left unsaid.

I can't do this, he thought. *I can't fight back. I can't face a Lanke. He'll slaughter me and use my bones as a pick for his teeth. I can't. I can't be like my father. I can't be like Gladion. I can't...*

He had to run, trip, fall, flee, who the plos cared, just do whatever he could to stray away and go somewhere far, *far* away. Staying was death. Only brave men smiled at death. He wasn't brave; he was dead. Better to run.

Aye. Never in a thousand Sons could I ever think to stay and defeat that thing. Never.

What about me then?

The voice was of a sweet scent, void of resentment. Aimee.

Will you leave me too? She beckoned.

I...Aimee, pray, I don't...

Will you struggle and defend those you say you love?

Sakes, Aimee, you know *me. You* know *I can't-*

Have you forgotten our promise?

No but I...

Have you forgotten?

Her words rushed through his blood. He tried to think of another excuse, but the ones he had were to say she was being foolish and shouldn't be asking this of him and that this was something well beyond his control. Though all of them could be true, none of them made much of a difference.

It wasn't the answer she was looking for.

No, of course not.

Then why are you CRYING!

Chry winced. His Lirda, his unworthy soul, leapt so far from his body it snapped back and rang his skin.

Why are you letting me die, Chry?

He swallowed.

I'd never—

Why aren't you FIGHTING then, damn it! Why are you always so damned SCARED to do ANYTHING!

Her voice seized his throat—that small, shriveled thing—and

50

ripped it out. He couldn't speak, but the heart beneath it tingled with…Thrill? Anxiety? Adventure? He couldn't tell. Something bizarre was happening. He was throatless but could speak through Aimee. His voice…Sakes, had it always sounded this *strong*?

No, not without her it hasn't.

Goodness Chry, stop that. I don't call you my courageous crow just because I wish *you to be courageous. I* know *you're courageous, and I know you can be someone more than the boy I met as a child. Chry, I* believe *in you.*

I believe in you too and me and, no, you're right, I can't let that big fat oaf lay one finger *on-*

A ghost of a hand brushed at his cheek and melted into what was considered a watery cheek. His coalesced conscious gave into a wild tingle.

Fight for me. It was a vanishing whisper. *Will you fight for me, Chry?*

His rattles were shaking. He couldn't control his toes or fingers. He didn't know what awaited him with the Lanke but for some reason, he didn't give a dry rattle about his fate. That cold dread had burst into flames, roaring inside of him. No, Aimee was right; she *needed* him. Right now, right here,

I need you.

and he would fight for her. Aye Aimee, you hear that? There's no way in plos I'd *ever* let *anyone* hurt you. Even if it means I die when I—

Live Chry. Live for me, live with me, l-

XIV

"I said leave her ALONE!"

Eyes closed, Chry heard a gasp sweep through the crowd. It was the most satisfying and terrifying sound he had ever heard.

What the bastard deserves.

Afterward came feeling, time, and place; he wore coats of sweat, his legs were numb from dangling, but above all, his fingernails were digging into the rigid wrist of the beast. A liquid warmth bled over his fingers. The satisfaction he felt became his victory.

Slowly, Chry peered his eyes open and was met with the beast's glare; its nostrils flared, teeth bared, its silver eyes like molten steel. Everything that glare touched boiled alive. Yet the more his eyes touched the beast's eyes, lips, cheeks, chest, beard, and arms, the more Chry was able to rationalize his fears. This Lanke was no beast; he was but a man. And an ugly man at that.

Chry made a raw, primal noise.

"*You're* the scum, you sack of shit," he spat. "Not her. And if you don't let me go, I'll kick your balls so hard they sit inside your mouth."

The last sight he saw before chaos was of Aimee. He caught a glimpse of her in the middle of his rant standing there tough and beautiful as always but also shocked and startled. Her light freckled face had a maternal Oh-Chry-what-are-you-doing look as though he should've known better. He would've laughed like a mad howl.

The rest happened in a flash.

His shoulder slammed against the dirt road, head whipping and arm crying, "Mama." Chry cawed pain. His head rang. Between them, there was a sound between a bark and a bellow, his name floating about. He couldn't reckon who. Drool dribbled down his cheek, his shoulder pulsed. There were legs, too many legs, like the Forest again. With his father. Trudging through to the Gardens.

He flopped onto his back expecting the scold of his father when he had dug his feet into the dirt and tugged at his arm. It wasn't his father. Above him was danger in the form of a cobra skin boot. The sole hovered over him, about to stomp. The dusty tread was worn thin.

I...

I...

I can see up his skirt, he thought through a daze. *Ha...Ha...Jest on you.*

Somehow, Chry didn't think he would laugh.

A muddled scream sounded from his right. Or, that's where he thought it came from; with his sight the clarity of mud, he couldn't really tell. Thereafter, the boot lurched from view. There were grunts and condemnations he couldn't reckon. Feet scuffled. His head rolled around like a Tōm Die. He pinched his eyes closed and open toward the sounds again and again until he could somewhat see.

Aimee, in her rags, had taken a defensive position in front of Chry before lurching forward to snatch the arm of the Lanke. Her ravenous nails, longer than his, drew blood. Her mouth flared words that Chry was glad he could not hear.

Something about getting away? Or else? He thought.

If that's what she had said, the Lanke responded in kind.

He had stumbled back from Aimee (*did she shove him?*, Chry thought) but recovered without a misstep. Snarling, he lifted the arm Aimee had gripped, cocked it back, then—as realization paled over Aimee—swatted her away with his forearm.

It was as though a rosewood club had struck a child and stained her lavish skin with the blood she had inflicted.

A cry escaped her. She flew backward and her body thumped down in front of the crowd. Her fall coughed dust. The folk shrank back in fear of becoming the next victim. From her slumped body, there lurked a moan which blew away his daze.

His heart burst; his thoughts ceded to savagery.

I'm gonna kill him. I'm going to fucking kill him. I'm going to kill him!

Chry was halfway to his promise: elbows thrust beneath him, legs bent, about to spring forward so his hands could wring the Lanke's neck. He could feel nothing beneath the rush and see nothing beside the cobra skin boot again, raised and ready. The sharp blade of his vision spotted the hair, nicks, and scars along his leg reckoning the latter from the arduous battles he had survived.

This was it.

The beast roared above him. Its boot jerked. Chry yelled.

"Vion, Vion, my ole friend, settle down, why dontcha."

Startled, Chry lost his footing and plopped down on his bony backside. He called out a whimper and then let out a groan.

Heroic, he thought, rubbing at his backside.

Yet, this did not concern him. Days of him and Aimee balancing and falling off sun-chipped yokes from long-dead oxen had prepared him for simple discomforts.

What concerned him was the voice. Looking around, he reckoned it had risen from beyond the crowd, a soothing melody played from the lyre of a human heart. If the beast and this voice were related, they were like the moon and sun: cool instead of harsh, elegant rather than scorching, one calling for hands, one calling for heads.

His reckless rage loosened its hold. A cautious interest and whining pain in his shoulder took its place.

The voice rose again, "Wouldn't want our fine warrior to bust a nut, es*pecially* over a feisty lad and his mistress. Wouldn't you agree?"

He squinted as if to see this bodiless man through the crowd before reckoning how relaxing the voice sounded, its speech plucking the strain from muscles so that any rage festering within shriveled like a plant beneath the Wastelands' sun. Chry only gaped then. He barely registered Aimee propping herself up on her elbows in search for the voice, too.

Contracting the absent, unknowing faces of donkeys, the Domumites had turned to gravitate toward the voice. There was a rustling of bodies further away from where the voice said things like, "Eh-scuse me my Scalies," and "Pardon your breeches, Simon."

Scalies? Simon? Who the plos is *this man? Creature? Thing?*

Many witty jabs thereafter, the outer circle of the crowd stirred between each other before opening outward like a gate. Gliding past them was a man most Rattles would call a "thirsty whore."

He was more beautiful than any mortal should be. Guile and charm carved the marble of his features, and a crow's nest of hair swept over eyes as green as the grasslands Aimee and he had dreamed about. One look promised adventures to the Grey Sea and an urge to climb the tallest mountain.

I wonder how far his boots have traveled, he thought. *I wonder where he had gone. Where he'll go next.*

However, this man was no god. His body was of common height, well-defined through his long-sleeved tunic made from cotton, a rarity in Domum. Even so, nearing the Lanke he called Vion, the man seemed short and thin, like a tall, lean dwarf. At his hip dangled a loose scaly-gray sheath with a dagger, its steel hilt beyond rusted and crowned with a silver pommel. Beyond all else, his most noticeable feature was a smug grin so natural it looked as if he had borne it while emerging from the womb.

This man, Chry thought, was far from a simple "thirsty whore."

He gestured with his hand.

"Let's think before we swing our slings around. Wouldn't want to cause trouble like you did in Dhymes. In all truth, Vion, you'd think an oaf like yourself would stray *away* from the gaol rather than waddle into one."

Apparently, he had a mouth too, one twice as wide as the Lanke was tall. Chry guessed if they were companions, it was not by choice.

Companions. Now that *would surely be a sight.*

Over him, Vion snorted. His boot balked from withdrawing as if still deciding whether to spare his life or not. Eventually, he abandoned the cause, caging a snarl.

This rattled Chry out of his wonderment. Somehow, he had forgotten the Lanke was even there. If he really wanted to (and Chry was sure he did), Vion could've crushed his ribs, back, and flattened him as other beasts of burdens had with the road. Chry wouldn't even have known it until the first scream ripped through his throat.

And what would you have done if you had *known? Screamed? Rolled away? Slapped him?*

He'd never know.

The gorgeous man looked down at Aimee. With a grin assuring the crowds he wouldn't leave such a beautiful maiden to lie in distress, he knelt down next to her, offered his hand, and whispered something Chry could not hear. He couldn't handle it. Thoughts of *no, no, no, pray, don't* scurried across his mind. Blessedly, Aimee refused—not by slapping his hand away or barking at him, as Chry had secretly hoped, but by simply ignoring it to push herself up onto her feet.

Chry couldn't prevent himself from grinning.

Still, the man's confidence would not accept defeat. Like a natural gentleman, he waited for Aimee who dusted off her rags and flinched when her hand touched her jaw. Her back was to Chry, so he couldn't tell how bruised she was from where that brute had hit her. Fortunately, neither Aimee nor the man looked as alarmed as he felt. That, at least, should've eased his worry.

Not enough though, he thought.

The man caught him staring, gave him a wink that would've patted him on the back and called him "my ole boy," then refocused on Aimee. Sunstones burned inside his cheeks, jealousy staked through him.

It was the eyes, Chry finally reckoned. The way they took her in. The man didn't openly lust for her breasts or ogle at her hips; that was for Rattles like Russel and Simon Hide. Instead, this man charmed with his eyes, praised her with his exuberance, and lured those in conversation like a Rusio ready with Hook and Tong for a Dry-Mouth to surface.

Like Vion, this man was another breed of danger.

Cupping her lower shoulder, the man leaned toward her ear as to tell a secret. This too Chry could not hear.

Of course I fucking can't, he thought.

But Aimee only nodded vaguely after the man pulled back. Chry reckoned she was bearing a grateful but courteous smile. His smug grin responded in full. Thereafter, he released Aimee from the twinkle of his gaze and offered his attention to Vion.

"If you're done intimidating innocent citizens, Bar would love us not to be late again. Many days ahead of us, as I'm sure you're aware. Even with a slab of veal for wits, it shouldn't be too difficult to reckon."

Locked inside Vion's glare was a threat to burn the man at the stake. The man's gaze did not crumble, welcomed the danger from what it seemed like. Chry did not think he'd ever understand that feeling.

Soon, and grudgingly so, Vion's silver glare retreated. It fell down to Chry. Unlike heretofore, the boy couldn't meet them. The elbows holding him upright threatened to topple.

Regardless of the nervousness he displayed, Vion just stood there, smoldering and bloodied. The wounds Chry's nails had inflicted were dripping tears down his wrist and hand. The battleaxe behind his shoulder glinted off the tired sun and the shadow Vion cast buried him alive. Suddenly, Chry couldn't breathe. He kept his eyes on those cobra skin boots. At least *those* serpents were already dead.

Before long, Vion broke his silence with a grunt, "They are not worth the effort."

He growled something else beneath his throat and passed Chry, nearly through him. Chry squirmed away. Every Domumite gave him the road as Vion stormed through. A murmur rustled between the crowd, hushed when Vion neared, then grew again when the strides were gone. Once they felt safe enough with only one fatherly Smar being shoved aside, bodies trickled back into the circle.

Finally, Vion was gone.

Chry did not believe this. He was expecting Vion to return roaring "*Die, Verten, Die*" with his battleaxe cutting through Domumites like a monstrous feller out at the Forest.

Instead, a swishing sound interrupted him. He twisted his head and there the man was—his face chiseled by the dying hues of the sun, bringing with him the pleasant scent of a salty breeze.

He was gazing along with Chry as a fellow companion. In that light, he looked more like a marble statue.

The man glanced down and sharpened his smug grin as if to tell him the secret he had told Aimee. Chry could only gaze. Even with how jealous he had been, the man was just so... so...

"Don't be too afraid of him now," the man said. He left Chry with another wink, so quick he had to wonder if the man had actually meant to wink at all. "Vion might act the brute but inside, he's just a big ole doll."

Then the man followed Vion toward the entrance and disappeared into the crowds.

Chry blankly stared at where he had left.

Well, he thought. *I'm glad he had such a great time.* Chry got to his feet and rubbed at the tenderness of his arm. It whined at his touch. *That "doll" was about to use my bones to pick the flesh from his teeth.*

The caricature he thought of would've been funny if the flesh wasn't his and the bib it wore wasn't laden with gristle.

He let out a shivering moan.

The crowds once gathered for the slaughter were now dissipating. Domumites had shed their silence for their usual rustle and bustle; rags and carts clumped by and stray bodies knocked against his bad shoulder. The screams of a baby receded into broken alleys.

Domum was back to normal. This gave him little comfort.

From behind, warm fingers coiled around his arm. Chry nearly leapt out of his trousers.

For fuck's sakes, that touch, Arbiter, Lanke.

He shouldn't have been so tense. The bronze skin of a hand and the fingers following into a graceful arm flushed him with relief.

"Aimee," he mumbled.

His lips peeled back into a smile full of crooked teeth and relief, but as soon as it was shown, the smile was spoiled. Vion had left his mark on Aimee. The first was a long bruise across her jaw, sallow in the center and inky around it like the yolk of an egg whose white had blackened. The second being a blush of black along the bottom of her cheek, cloudy and thickening.

"Sakes Aimee," he said reaching to place a hand on an unblemished part of her face. "We need…"

"Are you hurt, Chry? It looks like your shoulder's gravely bruised."

His hand retreated back. Underneath her natural compassion, Chry heard the tone of *if that Lanke lout* ever *bruises you again, he'll wake up licking dirt off the Garden floor.*

He paused.

"Aye, nothing too awful though, I guess." He passed a hand over his shoulder and restrained a grimace. It was as if a horse, one of the horses in Oscar's stables, the stallion probably, had galloped around the Market circle with him tied to its saddle. "It's just a little sore but, I mean, we should probably get your bruise…"

"Who do you think they were?"

Her sapphires had abandoned him for the path leading to Domum's gates. Not a trace of their former conversation remained. Her brow was creased into a rare frown of focus. The first traces of wind flicked golden curls off her shoulders. Her fingers still held his arm lightly as if gentle not to shatter Chry the Vase into a thousand, tiny shards.

With those bruises, Aimee looked as formidable as she was beautiful.

She'll most likely jab me in the jaw if I mention her bruises again.

But that was it, wasn't it? Chry couldn't just ignore his worry like Aimee did her injuries, even though he knew the most Gladion could do was slap a honey poultice over cheek and chin, toss her A Mother's Touch to drink, and suggest for her to stay home and rest. Even so, it's unlikely she would've remained fixed beneath his roof. Asking her to remain locked inside all day just so she could "heal" was like asking a finch not to fly away from the open door of its cage. Above all else, Aimee treasured freedom, the freedom to explore the folk and legs of Domum and pretend her injuries were like trinkets she could leave at home hanging from a peg.

At least, that's what it seemed like to Chry.

He rubbed his lips together and wiped the sweat dripping from his chin. The sun had cowered behind the squat hovels to create the blaze of a home burning. The first leg had thinned of Domumites, most having returned home to prepare for the chilling night to come. Before long, he joined her in staring off at Eulgash knew what.

Chry, too, had his thoughts on who these men were but nothing he'd go gambling at the Pits with. One thing he did know was that Vion was a Lanke. Even a blind Mi'Mal'Ren could see that. But why Vion was in Domum and how he had entered, being a Lanke and all, was harder to reason. Chry reckoned either the gorgeous man or the one they called Bar had somehow persuaded the guards. Not for a mark did he believe that Vion had approached the gates alone. If that had happened, he probably would've passed by the Lanke this morning, prickled with a litter of splintery arrows like a bloodied Thrones Green.

The other man though wasn't so easy to reckon.

If Chry had to guess, the man did seem like he hailed from Admah but not from the Wastelands, probably from one of the other three nations: Noma Devolum, Ontinia, or Etherine. He certainly wasn't from Domum or Poltuck Mines—folk were too rugged for a man like that. His clothing was clear of smudges, stains, tears, and dust gathered from living within these barren lands, and the man himself was well-washed—a foreign currency for Domumites who couldn't even see their arms through thick coats of dirt.

There was something else unique about him, too. His scent, as unusual as it sounded, was familiar. Chry thought he smelled it heretofore on Hatchen, a merchant from a Southern caravan company who sometimes traveled from the coasts of Etherine to bring Skinny Reds to the Market—their grey scales striped with the bloody truth of their name, the pinkish meat salted for thereafter. That salty smell from the carts and Hatchen was akin to the man's but not quite as raw, dead, and slimy. His was more like salt grains ground together in hand then tossed into a pleasant breeze. Under its spell, muscles loosened, thoughts cleared, and its only request was to close their eyes and believe in the wonders beyond the walls of Domum.

Mayhap the stories are true then, that the Grey Sea is as big as they say it is, that Cadaqu is built from crystal with Illum on every street, that there are such places as sandy deserts, an island where only fish lived, mountains reaching the heights of Nomanos, swamps filled with—what had Harlequin called them?—"blind, shaggy creatures whose own mothers wouldn't dare give them a smouch."

There was also the name the man had mentioned.

Bar.

Again it felt…familiar. It wasn't a name easily forgotten and Chry felt like Gladion had mentioned it heretofore, but it could be just as likely that he was thinking about the bar at the Brewing Beetle.

Regardless, Chry wondered if Bar was just as absurd and dangerous as these two were. His name was respected enough to at least calm Vion. Hard to believe the beast could ever be tamed, but his eyes had not deceived him. This Bar fellow could be somewhat of a leader then and those two must be his followers or something like that.

It'd explain a lot if it was true, especially why Vion and the man— opposite in approach, appearance, and tongue—were traveling together. They really shouldn't be. Vion could barely suppress his anger. The slightest remark—let's say from a blacksmith's daughter and a farmer's son—had nearly become their deaths. So how could Vion *ever* withstand a man whose mouth, every time it opened, spewed sermons that shamed even the heretic Ka'De'Coma.

It would also explain why there were so many horses inside of Oscar's stables, horses that really shouldn't be there.

A group of five, if I remember it right. Same as the horses.

And…well what? A group of five what?

Farmers, Rusios, miners, guards, mercenaries, Tanners, Drunkards?

Eulgash, was this any use to them? Really? The two, five, or twenty of them were still as unknown to him as the sands of Novania and the seas of Etherine. They could be traveling with an escort of Kemals for all he knew: Bar, their prideful leader, guiding them forward through a wave of its smoky hand.

Returning from his thoughts, Chry realized he wasn't gazing forward anymore but at the crusty blood beneath his fingernails. The blood of the man he had scratched.

His fingers wriggled like silver serpents.

"They're not from Domum. I don't think."

Aimee hmmed, half-acknowledging his response. For what seemed like another age, they remained silent, not talking, not comforting. Her sapphires dropped to her feet, brow wrinkled in stern concentration before loosening.

A smile softened her lips.

"Well, that's enough of them, I should think," she sent that smile to Chry, hinting at adventure. "We need to retrieve the rest of what Gladion asked of us before dusk falls. I would like to visit Ralesh's ladder too before I have to…" A faint hesitation. "I mean, before you return home."

Chry was too preoccupied with his fingers to reckon immediately as if he'd been viciously clawing at a wooden wall that blocked him off from the world beyond. Thereafter, he nodded, looked furtively back at where Vion and the man had left them and stared before leaving his musings to follow Aimee down the first leg.

XV

Ralesh's ladder was an unused, largely forgotten entry to the parapets of Domum. There were many ladders like this across town: one at the main entrance, another off the beaten path of Vassal Renega's home, two others in the Well, and one near Gladion's that they could've climbed to view the vastness of the Wastelands. But these sections of the wall were usually where the guards patrolled and where they'd most likely be caught (again) and thrown back down (again). Ralesh's ladder, abandoned since the Rattle Trade had lost control of Poltuck Mines, granted them an opportunity to sneak up the rungs and appreciate the Forest, free from the armored oafs.

Ralesh Sanal himself, for as long as Chry could remember, seemed wary to travel far from this ladder, hence the name. To leave its rickety rungs would mean entering into the Pits, Ironsmelt, or the Pools, all of which meant Condemnation either by Dry-Mouth, hammer, or drowning in pools of piss. Chry reckoned, just by looking at him now from afar, that these choices weren't too convincing to Ralesh.

As folk had come to reckon, Ralesh was a hard man to forget—and not in the way it was hard to forget Aimee. He was like a scrawny, bloody-eyed Lanke who had guzzled down five tumblers of Narthema, the strongest liquor known to the Wastelands, and held a worrying obsession in watching the heads of rodents pop like rare Rosemary Grapes. One eye was bigger than the next, but barely, just enough so it was difficult for folk who didn't pass him every day to spot the difference. Beneath the usual stench of Domum was his insufferable reek—burning rags and a mule's corpse basking in the heat. It was one of many reasons why Chry and Aimee were now hugging the walls of a long-deserted storehouse the Rattle Trade once used for ore, sidling quietly toward Ralesh's ladder.

The mage in question was huddled within a collapsing alley across a trickle of dirt they called a road. He kept snapping his fingers at a brown lump that looked as if Ralesh had eaten a bundle of fur and squatted it back out. From the lump curled a pinkish tail like a skinned snake. Every so often, a snap would yield a flame's flicker and Ralesh would squeal to himself in incoherent delight. His hands became the shake of a devout Nomatus who thought he had just experienced a brush of Eulgash's good grace.

The lump swelled and shrank.

Chry and Aimee made quick of the situation. They veered toward the splintery ladder—Chry's mind thinking of it as the contorted spine of an orphan cowering away from (*Vion's*) Miss Reselda's glare. Though Aimee and Chry were in what Rusios called "spitting distance" of Ralesh, the mage never gave them a glance. He was too gripped by his meal, his bigger eye bulging in hopes of lighting the fur aflame.

Their ascent went undisturbed. Aimee held the knapsack close to her to limit its clinking and thumping. Chry climbed close with each rung moaning at their weight. He refrained from looking up since he didn't want Aimee to think he was lewd and vulgar like Russel Hide and the Rattles. His eyes climbed the rungs with his hands.

They retrieved all of what Gladion asked of them. After bumping into Vion and that unforgettable man, they crossed through the Market again where Chry traded a bushel of carrot stocks for a jar of dried corn and a handful of moxam before the merchants abandoned their carts for the alehouses. Thereafter, they fled to the end of the third leg where they bought Gladion's iron blooms. As usual, the Caravans from Poltuck Mines were first greeted outside the walls by the Proprietors of the Rattle Trade. After the Rattle Trade traded for a sufficient supply, levies were enforced on any merchant who wished to sell within the walls of Domum. Considering the horde of guards around these gates from dawn to dusk, Chry reckoned Vassal Renega saw a share of the mox, too.

With the iron blooms *tink*ing inside her now heavy knapsack, the blacksmiths with the other Rattles at the Thirsty-Mouth Cobra, and Vera Ironsmaid, Proprietor of Ironsmelt, known to the Rattles as "Vera, the Iron Cunt," screaming and lashing at bloom merchants, Aimee dragged Chry through the outskirts of Ironsmelt where the residue of sooty smoke stung his eyes and dried his mouth until they slipped around the smithies, snuck passed Ralesh, ascended the ladder, and climbed over the last rung to behold the Forest of the Lost.

Chry could not stop himself from gaping.

The Son was mid-Ainason, and the trees were inclined to flaunt their leaves. Rosewoods roamed away as if unrolling a verdant scroll, North to the Forgotten Coast, South to Etherine, and East to the Void. Alders sprouted their fiery hair within the greenery, each branch groping for the sky to capture the last slivers of sunset. Leaves were set ablaze. White-linen lichen hugged the bark, and if Chry looked hard enough, there were corncob seeds hanging from the alders like little lanterns. Altogether, it was like watching trees forge a field of gold and green stars.

But this ideal was just as dangerous and misleading as the illusionary oases. Thankfully, the whispers, those he heard when his father took him to the Gardens, could not be heard from the walls, but he knew if he traveled beneath its canopy, he'd feel them crawling across his neck like sickly, squirmy worms. If he stayed too long, or if he visited too much, he might start withering to the likes of the Gardeners, speaking nonsense to themselves or speaking nothing at all.

If he escaped in time, he'd only end up like Simon Hide—a rowdy, fifteen-year-reckon Withdraw who had had enough of the Rattle Trade and one day decided to flee into the Forest. A day or two thereafter, he came back half the man he wanted to be. Where others like Salis Wood failed to return, Simon Hide came back numb. All he did was pick up his pliers, open the mouth of a dead Dry-Mouth, and limply pluck out its fangs, continuing his work for the Rattle Trade without complaint.

And to think, just beyond the Forest awaits the Void.

Chry shivered.

"—always so beautiful, isn't it?"

His face screwed in.

Simon...Beautiful? He thought but then awoke inside his body.

He was along the palisades on a walkway with a low wall facing the inside of town. Rosewood spires, their splintery skin bleeding with the sun, scraped at dusk and elbowed one another as if fighting for the last shreds of warmth before nightfall. Not a single guard was patrolling, and Aimee, a gorgeous woman, who was asking him not about Simon but about how beautiful the Forest was, stood next to him.

When she did not hear a response, Aimee turned her sapphire eyes of concern from the Forest to him. Her bronze skin glowed. He stared at her, his lips open like a loose hinge then tightening into a smile.

Never did he take his eyes off her.

"Aye, that it is," he whispered and laced his fingers with hers.

XVI

Night arrived.

The fingers of wind scraped against the parapet and ruffled his sweaty, slick hair. Behind their backs, the earth had swallowed the sun and dusk struggled to survive. Soon, the shadow of Domum would overwhelm them. They had traveled here enough during dusk to know they'd have to follow the candlelight within the shops of the Eduavel District or steal a torch from Ironsmelt to make it back to Gladion's.

This made Chry think of Gladion pacing beside a doused fire or huffing it to the first leg to search for a Chry and Aimee that he had heard were brutally beaten by a crazed Lanke. It was a worry, for certain, but when Chry glanced at Aimee beside him, when he noticed the serenity and comfort of her smile, he ignored these thoughts. If she wasn't worried about returning to Gladion's, he wouldn't either.

As if knowing he was thinking of her, Aimee's hand slipped away.

His hand remained grasping, but when he realized her hand was no longer there, Chry looked at her for an explanation. He received none. She was just staring down at the parapet, her brow brooding dark.

He reckoned he knew what that face meant.

"We can stay a little longer if you want," he mumbled. "I mean, I think we still have a ma—"

"It's not that, Chry."

Her whisper was a cold steel snake tracing up his spine and around his neck. It made it hard to breathe. Something was coming. A warning. Something in the way she diverted her eyes and spoke silently that told him not all was right.

"Then what's…" He swallowed.

Stop feeling so damn sorry for yourself thinking something bad's going to happen when there's nothing, and I mean nothing, *to worry about. The next words out of Aimee's mouth will be—*

Finally, Aimee looked at him and hinted at a smile.

"I've bought you a gift."

His throat shuddered a sound.

"A, uh, gift?"

Her lips curved into an adventurous smirk. Without a word, she shoved her hand into her knapsack, scavenged around before drawing out a lace of small links. Seeing it nudged his memory, but he couldn't quite remember where he had seen it heretofore until its end trickled out with a teardrop sapphire, enclosed in a river of silver. The necklace swayed in the wind and, in the last of the light, its gem winked at him.

Then he remembered.

Dry Trinkets. This was the item she had bought at Dry Trinkets and hid from him.

"Aimee...I..."

Chry reached a dreamy hand for the lace, gentle but firm in receiving it so the wind wouldn't whisk it away.

I mean, who wouldn't want to take this necklace. Look at it. It's just so...so...

"Beautiful," he whispered.

He couldn't contain his smile. That cold steel snake had loosened around his neck and dropped from his shoulders. The gift was both mischievous and exciting, just as he thought it'd be.

"I thank you for the gift," he said. "But how- how'd you even pay for this? I mean, no, that's not what I meant. I just know how scarce mox—"

"Enough about the cost, my courageous crow." She smiled. "Enjoy the gift."

The sides of his neck reddened. Without further complaint, he did as he was told and focused on the gift.

The necklace was utterly captivating. This wasn't a lie he'd tell his grandmother or Gladion so he wouldn't disappoint them and shove the gifts down to the bottom of a chest while they weren't looking. No, this was none of that. He enjoyed it so much, he almost forgot that folk usually put *on* necklaces when they received them.

When he glanced at Aimee, her face told of patience but beneath her mask stirred restlessness.

Chry hurried then. He looped it over his head. The silver tinked softly. The sapphire rested on his chest between the missing buttons of his shirt. Along his tanned skin, the necklace looked like a deadened Illum stone spreading skeletal wings.

His smile wouldn't stop revealing his crooked teeth. He admired the gem between his thumb and forefinger as the nightly gusts approached. His clothes rippled like a flag, his hair whisked, and the wind whistled. Beneath his feet was the groaning of rosewood.

He barely noticed.

"Chry..."

A voice from beneath water. The necklace shimmering.

"Uah…?"

That's a word, right? Aye, close enough, he thought giggly.

"I'm leaving…Tomorrow, at dawn."

His grinning paused and then fell. He looked up at Aimee but was meet with an ominous flatness: her expression calm, concentrated, and firm. Her eyes too…They weren't staring at him but below and to the right, unable or simply unwilling to meet his.

Only then did a claw clutch at his heart. His lungs were breathless.

"What…What do you mean?"

He knew well what she meant but couldn't reckon it as true. She denied him a response, just kept staring past him into the glowing remains of the sun. That's when the claw shoved through his throat and caught his tongue.

"I'm leaving Domum." Chry could barely hear her mumble over the wind. "I'm not returning."

Folk like Gladion and his mother once told him that shock struck fast and hard like being kicked in the teeth by a gelding's hoof: blunt, quick, and final before the victim could even reckon where the strike came from. They lied. It wasn't so quick to kill. It spread from his chest like insidious blood, piecemeal and destructive. First through the throat in which a lump the length of a spear jutted. Then to his skull where scythes scraped at its inner walls. Eventually, it'd reach fingertips and toes.

"But—"

Her hands cupped his as his eyes, round and numb, fell to them. They were the warmth of Gladion's forge but still failed to warm the cold, iron bloom inside him.

Across his neck, the necklace weighed heavy of sorrow.

"Let me explain."

His tongue had dried to the bones of the Wastelands as he gazed at her. Aimee's fingers kneaded the top of his hand, and he would have felt discomfort if the hole of his vision had opened beyond merely Aimee. Her eyes were veiled with water. She was peering in the wind.

She swallowed before asking, "Have you heard of the Black Rings?"

He struggled.

"The…The Black Rings? Is that a…trinket or something?"

He heard a quiet, disappointed sigh as if saying *what else should I have expected.* Hearing this was like a torturous needle to the stomach. What else should he have thought? That these weren't actual black rings he and Aimee could wear around town?

"The Black Rings," she started after a steadying breath. "Is a plague which has troubled Pulchrit, the seat of Ontinia's king, for years now. Most of Ontinia has been devastated by the disease but, as I have heard, Pulchrit is of the worst. The relief group, Hypenian, formed in response, has been sending several of its members across Admah for supplies: food, water, herbs, other ingredients for concoctions, potions, and poultices. Miss Maylord says if it can be of use, it will do.

"That being said, their sojourns to Domum are less frequent due to how far we are from Pulchrit and the dangers the Wastelands present to travelers. Nevertheless, they are necessary to acquire the Elos needed in preparing Goldendrake." She hesitated before saying, "I'd say they travel here every year or so, and if I don't leave with them tomorrow…"

She let that simmer. Gusts pushed against them lightly. Downcast, Chry was lost in what a life would be like without Aimee. Thinking about confronting Miss Reselda or mayhap Vion again without Aimee by his side was enough for a ghastly mist to cover his heart.

"There's…something else though."

He looked up, eyes almost pleading. She didn't respond immediately.

"What is it?" He asked.

"I…" She hesitated. "I want you to come with me Chry."

He retreated faintly, his eyes two O's blurred by the opening of the dreams he had envisioned with Aimee while gazing at the constellations of heroes and legends. It would have been hard to believe if her eyes weren't so firm with hope.

"Pray," she urged. "Come see Admah with me. Miss Maylord has already approved of you traveling with us, and the caravan will supply us provisions, so all you will need is your comforts." As if prompting, there came a comfort to her smile, something that he guessed reassured her. "To think, we'll be able to see the nations, cities, and places we've dreamed of visiting for Sons. Noma Devolum, Ontinia, Etherine. The Town of Vines. The River Twins... Goodness, Chry, even the crystal city of Cadaqu. Remember when we wondered how thrilling it'd be to see and *feel* the crystal? Remember how Hatchen's eyes glowed when describing the city, how he said the buildings touched the skies and ruled the Sea? Oh and the ships! Goodness, I can't even fathom sailing on a *ship*." She giggled, and he nearly melted. There were no more tears. "And to think we tried mimicking how a boat would rock with the wheel we stole from Kurt's wagon. How *furious* that little man was; Gladion almost couldn't calm him—merely two children not knowing any better, trying to balance on a stumpy man's wheel.

"Hard to believe that it's all coming true. Soon, *we'll* be the ones telling the stories, and it'll be—it—"

She grasped for words, but never did it diminish her charm. Her voice couldn't contain its excitement, her misjudgments coated in a hopeful honey.

Chry refused to respond.

Back in their dreams, Cadaqu seemed close enough for Chry to hop on Simul and ride to in a day. He could do all of what Aimee had hoped for; he could smell the salt of the Sea and admire the grandeur of the crystal, so high their heads confessed to the clouds and breathed air that tasted clear and sweet—an unDomum-like air—and then be back in time to eat Gladion's Dry-Mouth broth.

Why, then, after all these years of dreaming, did it now feel so far away? It was almost like the travel between them and Cadaqu had stretched to leagues, and between these leagues stretched more furlongs of dry and dangerous riding. This did not happen when he was dreaming. When he was within the safety of his dreams, Chry could fly through the streets of Cadaqu free from fear. Thinking more on it, he reckoned there was a certain freedom to this too—knowing that he could stay within the walls of Domum then return to Aimee's room or to the top of the Ruckers' roof where they could pretend to have thrilling adventures if only they were reincarnated elsewhere.

But now, now that Aimee was actually calling to travel elsewhere…

"Aye…" he said low enough for the winds to take. "It'll be amazing."

She wasn't looking at him but through him to lands beyond the Wastelands. This did not last. When she realized he wouldn't say anymore, when she returned to the present to find Chry here, sobered and aloof, her grin shriveled like a flower on hardpan.

"But you still won't come…Will you?"

He tried not to flinch, clamping his teeth together. This time, it was he who couldn't look at her.

Aimee bore an unmoving stare. Her next words were iron.

"All those times we dreamed of Cadaqu, the Grey Sea, Ontinia, mountains and seas and rivers…Were these illusions to you? Were we dreaming just so we could delude ourselves?"

"You know I—"

"*Nonsense!*" Her cry thwacked his forehead. Chry was so startled he thought a whip had bitten him. "You know as well as I do that Gladion has the mox *and* the patience to care for Clostra. He has a pen behind the hovel so your pigs can have their farrow and he would have no complaints about harvesting the cornfields until their tails green."

She was blotting out each of his excuses but, instead of huddling inside a fetal ball, Chry bristled.

"And what about Simul, huh?" He spat. "Who's going to care for him? *Oscar*? He'll butcher and carve the horse for hide. Within. The. *Day*."

"You must be as ignorant as a Smar. How are you going to travel with us if you don't have a steed to ride on?"

He threw up his arms.

"Well *I* didn't fucking know that! *You* were the one who said this lord person would have all that stuff for me and, well, give me the ride that I'd- I'd…"

Just when he thought he could defend himself, Chry stumbled on his words. Like a Lanke horde, Aimee was closing in, about to torch his home. He'd have to piece together *something* before she grew reckless, barged in, and burned it down.

His teeth ground together; his face gathered and worked.

"What about the farmhouse then," he claimed. "Am I just, what, going to leave it all behind me an-and let some Rattle use it as their Thirsty-Mouth? What would my father—"

"Your father isn't *here*, Chry. He's gone and he's been gone for three years now. Three *years*! And yet you *still* let fear rule you. Of him *and* of the Wastelands."

He opened his mouth, but nothing came out. At the deepest level, he knew Aimee was right. If he dug far enough beneath the dirt and soil, fear would be the hardpan beneath it. A pickaxe could break through it, like all those days he spent in the fields tilling for his crops. But every time he tried swinging that axe now, his arms locked and his legs rattled.

He convinced himself it was here at the farmhouse where he belonged. Kneeling by his cornfield, within his house, beside her bed, too scared to stand on two feet and stumble out into the Wastelands with a hope of finding Etherine or, mayhap, someplace better. And *why* folk would ask was he so scared? Because every time he gazed out into the Wastelands, far out, passed the comforts of home and habit, he pictured the face of Vion glaring down at him. He pictured that giant bird, hunched over a cattle's carcass, its snout rummaging around the pinkish cords of its stomach. He pictured unnamed and unseen creatures of the Forest lurching out for the flank of his steed. He pictured losing himself inside the Wastelands just like those wayward merchants who saw faraway oases and thought, "Oh Eulgash, he has saved me." He pictured losing his footing out on one of those ship things and plunging into a water so vast it rivaled the Wastelands. He pictured those Lanke hordes capturing him, pinning him down, ripping at his trousers as their cobra skin skirts steadily rose from their crotches. And every time Chry pictured them—any of them—he had to restrain the urge to run into his farmhouse and slam the door shut or urge his horse forward so they could reach Domum faster. How then could he think that some boy could ever see the city of Cadaqu when he couldn't even step beyond the shadows of Domum?

Here, in Domum, in his farmhouse, he knew what to expect. Out there, beyond comfort and consistency, was chaos.

Chry was no courageous hero.

Chry was no Simul.

The divisive lines of Aimee's face receded when she realized he would not fight back. In its wake remained a frank stare, her eyes glossy with the return of tears.

Eulgash, be kind. That stare hurt him more than any weapon ever could.

After a pause, Aimee dipped her head, mayhap so he wouldn't reckon those tears because just then, he heard the start of sniffling. It was suppressed, and her shuddering breath was so quiet it could've been the wind. Yet Chry had no illusions. This was no oasis.

Emotion rolled through his throat. The weakness of his heart drove his hands into a violent shake, not from the cold but from the fear he'd lose control and break down weeping in front of the woman he loved.

Aimee nodded to herself. Night huddled beneath her sockets like greedy, shadowy Kemals. With a voice low but firm, she said, "I understand Chry. Believe me, I do."

It was the last he could take.

Within his nose and eyes swelled an oppressive sob. Snot dribbled out of his nostril. He sniffled and pressed his lips hard, but it was of little use. Something trailed down his cheek.

The wind's in my eye, he thought. *That's all. That's it.*

Through the watery curtain covering his eyes, Chry reckoned the wind stealing her tears away.

"When we leave tomorrow, the caravan will be passing by the farmhouse." Her breath was unsteady, and there was a moment when even she could not speak. "Y-you can make your decision when we arrive."

Chry, with no words of comfort, could only nod.

XVII

Marks of the candle clock passed into monotony. Chry, squinting against the wind, gathered the reins of Simul into one hand and stuffed his hands into the front of his trousers, his legs pinching the warm flanks of Simul. The gelding was bowing its head and walking forward as to retain the despondency of its master. It couldn't be blamed. He was riding to the farmhouse when the gusts became unruly, cutting through clothing like tiny shards of glass. The excess of the reins whipped. Simul's dark brown mane yanked and tugged. Sometimes, the horse whimpered discontent. Far out to his left beneath a shining moon, two days from becoming Vigilant, was the rustle of the Forest. Chry could barely hear it. Anything other than the howling of the wind was hard to reckon.

The Wastelands had become as frigid as rattle balls.

That doesn't even sound right, he thought downcast, clenching at the reins. *But I guess Satch would approve. He can't take a breath without mentioning them.*

Even these thoughts manifested as a slug through the mud of misery. He could give less of a rattle about Satch, about snakes, about the cold night, about anything really. The only cold he cared about was that which leaked from within. Deadened and sluggish, sapping warmth from the farthest reaches of his blood. Every limb had become numb. It was like he wasn't even there. Soon, he'd just fade into the night.

It'd be better like that, he thought absently.

After descending Ralesh's ladder and parting from Aimee, both exchanging half-hearted reassurances they'd meet again the next day, Chry moped across the legs and Market of Domum in a silent fright. Back at the stables, Oscar was sitting in the same place he always was:

in his rocking chair with a candle clock beside him in a glass-cracked and iron-weathered lantern. Distantly, he wondered if the old man *ever* stood from his seat to enter the hovel behind his stables. Chry reckoned not.

Within the stables, the five horses he'd encountered heretofore were gone. Vion and the gorgeous man—both, Chry guessed—had taken their steeds to depart from Domum, probably traveling alongside the Forest until the road bent toward the river city of Viamous or branched off to the city of Dhymes. Either way, they'd still have to ride somewhat near the farmhouse. Mayhap not close enough to *see* the farmhouse (in the night especially) but close enough so that if they wandered too far from the swaying trees, they'd stumble upon a creaky, dying structure with a sleepy, greying grandmother inside.

If Eulgash wills it.

Upon a usual departure from Domum, Chry would've returned to Gladion's with Aimee and received the blacksmith's Obolio coat for the cold. This day he had not gone back. He did not go with Aimee. Their promises of seeing each other the next day were void of meaning.

It could be when she and this Miss Maylord came in the morning to his farmhouse, he would finally accept the shock and despair of her departure and be courageous enough to give her a decent farewell, embracing her in his arms, smelling the herbal remedy of her hair, cupping her cheeks and sending her off with a dawning kiss. Like what his father would have expected.

But it was also possible, more likely he thought, that he'd stumble out from the house toward Aimee, half-naked with his trousers on backward, grandmother rasping something from within the suffocating walls, his stare wild but devoid of life as those in the caravan would raise eyebrows at the sad sight. He'd shake his head "no" when she asked him to join her again, then he'd stand there remorseful as they rolled forever into the Wastelands.

Dawn was a terrifying thought.

Simul's hooves clacked along the hardpan. Threats of a rolled fetlock nestled between its cracks. Chry, upon further thought, forced his hands out of his trousers and kept a tighter grip on the reins. His jaw clacked. Though he wouldn't think on it, he was lucky there was enough moonlight to cross the Wastelands. If there had been a Blind Moon or even a Weary Moon, he might've had to reconsider Gladion's offer.

But he couldn't. That just couldn't happen.

This was when he saw it.

A flickering speck.

At first, he had not noticed it. Under him, Simul sensed the nearness of four walls, a trough of dirty water, and stale hay, hurrying onto a steady trot. Soon, they'd be back, the gelding neighing gratefully through its stall, Mister and Missus Swiggles squealing beside the house, and Chry slumped onto his pallet.

A farm, a grandmother, a field, and a Gladion every turn of the moon.

The life I live. The life I've asked for.

This is not your choice but your obligation.

Your father isn't here, Chry.

You still let fear rule you.

I'm not afraid. I did this because father…

Then why the *fuck* did he feel so nervous when Aimee asked him to leave? Why was it that Chry felt like some six-year-reckon all over again, glancing over his shoulder and expecting to see some-some reincarnated beast in the saddle with him caressing a claw across the hard lump of his neck? Why was he so *fucking SCARED* when there was no one, *no one* else around.

Well, let's just think about this then.

He didn't want to think about it.

The farmhouse isn't too awful to live in.

Aye.

I mean, you've been living in it for sixteen years now and you could be like those Rattles along the walls of the Residential district: no tongue, one eye, reeking, limbless.

Aye.

What ensued was a bout of silence. It wasn't the—

Chry stopped and stared. That speck. It wasn't a speck anymore but a single stroke of light where darkness should have been promised. It was as if the pointy end of a sword had stabbed through black cloth to reveal daylight.

The wind blew, but Chry stared.

He really didn't know *what* it was supposed to be. He guessed it was something like a wandering Kemal but instead of the dark clouds folk claimed their bodies to be, this Kemal descended from the sun, a body captured by light. But that was just absurd. Kemals were legend enough as it was with only deranged elders like Mi touting they've met one.

He could only stand by in anticipation. Beneath him, his gelding shied and whimpered uncomfortably.

The light burned bright from within the hollowness of his attention. Wind, shadow, steed, farm obscured beyond this hollow hole. From within, the light drew him closer. A grim curiosity tinged his blood.

It's growing too, isn't it? He wondered. *Could it be coming toward me? No, it'd be faster than that, wouldn't it? Something like, well, torches on horseback.*

That wasn't it either. He was *sure* it wasn't. It was steady in place, that he could tell now, and was flickering like the wavery illusion of a candle clock inside of his...his...home.

Chry's heart dropped; his blood numbed. He stared at that light for so long he reckoned his eyes would shrivel.

My house, my farmhouse...

It's burning...

He couldn't turn away.

This...

No, it couldn't be. It couldn't.

His throat thrummed, dizzying. Bellows of laughter, somewhere. Oscar. Vion. Aimee.

And yet that light stood in the exact place his farmhouse had for sixteen years and his eyes wouldn't lie to him. A ravenous tremble shook his fingers, his nose was runny and his- his-

He slammed his feet against Simul's flanks. His mind leapt thirty strides forward, but the gelding responded to the present: whinnying, jerking its head, then rearing its front hooves as if brawling with Eulgash.

Chry was thrown from his saddle. He had the vague recollection of still gripping the reins when a swish of its tail caught his eye. He cried out. His shoulder *thump*ed against the hardpan, his foot still caught in the foothold. There was metallic ringing. Grunts and moans which must've been the gelding's cue to gallop. Simul smacked its hooves down—a damnable smack—then charged forward without remorse. Chry was propping himself on his elbows when the foot caught in the foothold yanked back. His elbows flew out from under him, and his face kissed the hardpan hard. Crackles of pain radiated out like lightning. *How worthless are you* was the thought he had before hearing the crunch of his nose. There was a spurt of bloody warmth.

He screamed out a condemnation as Simul dragged him like a horse-pulled carriage. His body skipped, the plaything for some mythical Es'Tal'Mis giant to flail around. One moment it was the Vigilant Moon he saw. Another moment, his shoulder hammering down. The next, the ghastly apparition of his steed. Next, slippery shadows. Next, flying. Next, a faint, fiery speck.

His leg cried after every pull.

I'm going to die. I'm going to be crushed and mangled and unrecognizable like Eduala was, and Aimee's going to be like Reselda was, stumbling upon my shattered bones and blood and body, and I'll be rotting too and mayhap a carrion crow will…

His foot untangled. He landed rolling, his arms flopping madly. A clumpy rock punched his hip, a stone fist to the bone with the sound of crackling as the rocky hand flopped him onto his belly.

He finally sprawled still but the world…it…all of it just kept spinning. It was everywhere but somewhere else. The crack he glared at wasn't *a* crack but three, four mayhap, five probably. The core of his face was a dripping mess, bulged like a tender boil about to burst. The hard dirt cooled his cheek but couldn't submerge the throbbing bruise of his skin. His thigh a farmer's ache, his hip taken to with the flat head of a pickaxe. All of this with the taste of copper over his tongue.

My tongue

Bit it.

Did I?

Did.

Beyond the bleeding, Simul's neighs fled into the night.

Groans, eyes yawing for sight, Chry patted at the ground then groped for his nose, pawing at a nostril. His teeth sucked in a curt spit of air. The sound he heard from his nose was like ore rubbing against a stone wall.

What did you think *was...It couldn't...I...Aye...Hurt...*

Even his thoughts had succumbed. His limbs slumped. He laid still. His forefinger twitched. The sky bore against him. His stomach rumbled as if hunger were the first necessity he must satisfy. Behind his head, there was a ticking crawl that he knew only from a Desert Beetle, arising from somewhere, thrumming a reflection, then withdrawing back to where it came. He listened to the urgency of his breath.

His eyes dipped dangerously, fluttering back open. He...No, anywhere but here. Sleep. Back. On the pallet.

Pray, take me back home. Kill me a thousand times and resurrect me a thousand more but when I resurrect that thousandth and first time, Eulgash, pray, whatever you deem worthy, just...just pray, let me be back there. Let none of this be real. Just...let me have this one blessing.

Just this one.

He pried open eyes bleeding with tears but all he could reckon was that fire, blazing through his childhood.

Where were you?

The voice was as vivid as if she were next to him on her rocking chair.

Why weren't you here, Chry? Why were you with her? *Why did you* leave *us? Why did you let this happen to us? Why didn't you take better care of us? Why weren't you home by dusk like you said you'd be? Why weren't you a better son, a better farmer? Why were you so ungrateful? Why did you abandon us and your responsibilities? Why did you…*

These were his last moments before he slipped into the skin of the hardpan.

XVIII

There were five.

They rode toward the Forest from the speck. Their bodies were black with soot, speckled in blood, and scented by fire, like death arisen from coffins of ash. Some slumped across their steed in pursuit of dreams where screams died between a woman's loins. Another cast a silver glare out at the Wastelands, the coppery taste of gore tipped on their tongue. One appeared deadened to the tragedies of heretofore. And another held inside their gut an unease as if the night were accusing them with a limp, lanky finger.

Silent still, they followed forward.

The Forest neared—they could feel it through their years of travel—and its leaves would soon glow by their flame. The gusty night communed. The loose leather of a saddle flapped. Belt buckles rattled. Departing from the squeals of swine crept the indiscernible whinnies of a horse. The winds could be the culprit, manipulating what they had heard with what they had suspected. They thought naught and knew better than to be deceived. It was around here but the night had shredded its calls and scattered it skyward so the sounds could not be traced. No steed or rider, for no horse roamed willingly into the Wastelands.

Soon, they heard no more.

They pressed on. Most glances were an obscured nuisance. The Vigilant Moon shone the path forward, shaping sights and sounds in the likes of a world beneath the sea. Without its light, the lump would've been no more than an apparition. With its light, the body was a misshaped stone. A wandering eye would've known nothing of it. After they had tended to the fire and those associated, the last presence they'd be hunting for would be a boy. But the other—strange, empty, almost a limb to the darkness itself save for the firelight flickering from its black, robed hand—stared at it until its sheets of shadows were peeled off one by one.

Horse hooves whispered for it. Another departed the line, another. The vanguard halted, creaked its neck back, regarded the shadows hounding at their heels, observed, contemplated, then cautioned toward the rest.

A hive of others swarmed around the body. Their miasmas buzzed with the stench of curiosity and echoes of a conversation. Each word struck a spark, provoked a growl, or whipped a quip. But only silence beckoned at the end. A decision wafted within like the sighing strands of a campfire.

Enough time was wasted.

Limbs detached from their mounts, descended on the boy.

The Wastelands moaned its final farewell, and the night slept.

Bar's Discretion

I

Even before the body woke, Bar knew he would be a nuisance.

The boy was weak. Onvi described him as lean and, as the thief claimed, "fierce enough to wrestle with the big, bad Vion." Bar was not so inclined to praise. To him, the boy resembled a fishbone thin enough for Vion to break with his teeth.

He was also young and naïve. Imprudence was a natural trait for youth and a precarious one that would only lead to the death of innocents. Bar would not have this, especially now with how close he was.

The boy was thus futile to both him and the Runners.

Breathing deeply, he rested his arms on his knees. Alone, his well-formed shoulders revealed their weariness: hunched, knotted, the neck a lean spear of strain. His shin nagged in discomfort, the scars throbbed over his heart, and his countenance, always maintaining a face of fortitude in front of the others, experienced a bleeding effect; trenches burrowed into his brow, and blackish purple crests rocked beneath his stare.

When they first encountered the boy the night heretofore, he was sprawled on the hardpan and shattered like the remnants of a cart fallen from the face of an Ontinian mountain. The difference was that the body was still breathing when Ambia hovered her fingers beneath its nose; the carts Bar would search for in the mountains upon the request of the Hypenian were neither breathing nor alive, the closest description being that of unrecognizable debris.

Yet Ambia, once Bar's tent was built and the boy was placed inside, tended to his wounds without word. She doffed his ripped rags and donned him with clean linen from her satchel, washed the blood from his cuts and scrapes with the drinking water from her pouch then cleansed the wounds by dampening the foulard with Narthema, mended the broken nose and hip, administered remedies as needed, rested his head from her lap onto a bundled blanket of Black Wool. No one else helped her.

She could never resist mending those in need, regardless of their morality.

He stared at the wraps cupped around the boy's nose, pea-green poultice oozing out as mucus. Over his eyes soaked stripes of linen like the blindfolds the Silent wore in Asunio.

All these failings, he thought. *Whiles still suffering a state of debilitation.*

If traveling alone, Bar would've laid the body beneath the canopy of the Forest then left him for whosever god the boy believed in. But he wasn't alone, and in sooth, though he would not admit this, he wouldn't have a say in whether the boy stayed or left. Bar was the leader of the Runners and his orders would be followed. However, a leader only retained the loyalty of his men through the righteousness and valor of his actions. Abandoning a boy young enough to be their son would be neither of these. If the others desired to give this boy a chance, then he would have no choice but to—

Kill

Smile

He'll be dead soon

Bar rubbed at his baggy eyes, soot smudging them and clinging to his once pristine gambeson. His breaths became unruly. An ache rolled along the back of his sockets. The hand—

Slit their throats

His hand shook.

83

The voice. Again.

He clamped his teeth down so hard, his ears rang. Over his heart thrummed a three-scored recollection.

Slit their throats
Gouge their eyes
Keep a smile Barloc
Keep a—

He retracted his hand and tried to clench it into a fist. It resisted, clamped into a claw. The veins stood out like rope. The skin beneath his right nostril twitched. His flat stare struggled to keep form. He ordered his fingers to close but, again, they remained defiant. His arm wouldn't stop shaking. Every breath he took was stifling through a woolen mask.

He forced his eyes closed.

Admah will be purged, he concentrated. Moments taken to wash away the distractions and to envision the future gave him back his breath. *Soon, when the gems are retrieved, the suffering of the innocent will be eased.*

II

"He is in no condition to be traveling. Rest is what he needs."

"I did not ask what the boy needs."

"I know what you asked, and my answer is still the same. He has sustained too many injuries for us to voluntarily press on: contusions, lacerations, a Splinter fracture across the hip, Tearing Strain along the inner thigh, severely contused shoulder, a nose—"

"He is not our responsibility."

"He is since the moment you conceded to bringing him."

Bar stared at her. Most would have yielded to his stoicism by now, but Ambia was no such mortal. Her hazel eyes mapped defiance. They lived inside a dichotomy; they could comfort those who suffered as well as strike down those who opposed her care. It was another reason why she was perfect.

"Merely to leave him in Viamous with Sonias. She will know of a caravan that can return the boy to Domum or where—"

"This child, one Vion and Onvi *saw* in Domum, was lying in the middle of the Wastelands leagues away from any hint of civilization, beaten and bloodied with no one in sight to claim him. The nearest building was half a furlong away, and *it* burned to the ground without a survivor to its name. A person then has to wonder why a boy like him was far enough away from the Forest to make any traveler weary of losing himself to the Wastelands. Well, would you like to know where *I* think he was going?"

She was about to hear what he thought when she continued.

"That building was his home, Barloc. *That's* where he was going. And he would have died if it weren't for us."

Her hazels wandered over his shoulder towards the open flap of his tent. Her high cheekbones were knotted in scrutiny and her willowy neck was taut. Bar took these moments to consider how her countenance had reverted back to the innocent wont of a mother hoping to heal her child. It was beautiful in its subtlety. If he didn't already know what she was to him, he would have relished it.

After a while, she said softly, "How can you be so certain he will want to return to Domum?"

"Whether he does or does not is of no concern to the Runners. The Council waits for us."

"And the Council will still be there whenever we might arrive. If they wish for us to be there so swiftly, then they would have sent an entourage as they did for Lomano."

"Lomano was different."

"How?"

Her look nailed the question to his forehead. Bar took an internal breath, flexing his fist. The area where his shin had broken heretofore ached rhythmically. Ambia had drawn her arms akimbo like a Dry-Mouth brandishing its chest and threatening to bite. And though she had to bend her neck back to look at every Runner save for Cavas, her presence was never lost on them.

He tried persisting as dawn mounted behind him.

"Nonetheless, the summons from the Council are not to be dismissed."

She waved it away. "As I have said heretofore, the Council can wait. The healing of wounds cannot," her hazels flicked towards his shin. Her olive skin took on a pale shade. "I am certain you know best."

As if by command, the nerves in his shins crumpled and twisted. Men susceptible to pain might alleviate themselves through an utterance or by leaning on the other leg. Bar did not. He merely clinched his jaw.

She regarded him gently and thus cut through his stoicism like a stiletto across the throat.

"Another day, Barloc. Please. By then, the Amuias and White Wood will have healed him enough for travel. We can decide what his fate will be thereafter."

The tents' burlap stirred from the breeze. He didn't look back and only answered her with silence.

III

The boy did not wake that day.

Regardless of Bar's warnings, Ambia administered a portion of their Elos Amus to keep him submerged in slumber. Only the dingles of Ontinia, specifically those in Southwestern Halomotas, harbored the herb, and the merchants in Pulchrit tended to pair its rarity with an exorbitant price. In essence, the Runners always yearned for more. When reminded of this, the healer equally reminded Bar that the pain the boy would experience if awake would be like Bar's shin but tenfold. No amount of A Mother's Touch would soothe his screams.

Bar could not have cared less.

The Runners needed to be on their way, and the boy was becoming more of a nuisance than he could have first conceived. It irked him that the boy could be so reckless and be relieved of the consequences by the simple wave of her hand. Half the day was spent merely staring at the boy, thumbing at the keen blade of his stiletto.

Yet, upon further consideration, he reckoned it was necessary to appease her; Ambia would not forgive nor forget any acts of imprudence, those most with her patients. Four years of preparation and two years of camaraderie bound his hands.

As such, another day slipped by.

Camp had been pitched a furlong from the Forest, next to an Alderwood hut stripped and worn to its ribcage. They did not travel far the night heretofore. Once Vion strapped the boy into Ambia's saddle, their steeds started back to the Forest where they rode along its boles and leaves, its whispers crawling across their necks. They barely noticed. Bar led them forward until he thought it far enough from the Ker to reassure him of the Runners' safety. This was merely a precaution. He was not disillusioned by the supposed feeling of comfort, for the Cev and Ker roamed free in these parts of the Wastelands ever since the Lanke clans invaded Etherine. It would be ignorant as well as unwise to think these parts of the Wastelands were safe.

Per usual, Cavas remained as vigil for the night.

Sleep came and went.

The morning thereafter brought with it the mundane. Onvi, with a grin that spoke of misadventure, ventured out into the Wastelands to catch a Dry-Mouth. In his hands were the Hook and Tong the thief "borrowed" from the Rattle Trade upon their departure of Domum. As usual, Onvi was spouting his proficiency with the tools under the teachings of Satch, a Rusio for the Rattle Trade, and how "influential and insightful" their exchanges were. Yet Bar found the actual "training" unimpressive with their "influential and insightful" exchanges consisting of a plethora of Narthema, moxless pouches, and the two insightfully pissing through the second-story balustrade of the Drinking Fountain yelling "catch the Rattles below!"

Needless to say, Onvi returned cobraless.

The failure of Onvi was expected and thus accounted for. Their provisions (resupplied within the Market and consisting of Obolio and Dry-Mouth meat—dried or cured with salt—along with two cobs of corn) were enough to sustain them for their journey to Viamous. Despite these luxuries, the victuals they ate this day were seized by Vion. Perhaps knowing Onvi would fail, the former Vex left after Onvi did and returned periodically, each time with a Dry-Mouth writhing and hissing in his fist.

Ambia cooked the Dry-Mouths after Bar skinned and butchered them. Each diamond head and cobra skin he saved for thereafter. The venom Ambia or Onvi would use for poison, and the cobra skin would be salted, preserved, and sold to tanners in Viamous. Any inkling of mox would not be wasted.

They ate in silence. The sun blazed from overhead. Tendrils of smoke danced around the spit as flames sizzled the juices dripping from its cast iron. The Runners sat around it as did their tents. Their steeds nickered. The tent behind Bar where the unconscious boy recovered sustained a stillness like those of the dead he had left behind. The only Runner who did not sit with them was Vion whose hefty arm and shoulder peered from behind one of the tents. This was as expected.

Opposite the fire, Onvi slurped the tail of a Dry-Mouth. Upon consumption, his throat would rumble with satisfaction. His grin and fingers glistened with grease. Beside him sat Ambia, knees tucked beneath her inside a forest-green dress—tattered, smudged, and dusty as it always seemed to be. Unwashed brunette hair frizzled down her shoulders and over the strap of her Ironskin satchel. She ate delicately and sparsely.

Cavas was to Bar's left, cross-legged, back straight and still. His robes concealed every knuckle of his skin save a slit exposing his eyes. The irises were ebony, and the skin around them beamed as pale and bright as a Vigilant Moon. He did not eat. He simply stared at a point that could not be defined, past the fire, past Ambia, past the tents, past the reaches of the Wastelands and forever onward.

His presence here at a meal was a foreign one, but Bar did not question it.

Onvi belched vigorously, wiped his fingers on his trousers, then rested back on his elbows. His grin bore a pleasant triumph as if he was the one who caught the Dry-Mouths. His eyes glistened as much as his juice-covered lips and chin.

"I do say, my dearies, wasn't *that* a pleasant treat from Vion? Would've thought the oaf was empty of such kindness. Actually, on second thought," the volume of his voice rose a knuckle. Bar presumed he wanted Vion to hear. "Our lustful oaf *did* show princess Astrada how kind he could be. And from what *I* saw, his little missus made sure to repay him in full. If I wasn't an expert in the throes of love, I would've thought their relations bashful." Onvi flicked his hand up to the sky and paired it with a theatrical sigh. "But alas, even the best and brightest of us can be fooled."

Vion did not turn. The muscles in his back pulled and pushed as he ate. Unlike Onvi, Bar and Ambia kept eating from their chipped, pine plates. Cavas went without touching his food.

Grin fading, Onvi stared at them thoughtfully. He flicked his beautiful, blue eyes past Bar, back at him, then hinted at a smile.

"I'm reckoning one day we'll talk about what you have hiding inside that tent of yours, Bar. And, mind you, I don't mean what's inside your trousers."

Shameless and vexing. These were the words he would use to describe Onvi.

Despite the provocation, he deprived Onvi of the retort he desired. His prying was normal—little could happen within the Runners without Onvi wading to the source. Thus, when his mouth opened, etiquette dictated silence must ensue. As Bar came to realize over this last year and a half, all the thief wanted to do was to provoke a Runner into speaking and then prod, guide, and listen to gather any information he didn't already know. Eventually, Onvi would relent.

Bar sopped the meaty juices of the Dry-Mouth with his wheat bread.

"So, it's silence then? Come now. I'm certain there are questions about the boy we'd all like to know. What's the boy's name? Does it rhyme with shy? Pie? Why was he stranded in the middle of nowhere when Vion and I had the unfortunate pleasure of meeting him and his pretty mistress in Domum? Where might he go from here? Back to the pigsty that is Domum? What will he do when he wakes to find out that the oh-so-charming farmhouse was oh so inconveniently burned down?"

He worked himself to a sitting position.

"What do you think Cavas? You've deigned to sit with us on this fine eventide. Are there any words of enlightenment you'd like to share? Tokens of wisdom? A joke? Why did the trout cross the sea?"

Cavas stared at the hardpan. Bar reckoned he would simply ignore the thief, obliged to remain silent rather than risk rousing those inside. Instead, like ancient and rusted gears shifting, he rotated his head to Onvi.

The stark black orbs of Cavas looked at Onvi but seemed not to regard him. The thief did not falter. In truth, his grin seemed larger now, more eager and pleased with the result. Bar peered from his meal, smoldering at the grin.

We'll

Slit

Keep a smile

hook

tug…rip…laugh…tear…

Bar looked back at his plate. He meticulously chewed his meat.

Eventually, Cavas, as if tired of looking at Onvi, rotated his head back toward the Wastelands. Onvi digested this with another sigh.

"I'm guessing that's a steady 'no' then. Our mystic mage has left us to flop on dry land once again. Really, if it were me making the decisions and whirling the hammer, I'd knock the boy upside the head until he was wide awake and smiley. Wouldn't hurt him *too* much. It's not like he can become any uglier than Vion is now, which is, now that I think about it, pretty damn ugly. Sadly, it isn't my say in these matters. I am but a mere tadpole in a pond of Soulious Depan, bottom feeders sucking the skin off the bottom of my tail."

No one stirred. Onvi continued on.

"But if I *were* the top scale in the Scale Index, there'd be some real changes made around here, let me tell you. Yeah, yeah, you're a star, Bar, and I do not envy you a bit. But there's something about sitting around mindlessly until the sun flays our flesh and the Desert Beetles defecate on our skulls that hasn't been too exciting. Where's the fun in waiting? Where's the *thrill* in it? Didn't you, Ambia, retrieve a mote of Pios Amus from Raggedy Reselda? And don't think you can lie to a soothsayer like me; I've got eyes so far up my ass I can see my tongue.

"It isn't a stretch to say then that if we wake the boy with some Pios Amus, he'd be one step away from spilling his guts. Truthfully. Not that we'd want to see any more of his flesh, mind you. At least, *I* wouldn't want to. Young men aren't my favorite kind of meat unless we visit the Lucky Ladies together. In which case, mistakes can be made, secrets can be lost, and fun can be had. I only hope—"

"Onvi."

He halted mid-word. His grin hesitated. His name was spoken by Ambia who had her eyes on her plate. Her Dry-Mouth was untouched since he started talking. Bar could sense the feeling of weariness exuding from her like an untended wound. It disturbed a puddle inside his heart where the water vibrated red. His fingers clenched his plate, his stare blank with the visions of what he would do to the thief. He used a fleck of effort to restrain the violence locked inside those hands.

Why...why...?

Ambia's next words were gentle but firm, her eyes a sadness as though the plate were a crimson crypt for those she had forsaken.

"That is enough."

Onvi's grin disappeared. His lighthearted demeanor hardened, his features shaping into a somber song.

"And what would that mean, my dear."

"It means we wish to have a moment of peace. That is all."

Onvi stared at her. Even during these rare moments when the thief was quiet, his eyes could not stop asking questions.

After a quiet thought, he left Ambia to her silence and gazed into the flames. The last of its branches whimpered. There was a short, steel poker beside the rocks edging the fire. Many years heretofore, Bar retrieved it from the blacksmiths in Whitewall. Onvi picked up its oakwood handle with his right hand—that greasy, filthy, impure hand—and prodded the coals. The fire giggled as the steel tickled the branches. A pile of them collapsed. A spectacle of sparks puffed out like an elderly cough.

For the rest of their meal, Bar's stare never left that hand.

IV

Monotonously, night descended. The eyes of many shut, and sleep arrived for the few. Bar retired to his tent, third to leave the day behind. Before entering, he took his eyes away from the flap and saw Vion, sitting and staring out at the Wastelands, isolated and alone.

It was another sleepless night.

V

Bar opened his eyes to cold steel at his neck. It was rusted, Bar could feel, each flake digging into his flesh. Something wet dribbled down and puddled at his collarbone. Above was the boy with a breath seething.

Aside from the dagger, the scene was unfolding just as Bar expected.

The first thought was from a depth manifesting seven years heretofore at Caravan's Demise. It was the voice. It called for annihilation—snap his neck, break his legs, gouge his eyes. Self-preservation. The others would understand or come to understand. They'd ride out, they'd leave, they'd be off to the Council, they'd never return.

And yet his ambition steadied him. He concentrated on the dagger.

Must have concealed it within his trousers, he thought. *Dull and rusted—passed down over the years, neglected by its owner, or both.*

Before the Runners constructed camp, Vion confiscated the boy's sheath and sword. Yet why the brute had not thoroughly inspected the boy and located this dagger was a question he would need to deal with thereafter.

Should have never trusted him. Should have killed him years heretofore.

"Who-who *are* you, what's happening, what's going on, what's—"

Terror seized the boy's eyes and voice. His sleek hair jutted to one side like a hirsute horn. Wraps of linen and poultice clung to his nose like loose paper, and the skin around his eyes gleamed wetly from the damp linen Ambia had applied. In his hand, the dagger trembled.

Bar answered with stillness. It was a familiar feeling: death. The decisions he made heretofore compelled him now to believe it was inevitable for him.

"I would ask the same of you, but it would seem I have little choice in the matter," Bar breathed. As he talked, the dagger wiggled to the bobbing of his throat. Cautious not to provoke a slip of the boy's wrist, his lower body shifted. "I am Barloc, known to those of the Runners as Bar. And to you as well, if you so choose."

Doubt fleeted across the boy's countenance. The deep creases of his anxiousness loosened. Bar felt the blade's teeth release its bite and leave the skin altogether. The boy hovered over his neck like a weakness. He was condemnable. Callow. Witless. Rash.

"The Run—"

Bar's moves were ethereal; in half a blink, his foot slid under the stomach and propelled the boy away. His hips lurched back. With it came a muffled yelp.

The boy was disorientated and confused. Bar seized the advantage. He swiveled onto his knees, plunged forward, detained the elbow, hooked fingers around the boy's wrist to flow and guide the arm into locking firmly behind the back. Hands switched, nails clamping into his arm.

Tight grips. Smooth transitions. Easier detainments.

Bar's weight dropped down, impetus forcing the boy's head and cheek to strike the Black Wool blanket Ambia so graciously, so *thoughtfully* bestowed. There was a crying call for a name. From below. But Bar shoved a knee into his chin and neck.

Whining. So much whining.

Fingers bit into the boy's wrist, bent him down over his forearm and twisted, twisted, and twisted until there came the body's natural resistance. The boy tried wailing again yet couldn't. Flesh flailed beneath Bar like a speared fish. He kept hold with his other knee securely pinned to his lower back.

The boy was desperate to squirm free. He failed.

"I would suggest you let go of the dagger, lest you enjoy a torn socket."

The boy's response was garbled. Rust from the blade shed a bloody tear from its tip. The hand wielding it squeezed in desperation.

Afterward, Bar's body realigned with his Discernments. He finally took notice of the injuries he sustained. There was a faint sting somewhere along his skin. A cursory inspection found the side of his wrist scraped and a depression across his elbow that would have bled if it were not for the padded sleeve of his gambeson. The cut across his neck cried, his collar dampened with crimson.

There is merely the reduction of threat. Never the elimination.

Old words from a pompous bigot.

Bar contemplated tearing the elbow from the boy's socket—it would merely need another pull and he would scream, and Bar would wait until he stopped screaming. But the boy reluctantly released the dagger. It tumbled off Bar's thigh and onto the fleecy blanket. Once still, the dagger was no more than a harmless prop, the wool around it stained by gore.

The boy was in incessant pain. Bar applied a little more pressure and the groans soon magnified. The body squirmed.

The voice was enjoying this.

"Now, if you do not wish to risk losing the ability to move your arm…"

Push…More…More…

"I'd advise you to then calm yourself and listen to what I have to say…"

Listen to his arm breaking.

"Are we in agreement?"

Cheek smothered by the wool, the boy mumbled incoherence. Bar retracted his shin slightly from his head and heard a greedy gasp for air.

"Again, if you will."

The boy moaned in discomfort and within it was the soft hitches of a cry. His words and nods were the quick fire of arrows.

"I do, I do, aye, pray, aye."

Bar, thinking that no one would miss this boy, held the position for longer than necessary before releasing his arm. The boy moaned and dropped like a corpse.

Whiles the boy groveled, Bar seized the dagger and took the opportunity to examine the metalwork. It calmed him. Concentration always calmed him. Afterward, he stowed it away into one of the sleeves of his gambeson. The dagger had relinquished its origins—a common mold from Raminus yet bearing the durable, worn leather of an Opinel Bear known only to the Southern coasts of Noma Devolum.

It was a queer blade.

And I do not expect the boy has ever left the Wastelands. Most in Domum do not.

Thus the dagger was an anomaly and was accounted for as such.

Bar regarded the boy. He was rising to his knees and had his back turned toward him, holding his shoulder as if letting it go would mean the loss of an arm. From him whimpered a shame repulsive to Bar's nature.

Foreign to combat, he surmised. *That much is clear.*

Regardless, he waited.

Finally, the boy rolled over onto his rump. His shoulders were hunched, chest caved, and his arm limp. The linen wraps of poultice were smeared across his face as if a second layer of skin had slopped over his nose, revealing pasty green flesh beneath. His expression grimaced alongside his whimpers like a doe struck by an unsuspecting arrow.

Nodding as if to confirm his suspicions of the boy, Bar tucked his knees beneath him, placed hands on thighs, and breathed. He was bleeding. He was tense. If he could, he would have closed his eyes to calm himself, but these were matters he must attend to even if he deemed them trivial.

After a moment, he reached for the sleeve of his gambeson and drew out his stiletto. Its lightness was readily apparent as he caressed its keen edge. They sat across from each other, and when the boy reckoned Bar, he stopped picking at the linen wraps. His gaze bore twin shards of unease.

Outside, there were shuffles. Light mourned through the tent. Bar's cuts stinging.

"The word 'sword,' as you might reckon," Bar said, beginning with an introductory hum. "Originates from Elonamos, otherwise known as High Speak. 'Swo Lirda'—an archaic expression scarcely used within the current vernacular. The closest rendering Nexlor scholars can agree upon is 'breathless life' or 'soulless vitality.' Yet, I regret to say that many scholars still contend with how our Isaam ancestors meant for the expression to be interpreted."

Bar thumbed the blade, the sparse light inside the tent shimmering off its steel. The boy's eyes would not leave the stiletto. Bar's chest throbbed. The scars ached in their remembrance.

"But regardless," he said. "Do you know the reason why they adopted this expression for the word 'sword'? An object which is neither living nor dead?"

The boy's speech was unsteady and uncertain. "Um, no…"

"Because a sword by itself has no life to speak of. No Discernments to distinguish whether an action is righteous or wicked, justified or senseless. It cannot feel pity. It cannot feel rage. It has no need to kill, though its purpose calls for it. Nor does it hope to prevail under the flag of a broken king. It cannot feel shame in its defeats or joy in its victories. It is but a mere servant to the whims of its beholder.

"And yet, the mortal can. When a man comes in contact with his sword, when the blade is unsheathed and relishes its first bout of warmth, it is no longer lifeless. It becomes an extension to the wielder. Woven through the eyes, heart, and hands as one. It has no breath, yea, but it breathes a thousand lives. It assumes the vitality and verity of its owner. It is the executioner of your being that sheds the flesh when nuisances need to be dealt with. It bears no flesh and blood, nobody to guide it toward ambition, no sight to know prey from friend, but is very much alive, the embodiment of the wielder's warnings."

Bar gestured with his stiletto. It glistened madly.

"Do you understand?"

The boy's blank look was that of a fish gawking at an open ocean with its path unknown and unclear. Bar allowed a faint frown.

Not what you were expecting, buddy ole pal?

Hearing the voice of Onvi inside his head was almost as infuriating as the boy was.

"It means," Bar continued slowly. If he talked too fast, he might have raised his voice. "That I will not hesitate to use this dagger if you prove to be unappeasable."

Then the satisfying acknowledgment of the threat dawned over the boy. He became the Grand Mausoleums in Whitewall: pale, stony, and grave.

Bar released a sigh.

You could end him now…

Slit his throat…

Gouge his eyes…

He sheathed his stiletto back into his sleeve.

"Let us commence then. As I have already disclosed my title, shall I know yours as well?"

He planned for the rest of this conversation to be brief. The Council of Crystal was awaiting their arrival in Cadaqu. As such, Bar was expectant of their tidings and aimed for the boy to be gone before arriving at the crystal city. However, Bar would be disappointed in its brevity, for the boy retreated back from their conversation and reverted back into himself. His mind seemed lost inside another time and place.

Bar, as the subtle satisfaction of his threat condensed into stoicism, held in a twitch and said, "What is it."

Without meeting his eyes, the boy hesitated, opened his mouth, closed it, and then whispered to the shadows, "What...What happened?"

"Elaborate."

The boy was taken aback as his face, lips, and throat worked.

"Well, I mean...What happened to the farmhouse? What happened to grandma?"

Bar allowed him to think.

When the boy did not receive a response, he mumbled to himself, "The fire...it...it was burning at the farmhouse, wasn't it? I think it was, I *thought* it was but I...I don't...Were you the one who—"

"No."

He winced as if Bar had struck him. Inwardly, he wished he had. The boy was pathetic and appeared as so with the wrappings still clinging to his nose. Still, it was not called for at this time.

The boy hesitated.

"Then...Then it might not have happened, right? If it wasn't you then...then it might've been just some fire out in the middle of nowhere, not at the farm or near the farm, right? My house could still be there and I can still go back and...and...Do...do you know? Have you seen it? Is my home still there?"

Bar stared at the boy for a long time; he knew it made the boy uncomfortable.

"Would my answer make any difference to what you already know?"

Despair flickered through the boy's eyes.

"So, it's true then..." His eyes filled. Sorrow carried his voice. "My farmhouse...It wasn't a dream...Grandma, Mr. and Mrs. Swiggle. Simul running off." The boy sniffled, swallowed, wiped at his eyes with the back of his wrist. He merely succeeded in smearing the poultice. "They're gone...All of them. B-before I could even see them again." That's when the boy looked at Bar. His eyes were wet and glossy, vulnerable, but Bar merely watched. The boy tried nodding, yet the nod was shaking too violently to be considered notable. "I should have been there...Aye, I should've. I know I should've because I could've saved her if I was there with her and not with Aimee or, or I would've at least died with her an-and that would've been..." He squeezed his eyes shut. A tear escaped. From then on, he had difficulty speaking and soon devolved into a mumbling mess—snot dribbling from his nose, sobs overcoming his words, crying, so much crying.

Bar had seen this too many times heretofore to be moved by it now. Grief, misery, and remorse appeared in a variety of forms but accumulated into the same. The Runners were all similar—outcasts abandoned by the corruption of society with no place to call home. The Runners were their home now. This was where they stayed. This was where their hopes lay.

Now there came another, one he did not want, one he did not seek.

Bar waited for the sobbing to end, listening as an unappeasable bystander.

In the middle of his woeful display, the boy used his hands to wipe away the tears and rip away the wrappings. When his arms dropped, they revealed a countenance swollen with bloodshot blotches and a watery honey poultice. His breath soon steadied. Bar made no sound; he had waited seven years since Caravan's Demise—withstanding grief and lies, surviving the War for the Split, breaking from the Lanke, recruiting the Runners, waiting for word of the gems—yet waiting for the boy to calm seemed a more arduous task.

When he had, the boy tried resuming the conversation as would an inept elder pleading for another morsel of bread.

"Hu-how'd you find the farmhouse? Or, just, how'd you find *me*? I thought...I just...?"

"We were not expectant of you nor your home," Bar said. "Our travels bring us South to Etherine, yet we were halted by a sight in the

99

distance. That was where your home was. That was where we found the fire. As for you, one of my companions led us to your body. Without his presence, we would have ridden past you unawares. You may ask him how, but I doubt you will receive an answer."

The boy brooded on this. He sniffled. "What about my grandma then...? What actually happened to her?" He paused. "Could she have...well, survived?"

"No."

"No?"

Bar did not answer. He stared, and though the boy's discomfort was evident—rocking on his rear, rubbing his thigh, the restlessness of his limbs—his expression narrowed toward the truth.

The boy asked, "But what actually happened to my farmhouse? I mean..."

"Do you truly want to know?"

"Aye, I would," he challenged but retreated just as quickly. "I mean, I just...I'm..." The boy sat on his words then said, "I...I just wish it had not been like this. I know she's gone, I do, but she shouldn't be, she *shouldn't* be dead because I should've...I..."

Bar expected more tears but was pleased by their absence.

"Just, tell me what happened already..." He asked. "Pray..."

Bar held nothing back.

"The Lanke. They burned the farmhouse down and butchered your grandmother. Your horse was never found. Nothing is left of your home save for ash and bone."

No snot. No sniffles. Merely a desolate silence.

"Did..." It was barely a whisper from the boy. "Did you kill the Lanke?"

"What do you—"

"*Enough!*" The boy barked.

Bar raised his brow. He had not flinched—a creature such as this could never achieve such a feat. But his vehemence had been unaccounted for.

"I'm tired of all these...all these *questions*," he said. "All I want to know is if you killed them or not, not to have questions thrown at me like-like-like, just, *fuck…*"

The boy rubbed at his eye but this time smeared the poultice into it. He condemned Eulgash's name and then cursed profusely when the burn exacerbated. He tugged at the tail of his shirt to wipe away the rest but there was still much he had missed.

When the boy ceased whining, his eyes a stinging red, he mumbled, "Just, pray, tell me if you killed the Lanke. Just…just tell me already."

A drying, maroon crust traced down Bar's neck like a straggling finger. It had ceased to sting.

"Yea, we did."

It barely stirred now—merely a nod and then a mumbling of something that Bar did not hear. It clearly had asked all that it had wanted to know, and Bar now took it upon himself to steer the conversation.

"Besides your farmhouse and its resident, is there another in Domum that can watch over you?"

The answer he received was detachment: a gaze deadened to common courtesy and then an imperceptible shrug.

His nose twitched.

"If there *is* another in Domum, then I shall make the necessary arrangements to escort you back."

"What's the point." The boy asked, more to himself than to Bar. "Aimee's gone. Grandma's dead. The farmhouse's lost."

His next shrug was dejected. His response was absent. Gaunt fingers of despair hollowed the boy into a vacant skeleton.

Bar let out another sigh, irritated and impatient. It was but another inconvenience. If it was not him to deal with the boy, it would be Ambia or perhaps Onvi. If Ambia, her benevolence would certainly mean the boy's adoption into the Runners. If Onvi, his persistence. These were not preferable alternatives.

Bar leaned forward. The face did not reckon. He cocked his hand and then backhanded the boy.

101

The smack slapped through the tent, a sniveling cry, his skeletal body flinging to the side.

Someone heard. Someone saw. Someone's listening.

His body made a thud like dropping a corpse that now groaned and squirmed. A hand concealed the welt Bar inflicted, and his fingers unknowingly smeared the poultice across his cheek.

Sprawled, the boy threw an eye at Bar.

"What the plos was that for!" He whinnied, keeping his hand on his cheek as if this would heal his pain. Beneath strands of ungainly hair beamed his accusatory scowl.

Unperturbed, Bar leaned back.

"Reality," he said.

The boy's anger tried to boil but simmered and eventually cooled to lukewarm anxiety. He had reckoned Bar, what he was doing, caressing his sleeve where the stiletto was, feeling, warning. Bar assumed this was enough to convey the truth. The boy would soon learn. If not, it would die along with the others.

He rolled back onto his rump as his hand lowered to reveal an inconsequential welt at his cheek bone. With all his scrapes, bruises, and bandages from the previous night, Ambia would most likely not reckon another injury.

This time, the boy bore a sheepish air of caution.

"I…" He gulped, sniffed, crossed his legs, wiped the poultice off on his trousers. "I…It's just—"

"I will only ask you this once more," Bar muttered. "Is there another in Domum that can tend to your needs or not?"

Hesitant, the boy opened his mouth but then dropped his eyes.

His pretty eyes

Take them pretty pretties

Bar strained to hear his mumbling.

"I mean. I could stay with Gladion and…"

The boy stopped himself, but Bar's concentration veered towards the spry blacksmith in Domum's Eduavel District.

So he knows the blacksmith, more than knows, enough to address him by name when in need of aid. Onvi and Vion did say he was travelling with a girl when they encountered him in Domum. Perhaps it was the blacksmith's daughter?

Bar reckoned the knowledge as notable and stowed it away for thereafter. The boy might not be a hindrance as was once expected. From the handful of interactions Bar had with the blacksmith, he knew Gladion could and would receive the boy willingly.

But what it whimpered next was not what he cared to hear.

"No…no, there's no one."

Bar reined back his hand, resisting a primal urge to lurch for his neck.

He muttered, "And why would Gladion not accept you?"

"He, um, would." The boy tentatively scratched the back of his head, shrinking into himself three times smaller than he actually was. "But, well, why should I go back? My farmhouse is burned down, my grandmother is dead, Aimee has left me and won't come back for a year, mayhap never. And Gladion, aye, I love him like a father, but I just…I just can't face him, not after all that has happened. Not after I let the farm and his best friend's mother…"

Bar thought the boy's head and hand were trembling. The grief of what he revealed lay heavy on his countenance.

The boy whispered, "I might as well die and be resurrected as a housefly."

This almost put a smirk of Bar's face.

"Yea, so you can."

He rose and then crouched toward the open slit of the tent, not even giving a glance behind him.

As expected, the whines of the boy called for him.

"Wh-what are you doing? You haven't even told me what's going to happen or where… Where we're going?"

He stopped and gestured to the morning light slicing through from the outside.

"As you have said, you will stay and die. Your decision is of no consequence to the Runners."

"I didn't- I just meant that I *feel* like that but I, you can understand—"

"Nay, I do not understand, nor do I understand what either Ambia or Onvi sees in you. Their concern is perplexing and, as far as I can tell, groundless." His voice bore its usual flatness. "Regardless, I have made my decision. When we reach Viamous, if you are still with us, Ambia and Onvi will find you a merchant traveling North. There in Domum, you will live the rest of your days, with or without Gladion."

With the back of his hand now smeared in poultice, Bar opened the tent's flap. Through it bore a new dawn: the cruel emptiness of the Wastelands, scorches of fire and smoke, tents crowded in submissive solitude, their shadows stark against the dawn. Ambia and Cavas were the only Runners awake, as far as he could tell. They sat beside the flames, facing each other with Ambia's back toward Bar. Cavas's eyes were closed and his robed hands laid on top of hers as if she were preventing them from falling. Between their palms glowed a warm, fuzzy gold.

She was beautiful. Tempting. So tempting.

He planned to join them but had not crossed the threshold before the boy's voice infested the air.

"I don't even *know* anyone in Viamous. And who's Onvi and this…Ahm-be-ah? I mean, I don't really think any of it matters anywise. There's no one in Domum for me to go back to since everyone I used to know is either dead or gone and, well, I mean besides Gladion, but just how am I…"

"Decide for yourself."

He motioned to leave. The boy panicked.

"Shouldn't I at least, well, have a say in where I go? Shouldn't *I* be the one to choose where I end up, and where I should be? That's how it should be, right? I shouldn't just not have a say in this because that's just not right, right?"

Bar turned his head over his shoulder, unrevealing of what stirred beneath.

"Where you should be and where you wish to be will always

differ," he drawled. It was an ominous warning. "And yet, I assume you have someplace where you would like to be. If you do, then speak. I am scarce on patience."

The boy was thinking as well as staring at the Black Wool blanket he sat on. Eventually, he looked up at Bar. His eyes kept flicking elsewhere so he wouldn't look directly at the leader.

"Well," he mumbled. "I was just, well, thinking that, if it wasn't too much to ask that, well, I could mayhap stay with you for a…"

"We have naught the resources to support such reveries."

This was a lie. Although their resources were not plentiful, they retained enough to be at ease. Another mouth for another two or three days would be unsatisfactory but not unbearable.

He must have recognized this.

"I…I know you don't want me." Gloom billowed around him like a nimbus. "I can see that much, but even so I…I want to find Aimee. She said she'd pass by the farmhouse, sometime. I can join her there and travel with her to wherever she or they would want to go. Mayhap we could wait for—"

"When was this?"

"Huh?"

"When was she supposed to visit the farmhouse?"

There was blankness to his expression that quickly reverted to please.

"I-I mean. Well, it was the morning right after the night I was supposed to come back to the farmhouse, when I saw it burning instead."

"Then your request is impossible."

His lips and mouth scrunched into an unbelieving frown. He opened his mouth to speak, but Bar cut him off.

"You have been unconscious for more than a day. The morning you were meant to meet this Aimee has already passed."

At first, the realization dumbfounded the boy but then succumbed him to a pit of despair. His head sank into that pit.

"She…" The gap of silence was grueling. The boy swallowed.

"Then, could I, well, go with you until I find her? I think I can help you if you just, well, let me."

Bar was unconvinced.

He left the entrance to approach the boy. The fear in his eyes swelled as Bar hunkered near him. Despite being eye-level, his presence exuded an immense pressure that could have crumpled innocence. It was suffocating. The body of the boy cringed the slightest but tried his utmost not to cower.

The boy smelled like spoiled honey.

"What could you possibly offer the Runners?"

Nothing. Bar squeezed his hand into a ball.

"What could you, a callow boy deprived of caution, care, and wit, offer the Runners? All that you have proven thus far is the promise of death and failure." He was so close he could hear the beating of his eyelashes. "Your farm is burned, your grandmother is dead, and yet you remain. Nay, you are merely a coward."

Bar could tell he wanted to argue, to say something, anything, but he knew what Bar said was true. The boy was a coward for failing. The boy was a coward regardless.

The boy gulped, trying not to move. A dire plea of fear reverberated from him.

Bar bent his neck to scrutinize him.

"Tell me. Is this confidence you espouse or merely arrogance?"

A dribble of sweat cut down the boy's knife-thin nose. Within Bar grew a lightness that not even the promise of the gems could evoke.

"I don't…What…"

"Answer."

"I-Nu-no…it's…it's arrogance."

"And what does the arrogant boy want. Tell me what the arrogant boy wants."

"I…He…He…"

"I cannot hear when you stammer."

"I, I just…"

"Say it. *Say it*," Bar spat.

The boy winced away from his spittle. Welts of tears beaded in his eyes. He shook his head in a nod as if this was what he *fucking ASKED FOR*.

"Pray, I, I just…I just want to know who you are, aye, who the Runners are, and if I can help you and go with you and find Aimee and do something useful and, aye."

Useless

Useless

Useless

Useless

Useless

"Tell you. Who we are."

His raw breath stroked at his cheek, and from the bottom of his throat rumbled a pleasant purr. Bar could see the boy's skin shuddering and picked out the popping of sweat on his pores.

The voice inside cackled.

Bar recast his countenance for thereafter. What remained was a bare stare. He nodded ever so slightly.

"Yea," he said. "I suppose I can."

He leaned away, and it was like a dam to release tension. The boy drew in a shuddery gasp and then panted like a thirsty mutt. His cheeks ran tearful deltas. He wouldn't stop sniffling.

Bar returned to where he sat heretofore and glanced back at the boy. He was a forlorn sight and would have made any patron of the Pig Pen chuckle with malicious glee.

Bar did not. He continued as though their casual conversation had never ended.

"The simple answer to your question is that the Runners are akin to mercenaries. We journey throughout Admah and, on occasion, to other Nomases in fulfillment of varying contracts. Yet, as with life, simplicity is a blind beast."

He touched the meager slit of his neck. The blood had begun clotting.

The conversation is persisting longer than was expected.

It could not be avoided; if he truly meant to throw the boy into the Forest or forgo him to the worries of Onvi and Ambia, he would have by now. Yet, there had arisen another possibility for the boy—one Bar had not considered in his narrow-sightedness and one he did not necessarily disregard as impractical. Despite the words he had spoken heretofore, the boy could prove useful, if only under the title of a boy.

Another child for her to bear, another for her to tend to, another to prepare her.

Perhaps.

Bar shifted off a rocky lump.

"The word 'mercenary' implies an immorality which is, in of itself, a defamation to the Runners' name. A more honest description would be that of a haven or, better yet, as a family. We eat together. We travel, survive, and commune together, cross rivers, valleys, and nations alike. We suffer, then we mend."

(*Lies*)

"We live through one another."

(*Lies*)

"We form bonds that last an eternity."

(*lies, lies, lies*)

"Thus 'mercenary' is merely what we do but not who we are. Can you understand this?"

With hunched shoulders, the boy gulped again but then nodded. Bar eyed him.

"In affirming this, you also affirm that you understand the consequences and dangers of joining a group such as the Runners. Can you fathom these dangers as well?"

The boy hesitated again before giving another vague nod. The resemblance to an obedient and naïve child was too uncanny. The boy would never fathom how cruel life could be. A simple fire and death were motes to the sandstorms the world could create.

"Then I implore you to reconsider what you have asked. We are not a group to accept members willfully for our tasks are those that cannot be taken lightly. Death is a constant, hardship a must, hunger a possibility. These are the least that will be required since the road ahead is a perilous one." He paused. "You have asked to join us whiles you search for Aimee. I ask if you can."

The boy was paler than the whitewood birch of Volumanos. Another word and it might just vanish.

"I…I think so."

"You think?"

"I know. No, aye, I can. Will. No, I will."

Bar's thumb and forefinger rubbed together in meditative habit. The cuts along his neck and wrist tingled.

"Very well," he affirmed. "However, as with any prospect, before I induct you, I must know what skills you possess that would ultimately benefit the Runners."

A silence dawned before the boy realized Bar was waiting for him to answer.

"Oh well, I." The boy squinted his eyes, biting at his lower lip whiles sawing through it. His countenance turned through the rusty cogs of thought as his gangly hands wrung together. "Well, I can cook, even though I let grandmother cook most of the time, but I can also clash swords if that's what you are looking for."

Cooking

The word and the being which said it induced an unpleasant scene: the first time Onvi offered to cook for the Runners. Merely remembering the incident upset his stomach which had once tolerated the skewered and boiled bowels of a Kil'ri Frog during their first visit to Caris'ma. The victuals Onvi served were nothing apart from deplorable—every slice of bread and Cacusan cut burned black and unpalatable. If it were not for his exceptional skills in thievery and the quick wit of his tongue, Bar would have reconsidered his decisions back in the Silent Swamps, separated and secluded over its waters.

But, in soothe, despite the contempt he had for the boy, the latter of his supposed skills intrigued him.

Clashing swords, he thought. *So the boy thinks he can fight.*

Bar would not be convinced until he appraised the statement

himself. If his words were true, the finding would be, overall, advantageous for the Runners, for well-trained and reliable warriors were difficult to come across. Ambia, despite her unquestionable loyalty and ability, would not wield a sword. Nor was her magic of a destructive nature. Even if it was, Bar doubted she would wield it to harm another, regardless of their hostilities. It was understandable and a reason as to why she was ideal. Yet the circumstances limited the Runners considerably.

As for Onvi, his skill as a thief was a complement to the shadows. It was true he was becoming sufficient with a bow (training from Bar had taught the thief the fundamentals of how the Ras clan wielded the bow and arrow, on and off horseback) but Onvi was still well away from mastery. This left Cavas, Vion, and Bar to endure their physical combat, proving problematic. It was pivotal to divert attention away from Cavas and, in soothe, having him engaged in the violent vehemence of warfare—that of which could incite emotion—was a circumstance Bar would rather avoid, if not extinguish altogether. The idea of even hiring mercenaries crossed his mind, but their swaying loyalties and unseemly manners were an unknown too detrimental for his expectations.

Nonetheless, if the boy was telling him the truth, then there could yet be another use for him.

"And what do you mean when you say you can clash swords?"

He rubbed the back of his neck. Poultice was lumped on his chin like a mole.

"Well, I can use a sword well, I guess."

"You guess."

"I mean I do, really well. Me and Gladion, or, no, the blacksmith I mean, from Domum, aye, we'd always clash swords every Moon because, well, he said that I needed it to…to protect the farmhouse…"

His eyes contracted guilt and solemnity. Bar looked for tears, but the well of the boy's being was dry and gloomy.

"Yea," the leader said. "And we have seen how skillfully you have protected the farmhouse."

The boy shrunk further into his silence.

Bar studied him. From within, a finger plucked at a string of regretful recollection; the immediate image was of a home years heretofore. Many years heretofore. One undamaged by war and tragedy and one still homely and healthy. Those inside alive and well.

"Nevertheless," he resumed. "We shall test your swordsmanship."

Bar rose for the final time, and the boy's eyes followed him like a realization. They were filled with unacquainted concern. At the flap, Bar stopped and tossed an eye over his shoulder.

"What is your title?" He asked.

The boy blinked profusely before comprehending.

"It's, um, Chry. Chry Esolious."

Bar *hmm*ed and then looked out at the rising sun.

"Chry. How fitting."

VI

He followed the man named Bar into the morning bloom. It was a struggle. Moving his body was like goading a stubborn mule to drive. Every movement spoke of soreness and every step brought with it a groan, yet not all his pain could be seen. Actually, the pain he felt inside, he reckoned, wasn't really pain.

It was emptiness.

Everything he had learned…Everything that had happened…None of it felt *real*. He knew it was, but there was still a piece of him that hoped beyond hope that he'd wake up on his pallet in his farmhouse filled with the folk he had loved and lost: grandma, Aimee, mother, father. He'd rush downstairs where a cauldron of Dry-Mouth broth would be boiling, where each of them would receive a bowl to warm their hands, Chry's stomach growling. They'd slurp under a communion of warmth and nothing, nothing would be misplaced. And never would he complain about the broth again.

This would never happen. The hope he had was shriveled until there was nothing left but a stunted Lirda, an unworthy soul to be resurrected again by Eulgash to continue living in this wretched world.

You can still go back

It was the voice of comfort. He could hardly hear it over the absence of care.

Gladion still lives. He'll be waiting for you to come back so you can go to Poltuck Caravans and Halorda Herbs and retrieve ore and herbs and all those little things that he's too busy to pursue. That doesn't sound like a terrible life, does it?

Mayhap. But he also didn't think he could ever face Gladion again. Bar was right. He was a failure. He let the farm burn to the ground and let his grandma die screaming when he told her he'd be home before dark. He failed everyone he had ever known. His father, mother, Gladion, Aimee...Grandma. They looked to him for support, and he betrayed them. Going back to Gladion's now, all Chry would see in those tiny eyes were inklings of regret and disappointment. It'd be pinned to his forehead as shame, and he'd have to wear it around Domum for the rest of his days. Others would say there was nothing wrong, that they bore no resentment toward him, but he knew. They'd toss their sidelong glances at him from afar and murmur as he left. Satch would stride past him without stopping to tease. Carp would somehow forget to sit down with Chry to ramble about the hearsay of Domum. The cackle of Ingrid and the lute of Harlequin would cease when he entered the Brew Beetle. And Reselda...No, he couldn't go back to Halorda Herbs, not with her accusing glare.

Although the sun was at his back, Chry squinted against the morning glare. Scrunching his nose brought forth a stiffness that he could not remember having heretofore. He wiped away more of the poultice from his chin and nose, and when his eyes finally adjusted, he reckoned the Wastelands, tents, a fire, and...well...folk. Two of them. They sat beside the flames and, from what he could guess, were trying to sleep upright. One of them—a man, a person, thing, wrapped in black robes with only a slit of skin visible across the eyes—had laid its hands on top of the other's, flushed with a golden glow in between. The thing did not stir as they approached. The other woman, though Chry would not admit it, was much prettier to look at. She had a slim frame that suggested a pleasant grace and thin, brunette hair tousled down her back. A satchel crafted from a hard-looking leather hung from her shoulder. Branded on its corner was a chicken-like symbol.

She had not turned to greet them yet, but he felt at an immediate ease with her. The screws of his shoulders loosened, and the vise clinching his ribcage slackened. Yet, as much as this might have been a comfort, nothing they talked about would comfort him. This woman was not Aimee. This woman was not his mother or his grandmother. She was just some random stranger.

The footsteps of Bar and Chry eventually alerted the two. The black-robed person was unhurried in opening its (his?) eyes and carried that same behavior into its stare. Its irises were blacker than the mouth of a mine, and it wouldn't stop staring. Not at Bar but at Chry. The eyes stripped him naked, and he nearly squirmed out of his skin.

The woman noticed shortly thereafter. The glow of their hands faded away as she looked toward them. Features of her face were willowed into a motherly compassion. High-cheek bones with olive skin. Relief billowed over her hazel eyes upon seeing Chry, and the smile that followed was soft and warm.

"Blessings, I am glad you're well," the woman said. She had a lilting voice that floated and there was no indication that she thought differently of her words. Rising to her feet, she dusted off her skirt. "I was beginning to worry—"

She stopped. Her hazels narrowed then broadened. Seriousness burned through her smile, one as intense and as steady as Bar's.

"Goodness Barloc, what happened to you."

It came out as a whisper. Her uneasy stare clung to Bar who, otherwise, looked unconcerned. For what seemed like the first time, Chry noticed the beard of dry blood down his throat.

The woman stepped toward Bar as if striding blind through a fog. Her eyes never left his throat. Stopping at his feet, she swallowed. Bar remained still. When she raised her hand, it trembled as if frightened of what she had discovered. It hovered over his neck then, without touching, drifted down to the wrist where another cut kissed the bone. Bar allowed her to gently examine both wrist and neck.

Her eyes were pale; her words were stony.

"How did you suffer this."

"A rusted blade."

Her expression twisted in disgust.

"Goodness Barloc, you *know* we don't have…" She struggled with her words. Her head hitched quietly. "Enough…enough Goldendrake to…"

She clamped her eyes shut as her breaths came out fitful. The struggle wavered between an expression that wished for seriousness, even condemnation for Bar, and nausea that rejected these notions.

She turned her face away from them, trying to hide her repugnance. Her hands were clutching his palm.

Bar slipped his hand away—she hardly resisted—and guided it across her back. He led her toward one of the tents, his movements carried out with a gentleness foreign to Chry. The woman didn't protest.

"Rest," Chry could hear Bar say.

There was a shake of her head.

"Your…your neck needs…"

Another look at his neck contorted her face. Right then, Chry sustained a thin needle to his heart, a feeling of emotion he tried desperately to hold onto but that soon vanished. His heart dried again as a molt of dead skin.

Eventually, she did as she was told. Bar kneeled her down before the tent. Their backs were facing Chry, but he still noticed the shuddering of her breath from her shoulders. Her body leaned forward as if the contents within the tent talked of an irresistible pull, but she didn't leave him. Not yet.

Cavas was near but only watched with a stare of empty intensity. Bar whispered something into her ear. Chry risked a step forward and tried listening since he couldn't outright believe how Bar was acting.

It's almost like he's comforting her, he thought.

This was difficult to imagine. For him, at least. Nowhere in their conversation had Bar released his stoicism or forcefulness. Chry just assumed this was how he always was. And why not? Every word and gesture he expressed was deliberate, scathing, and unpredictable, like juggling knives where one inconvenience could mean the nicking of the skin or a severe gash or worse. It disturbed Chry. He had cowered when talking to Bar and now the man acted as if that person never existed. For all Chry knew, he could've rocked a baby to sleep in one hand while drowning a child with the other.

Or, that's what it seemed like at least...

After what he thought was initial resistance, the woman relented. She nodded wearily and whispered so low he could not hear. Bar didn't reassure but instead helped her into the tent as she crawled in. The flap draped behind her and swallowed her. Then she was gone. No one left but him, Bar, and the hooded being.

When Bar turned to face him, his features were unrelenting. Now they *both* were staring at him and his discomfort was like stripping naked on top of Simul's statue inside the Market for every merchant, sot, and Devout to see. Chry thought it'd never end, mayhap forever, until Bar unbuckled one of the sheaths from his waist and tossed it casually to him. Chry shrunk back as if the foreign leather were uncoiling into a vicious Dry-Mouth. It knocked and bounced off his elbow, clattering onto the hardpan.

"What," he said before Bar lunged forward, hand on his hilt, about to strike. Chry couldn't move. He wasn't moving. The blade hissed and cut through the dying breeze.

His strike was effortless, and Chry would've drowned in his blood that day. It was only because of his body's natural desire to live that he stepped back to dodge the blade's tip. Even so, it was knuckles away from his throat, close enough to taste the sweat.

He's trying to kill me. I'm going to die. I'm about to die.

The slicing air whistled through his ears. He was stumbling back when Bar came again, this time from the right, slanted and seeking. Off to his left laid the sheath Bar had thrown, stiff as a limb.

The slash missed again but Bar, true to his character, did not relent. Somehow, Chry's legs and mind worked together to roll him towards the sheath beneath the following strike. The scene spun like a Vorsio while behind him he heard the whoosh of steel bitting the breeze.

He didn't roll onto his feet—he was never so graceful—but tumbled into a sprawl. Heart pounding at his wrists, he scurried to face the man. His head was looking over his shoulder and…and…Oh Eulgash, those eyes…

Pray, he pleaded. *Whoever the plos this man is, Eulgash, pray, save me.*

He tried to speak, to mumble, but his skull was empty, and his throat shriveled.

Bar was so still he had become insurmountable. Dawn had thrown a shadow over his expression, one lost in secrecy. Chry trembled too much to reckon. He wished he wasn't here, wished he wasn't looking at him, wished he had died somewhere else. If he just shut his eyes and opened them again, he'd wake from this dream. Gone forever.

The fire guttered beside him, there were eyes hammered to his back, and the voice which spoke was tireless.

"You shall never know your enemy."

Chry tried, oh he tried to know. But the cowardice in his bones impeded thought. Around his neck, the sapphire necklace bore the weight of Admah.

I'm dying, dying, going to die, dying

Bar stepped towards him. The sun blazed behind him, and the intensity of his shadow consumed Chry. Life became as real in those moments as they were a Son heretofore.

The words Bar said were clear.

"But you better well be ready for them."

Then came the blade.

VII

It was his body that saved him. It had done it heretofore and now it had done it again. Why? Why did his body care? Death lived below where he lived now: no more concerns, no more grief, no more laboring for life. It was the reflection of an emptiness he felt from within, sweet, sweet echoes foretelling of the day when he'd straddle the edge of that abyss, close his eyes, and fall.

But when the opportunity came to fall—days after tragedy—his hand instead groped and seized the leather of the sheath. It was his body's desperate attempt to survive.

What are you doing? His thoughts asked. *Why are you doing this? What do you have to live for?*

He couldn't answer, and that was why it was all the more confusing when Bar's sword descended and the leather sheath appeared above him, clinched by two hands.

My hands, he noticed and was just as surprised to reckon that, aye, they *were* his hands.

Bar's blade struck from overhead like a butcher's cleaver. Steel against leather resounded a thinned *thud*. A shudder rippled down his arm and threw him onto his back. He cried out. His elbows nearly buckled from the blow.

He tried pushing the blade back, grunting, teeth clenched as his arms shook, but the sword wouldn't budge. His eyes—frightened, hollow, confused—caught glimpses of the man above. Eventually, they could only stare. Beneath the shadow of Bar's expression, there was indifference—no remorse but also no pity. It was as if Chry's death was another obligation needing to be executed.

He thinks of me as another Dry-Mouth to behead. Another day. Another inconvenience.

What pictures arose from this—Bar hunched over, cleaver cocked back in hand, Chry's snaky form motionless on the rosewood—seemed not so far from the truth.

Bar leaned into his blade and Chry had to lock his arms to keep from giving in. The blades trembled relentlessly. Bar's shaped jaw was fixed. Visibly, the effort did not seem to strain him.

Chry was trapped, he needed out, his muscles were expecting to tear, blackness was closing in, the Wastelands were dying.

One more push, Chry me boi, n ye can say farewell to dat 'ead of yars

The echoing voice was Gladion's, and Chry thought, *And you don't think I already fucking* know *that?*

The blacksmith would've surely laughed.

Pieces of metal tinkled over him as Bar lifted his sword. Chry had a moment of release before the man, just as swiftly, swung down again. The *thud* slapped him onto the hardpan. A squeal whimpered from his throat. He squinted to regard Bar, but a sweaty tear dripped down from his chin and fell into Chry's eye. A stinging blinded him as he let out a string of condemnations. Movement from above, a weepy blur, lips mayhap. Chry couldn't make out what it was or what was said or if any of this was right and true and just.

You need out. Run. Your arms, chest, they're failing.

N remeba wat I taught ya, Chry me boi.

This time, Gladion's voice came to him so clear that his defense buckled. Sharp steel sniffed at his cheek. He recovered and gained back a knuckle. It was a struggle to both fend off the onslaught and listen to what that scruffy, fat old man was telling him heretofore. Chry tried regardless.

I don't play easy, ya should know. I come after ya hard like it's real cuz one day it will be real.

I guess Gladion did fight like Bar, he reckoned. It was enough to begin straightening his spine. *Gladion never relented when clashing sword...Actually, I think he's just as fierce as Bar is now.*

The swelling of remembrance strengthened his blood. His expression turned inward as his muscles remembered their purpose. *Aye, you* have *clashed swords heretofore. You* have *prepared for this. Stop cowering and* focus *already.*

He did. He was. A clearness returned to him. Arms were about to give out. Bar was pressing down harder. Resistance. Lessons from the days he trained with Gladion pierced through the haze and revealed a thin thread.

This was where he started.

Opening the fingers of his left hand, he shifted his right hand up so the sheath would slant down. With the pressure from Bar's blade, the foot of the sheath staked down into a crack beside his shoulder. The blade jerked and scraped across the leather. Even so, Bar did not lose balance and leaped back before a strike could land. Chry took the opportunity to hurry to his feet. He was too exposed on the ground. He needed up. He needed to face Bar.

Chry steadied himself. The sapphire necklace rang softly in his ear when Bar was there, again. Steel swished. Chry stumbled back to dodge the first, unsheathing his sword (*Bar's sword, you're using his sword*) to meet the next blow. Blades clanged together like silver thunder.

Get ya bearin's. Understand who ya fightin'.

Chry shoved off to disengage. The breath was spent in thought.

He's using one arm, his left, only. He's at half strength, exerting half effort. Swings are wide and powerful but controlled, so he can retreat if need be. Attack from the right. Mayhap a heavy swing from the left will reveal an opening.

The next swing was arching. He dropped the sheath and stepped back, and the strike fell short. Behind Chry was a presence that he knew as a tent. From it came recovering breaths. Along the edge of focus lingered black robes that had not moved.

No more dodging

Attack

Fight

An opportunity opened to strike. Bar had cocked back for another sweep and once the blade missed, Chry thrust forward, sword seeking his side.

Open, defenses open

Until it wasn't.

Bar shifted his torso the slightest, enough for Chry to miss. Then, he stuck out a foot, almost casually, and tripped him. Chry went tumbling onto the hardpan, nicking his face, cheek, sides, elbows. When he found himself rolling onto his knees, scurrying to his feet, preparing a stance to face his opponent, his ears latched onto what Bar had to say.

"As to be expected."

As to be…

His emotions boiled.

As to be expected, as to be expected! Who the plos *does he think he is saying that it's "to be* fucking *expected!"*

These whines from within were the rally to loosen his joints and revolve his being around the total and utter defeat of Bar.

No holdin' back. Exploit da weakness ov ya opponent. N don't tell me dey don't 'ave one because dey all do.

Chry was unhearing.

Bar did not approach, so he took the action upon himself. Their blades met and what occurred was the elegance of crows: the soar and pull of a dance captured within reverberations. Chry led. Resentment backed his swings as red waves washed into the abyss with the flotsam of frustration, aggression, and whatever the fuck else there was. Somehow though, Bar was unconcerned by this. One-armed and retreating, he wore his usual stoicism without a mote of panic.

Even so, Chry was pleased, exhilarated even, to be pushing Bar back onto his heels. The rattle fucker deserved every moment of suffering that he had experienced inside the tent. All the hatred he spewed, all the humiliation

Worthless

Witless

Coward

He deserved this. He deserved it. Everything. He deserved it all.

Chry pressed. His focus was on his right side. Bar compensated by turning the body so his left arm would face him. He persisted despite the Wastelands melting around him. It was just him now. With Bar. The two of them. A boy and a bastard between tents with dirt, sweat, blood, a raging sun, and screaming swords.

It was the most alive Chry had felt since waking this morning.

But he soon reached his peak. After every swing, his arms started to show flecks of exhaustion. He was weakening; his blows lacked the power, his swings the quickness.

Neva exert yaself. Ya opponent mayhap be waitin' for ya to tire before strikin'

This was a warning, but his mind did not acknowledge it. Inside was chaos. His flame burned into uncontrollably shaky hands. It deepened when his next strike Bar flicked aside with ease and strode forward. Panic quickened his heart as Chry found it hard to breathe.

He's gaining. He's going to kill me. Strike, strike, strike, strike, strike

He let out a guttural cry like some Lanke, gripped his sword with both hands, and swung with deranged desperation. His strikes only became wilder when Bar effortlessly dodged the first, half-deflected the second, dodged the third.

Steady yaself Chry. Ya letting yar—
Kill him already! KILL him!

Every blow was deflected or dodged. Bar closed in. Harder. Faster. More, more, mo—

His downfall came through his own distress. He had released one of his hands from the hilt to thrust the sword at where Bar's heart should be. Bar seized the opportunity again to deflect it, lower his shoulder, and ram into his chest. A gasp of air left Chry. The thought that filled the space was *I'm dead. This is the end.*

He crashed onto his back, his head knocking against the hardpan and his teeth clacking together. There was a ringing between his ears and a wetness in his mouth. An estranged feeling told him to rise, move, fight. But his eyes had been thrown into a daze and the sights he saw were scattered across a plain that held no clarity nor direction.

There was clattering from afar. His fingers grasped at nothing. His eyes had closed to help the slightest, for now he felt a warmth across one side of his face.

The fire, he thought. *I'm near. The fire.*

Opening his eyes took a groggy effort. There appeared a form and a vomit of color. A sharp kiss touched his throat. It felt like a lovely caution.

Soon the blurs cleared. The shapes defined themselves into a snake extending from a human limb. Metal was the snake's body that straightened into a perfect edge. The kiss against his Cor's Crux, the vulnerable lump of his neck, became the tip of the blade. When he reckoned this, Chry restrained his movements, still as a tree trunk. The man above him was expressionless. Bar had not forgotten to hone his blades.

Chry's panting was inconsolable. He tried not to swallow but did so anywise. His Cor's Crux lumped down and softly resisted the blade. A prick of blood bloomed from the exchange. His temple still throbbed from the frenzy of their fight but was swirling back into the abyss where color could not manifest. It was returning. Again. That emptiness. And as it opened to him, his lips whispered, "Kill me."

A horse from afar would not stop neighing. Another neighed too but only once. The fire crackled soundlessly.

In the end, Bar did not kill him. The blade parted from his neck and strain sighed from his throat. The sword rose, and as it rose, Chry regarded it for the first time. It was…It just wasn't normal. The longer he stared at it, the more he traced its rudimentary engravings edged across the blade; exotic webs contained within circles as if stamped into the steel. With how unique the symbols were, it's a wonder how he had missed them heretofore. They were even on the blade he had wielded.

Who the plos is this person?

Bar slid the sword back into its sheath with a hiss and click. The Wastelands were deafened by the sound.

Bar wouldn't lift his stare, and Chry could not tell what he was looking at—the hollowness of his eyes or the blood on his throat. He soon didn't look at either and regarded the black-robed person who had given no signs of life. Just the faint turns of the head.

He's going to leave me here to die, Chry thought, his body a numb tingling. *Not enough to kill me, is it? Better just to watch and wait.*

Like a coward

Like me

But the response he heard startled him and stilled these thoughts.

"We leave at dawn. Stay, come, the choice is yours."

Chry's expression blanked. His mouth trembled open to ask, "what do you mean?" but closed just as quickly. There was no use.

Bar was already turning away.

VIII

Shortly thereafter, the Runners tore down camp, readied their steeds, and traveled South. Upon horseback, huddled behind the woman now known as Ambia, was Chry, silent, sore, and unfeeling to the dawn of a new horizon.

IX

Onvi allowed him to sleep in his tent for the following night, but Chry, after retiring early seemed the only solace for his heartsick bones, could not sleep. He woke groggily to the rustling of the canvas, his droopy eyes rolling in their sockets to find an empty tent.

Onvi must not have gone to sleep yet, he thought as if the words were yawing. *Still must be out.*

He let out a sleepy moan. Oddly enough, though the grief of the farmhouse still felt like stone blocks tied around his neck, its presence was not so suffocating right now. It seemed…Well, bearable. He couldn't quite smile, and the clamp over his heart had not released it from its clutches. But for some reason he reckoned that everything onward—his trek with the Runners, his search for Aimee—would not be irrevocably devastating. That there was still some hope for him.

Wait until Onvi returns. You thought grief was going to keep you awake? Let's see how well you fair against Onvi's mouth.

Chry could have chuckled, but the opportunity left him when he realized that he could not move his arms, legs, or torso. Face falling, he tried rocking his neck and head but they, too, were numb like being flattened beneath a boulder until the pressure receded into a myriad of stinging needles.

He was stuck inside an unresponsive body. Only his eyes, now as vigilant as the full shine of a Vigilant Moon, could move, jerking to and fro until they caught onto a shadow in the opposite corner of the tent: a slab of unholy strength. He couldn't see more. The stench of shit squeezed his gut, the thought being that something had smeared it across the burlap of the tent. He didn't know why he thought this. Onvi wouldn't do this, the Runners wouldn't do this, *no one* would do this.

The broad shoulders of the thing, that which his disturbed mind conceived as a beast, skulked forward.

"You're a worthless fool."

Its growl was between a gurgle and a scratch like a rabid mongrel with knives in its throat. From the shadows preyed a grin with the blackness of its glistening beard. The beast was hunkered beneath the canopy, a cross between the Hunchback and a Lanke, a true Lanke thirteen hands tall. Its chest was bare and scarred, and the matted fur of its war skirt loathed to conceal its manhood. It snickered.

"I'll fuck her. I'll force you to watch. I'll rip her throat out. She'll die. You can fuck her thereafter."

Frozen, Chry could not distinguish between what could be heard from what could be perceived. Fear urged the eyes to accept the beast but would not, could not allow him the freedom to flee. He was trapped inside a fleshy prison like those Brown Mice he'd catch behind the back of Gladion's home. How they had squealed within their metal cages. How he wished he could now, his throat clamped shut.

Arbiter, what have I done? Why?

It stalked forward with an oath. Through each stride came another scar on its leathery and sallow skin. The face offered its sockets and from them slithered out twin serpents, their silver scales hanging and unraveling until they thumped down at its feet. He could hear the hissing in his ears. The sockets left behind bore the empty hollows of the Forest.

Malice approached.

"You think you can be one of us."

Its soles crushed the stalks of grass. Contorted bulk, grumbling senseless things. The mouth was a gorge where a sickly yellow chip fell. A tooth. It dropped but rolled onto its tongue and into a throat serrated and fleshy as though its unclean and jagged nails had clawed it open. It swallowed. The rot of its tooth peeked through the ruptured tunnel of its throat, almost dropped forth before his feet, but then disappeared down into its chest. It did not flinch.

Chry's fingers rattled. His breath became unreal husks. Lying like a corpse, he held a cold stare. He reckoned (though not knowing why or how, more like with an empty acceptance of it) that this was its last tooth and each gape in its mouth was bleeding generously onto its beard.

Get away from me. Leave me. Leave. He had meant to move his lips to say these words, but the thoughts were unfulfilled.

Its words, though, were inescapable. The serpents sniffed at his feet.

"You thought you could be brave. You thought you could endure."

No, that's wrong. He couldn't. He wasn't brave, he couldn't endure, he ran, stumbled into Ambia's tent, shook her awake, yelled and pleaded for her to come see the beast hiding in the tent, but that was just an illusion like the rest of them as his body was the stone at the bottom of a well; motionless.

"But you will never be—"

It hesitated. Chry almost felt a tinge of relief before a twitch contorted through its neck to where the heart should be. Its bald pate jerked, and its throat leaked even more. The serpents yawned to bear fangs, hissing, venom dripping.

"Will never be, never *be*—"

It gargled a sound inscrutable through its mushed mouth and curved inward on itself as to protect its chest. Its spine hilled along its back. Its manhood spasmed.

He prayed this was it, that this was all the beast would do. He couldn't take it anymore. Anything more and he would pop…

Pray, leave me—

It lurched. Inhumane gurgles, Chry helpless. He could not depart from himself, closed his eyes as a fist plummeted from above and caved in his skull like an adze with a log of wood. Twin needles punctured his thighs. A knee crushed his—

X

Chry whipped up, jerking to find out where- where that *beast* was and why and what happened, how was he moving again but the answers he received were a bursting heart, soaking sweat, and a stone in his throat. The frantic search of his eyes only returned with an indifferent tent and a noise: the steady flapping of its canvas against an innocent wind.

A dream, he thought. *It was all…just a dream.*

He licked his lips, gulped, and tried to steady his heart, placing a hand over it to feel its pangs. It wouldn't stop sprinting, even after moments of waiting.

He had to get out. He had to move.

He wandered through the slit of the tent and out into the night, hoping in the back of his mind for something to calm him, but what he found was the Wastelands' endless hardpan, a sight that reminded him all too much of why he could not sleep.

I shouldn't be here, he thought but reckoned that "here" wasn't actually in the Wastelands or with the Runners. It was here living this life. He didn't deserve to be alive while his grandma was dead.

Tents pitched and circled around a dying flame that was already becoming familiar, Onvi was nowhere in sight, and he reckoned the others were inside their tents sleeping. The only other Runner he could see was Ambia. She was at the edge of the small knoll they had camped on, the first signs, Onvi had said, that they were nearing Etherine. He could see her from the light of the waning Vigilant Moon, and it looked like she was drinking from a vial that contained, he thought, A Mother's Touch. Her Ironskin satchel hung from her shoulder and was where he reckoned the vial had been. He also hoped—No, he *needed* for that satchel to have Elos Amus, so it could ease him to sleep. Hopefully, the Elos Amus would be strong enough to ward away the beast from crawling back into his dreams. It was of little use though: Its remedies were snug inside that satchel and Chry didn't have the courage—*You thought you could be brave*—to bother her with his petty problems. He was an outcast. No one. Why would she help him? There was no reason. He didn't stay. He didn't greet her. He slunk back inside to watch their names echo off the canopy of the tent.

Aimee

Grandma

Aimee

Aimee...

Onvi's Reminiscence

I

Onvi guzzled down the last of his tankard and slammed it onto the bar. Froth splashed onto the dust-colored wood, and Chry winced from the blow. He reckoned this loud and lively creature—through his giggly grin and giddy mumbles—was beyond pleased.

Onvi rapped his tankard against the bar. It eagerly clacked. As if this was not enough, he called for another with a wheaty breath and by swaying his tin. Turning from the casks, the tapster glared at the thief, his gaunt temple throbbing with a blue tree branch, the skin of sun-spotted rawhide stretching across his skull. Despite the discomfort Chry felt beneath that glare, Onvi giggled as if at a joke. This was just how he was.

The tapster scrunched his weary eyes, grumbled something to himself, retrieved, tapped, and brought Onvi another tankard, his fourth before dusk.

"Much appreciated, Ryder my old friend!" Onvi swiped it from the bar. "Greatest Tapster on this side of the River Twins, I swear it! Plos! Across the Four Nomases! No equal, I say!"

Onvi toasted him. Ale spat over a lip bent and drooling. Ryder, apparent owner and tapster of the Restless Ryders, responded with a disgruntled grunt and tried hard to ignore Onvi by washing the empty tankard with water from a pockmarked pail. The frayed rag he used looked even dirtier than the tankard he was washing.

Chry was sitting beside Onvi, drooping on a rust-eaten stool and gazing through a deadened fog. In his lap, his fingers were like numb worms.

It had taken the Runners three days to reach Viamous, the former heart of Etherine trading. He guessed it would've been less if Bar had led them through Dhymes rather than around it; from conversations he had overheard from merchants and travelers, traveling through Dhymes was faster, more reliable, and allowed for further protection from the Lanke. It was probably the route Aimee had taken, too. But Chry didn't ask Bar why he did what he did. He kept his words to himself. All he heard of it was Onvi babbling about how Vion had imprisoned himself within Dhymes and how only a rooster with cumbersome hands could have done worse for themselves. He didn't listen to the rest.

At the end of the second day of travel, the Runners were greeted with their first blades of yellowish, straw-thin grass. It lolled across the heads of mounds like shaven hair, hardpan having retreated beneath the scent of natural farmlands. From then on, the sight became greener. And no, it wasn't an illusion. This was the green folk could touch with their fingertips or wiggle between their toes.

He saw new creatures. Six of them beneath the endless limbs of a tree. They had light tan fur, round eyes, and stood on four hooves but were smaller than any horse, ox, or mule he had ever seen. Well, besides one, bearing a pair of horns that looked like a pair of claws.

"Fawn," Ambia had whispered over her shoulder. They were riding on her saddle with his arms wrapped around her. "With their father, a buck." She waited before saying, "They usually travel in groups like this one, otherwise known as herds. And the tree they're under is titled an Etherine Live Oak. It's the second-largest tree in Admah and is adored for how far its limbs can sprawl. If you'd like, we could stop and look for a time."

He didn't respond, only watched on with a thousand-league stare. When first seeing the greenery and fawn, things he had rare experiences with in Domum, there had been a spark of fascination burning within that harkened back to days with Aimee dreaming. He

129

had tried to reach out for more of its warmth, but every time he tried, the fire retreated two paces to his one. He couldn't catch it, no matter how fast he ran. It would always abandon him to a frigid and mirthless cell.

These cruel retreats became readily apparent when they rode into the city of Viamous. The bridge they rode over was a never-ending road, its rivers (those that should've amazed him with how much water they could carry) turned into recollections of a pail being spilled, those Illum lamps hanging from cast-iron spikes shined against the shadows of his being. Every aspect of the city was that flicker of fascination, its wraith, and then emptiness. He tried looking over the balustrade at the shimmering water or at the stone buildings potted beside each other, but none of it captured what Chry experienced; they saw the city, they rode over the bridge, they rode into the city, they rode along the road, they rode into a stable, they walked out of the stables, they walked somewhere else, they went through doors, they sat on stools, they stared at walls.

This was all. Viamous became another city…A bushel of folk, rich and poor, that would soon die and waste away. There was no home here. All Chry wanted now was to find Aimee and hide in her embrace. She would understand.

But they were here instead, in the Restless Ryders, around so many…Well, women… Women of Proper, as Onvi liked to call them. It didn't matter. The lack of guests called for either boredom or a swarm of lust in which Onvi reaped the rewards. At least two women (or more, Chry did not count) had recognized Onvi and reintroduced themselves to the slithery-tongued man. Each time they did, Onvi made it his first concern to introduce Chry as another scale to swallow. He didn't know what that meant. He didn't *want* to know what it meant. And when they tried their tongues on him, he made no effort to respond—never looking into their eyes, never talking. It was easy not to and was usually enough to discourage them.

"And how do you expect to catch one with an attitude like that, Chry my friend!" Onvi had claimed.

He wasn't. He didn't want to think about these harlots, and he surely didn't want to haul himself up those spiral stairs to empty rooms where there had not been a prosperous man since the War for the Split. The Restless Ryders and Viamous, if it were not obvious from its lack of patrons and citizens, were on the verge of death. Or, that's at least what Onvi told him, that, since the War, trade on the River Twins had declined and ships on the Grey Sea had grown, for the Lanke now maintained control of the riverways flowing into and back from Ontinia. The only reason the Restless Ryders seemed to be still riding was because of the man sitting beside Chry and, with how belchy, giggly, and giddy he was, Chry did not think Onvi could continue on filling either their coffers or his tankard.

Onvi swallowed half of his beverage before burping. He turned on his stool to peruse, smiled crooked, then gestured at another harlot.

"This one's a looker," he nudged at Chry, then chuckled.

He did not know what a "looker" was. He had convinced himself that he wouldn't turn to find out. Then there came a pleasant purr beside him. Its suddenness tempted him enough to take a peek, which then lingered into a stare.

His face paled, eyes still.

The harlot was shapely. That couldn't be denied even within his fog. Her amble lips suggested desire, her hips were as curved as could be imagined, and her frame carried its weight in mox. She had carelessly covered herself with a holed and faded silk that was supposed to be the scarlet hue of her hair. One of her breasts, plump and heavy, was bare. The other wasn't too far behind. Across the skin was a spectacle of freckles, and the mole above her bare nipple made her allure imperfect but oddly sensual.

Worse was the sapphire gaze she tempted them with. It was impossible to break free from and enticed Chry for reasons he would not admit. Unconsciously, he fingered the sapphire necklace around his neck. A coldness sank down from its silver to where his heart was thumping.

She isn't Aimee, his thoughts reminded him. Chry barely noticed.

131

He could only hear his heart. *She has the same sapphire eyes, but they aren't Aimee's. They aren't. She'll never be Aimee. Never.*

What he thought could not save him.

"Well now," the woman purred, her voice smoother than the silk she wore. Her eyes appraised Onvi relaxed on his stool and stopped at his adventurous eyes. She responded with a leer. "If it isn't Onvi the Merciless, back to fuck his dearest whore."

Chry shifted his bug-eyed stare to Onvi but regretted looking. Any shame Onvi should've had was overcast by a grin too smug to be shameful. Instead, Chry had to watch him lick his lips as his eyes crawled over her skin.

His insides shook.

I need out. Bring me away. Far, far away.

In a fluid motion, Onvi slipped from the stool, snatched her hips, tugged her close so her body would feel his. His fingers clawed into her rump which compelled her to press harder. From the edge of his vision, Chry noticed her hand descend into Onvi's trousers. From then on, he did not dare look lower than their necks. He had the feeling he knew what he'd find.

"So crude of you, Volumous," Onvi said, teasing. There was the movement of fingers on a breast. She let out a moan and moaned even louder when his thumb passed over her mole. Beneath his words was a suggestion. "Must've been lonely since my absence."

"Lonely? Never," she moaned. Chry tried not to watch but caught a glimpse of her leaning closer to whisper, "Only hungry."

She bit his earlobe.

Chry did not see how Onvi reacted. Chry did not want to hear. Chry felt like he was tied to a bed of nails.

And yet he was forced to listen to the smacking of their lips. He squirmed in his seat, not daring to look until there was a shift above their necks. For some reason, his childish curiosity won him over again, and his eyes wandered away from the bar. The movement was of Onvi kissing her neck then biting her shoulder, lower to the collarbone and down to…Oh…Oh Eulgash pray, no, no, no, nooooo

His cheeks burned from embarrassment, and his virgin eyes melted with how intimate and ferocious Onvi was. Why? Chry couldn't say. It wasn't like he had never seen this stuff heretofore. Mister and Missus Swiggles had acted together in their pen, and brothels in Domum, like the Thirsty-Mouth Cobra when Chry would pass it tailing Gladion, were telling to what would happen in the Restless Ryders. Yet he himself had never opened the gorge with Aimee or anyone else. That's probably why he was so embarrassed when others did; Chry was so close to Onvi and the harlot that the chance it *could* happen to him, that it could just hop over and corrupt him like an untamed disease, was beyond uncomfortable.

He had to look somewhere else, anywhere else, but the hard sucking sounds Onvi made came, and the unruly moans the harlot made came, and they weren't leaving him, and they would never leave him even if he closed his eyes and pretended the sounds weren't there but somewhere very far away.

If I just forget about them long enough, she'll leave like the rest of them. This sexual stuff will end, and I can think about Aimee and us together again. Aye, that's better, I guess, me and her, not me and the harlot.

For a moment, he actually thought he could escape to her, to Aimee. Pictures of her tried to form from the blankness but were stunted. Her image, though he knew it was her, though he recognized her and her beauty, was distorted, somehow veiled by the fog of his mind. It wouldn't relent. The most beautiful woman he had ever set his eyes on and Chry couldn't even see her.

He tried cutting through that fog when his body leaned and the stool he sat on squeaked. The sound startled him awake—his mouth as dry as the Wastelands, his throat reed-thin. He had forgotten where he was.

Sounds beside him stopped. Somehow his mind reckoned this as good and even had the boldness to sigh. But when Chry reckoned who was next to him (the Woman of Proper), where they were (the Restless Ryders), and what they were doing (sex things), the coils of anxiety

133

seized him.

Oh Eulgash no this can't be happening, not now, pray.

"And who have you brought to me this time?"

Uneasiness simmered from his stomach.

Onvi's brought others too??? This has happened heretofore??

It was a silly thought. Of *course* Onvi had; he'd probably visited the Restless Ryders a hundred times heretofore and that meant a hundred different chances for him to bring an innocent guest into this spiderweb of lust.

Chry wouldn't look at them.

You're going to have to. You can't pretend this isn't happening because it is happening because this is real *because everyone's—*

He heard Onvi snicker and immediately pictured him bearing fangs as his eyes blackened, ready to bray laughter as would a Lanke.

"Him?" Onvi said. "His title is Chry. And don't let the name fool you. The boy is anything but a weeper. Mayhap shy in bed, but I'm certain a woman of your," he cleared his throat. "Expertise can show him how restless a Ryder can be."

Chry became a swelter. His armpits were sweaty, and his loins were chafing against his trousers from how much he was squirming. He still would not look but felt her loom over him. She had left Onvi, The Forgotten Pleasure, and had taken on new prey. He could sense, almost *feel* the seductive smile contorting across her bloody lips.

Pray, for the love of everything holy, pray.

"I can show him much more," he heard her say.

He wished he would've prayed out loud so he wouldn't have heard this. Even if he did, the nails strolling across his shoulder made certain he could feel her instead. They were scarlet and like the legs of a spider, strutting over the jutting bone of his shoulder, suggesting that the woman who owned them would drag him upstairs screaming if that's what it took.

She coiled around him like a Dry-Mouth so her cheek ended on his, brushing. Chry shivered at being so close and couldn't stop the shiver from spreading to his loins. It was wonderfully horrible. He could feel her breasts, those ungodly plump breasts against his back. His body missed them when they breathed in. They were warm in threatening his resolve which only deepened with her quickening breath and the scent of her foreign oils, of lilacs—he at least thought that's what he smelled, those from Halorda Herbs, with Aimee, luring his nostrils.

The harlot had petrified him. He could not stir free. He tried resisting, but his lower body would not yield its iron rod.

Her delicate caress slipped down his neck, so her nails could play with his necklace. The silver tinkled. She stroked her thumb across the sapphire and hinted at what would come thereafter.

His bones were shuddering. The throb from below was so intense he felt it would burst like a Capar Weed popping over the flame. He knew that she knew he couldn't stop himself or her hand before crying cobra. With her touch, he would expel. And what then? He'd exit the brothel, shamefully, head hanging, as the passersby looked down at the wet spot on his trousers and thought either one of two things: that he had been too dim-witted to pull his trousers down and aim, or that he had not the rattles to last before the harlot could undress him. Either way, they'd laugh at him. They'd mock and ridicule him, and Onvi would bear witness to it all and tell Aimee if they ever met and that couldn't happen, he couldn't have that happen, so he had to say something before that happened and say it now but what stumbled out was a stutter, "That's- That's mine, I-I don't-"

"Such a pretty little thing," she replied as if to herself.

The breeze of her breath hushed him like a silent whip. Somehow this and the possibilities it brought were more arousing than the rest.

It's the sapphire. She's talking about the sapphire, and only the sapphire, and that's it. Nothing else. Just—

"Pu-pray, stop, I can't…"

"You'll have to pray louder if you wish for your gods to hear you."

The chaos within leaked onto the flesh. His stomach was queasy, his manhood eager, his blood panicking, his mind failed to steady—a lust that would not abide by reason. It tingled between his toes, clattered in his teeth. There was too much to control.

His eyes brimmed. He was about to cry. He was going to cry.

Her stout fingers wrapped over his hand to manipulate every finger. He could not defy her, his flesh so very numb. She guided him down through her silk to where her crotch was and rubbed two of his fingers to where the pressure compelled her to moan.

This. It was his first. His breaths were sputtery, on the verge of weeping. The numbness of his fingers could not register the wetness of her.

All he could think of was Aimee.

Just pretend it's her. Pretend Aimee's here with you or you're there and it's just you two sharing the same bed, that feathered bed Gladion saved for her, aye, just go to that place and kiss her skin and smile, just smile again pray.

"You," the harlot moaned into his ear. Her voice was flustered with pleasure. He had nearly forgotten about her but by now, he did not believe this was possible. "Will learn to play."

He felt the thrust of her hips as his fingers moved in and out. His palm dampened. This was not helping him separate anything and everything his body yearned to convey. He tried anywise. Yet it was her other hand that he had trouble being rid of. Wrapped around him, it descended from his stomach to strangle his inner thigh. This was her teasing him. Her moans were a note to her willingness.

Shoulders rolling back from his seat as far as the harlot would allow, Chry clamped his eyes closed. He thought, *Aimee's hand, Aimee's hand, Aimee's hand, Aimee's hand, Aimee's hand...*

But the hand that groped him was not Aimee's, her touch firm and tight.

Despite the fear which petrified him, the throbbing he had below was an ecstasy of untold potential. It was the beginning of something he had only experienced with himself and never of this intensity. No place in his childhood was safe from Chry imagining with his hand that him and Aimee were engaged in endeavors that did not end with just a kiss: his room on the pallet, the porch on the rocking chair, the threadbare velvet chair his mother and father had brought home before he was born, the farmhouse stable while Gladion was fastening iron horseshoes to the hooves of Simul. He did it everywhere but never with anyone. There really was only one person he ever truly wanted to love.

And now she was gone.

Forgive me, he wept within. Guilt struck him like drops of lightning. *Pray, forgive me, Aimee, I never meant for this or any of this, it's all my fault, if only we had more time in Domum, if only Gladion had not walked in on us.*

Her grip tightened and his crotch gave in to an expecting jerk. He squirmed back as far as he could into her bosom. She welcomed his invitation.

His eyes overflowed and the tears cut scars down his cheeks. He wept openly.

Just kill me. I shouldn't be feeling this. Throw me in the River Twins. Bring me back to the Gardens bloated.

Then there was his hand lifting from below her and moving up and something seductive and slobbery cleaning his finger.

She's licking my-my- oh Eulgash, help me, she's-she's-

Her lips claimed another finger, her hand another tug.

Long. Intimate.

His mind retreated into the void. A last desperate effort to blot this from thought—breasts, hands, licking, his mental eye tracking her hands but helpless to tell *his* hands to grab them, stop them, toss them aside. His spiritual skin began floating high into the sky so that it could not register what was happening below.

The last whispers he heard before he lost his mind were, "You'll become another toy for—"

His Lirda lifted from his body, and he remembered no more.

II

The next moment Chry could remember was gazing at the cask of ale, its wood stark against the grizzled stone. The throbbing of his groin was withdrawing. Through its wake was the tingling residue through his limbs like puddles after a storm. Another moment passed until he reckoned where he was again.

The Restless Ryders. The brothel. Onvi. Ryder cleaning the same tankard as he had been heretofore but farther away. Much farther. Chry's hands were clenched on the stool, his right trembling and clammy. The memory to why it was tried sneaking above the surface, but Chry shoved it down a hundred hands until it disappeared and dissolved into the watery depths.

Nothing happened. I'm well. It was nothing. It never happened. Never.

Even so, he expected shame, dampness of trousers, mockery of others. All three were inevitable. But when he descended from the clouds, Chry noticed his body felt…Well, normal. His trousers were not damp, and saliva sloshed between a tongue that had been too dry to taste heretofore. There was no rush of shame. Nothing about him was different. Besides, well, the clammy hand. That and the sweat still beading under his armpits.

Mayhap what happened was just a dream, he thought. *All in my head.*

"I take it Volumous doesn't flatter your fins."

Chry was startled from his daze. He shot a frightened look at the voice but there Onvi was, lolling beside him on the stool, gulping down another tankard as if this were just any other day at the Restless Ryders.

His fears lifted but his gaze didn't. There was just something about Onvi that asked folk to stare longer than was needed—his straw of gracefully unkempt hair, pronounced jawline, twinkling eyes of water, and long eyelashes but not long enough to be considered womanly.

If a man could be called beautiful, Onvi was that man.

He finished his fourth tankard (*fifth? Eulgash I do not know*) and set it on the bar. Beside it laid a crystal dagger and a gilded metal object that Aimee had called a compass. It was open and held glass so harshly cracked that North and South were unreadable. He'd heard some merchants mention them, like the Hunchback, but had never seen any heretofore. Nor were they prevalent within the Wastelands, even by those who traveled throughout Etherine.

No matter how unique and appealing the compass was, his interest drifted. His face slackened, the bags beneath his eyes drooped like the melting of a candle clock, and his manhood, once vigorous and pulsing, was easing away. He dropped his gaze from Onvi to the bar where tree rings rounded and rounded with age. He wouldn't look up. They were all the companionship he needed.

Onvi did not notice. If he had, he did not say anything about it.

"If you're wondering where that fine piece of work went, she's upstairs now. No doubt fawning over you and your…Ahm, assets." Onvi peeked down then looked back up. Chry did not care to notice. "For some reason, she still thinks you'll flock up the stairs to see her soon. I do say, Chry my friend, of all my days here, you are the first to have so effortlessly bewitched the Ryders' most dangerous creature. Most men like devouring her whole and that just ain't going to do it for our little Missus. Nope. Ain't happening. That's why it's all the more tantalizing for her to discover a young man so impervious to her attractions." With a bubbly grin, Onvi shook his head as would a peasant heading toward an unremembered night. Before drinking again, he belched and said, "You're a wizard, Chry."

He didn't question what a "wizard" was. What was the point?

Onvi gurgled the rest of the ale, slid the tankard across, and slapped the bar once for another. Without losing a breath, he spoke.

"You shouldn't be embarrassed either. Last time I visited, there was this poor, *poor* soul, Lloyd, I think his name was. Unique title, if we can say nothing else. His wife died, oh, not a Moon heretofore in Cadaqu from what he had called 'the Slum's Plague' or something like that. Not important. Departed Cadaqu for a new life but ended here instead. How about that." He made a noise between a giggle and a hiccup. "Poor lad never even found the mox buried inside her crotch. Truly a shame."

Chry gloomed down at the rings. He did not respond. Above them, the Restless Ryders groaned of wood and harlots. Beside him was an exchange between Ryder and Onvi that he did not try to grasp. Afterward, Onvi took notice of him again. His grin flattened. Suddenly, the thief did not look so drunk nor carefree.

He asked, "You want a tankard?"

Chry didn't respond. Onvi nodded.

"I'll get you a tankard."

Ryder brought another but his scathing glare toward Onvi said that he better have the mox ready to match what they were indulging in. Onvi did something in response, but Chry didn't reckon them.

The tin butt of the tankard entered his view but covered the tree rings by which Chry had been so allured. He didn't look at the culprit. It wasn't Onvi who placed it there but an impossibly hairy hand. Ryder probably. He could feel irritation somewhere inside of him but only for a stroke like the flicker of fascination he had for Viamous. He heard the voice of Ryder say, "Volumous 'ould sleep with ah dead horse if it meant she'd receive 'er mox." Thereafter, Ryder snorted laughter. It was raspy. There was another chuckle. Chry didn't stir.

There was another exchange between Ryder and Onvi. Soon enough, there was only Onvi. Chry reckoned the speech of "I must say, Ryder *never* disappoints me with his enthusiasm. Dontcha agree?"

Chry was quiet.

Onvi bridled his grin. He spoke his next words with genuine friendliness, but Chry could hear the unspoken concern.

"I'm assuming you don't grieve well. Not with women or ale?"

He was quiet. He could hear Onvi sigh.

The thief was restlessly tapping on his compass. The glass tinked. From far away, someone muttered something. There was the shuffling of feet behind them, bodies beside them, then the words of "Not now my lovely" spoken as if with a casual gesture. The shuffling shuffled away.

Onvi rested his elbows on the bar. Chry's nose twitched to the brothel's yeasty stench. The back of his eyes became numb with how long he'd been staring at the tankard, and the silence between them was as thick as the black smoke of Gladion's forge. Not a dribble of ale was sipped.

It felt like ages before Onvi spoke.

"I don't expect to understand what you've been through," he said. "I don't expect I'd ever understand. These feelings of sorrow and grief are, shall we say…They're…"

He hesitated, and it was this out of everything Onvi did that brought Chry from staring to listening. Mayhap because it was unusual for the talkative thief to hesitate when speaking. It was almost like he was being careful with his words which was something he did not do often.

Onvi sighed again, rubbing at the back of his neck.

"I suppose you can call them little walls. Break down one wall of big bad sorrow and then bam, there's the next, waiting for you on the other side. Shittin' while grinnin'. Some might even say that if you wait long enough, these walls will soon deteriorate, crumble, and then blow away on a sea fairy's fart, never to be thought of again." The smile Onvi bore struggled to stay but didn't. He paused. "They're lying to you if they did."

He cast his eyes over Chry. His lips were a scar, his stare gorgeous in its penetration. Though the numbness felt encompassing, Chry gave an offhanded glance and shifted in his seat.

The tankard remained where it was, unbothered. Onvi did not take the tankard even though Chry was beginning to think he wanted to by how he kept staring at it.

There had been harlots who descended the stairs, but Chry did not look to see if any of them were Volumous returning for a second filling.

Onvi breathed deeply before speaking again.

"The past. Yup, that beauty is a bitch alright. Not like I was much better. If you were to see me back then, causing mischief not only for Heclar and Noctito but the Guild and all, you'd think of me now as a Nomatus—prim, proper, modest in his habitual drinking. And I would wholeheartedly agree with you. I was unruly, advantageous, reckless, and, back then, unreasonably stubborn. A hard-headed child wanting to climb the tallest tree in Noma Devolum just to prove to others I could. And I regret none of it. More importantly, though, I wanted to prove to myself that I, Onvi, the offspring of a shit-bag father and long-dead mother, was *the* best climber around. My pride would not have it any other way."

With a finger, he rubbed at his lips. Something crossed over his expression before he could birth a wistful smile. "Now, when I met *her*, oh now *that* was different. I swear the first time I saw her, I was hook, line, and sinker. Only because of the hair. A dance of flames against the moonlight, I'd say."

He chuckled and Chry could not tell if he was joking or not. He kept staring at the tankard, sockets cowled with the purple bruises of sleeplessness.

"I can remember her the most when she cooked. Those days were much like this: I'd go out, try to fish, usually fail despite my pride, go trade with the Clawers for a Rubberneck Trout or Gulf Crab, come back, pretend I caught it myself though she'd know—just with a look Chry, one *look*—that I was lying through my ears. But, really, this was of little importance. She'd boil whatever I brought home. Then we'd eat together with Ferax panting beside the table. Remarkable for a former thief and widow."

Retelling the story blossomed the grin for which he was notorious, and his voice recovered its light-heartedness.

Shaking his head, he said, "I can even remember that pretentious mansion of hers. Goodness almighty that place was a stick up my ass. Each piece of furniture was—and I swear this to be true—more expensive than my childhood home. Swear it across my thievin' heart. But, no. No, no, no. She *insisted* we stay, saying, and I quote, 'You'll have to drag me out screaming before I leave my home.'"

He gave a bark of laughter, Chry not knowing whether it was out of contempt or affection. Merry again, Onvi reached for Chry's tankard and stole it.

"Should've told her, 'You already scream in bed, why not scream some more?'" He shrugged his shoulders. "But oh well."

He leaned back and took a long, satisfying swig of the ale. Around them, the brothel seemed shrouded like peering through a hazy foliage at its women and stone. That's why the little voice that did speak was so striking.

"How'd you meet this woman…?"

For the moment, Chry had convinced himself that the voice had rustled through the foliage to ask Onvi the question. But from how Onvi suddenly stopped, lowered the tankard, and was now regarding him with that lop-sided smile as if to say, "why, I'm so glad you asked," Chry realized that, no, it wasn't Ryder or Volumous or another harlot who had spoken.

It was him.

Onvi did not wait for the opening to close; he slapped Chry on his shoulder and made him flinch. Chry was already regretting his question.

"That, my friend," the thief exclaimed. "Is one plos of a story."

III

Three years heretofore

He snuck into her mansion on the 2nd day of Ainason in the year 816th.

It was a decision of indecision, but after he had slipped through the third story window of the estate, there was not much of an option to reconsider. He was already six hands under, and Onvi the Conqueror was no quitter.

He rolled across a bristle of fur into a crouch, his cloak dripping.

Carpet was his immediate thought. He couldn't see a lick but felt the fur along his skin. *Vvuladev hide. What Noctito showed Jun and me during training.*

This was subsumed by his next observation, not what he saw but with what he smelled—a burnt, homely scent, wispy and damp—as horrible to a thief's nose as soiled scales. It meant a doused flame, and a doused flame meant that the infamous widow of this mansion was here. Or had been.

His eyes sharpened and perceived that there was no lump in the bed, no shadows lurking, no one. The Cross bitch had gone. The door to his left was ajar, the natural sounds of a drizzling rain and howling winds covering his entry. As his eyes attuned to the gloom of the room, its layout reaffirmed to the sketch Noctito had provided—feathered bed with a pretentious canopy and rumpled bedsheets of silk carmine, coals cooling in the hearth, thin whitewood bookcases, a stuffed Opinel Bear head, Ironskin Goat, and a third animal with a ribcage tusk that Onvi didn't recognize, a Maplewood crossbow in a case—before he spotted a nightstand with a stone display case on top. Within its glass was his mission.

He had a shadow of a breath. In his mind, Noctito's words arose from beneath an intoxicating haze.

"Isadora has arranged for the dagger's delivery upon morntide. It's ancient. Rumored to be forged from the crystal brought back from Soluim Imes's expedition to World's End, from the island of Omna."

The grin across his lips rivaled a mischievous god.

The mansion he had snuck into, The Cross Mansion, was one of many estates on the island of Noma Devolum, a nation with a humidity that made the skin under his armpits chaff, a clammy stench of scales that damped his mess of hair, and nights upon nights of drizzling rizzle. Since the island was largely free from levies and easy to build on (compared to the mountains of Ontinia) with views of King's Channel and the Western Sea so sublime that lungs filled with awe, homes like these were common. But since it *was* a mansion, the fangs of Isadora's Guild had latched onto it. Noctito, his pseudo-mentor, had been asked by the ever-invasive Isadora to send someone to retrieve that ancient dagger from this mansion even though two of their prior thieves, Jun and Makathiel, were either captured or executed in the town square of Wilcom.

Onvi was none too pleased with the assignment, going as far as to say, verbatim, "I'm not going, and I will be *damned* if I let anyone else go."

But, then again, here he was.

It's because you love it. You love the possibility of being caught. You love the race of your heart and the buzzing of your fingers. You love thieving. It gives your little man a thrill, doesn't it?

And you don't want to see anyone else get hurt.

He shoved this latter thought aside. The excitement of the hunt was on him.

From outside, he heard the yelling and scrambling of guards chasing after his illusionary goblin, the supposed intruder.

The widow went to check on them. Not much time left. Grab the dagger and go.

Ain't that the damned truth. Mayhap the goblin could distract her by lifting her skirt so all could see those smelly knickers.

Onvi gave off a secretive snicker before going to work.

He hastened to the nightstand. Its handle was of golden filigree and hard to overlook, and the Black Glass candle-holder on top could only have originated from one of the islands in Ashes Fall. Most likely Cavuln's Landing, if he had to guess. Behind the candle was the case of fine stone flushed with the brick. Its material was timeworn like what he encountered within the ancient city of Valaalama. Flowerings were carved across the stone, though this, too, puzzled Onvi. Usually, he'd recognize the designs of artwork and of the like since Noctito (and Isadora at times) taught him the cultural tendencies for countless regions—Eastern Devolum carving poles in mimicry of a scale, the wicker weaved from the Mushroom Willows of Noma Devolum, the harsh masonry known to the Ontinian city of Raminus, the hundreds of different styles associated across the islands of Ashes Fall. All of these and so much more.

But this design...This design he did not know of.

The closest he could think of was the long-exist Farramaa who were the same species (same humans?) that had lived in Valaalama located within Noma Devolum. Even this was doubtful; he and Noctito had recently stalked through the Valaalama Vaults, and Onvi could be the first to attest that the "god-like" sneers he'd seen carved onto the coffins were aesthetic, somewhat, but only in that sinister and damning way. Nothing like the stone before him which screamed of butterflies and harmony.

At the very back of thought, this uneased him and would've uneased him more if it weren't for what lay within the stone case.

He couldn't stop himself from snickering.

And there she is, my prized beaut.

Behind a sheet of glass, dressed in an Ironskin leather hilt, simmered the crystal blade. His reflection swelled to the eyes of gems. And his fingers trembled with desire. It was a feeling common among younger thieves, naïve and impatient. It never left, was only ever tamed.

Silence. Rain trickling. Shouts.

He blinked, and his hand was hovering over the glass, as if in pursuit of a harlot's irresistible bosom. His fingers ached with how much they shook. They were so *close* now, so very close to caressing and clutching and squeezing. Why not come closer then? What was stopping him? What was loved was needed. It wasn't like they paid him *not* to touch…Right? Noctito was the one who told him to steal the damn thing, and if he could, he would because that's what good little thieves did.

Touch.

If only for a moment.

Go ahead, Noctito murmured to his mind's ear. *Grab it.*

Onvi resisted. Seas be damned, there was a rigid wedge sliding down his throat at agonizing speeds. He tried swallowing, sending shivers down to his toes. Sheens of sweat lined the back of his neck. He had a sudden realization that he couldn't move his hand and another that he didn't *want* to move it.

Dammit. Is this what took Jun and Maka?

After the thought formed, Onvi became certain it was true. It straightened his control. He clutched his hand into a fist, fought to tear

146

it away from the glass.

His hand fought to stay. It shook.

He knew exactly what this was.

I love that fool Tilugo, but his incantations are one mother to fuck.

His lungs felt like they were breathing through metal prongs. A drop of sweat hung from the tip of his nose. His knuckles cried in disappointment. However, no discomfort could thwart his grin. It hooked from ear to ear in surging triumph as he gradually reined his hand back to his chest.

Onvi expelled a weighty sigh.

Who would've thought a widow could create such a powerful incantation or even know anyone who could, he thought. *If she wasn't so damned troublesome, I might've liked to play along.*

From this feeling came another that Onvi couldn't quite reckon. Was it lust, allure, admiration, or a hodgepodge of all three? His friendships with Maka and Jun (mostly Jun) would've made the feeling worth being disgusted over. But it didn't. Whatever he could say about the widow and how she ruined the lives of two of his closest friends, she was no halfwit. She knew what she wanted to defend and knew the right people to ask. Onvi liked that. He could admire it, too, even if he foiled each of her precautions thus far.

Outside, the cursing of the guards dispersed into a clacking of armor and the shouting of commands. Onvi mumbled a vulgar insult, his hand still shaking.

Enough lovey-dovey stuff then. You can think of sex, love, and fascinations all you want after *you're back at the Guild.*

Righty-o mate.

Onvi tilted his head behind the stone display and found, as expected, another carving. This one was unique to the stone and quite rudimentary: a diamond inside a circle with lines drawn horizontally and vertically within.

Obsession.

He made a fake, disgusted sound then unsheathed his knife.

Tilugo, you really have to stop teaching random folk what you

147

know. It's bound to kill me one day, I'm certain.

He could hear his pedagogue laughing from the Temple. So Onvi decided, whenever he saw Tilugo again, the man of the round paunch and ruddy cheeks, he'd tell him exactly what was on his mind. Whatever that might be.

To nullify the incantation, Onvi had to lay his back against the wall, stretch out his arm, and whittle his blade across the edge of the circle. From the incantation rained stone dust. His wrist strained after a while, and he couldn't help but think how a guard (or widow) would react if they walked in on him.

Probably poke me to death with their pointy sticks.

From far below, one of the doors shrilled open. Footfalls rolled through the halls.

Shit, he thought. *Goblin caught. Alert, alert. Goblin caught. Now they come for me, thy master.*

He better hurry or else chop suey.

His hand danced to the quickness of the footfalls until a tiny nick severed the carved circle. Nothing special happened to indicate this— no sparks or voices over his shoulder saying, "nice work, old sport." Out of all the troubles Tilugo's incantations brought, this was probably the worst; there was no definite sign in knowing when the enchantments had ceased besides actually touching the object.

Another nuisance he'd tell Tilugo about thereafter.

Despite his cockiness and urgency, Onvi checked for anything he had overlooked. He peeked under and around the nightstand for unsuspecting wires (the nigh invisible ones that had nearly ended his thieving career early on), inspected the display a second time, glanced above for any large axes about to swing from the ceiling (*Aye, these things do happen*) or the floor and walls for skillfully-placed trap doors. Then, when all the crabs were cooked and served, Onvi hovered his hands over the stone.

Even now, at an age where he had stolen too many treasures to think about how risky each one was in obtaining, there still welled in his chest a restless pressure. He never acknowledged it (why should he?), but he also could never be saved from it. Somehow, he even thought the pressure contributed to the excitement of being a thief. An essential reason why it never dulled and why he still found the trade rewarding. How could something be so exciting if it weren't so absurdly dangerous?

Behind him, the drizzle became heavy and the growl of thunder issued an ominous warning. He breathed in—metal boots clanking, hands of haste digging nails into his shoulders, shoving, urging, pushing—and breathed out.

He set his hands on the stone.

Nothing.

The hinges opened. Squealed

Flinch of the heart

Dead

He held it there.

Nothing happened.

A prick of relief released the tension from his shoulders. Triumph became the ache to which his body yearned.

Too easy.

Onvi reached in.

The touch of its leathery hilt eased upon him a smug grin. Elation focused his vision. Its keen crystal edge simmered for him. The silver pommel dazzled. Feeling it in his hands brought forth a satisfaction that only a fisherman could have after reeling in the legendary Soulious Depan who'd been evading fishermen since the days of the Farramaa.

But this was a poor comparison, wasn't it?

Fishing couldn't match what he felt now. It never could. It never would.

Unfortunately, the feeling would have to be bottled up and stored for thereafter. His first thought should be to escape which inevitably called from the window he had entered. He gauged his chances in climbing down, hurtling over the hedge, and dashing to the sewers. If the risk of being seen or slipping on wet brick was too high, he'd instead climb to the roof and wait. No one had actually seen Onvi yet,

so no one knew he was still here. If all they saw was the empty stone
case with no trace of the thief, they might reckon he was already gone
from the grounds and expand their search beyond the mansion. And
who'd be right behind them? Sneaking through the wetlands?

The one and only.

Onvi hastened for the window.

Rather not wait that long either if I don't—

A hinge squeaked.

The door. *The* door, the fucking *door*.

Run!

If he didn't want to be murdered like Maka, chained like Jun, then
run, open the window, fly down, topple over the hedge, sprint, tumble,
bolt through the sewer entrance, bled into the shadows like there would
never be another morntide.

His legs did just that. His cloak ruffled. He was a step toward
freedom before catching a glimpse at the door. Then he stopped, dead,
and...and just stared. His knees stiffened into obsidian spheres.
Urgency twittered off. Salvation awaited him, but all he could do was
stare.

Standing strong and defiant within the doorframe gleamed a
goddess.

With bounties of time spent in brothels such as the Lucky Ladies,
Onvi was proud to have encountered and canoodled and escorted to
rapture many a fine woman. They all arrived at his doorstep in their
own parcels—each a unique shape, size, lust, and personality. True,
Onvi had the world to pick from. Each would give him exactly what he
needed when he wanted it (aside from Lamiaa Masuaa). Mayhap this
was what made the idea of brothels not as thrilling as thieving: A thief
could never know what would happen next. They could prepare, they
could connive, and they could observe, but at the end of the eventide,
execution would always linger as an unknown. Chaos reigned here, and
Onvi bathed in it joyfully.

Not to say brothels were boring. Oh, they were never such, my
friends. But Onvi—and he was quite certain of this—had never met a

woman like this heretofore. The goddess had not spoken a word but spoke with her body like so many do. And the words it spoke were of a nature that was unclear, unknown, and unpredictable. It asked Onvi, bluntly like a battle, to come discover what he might never know.

He first greedily gathered as many details as he could by looking at her. Fierce fiery coils of hair. Freckles. A Sea of them and eyes that had stolen the water's magnificent blue. A rough-hewn nose cut from a feller. What about her teeth? Where? Have to wait. The discoloration down her neck to a buxom bosom, stout hands that could fight with an Opinel Bear, her backside unexposed but no doubt plucked from his dreams and offered to him by a merciful god. Was Eulgash real then? Did he really exist? He must be. The Sea, too. There was no other explanation. His smell was sharp enough so to smell from her the sugary scent of a maple's sap. It reminded him of when he climbed trees as a child.

His little man was not ignorant of the goddess either. He, too, was quite aware and showing and throbbing.

How the plos did that happen so quickly?

Then, from her ample lips, the goddess uttered a blessing to Onvi. He was her one true disciple and she spoke to him from a plane of existence higher than he could ever possibly comprehend.

"You sniveling *thief*!"

Her words were a lightning bolt that struck him dumbfounded. He descended into a deeper daze. His mouth opened to give a clever response to her freckles and her hair enflamed and her demanding, sexy, downright-

"I-uh-I…I du…uh…"

His tongue was pinned to the roof of his mouth, and he felt something wet dribbling out the corner.

That's drool. You're drooling. I'm drooling.

At the door, she bore the posture of a queen about to call for her guards but hesitated.

Her chest. It jiggled when she spoke.

Sea be damned, how he loved her.

Her freckled brow narrowed. "What are you…?" Her head shook as she muttered, "Forget it."

She turned from him, her callus hand gripping the whitewood frame, swinging those hips, those *voluptuous* hips. Onvi ogled but recovered somewhat when his mind equated jiggling hips to a departing widow. Widow. *The* widow. The one who had sent both Jun and Maka to their figurative and literal deaths.

The Cross bitch.

Somehow this version of her did not register with Onvi.

His hands shot up. Likewise, he did not realize he was holding a thousand-year-reckon dagger from the times of Solium Imes in his left hand. It flew from his fingers and landed on the black fur carpet with a deadened thud. Thankfully, it had not chipped.

Noctito ain't gonna be too happy about that now will he?

Granted, mistakes like these were a rarity for Onvi but this whole situation seemed a rarity.

"Wait, my love!" He called. "Let us not be *too* rash. We've just met, after all, and I wouldn't want our relationship to start off spoiled."

His words were fluent and eloquent but also fleeting as a heron fleeing from a forest fire.

The goddess tossed him a glare telling him explicitly that no words were needed. She had already decided his fate with an assertiveness that no harlot could match.

She turned back to the hall, her penetrating glare departing. That's when the realization he was about to be caught and turkeyed slapped him. He needed to think, do, go if he wished to live a free man. And quickly, at that.

So, he made a decision. Like so many things in his life, he didn't think about it before he did it. It was made through pure impulse and was, in essence, the smartest and stupidest decision he had ever made.

Onvi rushed for her.

She caught him at the corner of her eye (*those beautiful eyes*), looked briefly puzzled, and then gaped in astonishment when Onvi tackled her. She let out a groaning cry that probably woke half of Noma

Devolum, even though Onvi tried his very best to be gentle.

They hit the floor together with the thud of fallen swains. He ended on top (he wouldn't have it any other way), maneuvering to straddle his knees beside her chest. Through the back of his thoughts, he hoped he had not harmed her but immediately reckoned that she was far from hurt. Actually, she was thrashing violently beneath him, her back thumping against the hardwood like a scale pinned by a spear. She would've added her voice, too, if Onvi hadn't slapped a hand over her mouth beforehand, his palm cupping her chin so she couldn't bite at his skin.

Nevertheless, her fingers clawed at his forearm, nails gnawed to a rugged edge, his skin crying blood. Onvi didn't call out. The blood rushing through his brain and cock was already too much to attend to. Pain was secondary. He needed to restrain her, calm her enough so he could at least *talk* to her. But something told him she wasn't in the mood for talking. Her eyes of the seawater blue were roaring into a raging flood plos-bent on ripping off his little man and shoving it down his throat. Her muffled yells tickled his palm like a lover's kiss and aroused his manhood to the brink of bursting. If he leaned too close, he reckoned she'd take the opportunity to tear his eyes out.

It was one of the hardest, sexiest, and most awkward moments he had ever experienced.

Alas, sexy times were doomed to end. Down the hall, beneath the floor, he could hear metal footfalls pursuing him from below. They'd be here soon to ruin any redeeming qualities the moment had. And *that* Onvi could not have.

So, he eased his knees into her armpits, snug. Her bum flailed and thumped against the panels. Thunder rolled above. With his free hand, Onvi pinned her arm and planted a kind knee on her shoulder to keep the arm in place. Her chin was slipping from his palm, and he could hear the ferocious mumbles leaking through. One of these was "fa-ck-in qu-wok-sa-ca-ker" translated into "fucking cocksucker."

Our first fight. How adorable, Onvi thought teasingly.

He briskly switched his hands. She gasped before a hand clamped her mouth shut, again. This only sent her further into a frenzy. Her hair splayed behind her in a red rage.

After the exceeding trouble in snatching her arm (like catching a slippery trout with a bare hand), Onvi pinned her other arm beneath his knee. He returned both hands to her mouth and leaned slightly back on his haunches. His breathing resembled that after rough sex. She did not think along the same thread; the fury he encountered in those eyes narrated to him the scenes of a spear skewering so far up his ass, he'd feel the iron prong tapping his teeth.

As gruesome as this was, he could not reckon why it still aroused him. Doubly so, he could not reckon how she had come to have a full view of this arousal. Like a crudely erotic play.

Oh Bear, what the plos have you gotten yourself into?

Onvi Basileus had no earthly clue.

He tried to reason with her anywise, however little that might be.

"Listen to me, my love. This only ends well if we continue on civilly."

If he had said these words thinking they'd sway her, Onvi should've reconsidered. The woman would not hear a word of what he had to say. She listened only to rage and *that* would not help him live.

You could just dispose of her, like what you did to the guard.

Onvi pretended not to hear this.

He tried once more, speaking to her in the soothing silver of his tongue, but, once again, he encountered the same stubbornness, digging her heels into the wood, stabbing her fingernails into his thighs.

Her greatest appeal had become his greatest challenge. And Onvi loved a good challenge.

He resorted to Plan B, i.e., the worst of plans. The smug grin he carried flattened, his brow smoothed, and his eyes softened. What remained was a somberness rivaling that of Maka's death.

From here, he waited for her to calm.

For the longest time, she didn't. Onvi in the meantime concentrated on two peoples: the woman, first off, and the guards he heard below them. If it weren't for the pouring of rain and the crack of thunder, they would've surely heard their lady struggling from above.

Anticipation seethed through his breath. His nose twitched. Another urge to silence the widow, quicken his escape. Onvi resisted; it was easy to be patient when staring at such beautiful freckles.

Sooner or thereafter, her fists slowed in slamming against the floor. Her leg knocked again, her arm waved weakly in its net. There was a grumbling of frustration, and in her eyes dampened tears.

Onvi had to conceal his discomfort.

In the time he had known of her, he merely reckoned the Cross bitch as fierce, firm, and unwavering. There was no space for emotion, even after meeting her; if there was a thief that needed killing, he'd be killed with the straightest of faces. But now she was crying. *Crying.* And Onvi didn't know what to do with that. He was a thief. He was a debauchee. He was Onvi the Sordid, Onvi the Faithful, Onvi the Wise, Onvi the Conqueror, and much, much more. He was always, *always* gone before they wept. That was a motto. If not, he'd string together pleasing lines from his ass to soothe the woman. And then he'd leave them better than they'd been when he had come.

Now he was stunned by the tears of an incomparable woman.

Soon there was quiet. Her limbs were stilled, bosom shuttering with emotion. A tear trailed from the corner of her eye. Though she had ceased flailing, the fury she bore in her glare would not leave Onvi. His gaze would not leave her either. Frantic footfalls below were followed by doors jerking open. But, truly, it was only them now.

Onvi, despite every warning Noctito and Piama and Roland and especially Jun and Maka would have for him, retained an insatiable desire to lift his hand, lean down, and kiss her. He, unfortunately, didn't do this. He could not think of a faster way to kill himself, yet he did have to wonder what the plos this woman was doing to him— physically, mentally.

Time passed. The guards swept across the second floor as storm covered their ruckus. A husky howl bellowed from the lowest floor, like a dying wolf trying hard to warn of danger even though its throat had collapsed.

Now that he had her full attention, Onvi didn't really know what he was going to say. Like always, he had not thought this far ahead. It was but a miracle she stopped flailing. Nevertheless, he thought of something.

"My love," he felt her body flinch at the title. *Good, she's listening,* he thought, although he admitted that disgust wasn't the first reaction he was looking for. Onvi pressed on. "I know you think of me as nothing more than the dirt you scrape off your boot."

Her glare confirmed this. If he did not get the gist, she muttered something into his palm. There was no translation needed. He could guess what she said.

He leaned closer and spoke softer.

"But, pray, think of the situation we find ourselves in. When you opened the door, I could have run for the window and left you here to yell for the guards. As I have proven, I am nimble, skilled, and beyond handsome, no doubt capable of eluding the guards and escaping into the wetlands with the dagger I have come here to steal. You would've had no scent to track down since I can change my scent at will. I'd never be seen again, and you would've been made a fool.

"But I didn't."

She didn't look convinced. Though Onvi could change his scent, he conveniently forgot to mention that he'd probably faint from over-exertion if he tried to cast another spell after having summoned the goblin illusion.

Oops.

"I could have hidden after I retrieved the dagger," he continued. "I would have sunk into the shadows, waited for you to enter the room, to search for a thief that could not be found, to stare at the dumbfounded head of that Ironskin Goat, and then to leave unbeknownst to my presence.

"But I didn't."

This he had stretched too. He didn't have enough time between stealing the dagger and hiding to when she opened the door.

But lies were lies only when someone discovered them as such.

"I could have dashed forward and incapacitated you. You could've reached a pain-staking breathlessness that could've taken years to lose. The lights would've extinguished from your sight. I could've found a closet, set aside from the rest of the mansion. I could've gagged, bound, and stuffed your body in there and left you for a solitary drink at Pike's Pier.

"But I didn't.

"I could have killed you—a quick and quiet death. You put on a tough face, but the truth is, I had a dagger in my hand and any other reasonable thief would've seen you and counted their options—kill and be free or save a life and be caught. You're clever enough to tell me which option a thief should've chosen.

"And most of all I could have told you none of this. I could have withheld these details from you, and I could have forgone speaking with you. In another life, you would've known nothing of my presence."

He furrowed his brow with as much sincerity as he could muster.

"But I didn't. I did none of this because, in the end, my only hope is to speak to you." He spoke his next words inside a breath. "I'm risking my profession, my pride, my friends, and my life, just so I can be here with you."

She didn't believe him—he could tell; it was all a load of toadshit to her. But the tears had stopped, and her limbs loosened. The enticing curve of her bosom had regulated its breathing. Her glare was still there, distrustful within their sea-blue sparkle, but, really, he could only hope for so much.

Onvi was making headway.

He set his voice to a shudder as though about to cry.

"So, I ask you, give me a mark of a can—"

Hinges screamed between the rain. It shook him out of focus and sent an ominous chill through the flesh.

They're here, I'm dead

But they weren't.

The squealing was down the halls. He had neglected the steel steps

157

storming up the stairs and now the guards swarming onto their floor.

This is no jest, Onvi. Noctitio's voice. *You either stay and die or leave and live.*

The guards were on the opposite side of their floor, but fat shit that would do him. They'd tear him to pieces.

His eyes flicked over his shoulder, back toward the open window. A cascade of rain poured through and puddled at its mouth. His joints and fingers and toes ached for freedom. He couldn't hide on the roof any longer since the widow knew he was here, but he could flee and get a furlong ahead of the piggies before the widow cried wolf. The storm and its gales could cover his trail and scent but it'd be a trek through Plos if the storm became anything like the Swaya Alasa that tore down his childhood home, not to add he was at a numbers disadvantage when fleeing from the guards—eleven to one.

Every instinct called for escape, but now he didn't *want* to leave. Now, what he wanted—love and passion—was not in line with the Guild's intentions. This naturally would piss off Noctito, but most of all, it'd irk Isadora who'd never release her grip from his balls, both figuratively and literally.

Remember who gave you purpose, her voice whispered, over his shoulder, leaning on him, touching him.

This time, Onvi made a conscious decision. Whatever the plos happened here in this mansion would be his sentence. If it was death, then so be it.

He tried to hone this desperation into his expression: a pleading in his eyes, his mouth a straight scar, brow creased into seriousness. All the widow returned to him was impartial contempt. She gave nothing away.

"I know you hear them, too, so I'll make myself brief," he breathed. "I'm about to hand my life over to you. I have every reason not to."

What are you thinking, what are you doing, what are you planning, what are you thinking, what are you doing, what are you planning, what are you…?

The storm smote the roof. Doors swung open then slammed shut like artificial thunder. The thudding rounded a corner and hunched into a beast grander than an echo. A glow down the hall bore the shadow of these beasts, malformed and shifting. Between it all came a feeble howl.

He gazed into her once more. She merely glared back as if impatient for what he was about to do next.

The thief gave a lasting grin.

"But for you, anything."

Onvi lifted his hands.

✳✳✳

He'd be lying if he said he wasn't expecting her to scream. Just as he had every reason not to lift his hands, she had every reason to alert the guards. His slippery tongue, he knew, could only leverage him so far before folk broke with frustration.

That's why her silence was all the more relieving.

Score one for the thief.

That being said, her glare was not in the least bit reassuring. He could see now the easy curve of her lips that did not bear an easy smile—more like a harsh, unforgiving slit his mother would have when catching him and Merek stealing mox from puppet "master" Rida. If it could, her eyes would've burned holes through his skull, and as the boots pressed closer, the only thing she muttered to him was "Get off me."

The words were said as if roasting over a flame. They were like oil and could've easily caught a tail of the fire and burst in his face.

Onvi did as he was told. Like an obedient slave.

A little role play never hurt anyone, he thought while hunkering down on her thighs. If this annoyed her, she did not show it. If this excited her, she equally did not show it. If Onvi did not know any better, he would've assumed they were preparing to move this show into the bedroom.

Really, his booties should've been shivering.

The widow propped herself on her elbows. As a product of habit and nature, Onvi's eyes latched onto her bosom. She did not notice; she was glaring down the hall at the dusky shadows painting the brick by torchlight.

She called, "Who goes there?"

Halt in the rush of footfalls. Shadows rustled on the wall, undecided.

A resonant voice, like the beat of a young drum, responded: "My lady Maaria." Armor shuffled as a shadow knuckled closer. The rain let up enough for Onvi to hear the click of the man's throat when swallowing. "There has been a breach in the grounds of the mansion. We suspect another thief in need of disposing. We assume he's on the third floor and could be in your—"

"In my what? Last I checked, my bed only knows of one to sleep under its sheets."

Chuckles squeezed through his lips. The widow silenced him with a venomous glare.

The shuffling stopped, hesitant to proceed. Out of fear? Out of fear. Fear was what possessed the shadow. Huddled behind the speaker, Onvi could imagine the unsettled eyes of his subordinates, pleading to be anywhere else but here.

He would've died to see that.

"Yes, my lady Maaria," he was speaking slower as if handling a viper. "We do not deny your word, but we do have reason to believe that an intruder has—"

"If they have, then they are well on their way to enjoying themselves at the Lucky Ladies. Thus you have failed in your duties to protect the Cross Mansion."

"But my lady, what if—"

"What if naught? I would be long dead if the thief had decided so, and it would not be in light of your prudence. I suggest reconsidering your patrols and the guards you have posted, Rucker, or come morntide, there will be a new Alor to speak of."

Gloom answered her. Thunder beckoned once more at the Sea's

retort then whimpered away. A light drizzle pattered thereafter. They listened to the dog-o below, its howl catching inside a throat that sounded crushed.

Instead, Onvi's manhood answered her, vehemently, despite sobriety. It throbbed thru and thru before Alor Rucker spoke again, his voice whipped into obedience.

"As you wish, my lady Maaria."

The last blessings he heard were those same footfalls retreating down the hall.

***

She locked the door behind them. Onvi gave a grin that was anything but bashful.

"Maaria," the name rolled off his tongue. "Such a beautiful name for such a beautiful woman."

The voice behind him was cold, "You have less than a captain's breath to tell me the truth, or else I will call the guards back."

"Easy now, why so serious?" He grinned.

She didn't.

Instead, she hunched down to retrieve her dagger from the Vvuladev rug, her eyes never leaving the thief. Onvi refrained from glancing at the crystal. From the floors below, armor scraped through dejection, and the howls quieted to a faraway panting.

"The truth…" Onvi nodded. The grin he had withered away. He was next to her bed but did not feel that same urge to jump into it as he had heretofore. "You want the truth, huh…? I suppose that's not too much to ask for."

He looked at her dead in the eyes.

Third rule to being a thief: Never tell the truth.

"The truth is that I was sent here to steal that dagger. I'm a thief: This is what I do, but not what I have always done. There were days when I was innocent if you can believe as much."

She maneuvered between him and the window, suspicious. Fine by him. He had stepped past the dagger without laying a finger on it and adopted a pose unthreatening to the eye, hands free for perusal. He had nothing to be scandalous about. He wasn't going anywhere, so he didn't act as if he was.

No, he was going to persuade her to be his. *That's* what he was going to do.

"As a child," he said. "My family lived inside a dilapidated hut outside of Palm. Before I was even born, my father left us. You can say I should loathe the man, but how can I when I do not even know him? Instead, throughout these early days, my brother, Merek, became my guide. I revered him. Each time he went outside to explore Noma Devolum, I dutifully followed. Mother would imprison me at home when I was two and three but when five rolled around, she stopped resisting. It was too difficult."

Onvi paused, his grin of reminiscence fading as if the night were drawing it away. The drizzle tapped on the window-sill. He glanced at Maaria. Against the light from outside, her countenance was a shade, and beneath this, her countenance was as flat and impenetrable as the face of Mount Blemeron.

He continued on.

"Merek left us when I was seven years reckon. Two years thereafter, my mother became ill. Her forehead burned like a furnace, and she kept me awake with how loud she groaned. I visited lady Woodwhite in Wilcom and, when I got there, drenched in sweat and starved, she told me my mother had the Fisherman's Sickness, probably caught it from the air or a bug or something. I asked what else she had to say, thinking this Toad of a sister wasn't telling me everything I needed to know. She wasn't but you know what she said to me? She looked me in the eyes with that no-shits-given glint that hangmen give to the condemned" (*Makathiel*) "and said, 'Son, we ain't got nothing else to talk about. In three days, you'll be sitting your scrawny ass at the Departed Pier, crying buckets as your mother sails out dead to the Sea. *Dat's* what's going to happen, kid, and *dat's* how it's going to be.'

"I didn't believe her. I was startled, upset…scared. I slept only a lick in Wilcom before returning home, dragging the cart I brought mother in through ruts of mud and mire. It took me from dusk to dawn to return with my shoulders and thighs a burning thereafter. By then, mother had worsened. She had vomited over herself and would've died right then and there if I didn't hear her choking on her own vomit. It was all just so damn ridiculous. My mother couldn't die. She was my *mother* for a fisherman's sake."

Silence marched on.

"Well, she did. That bitch Woodwhite said she'd die in three days, but she didn't. Mother lasted another turn of the Moon until her fighting spirit tired, paled, and stilled. For another Moon, I wept. For another two years, I lived alone. Not long after her death, our hut was flattened by the Swaya Alasa which left poor boy Onvi scavenging for food and shelter. After some thought, I left for Wilcom. Palm had three families living there and two had forgotten about me. Wilcom had more homes, more scales, more chances to survive. So, from then on, I drank from puddles and slept beneath maples. It was always raining, and I was always wet and sometimes I—"

"Enough. I've heard enough."

Onvi looked up at Maaria rubbing her eyes. The voice she had spoken with was anything but searing: hard, yes, but tolerant and tired like a patient pedagogue who had just listened to the life story of a naughty truant.

He stared at her. She didn't look back, yet that didn't stop him from admiring her figure. Caressed by the glow of the Illum light outside, diluted by the drizzle, her curves beckoned him to investigate.

Give me another night, and soon I'll be waking beside those freckles of yours. Onvi did not think about this. He knew this. Freckles like a thousand, splendid stars.

She finally looked at him. The light behind threw a gloom over her as if about to steal her away. Her sockets were the caverns of a deadly, dank prison cell. He could reckon none of her, couldn't even idolize her, but did feel a brooding that would've smothered a weaker man.

His heart pounded. It had never done that heretofore. Not during his heists. Not when he had nearly died in the Valaalama Vaults. Not during sex with Lamiaa. Actually, it did with her, of course, but nothing like this where he was beginning to think it'd burst if he didn't tread on the right word or touch her passionately or fall to his knees to express his undying love (*now, don't you think that's just a little over-dramatic?*) or eat with her downstairs before eating her upstairs.

It took every effort to stop himself from tapping his foot or licking his lips.

"Tell me," Maaria whispered. He could barely hear her, but her voice was the only focus. "What's your title?"

He reacted immediately. Any time left for hesitation would give the impression that he was lying. As they all knew, lying was for thieves as water was for scales, especially when they were talking about their titles. The Guild might as well write another rule stating that "no thief, present or past, shall release the title of their identity over to suspecting parties, affiliations, or individuals, willing or otherwise." Thus Onvi had even given proxy titles to each of the Guild members: Roland was Hardass, Noctito was Harderass, Piama was the Softest of Asses, Crissa Buttercup, Lomisar Blind Side, Isadora the one and only Whore's Bane.

No one ever used their titles.

"Onvi Basileus. Others call me Onvi the Lover, but, upon seeing you, I've found the only one I wish to love."

He reckoned she was resisting a blush, but this was another one of Onvi's delusions. "Blushing" might've been the distortion of a few shades across her shadow because, despite his desires, Maaria tossed a hand and said, "Your flattery will do you no good."

Nevertheless, Onvi hinted at a smile.

Maaria crinkled her nose, crossed her arms tight across her bosom, and sighed so her breasts lovingly pressed against her arms.

This was a ploy. She did that on purpose. She knew, oh she *knew* this was his weakness.

"I can't say I feel sympathetic to you nor to the thieves you call friends."

Through the darkness, Onvi caught the pupils of her eyes twitch. A lie, and no delusion this time. This was very much real.

"Everyone suffers, whether their trials be slight, significant, or life-threatening," she said. "And yet I will admit that, throughout my time confronting men as doltish as my late husband and as greedy as your crowd, I've never had the chance to know a thief to be so honest. You might not be capable of the full truth, that is easy enough to tell."

Damn it, beautiful and *clever? Now listen here master Onvi, this might mean trouble with a capital T.*

"But your willingness to reveal some of your personal tragedies is admirable. Perhaps not you and what you do but at least what you've had to endure."

Then, Maaria did something that she probably never thought she'd do as long as she lived. She smiled at Onvi.

"I thank you for telling me this much, Onvi Basileus."

Onvi did his part and smiled back. It wasn't his notorious grin that had bedded every Lucky Lady or the why-not-share-a-mox grin every regular at the Drunken Depaconaio was inured to, but a warm and heartfelt smile. It was like reliving his childhood, Merek and him climbing a Mushroom Willow, mother playing the viola within.

Maaria stepped aside from the window. "Despite your honesty, my mind is decided; I have no more use for you and, against my better judgment, will allow you to leave. I will not stop you. Some part of me even hopes you succeed in fleeing from the guards. I doubt you will. You boast of skillful excellence but were otherwise caught by a widowed woman."

"Only to see how gorgeous she is."

"Like I've said heretofore, your—"

"What if we make a deal? You and I?"

Another impulse—like he really had a deal for her.

But as he said this, the first pieces of that deal started tossing themselves into a heap before the forefront of his mind. Good thing, too. She was about to release him like a dog who had served his time and was now being laid to rest. Onvi would have none of it. He had come too far to be given a free pass to World's End. Nope, ain't

165

happening my love. You're stuck with me forever. For better or for worse.

The widow pressed her lips into a serious slash; she might as well be attending a beheading.

"And what would this deal entail?"

Her voice was low, neither approving nor disapproving.

Reel her in Onvi. She's all yours.

"The deal is quite simple, in truth." The thief unleashed his pride and joy: his smug grin. Deadly potent. "Since you're still unconvinced of my abilities as a thief, allow me to convince you otherwise. For the next two turns of the Moon, I shall sneak into your mansion and meet you here, just as I have done this night. If I elude your guards, you, in all your graciousness, will not imprison me. But, (he raised a finger) if I am caught by a guard, however unlikely that may be, or if I do not attempt to enter your chambers on one of these nights, then you can treat me as the deplorable criminal you claim me to be. Lucky for you, this will never happen."

She gave a hand, "And how does any of this benefit you?"

"It allows me to speak to a goddess."

"And how will I pursue you if you decide not to return?"

Onvi bore his grin with expectant pride. "I'm glad you asked."

Now came the exciting part.

He reached cautiously into his cloak and uncovered a dull dagger. It had no place in being called lethal. Its iron edge was rusted and chipped like the tiny teeth of a cannibalistic fish, and the white cloth of its hilt was already unraveling and splotched with faded blood.

Her body was taken aback, the whites of her eyes broadening to eggshells. She reacted. Her hand clenched the crystal dagger as it glinted, begging for blood. A scowl twisted itself as to shatter any benevolence she had heretofore (which wasn't much). Her chest expanded to call out. By all accounts, Onvi wouldn't be surprised if, at that moment, Maaria wished to rip out his throat.

A natural reaction, if he can say so himself.

He snapped to an innocent position: hands up, palms up, fingers splayed, dagger held with a single thumb so there'd be no way in plos he could strike her or her mother or her mother's mother. Frayed cloth bobbed from the hilt.

Easy does it, Onvi, don't go poking the bear.

"No need to be alarmed. Harm is not my intention."

Onvi swore Maaria was going to call out (and by golly, she should have), but instead she lathered her voice with bitterness. Her knuckles were white beneath the shadow's swath.

"It better not be, or death will be the least of your worries."

Onvi resisted a playful grin.

Oh I hope so, my love. I hope so.

From then on, she did not let a single act go unnoticed; every twitch, glance, cough, and fart recorded for its likelihood of danger.

Wary in provoking her further, even though his loins ached for it, Onvi touched the dagger's lip to the tail end of his cloak. The wool was cool to the touch, still damp from the Noma Devolum rain as the dagger's teeth seesawed through. There came tearing like the skinning of a muskrat, a tug, then a rough rip. Finished, Onvi leaned lower to rest the dagger on the carpet; some might even call this an act of innocence. He straightened up and held the wool swatch plainly between his fingers, so Maaria knew there wasn't no funny business.

Her fury converted into suspicious puzzlement.

"In the unlikely case I do not return to your abode, you can have a dog, or your dog, trace my scent from this piece of cloth. If you don't have your own, there's a man in Sins by the name of Sneas who has his own furry friend. Both are as ancient as Farramaanina shit, but the hound has a nose that can track down any man hiding within Noma Devolum. He'll help. Just tell him the Amola sent you to find a thief, and he'll be on it quicker than you can scream 'Alor Rucker.'"

Maaria narrowed her brow, both in suspicion but also in, he knew, contempt. It was an expression to say that she was not impressed with his wit.

Only fooling yourself, missus.

"You said yourself you can change your scent," she said this as if sifting for the truth through a chest of needles. "So what will having a piece of cloth do for me?"

Onvi could not conceal his satisfaction.

"As usual, you are brilliant as you are beautiful. Unfortunately for me, the spell is not a permanent one. When I sleep or lose touch with my concentration, the illusion will leave me naked to my natural scent." He held the swatch towards her. "In other words, you will be able to track me down while I sleep."

You Toad*! What are you* thinking*! She's going to find the Guild and kill the rest of us!*

She could. She probably would. But Onvi was willing to take the risk.

Trust could only be bought by leaping.

Her face was abandoned of expression.

"And if you leave Noma Devolum?"

Onvi smothered a chuckle, bending to lay the piece of cloth beside the dagger. On the carpet, they were like two puppies in a pocket.

"I never intended to," he said. "But, since you worry so, allow me to reassure you that Sneas' furry friend can track a man across seas and mountains, towns and cities. I am certain, too, that you have certain friends in certain towns on certain mainlands that could help hunt me down if I do turn rogue. It won't come to this. Your guards are much easier to elude than those across King's Channel, I can assure you."

From her lips, through a spell, he swore, curved a faint provocative smirk.

"Is that so?" She challenged.

Her light-heartedness was unexpected. Onvi had to blink first then glance at the smirk once more, no, twice then stare to access the accuracy of what he just witnessed. A smirk. No deceptions, no illusions. Maaria was genuinely smirking. And this time, she was here to play.

Just when I thought I understood you, he thought. *I get lost in that storm we call uncertainty.*

Like most pleasures, the smirk disappeared shortly thereafter; it receded as would a wave during low tide. Remaining was the rocky, barren coast.

Onvi forced himself out of his surprise by biting the side of his tongue. That brought back its silver as his expression regained the elusiveness of his charm.

"So, what does the widow of the Cross Mansion think? Does she think the terms sufficient enough? What else might bother you?"

This was, as an old friend would call it, his dog-and-pony show. He already had every response to every question she wished to protest with, and from what that smirk told him not so long heretofore, Onvi already knew what she would be saying next.

However, what she said next did not conform to his confidence.

"I should not be conversing with you."

Blimey, why noooooooottttt, he thought.

Maaria turned herself from Onvi so she could gaze out the window. (*Wonderful move, distance self from the persuader. Good, good.*) The rain persisted in its patter. Below them clanked the armor of a guard searching the mansion's face. Onvi could hear, if he strained, a clatter of metal in the front and a distant yell asking *where the plos Darest was.*

Oh, he's right beneath that bush, little one, Onvi thought with an inward snicker. *You're just too blind to see him.*

"Father would not approve of having a thief in his mansion. Nor would Alan," she said. Her words bore a wistful longing. "They'd do things differently. My father would've shot you between the eyes with his crossbow the moment you peeked over the window sill. Alan would've screamed obscenities loud enough to alert the guards, although what he would've done means little to me. I, on the other hand, seem less shrewd. My father and husband have long since departed from Death's Departing, and now it is only me to say that you interest me, Onvi Basileus. You bear a clever tongue and retain a confidence that does not trend on pomposity. I like that in a suitor and shall admit that these last Sons without another to warm my bed have been less than ideal."

169

She turned back to stare at him intently. He thought he saw a chink of her smile.

"I do hope to find another to warm my bed."

I'll do more than warm you. I'll make you scream.

Instead, he bowed his head to say, "If you are willing."

"Then I ask for one more request."

"Anything for you."

You've reeled her in, Onvi. She's flopping on dry land, and now all you must do is scale her.

A pause in the drizzle. In its place was the heavy hand of humidity, damnable through the curtains. Buzzing swarmed into their ears, pestering, and every absent comfort introduced him to another long and weary eternity.

"I request that if you are captured by one of my guards during one of these darktides that you will divulge to me everything you know about the thieves you work for and with. You will tell me their titles, who they are, where they live, sleep, drink, which mansions they have stolen from, where they will steal next, how you managed to navigate through the sewers, who they partner with; everything you know about what the Devolumians have named 'Night Prowlers,' as I am certain you are part of, will be disclosed. This is my request, Onvi Basileus. Any other offer can be negotiated without me."

Throughout her explanation, the grin shining through his ears shrank until his expression was devoid of mirth. He did not take pleasure in what Maaria asked of him. She was playing the game by serving it back fast and hard; in other words, she was testing how committed he was to her. She said his name as a warning: "I know who you are. I know who you are associated with. If you run, you will be caught. I will hunt you and every friend you have to World's End and back and then introduce them to one of my three friends: the gaol, the gallows, or the Sea. There is no running. There is no hiding. You will obey or you will disobey." She gave him an insurmountable choice to betray his friends. There was no conceivable way he would be caught (that he had already resolved) and so the betrayal was nothing more than a measly cut across the arm. But the mere acceptance of her offer was to allow for that cut to one day catch Sepsis and infect the rest of the limb in which he'd have to amputate it or die painfully.

Either way, it would hurt.

She must've noticed his disfavor because she left him with a you-should've-known-as-much smirk and strode to the grey wood trunk at the foot of her bed. The window was left free for the thief. She did not bother picking up his dagger and cloth, another jab as to say, "Take both. Won't make much of a difference."

Onvi stared in contemplation.

Maaria had become his golden egg on top of that treacherous mountain: Every step and climb were peppered with the threat of slipping and falling to his death, boulders the size of his pride would tumble overhead and crush a careless man, creatures of dark descent prowling inside the caves in hunger for an Onvi stew. That egg would not come easy. He'd have to sacrifice, and that he could not bargain against.

In the end, they both knew what he would do and knew that he was reverting to a childish fry: anxious, horny, and desperate.

She wants you to feel like this. She wants you to be on your toes and distracted so you can make a mistake.

He understood this. But this was also when he was at his best—when the rewards were the richest and the dangers were the darkest.

Maaria could not cripple him so easily.

He swished spit inside his mouth, reconsidered spitting on a floor that probably cost more than the last three objects he had stolen combined (a necklace, a puppet, and a cock, don't ask), swallowed, and approached the window. He did not look back at the dagger and cloth.

Boot propped on the window-sill, he hesitated.

"I do hope you like having another man to keep you company."

His words were grinning, and yet if anyone with a brain would've scratched beneath it, they would've discovered the mirth he had was a scant veneer.

Sifting through the silks within her trunk, Maaria said, "If they're competent."

A fighter here, the voice in his thoughts drawled as would a hoary sailor with a cigar between his teeth. *Ain't no telling how dis goin' to end, will it now?*

He decided then he'd leave while the day was still at high tide. There was nothing left to say.

His cloak swirled, and the night emptied itself of suspicion.

***

Sneaking into the Cross Mansion was like strolling through the sewers—straightforward when repeated. After his second night, Onvi became familiar with the tendencies and inclinations of each of the guards that he played with like Jun with her viola or Rida with his puppets. He even knew five of their titles and three of their wives.

Names hold thy power, oh yes they do!

Maaria (i.e. damsel inside Cross Mansion) was another beast entirely. During their first night together, she refused to acknowledge his existence. A fisherman hearing the story might've thought he was a despicable thief or something. Anywise, despite his chivalry, they did not sleep together in the same bed but with him curled on the fleecy carpet like the late King Ventem's baby. As well as depriving him of warmth and companionship, Maaria did not speak to him that night or the night thereafter.

At least the fur was soft.

By the third night, she asked him to sit at the foot of her bed. No closer. Stay exactly where he was or else guards. She spoke formally, he flirted openly, but they both avoided anything related to thieving, Maka, or Jun.

By the fifth night, they conversed as if they had known each other since birth. Each exchange excavated another truth. Maaria was the single child of the Cross family. Her mother and father tried their damndest to bear that button-nosed boy so he could marry and haul his wife to the Cross Mansion and litter it with mini Crosses. Alas, the slimy and scaly Alan, Maaria's late husband and delegate for the Purple

Sails in Laguanio, was what they settled with, a marriage she still detested to this day. And contrary to his life's blood as a lying thief, Onvi, too, coughed up pieces of his childhood. Merek, his older brother, had left by boat with some random fisherman named Skier when Onvi was only seven years reckon. The two boys had listened to Skier for Moons about the stories of the Four Nomases—Voldev, Novania, Zoar, and Admah—each story holding a promise: If a man were courageous enough to visit these lands and islands and clean up their messes, their names could be written in stone forever. Merek's eyes shone bright like a diamond. Unlike Onvi, too young to think past the grumbling of his stomach, Merek became infatuated by the suffering of others and reckoned that he could do something about that suffering on the other Nomases. Probably not the best message for aspiring adolescents liable to have their balls cut off if they tried "saving" the daughter of a king, but what the plos did Onvi know?

By the seventh night, after their oopsie-daisy, Onvi and Maaria were like ravenous rabbits. Every lust and fantasy in which they could've indulged took place in the span of the following seven nights. Eulgash watched in awe and utter dismay.

By the fifteenth night, they lived happily ever after.

Yeah, right.

***

As unfortunate as it was, Onvi had to inform the Guild why he could not retrieve the crystal dagger, which had been returned (as he had neglected to tell Noctito) to its plush cushion beside Maaria's squeaky bed. Darktide was receding into the morn by the time Onvi ended this exquisitely detailed story of raving goblins, screaming guards, and drizzling darktides. How true this story was to what actually happened was less than flimsy; Onvi simply stated that the guards had seen through his illusion (however unlikely this was) and that, as stated by Isadora herself, he'd rather return another day than risk being caught. No incapacitated guard. No Alor Rucker. No Maaria.

Noctito was not pleased—the twitching of his scar never lied—but queerly enough, at the end of his story, Noctito held his tongue and simply affirmed with a grunt, telling him he'd have to either return to Cross Mansion in a few days' time or attend to another job entirely. After this, he left Onvi flabbergasted. Noctito was comparable to Sneas's hound when sniffing out a lie. Noctito knew his story was a load of poppycock. They *both* knew it was. When was the last time Onvi was cautious about being caught or cautious about *anything*? Answer: Never. Every adventure they had together ended with Onvi making a rash decision that led them into further complications. The Valaalama fiasco was one. Maiden's Port was another. Their mere existence together was the third. They could also attest that Onvi would never make a faulty illusion. Noctito did not train him to be incompetent, and Onvi did not have the pride to allow for such mistakes.

All in all, reining back the lie-lurching hounds was very un-Noctitian of him.

After this first night back from Cross Mansion, the days went by slower than a scale flopping across a dirt road. He turned towards a vital list of task which distracted him from the devouring thoughts of Maaria, Maaria, Maaria: playing tricks on Crissa (Crissa was *still* squirming about the thousands upon thousands of illusional worms), fucking Piama silly at the Drunken Depaconaio, listening to Lomisar tell his tales of Golden Nose as Onvi reorganized his bookshelf, repeating activity two with Lucky Ladies, diverting his eyes from Isadora. But by the end of each of these vapid tasks, his mind would always stumble back to Maaria, jittery for another dose. Each darktide he'd sneak into Cross Mansion, the jittering would settle, and a calmness would release his heart.

These were the best nights of his life.

When he won their deal after two turns of the Moon, Onvi continued pursuing his woman by religiously sneaking into her mansion. This night, the twentieth of their lover's escapade, was no different; the Weary Moon looked upon his mischief with a disappointed eye. Since he had endured the nights where the Vigilant

Moon exposed red brick and grey steel, attempts to sneak into Cross Mansion had become even easier. A mouse with mittens could not have done better. And instead of entering through their infamous window where Maaria would be expecting him, Onvi took on a different entrance: He reckoned the opposite face of the mansion had not received enough lovin'.

Strutting through the halls after startling the newbie guard, Olsen Halomis, into seeking help, he peeked his head around Maaria's door, his grin bridging the gap between its jamb and frame. His footfalls were those natural with the wind and rain and, as much as he could tell, though she always surprised him, Maaria could not distinguish between the two.

Although they had long passed the full sexual embrace he received after their first real argument (he did not count their initial meeting as a "conflict," merely an inconvenience), Onvi was taken aback by how somber the room felt. Maaria was upright in her velvet sheets and buried her stiff hands between the cradle of her thighs. Her cotton nightgown, usually puddled on the floor, clung to a sterile frame. The fireplace burned. Shadows born from her miasma. Her glare expressed a brooding that even Onvi could not illuminate.

Now, what do we have here? he thought before saying, "Hello there."

He strolled into her room. She greeted him with silence.

Uh oh, we're in for it now.

Onvi culled through the incidents that might have provoked her. Last time he checked, he swore he hadn't wedgied any of the guards (recently), and the necessary tributes were already bestowed to Ferax downstairs. For the last two darktides, the mongrel was privileged with ripping into a turkey leg—thick, succulent, and raw from the docks of Limous.

Onvi took a step forward.

"It seems something is troubling you, my love."

This was posed as both a question and a concern. From beyond the open window, a ferocious but faint bellow called for someone. Alor

Rucker's voice, if Onvi had to assume.

About to tear Olsen's ass cheeks apart, I have no doubt.

This slight distraction diverted his attention from what Maaria had just murmured. He could've wrapped his leg around and kicked himself in the behind, but it was also very possible she murmured this because she did not want him to hear it. His mistake would be collected, preserved, and utilized as fodder for an argument thereafter. She was clever like that, and that made every conversation worth tackling.

Onvi crossed the room and sat at the foot of her bed. The fireplace warmed his skin. He dared not move closer knowing his body was speaking in place of his voice. This maneuver quite simply said, "See? No sexual intentions. I'm here to listen."

He hoped this reassured her.

Beside him on the wall, a trinity of heads accused him of his deficiencies: an Ironskin Goat, Opinel Bear, and that foreign boar thing with its ribcage tusks. Their dumbfounded faces judged his every action, somehow, even if their eyes were as dead as pans. Onvi couldn't understand why this discomforted him more than Maaria's silence did.

Discomfort. Discomfort! When have I ever felt discomforted?

His ass shifted on the feathered cushion, his nose twitched imperceptibly, and he tried ignoring the black, bulbous eyes along his back.

Maaria raised her voice over a whisper.

"What does being a thief mean to you?"

She was not looking at him. Initially, he was puzzled but did not express it. His face remained flat.

Being a thief? What the plos does she mean by that?

Instead, he displayed a pleasant grin that wouldn't have known the difference between wading through this delicate discussion or caring for a delicate grandma.

"And what brings you to ask such a question? We both know my thieving is beneath you, and upon these nights, we should only know—"

"Enough, Onvi. Answer my question," she said in a tired sigh as if restraining frustration.

His mouth was ajar, but no words spilt out. Onvi was not accustomed to being interrupted, Maaria playing as if in control: she the fisherwoman reeling him in, the scant Sun-Dry Weln.

He finally said, "I don't see what thieving has to do with our nights together."

"Then tell me this; what makes you think you still need to be a thief?"

"Well now my love, that's—"

"I said enough with your toad*shit*." Her silence cracked. Her look snapped at him in that familiar, fierce, but lovely glare. If she was a furnace, he'd be scorched. "You have everything you might ever need in this mansion, and if you don't, I can surely obtain it. So tell me then without any of your pompous and flowery words—*why* are you still a thief?"

Onvi stared at her, jaw clenched. His hand was gripping his thigh, and he reckoned if he would've released his fingers, they would've trembled as to be unable to think.

He knew what she wanted. Why she asked. In her eyes, there was only one possible solution, and that solution was for him to hang up the cloak and dagger. Onvi knew too well where that road would lead. Lazy sunrises, late morntides, yawning, donning then doffing for spontaneous sex then donning again, Maaria telling him, "Nay, you can't wear that out in public," idle strolls to and through Wilcom, buying tiny tomatoes from Missus Woodwhite's garden (the mother Flora, not the whore daughter Sa), children running and ringing the bronze bells, hand-holding while returning to the mansion, loving each other again...

Children...

He dreaded what would happen in that happily ever after scene.

Despite the concerns presented, Onvi never faltered. He slid closer, now in reach to touch her. He didn't. Not yet. The maneuver was merely a whisper saying, "It's our decision to make."

He settled into pensive thought then said, "I need to produce my own wealth."

"That's not a valid excuse."

The voice was menacing as if hinting at the dangers that lurked below the swamp's waters, but nothing scathing. He could work with this. He had surveyed the land and now he meant to redirect.

"I would think that you of the two of us would adore the arrangement we have. My presence, my mouth specifically, as you have no doubt noticed over these turns of the Moon, is not as easy to live with as a single darktide would reveal."

Maaria was silent. A twitch of the lips would've reassured him of the amusement hidden beneath, but silence was just as good. Onvi was ah rollin'.

"And also why should I bargain with the life of the woman I adore? I am a thief not only because it is where I belong but because any other life would end in tragedy. I am but a simple man, Maaria. My thinking is not complicated: What we have here works and will work for as long as you deem it worthy. Have we not shown our commitment to each other? Have these nights not satisfied our promises of passion? If I have not displayed enough of either," he compelled her with his thousand-starred grin. His hand snuck onto her thigh covered with bedsheets. The silk was velvety, welcoming, but the flesh below froze his hand in place. "Then I can surely redeem myself."

She was glaring straight at him, burning a hole between his eyes that would've been bullseye if he didn't, right now, take his hand away.

Onvi took his hand away. Any urge he had to caress her thigh waned. He did not feel the sexy times anymore.

She did not look away.

"I swear Onvi if the next words out of your mouth aren't the truth, then leave me and never return."

Ouch, that's a stinger, he thought, but what he felt was much less flippant.

Lust drained from his grin.

Look at her Onvi. LOOK at her. You're going to lose her. You're greedy and you're going to lose her to a greedy and filthy Guild. Then what will your future look like? Stealing until your knees buckle, drinking until you know naught where the tavern is, fucking until your cock shrivels? Yes, what a wonderful life you will have Onvi. Doesn't this sound just splendid?

Yeah…

But it wasn't that easy. Simple, mayhap, but never easy.

It came down to the inescapable fact of his life—Onvi could not forgo the pleasures of being a thief. Thieving for him was a lot like fishing in that Noma Devolum could not survive without it. The children would starve and cry, the men would lose the will to carry on, and the woman would scavenge for the last morsels of meat to cook. This was no life to live. This was not how he wanted to continue living.

And everything would've been just so damn dandy if all continued on with how it was. Onvi had no quarrels about sneaking into her mansion every darktide for the rest of eternity, and she shouldn't either. A life like that would be sweet as peaches and cream. But now Maaria was spoiling the peaches and ditching the cream. He would starve because Maaria demanded him to forgo the pleasures of being a thief just so he could become a law-abiding husband.

He could never become a family man. If he had had any hope of bearing a child, he would've escaped from the Temple with Rena Cartine whenever they were idealistic adolescents. Back then, the thought of a settled life disinterested him so that the colorful adventure they envisioned together became grey with monotony. Now it was clear; he would not become a father, he would not become a fisherman, and he would not fucking settle for something he could never become.

But here he was, hesitating to tell her exactly this.

"Maaria…" Her name was weak on his lips. "I understand what you wish for, and the truth is I wish for the same."

"Then why do you leave before morntide."

"I leave so to appease the others. They would not be as accepting of us as you might hope for."

The spidery grin of Isadora implied everything he needed to know about how she would react to Onvi leaving: silence first, a purr next as to make the thief think that what he did pleased her, and then there'd be the beginnings of a new web. She'd spin it for as long as it'd take to lure the ignorant flies of Onvi and his mistress because Isadora was not one to ever surrender a member of her family.

How in the plos could Onvi explain this threat to Maaria who was just as fearless about death as he was? He couldn't. Death had less of a presence in her life than did a glass window.

"So you are frightened of them," she said accusingly. "Whoever these thieves may be that you have yet to name? Onvi, with the huge and haughty cock, is frightened of a band of thieves."

Onvi smirked.

"I am frightened of nothing in this jolly green world, of course, and yes, my cock is quite huge, but that does not mean I am not frightened of losing you."

"I can take care of myself."

"As you did when I tackled you? When a thief of extraordinary skill snuck into your mansion to try and steal your dagger? I do happen to recall you yelling to Alor Rucker that if a thief was already inside your mansion, they would've killed you already."

He offered his hands in a "well, how 'bout it" gesture.

She didn't strike back. Onvi had won the skirmish, but he'd be purblind to think he had won the war.

The wheels of her mind rolled before speaking. She left no room for argument.

"Listen carefully Onvi because I will only say this once."

She paused for greater effect. He loathed when she did this because it was too damn effective. As to make matters worse, noises filled the space between them. On the opposite side of the mansion where the guardhouse was, there came the crashing din of metal. From below erupted the trembling howls of Ferax, Maaria's hoary, blind mongrel. A gust of wind surged through the window as the Sea's breath, sweeping Maaria's burning hair off her broad shoulders.

The silks rippled beneath them. The flames crackled and whisked.

"I want you to live here with me. I want you to eat at the same table as I. I want you to stroll through the Amenol Genas beside me. I want you to become acquainted with the fishermen of Wilcom." *Like that would ever happen*, he thought. "I want you to wake every morntide in my bed. I want you to stay with me until the last breaths of eventide through the shadows of darktide to the first rays of morntide. I don't ever wish to walk through an empty home again, wondering if you will ever return."

"You know I will."

"Yes, but that is not my point, and you are clever enough to know that."

He nodded and said, "You want me to leave the Guild and stay here as if I were somehow a normal husband with leagues of lands and hordes of servants."

She conceded a smirk. "I would not say our situation is a normal one."

Despite the tyranny this future promised, Onvi still managed a small chuckle. Eventually, it died.

"And what should I do instead?" He wished for his voice to be harsher, so he could at least pretend to retain some control, but nothing he said rose above conversational. "I did not lie, as thieves so often do, when I told you that I live through my profession as a thief. I have nothing else. I *am* nothing else. I will be lost if I stay here and forgo my livelihood."

"I never said you'd be without purpose. Opportunities are plentiful in Wilcom. Halorigalos is searching for a new apprentice after Buyo nearly burnt down his forge. You and I both know how old the man is and, without a son or daughter to pass on his inheritance, perhaps you can work under him until he's ready to relinquish the forge. If not this, the companies within the Purple Sails are always in need of crewmen. Under the Cross name, I can arrange for you to become a boatswain or quartermaster rather than a simple deckhand. I wouldn't even be bothered if you taught at the Temple of Illusion. I have no knowledge of their occupancy—the happenings of the Temple are mysterious to me save for the supplies exchanged at Illusion's Pier—but from what you have told me thus far, I'd be disinclined to believe they would deny you."

He did not respond. The first option sounded horrid like drinking ale from a straw. The second option was possible—its adventurous nature prickled his fancy—but what was the purpose of leaving the Guild for Maaria to sail the seas for Sons without her? This mathematical equation did not compute. There was also the possibility of being told what to do and that he did not fancy. The Guild had its hierarchy, but jobs were hands-off. Isadora or Noctito would tell them what needed to be stolen, and it was up to the thief to conceive how that item would disappear into their hands.

The third option was the most promising and even somewhat exciting. *Listen to me, ya liddle munchkins*, he would pronounce to the Temple's grand round hall. *We do this my way or the highway.* But then he remembered all the days he would peek into Tilugo Daisy's chambers where his head would be ten hands deep into his work, that quill fleeting across parchment as though this was something a thief like him could enjoy. He immediately retracted his excitement. No profession where his ass touched the seat for more than a mark could capture his attention.

She must've reckoned this.

"Onvi, please know that your uncertainties are my uncertainties. I might not know of these thieves you call friends, but I can clearly see how much they mean to you. Your reactions to the names of Maka and Jun are telling enough."

As if to prove her right, Onvi's gaze snapped at her. Within it was a cold, faint fear bleeding from a chest he dared not open. Noticing this did not stop Maaria from taking a pickaxe to its frame.

"However, I will not allow myself to live under the same roof as a thief. Not only will it degrade the Cross name, I will also be deemed deplorable by others across King's Channel when they discover I've been spending my darktides with a thief. They will see it as a betrayal to the Cross family and to the late Alan. Nay, Onvi, this cannot be allowed. The only reason I can sustain myself here is because of my past and current standings with the Purple Sails. This cannot be risked. Your life cannot be risked. Not for these silly games you play with your 'friends' just because you wish to steal the possessions of others. It's reckless and childish, a fool's fantasy to think it will go on forever. I won't allow it. Not whiles you still call me 'love.'"

Onvi should've been furious when Maaria mentioned Maka and Jun. It was a dirty trick, something he would expect from a thief, not from a widow. He should yell at her, scream. He should tell her what a notorious fucking cunt she was, and that she should eat shit and die.

He didn't. He'd never. Not with her.

And, of course, she was right. The life of a thief, as seen with Maka and Jun, *was* duplicitous and dangerous. Perhaps that's why she named them in the first place. He supposed he should revise what he said about her then: Maaria regarded death as she regarded a glass window—unnoticing of it—until the heron of her lover was about to fly straight into it and break its neck because it did not know or, more likely, did not care that he was approaching it. Then, the shattered glass would be all she could think about.

Yet, still, he hesitated to give an answer. The Guild was consuming him. He was hearing Maka laugh in mockery as he often did and Jun playing her viola within her room and Roland inhaling that damned cigar with the smoke puffing on his face and Onvi coughing then asking how many Sons did he have left before those cigars killed him and Roland telling him to go fuck himself and Piama shaking her head with that simple smile which always agreed to a challenge and Lomisar snoring at the table next to them as Crissa fiddled with her liquids, Noctito gone again.

Isadora moaning within the shadows.

Yes, beyond any doubt, Onvi hesitated. Then, his hands reached for Maaria's and held them tight. He made certain he looked her in the eye so she was certain he was not lying.

"Of course I will stay," he said. At this, her lips hinted at something hopeful. "How could I ever say no to my love?"

The final thoughts he had before the night took them was, *I will*

183

love her forever, I will always protect her, and I will never *let her go.*

How naïve he had been.

IV

"'N there you have it, friend! Story of how ayyye meeted my lovely!"

By the story's end, Onvi's sixth tankard was empty and the sunlight through the glass had become sleepy and shrouded with a thin rain. Ryder had carried peelings of bark to the hearth, his don't-annoy-me glare not wanting to associate with others. Harlots lounged around within the air of stone dust without an act to pursue. Volumous was nowhere to be found. Between an indiscreet wall and clutter of chairs, one harlot was bent low over another, the woman moaning to Eulgash above. Chry would not glance over there.

At first, Chry didn't listen to Onvi. The tree rings on the bar's wood had become his world and that world was a devouring depth. He'd keep falling and falling back into it without the will to look around.

It was comforting, that timelessness.

But being forced to sit here while his rump became sore eventually forced him to listen to something other than his lowly thoughts. From then on, Onvi's story grew to fill in the depths and bring him back to solid ground. Chry even felt a crumb of amusement in witnessing Onvi's speech and behavior gradually deteriorate into a merry jester.

In a way, Onvi was a small blessing. His story was for Chry as Elos Amus was for the injured. It did nothing to heal his wounds; the farmhouse fire had inflicted an ulcer to his mind where the rictuses of his grandma, Gladion, Aimee, and even his father tormented him. He had resigned himself to believe these wounds would never heal. Not by friends. Not by family. Not by the passage of time. He'd sometimes forget why he was here, living. There weren't many reasons left.

But what Onvi's story did do was mask the pain he would've felt during this time and help him bear the suffering of another day. It was another depth Chry could immerse himself in but one with vibrant colors and a scene of lavish splendor. Onvi's personality couldn't be ignored either. His pride was untamable, but otherwise, his friendliness helped. They had known each other for less than a turn of the Moon, but Chry felt like they'd been traveling together for too many years to count, their relationship forged from steel.

Everything considered, picturing the thief tackle an innocent widow or avoiding Noctito's disdain by sneaking into Piama's room put a much-needed smile on his lips.

"So you left the Guild then?" Chry asked in a tired voice. He already knew the answer but wanted to keep himself distracted.

"Sssssssssssssure did," Onvi released a burp ripe for a bloated king. There were giddy titters thereafter. "Ain't no *way* ah thief like me passin' ah chance to snatch her ruby rose."

Chry could not comprehend what he meant, this being a common occurrence with Onvi, but he was no less content. Not happy. That was too strong of a word. But content. Aye. And by being content, he should've sat quietly and listened. Chry knew that if he did, Onvi would've babbled about every shop, brothel, and tavern across Noma Devolum including every type of woman, fish, and item he had stolen since his days as a baby. He should've sat there quietly. He should've let Onvi talk. He should've. But he didn't, and that was his first and fatal mistake.

"What happened to Maaria then?" He asked. "I mean, surely you wouldn't be with, well, the Runners if…if you were still with…"

Chry had gotten halfway through this path of conversation before words clogged his throat. Now, he gaped helpless.

The transformation of Onvi's countenance could only be described as sobering. His final tankard (the last one he had promised) dropped from his lips. Reddened eyes had receded so far back into their sockets that the skulls Chry found near his farmhouse portrayed more life. His grin emptied in a deadened stare. It would not look away from the opposite wall where the casks were and, really, it was the closest description he could name since it offered no recognition of its surroundings. There was something through those casks and beyond that could not be reckoned by a stranger but was all the misery needed to cripple a man.

His hand released the tankard, sheathed the crystal dagger, shoved the cracked compass into his trousers, then said in a hushed voice that would've made an elder and baby cry, "We'd better return."

He flung a mox coin, deadened Illum stone encircled by silver, onto the bar. It bounced off the rosewood, dropped off the edge, then clattered.

Chry was paralyzed.

Wa...What have I...?

"Onvi wait. Just..."

The thief was already making for the door where the lecherous looks of the two harlots—those that had been enjoying one another—leered him to stay and enjoy himself. Onvi shouldered past and left the brothel.

"Onvi, pray, I didn't mean...I just—"

Chry rambled on. He rambled on as he tumbled off the stool and away from the bar. He rambled on when he sidled past the two harlots who had, at first, looked upon Onvi in utter disgust then, somehow, forgot about him by touching each other again. He rambled on while they traversed through the rounded streets of Viamous. He rambled on beneath the sprinkles of rain. He rambled on as they crossed over the River Twins.

He rambled on and on, and Onvi did not say a word.

V

Chry did not stop babbling until he was almost across the viaduct. Then, he stopped and stared.

He had not succeeded in stopping Onvi. The viaduct they strode on was enormous and had taken them almost a full mark of a candle clock to cross. With Viamous residing on the confluence of the River Twins, the largest rivers in Admah, it had to be. Not only was it long, it bore a berth wider than Volumous's hips (*Oh Arbiter, help me, Onvi has corrupted my thoughts*). Three horse-drawn carriages could cross abreast and still its cobbled street would have enough space for residents on either side. The stubby balusters were a joy for small children to peer over and marvel at the vast, sparkling blue waters of the Twins.

That could not be said now.

The waters were contaminated with the glum of night and drizzle. Puddles sprang between the street's gritty stone. Not a soul revealed themselves. It seemed only him and Onvi were illuminated beneath the posts of Illum blocks evenly distributed across the bridge and throughout the main streets of the city.

That light was how he saw the child.

He—or at least he thought the child was a "he"—had tucked his knees into his arms on a stone, slanted embankment where a steady sheet of rain emptied into the untamed waters. He was too far away to know why he was just sitting there getting wet, but his presence immediately reminded Chry of Arya and Robert, the orphaned children in Domum, nibbling on the gristle of Dry-Mouth meat dirtied from grime beneath their nails.

The child had not noticed them yet, and Chry was glad his pleads to Onvi weren't too loud to alert the child even though he didn't rightfully know why that mattered. He wasn't going to talk to the child. He'd probably never see it ever again.

The child eventually noticed Onvi, but like Chry, the thief did not stop for the child either. The inn the Runners were staying at named The Stone Basin was the first building at the corner with its stables further down and an inconsequential alleyway behind. There could have been a time heretofore that a night like this would have captured the hearts of travelers with a warm fire and hearty meal.

Not anymore.

Unsettled silence gaped from beneath its neglected, stone façade, and the songs of old had wilted from the throats of its disgruntled inn keepers. From its glass windows passed the occasional shadow against the faded glow of an Illum stone. It was plain; the rooms were starving for the company they had lost from the Split. Chiseled along the curved head of the door was the inn's name, long weathered and never reshaped.

The child's head shifted toward Onvi then became stock-still. Onvi did not turn his head. He barreled through the front door as would Vion. Chry thought he heard the *ting* of a bell overwhelmed by the *clap* of the front door being slammed. Chry flinched. The child watched on, undisturbed. Then his head turned to Chry.

It was as if Chry had been flicked on the head. He had to hold himself upright with his hair a wet mop of black twine. He could not see the eyes or the expression or the condition the child was in but felt the suffering it hurtled at him instead. It was like being snapped at by a Dry-Mouth desperate to deter him from approaching but whose fangs had been plucked long heretofore.

Against the threat of a torrent of rain, Chry stayed still. There was something…pulling him toward that child. He should have felt indifferent as he had with their travels, as he had with the city of Viamous, as he had with each of the Runners…Well aside from Onvi, but look where that led him—here with his farmhouse burned, his love lost, his life ruined, and his last friend departed. Yet he *didn't* feel indifference. He *wasn't* swallowed by the fog. Instead, his mind had wandered into concern. There was no one here to look after that child, no one here to love him.

He probably lost his father too, a small voice whispered to him. *Just like you have. It's probably why he's here, abandoned with nowhere to go.*

The last day Chry saw his father was the first day he said he was proud of him. Chry was so startled he didn't even know what to say back. He guessed, thinking back, he should've just smiled and said, "I thank you." It's what he should've done. Instead, his father left, and Chry just stood there on his pouch dumbfounded. Leaving so soon was just as confusing as his praise; his father would usually stay home until his mother returned from Domum. That day he hadn't. He was alone with his grandmother for the first time since he could remember, and Chry was afraid. There was a rodent inside his heart, black and bloodied with fears, nibbling, and tearing from within. He couldn't silence it. He had waited on his pallet, crying for no reason. He never cried when his father was around, but he wasn't around, so damn it all to plos.

Days thereafter, when filling the trough with feed for Mister and Missus Swiggle, there appeared a speck in the distance. He gasped. His hands dropped the sack. They were shaking violently. Hope bloomed. Under his breath, he mumbled, "Oh thank Arbiter, thank everything-" and could not help himself from dashing forward to meet her. The wind ripped at his tears. Grinning wildly, he yelled something he couldn't remember, couldn't hear, before the words died in his throat. The strength from his legs lifted and they slowed and slowed until he stopped. He wasn't grinning anymore. There was a steady clopping as Gladion rode toward him. His knees were weak and shaky. He could barely stand. He shouldn't be here. No, not now.

Gladion reined his mule in beside him. It sneezed. The blacksmith's grin was gone. Chry was gazing forward, vacant. His throat was dry, but he couldn't…*No, pray, no. Don't. I can't. Not right now, not ever, pray no.*

"Da Lanky," Gladion whispered. "They…"

Chry dropped to his knees, eyes blurring with tears. He never saw his mother and father again.

Slants of rain peppered his cheek but then calmed again to a drizzle. With the regimented motion of obedience, the child rose. He never fully turned his back to Chry, climbing the embankment and entering the alley beside The Stone Basin. The Illum light from the street receded further before the child was lost to sight.

Chry gazed at where the child had been and then where he had gone and then at his feet where the rain tickled the stone.

I'm proud of you, son.

His feet moved him then. He ignored the front door of the Stone Basin and descended into the alleyway.

VI

He almost passed the child without even realizing it.

On his right, between two unfriendly facades, was an alley near the width of his shoulders. He could not see its end for the darkness had corrupted his sight, but just at its edge closest to him, sitting just as he had on the embankment, was the faint shades of the child.

Even though light was sparse, Chry could reckon the child was a boy but that this boy was not much younger than Chry. If he had to guess, the boy was about twelve or thirteen years reckon, three years younger than Chry, about as long as his parents have been dead. He couldn't really see the boy. They were too far from the street, and there were hardly any rooms from The Stone Basin that were lit. Those few that were had Illum stones faint from years of use. The drizzle diluted them. The boy looked more like a dirty, pile of rags than a child.

As if this was his trigger, Chry took a step toward the boy. There wasn't much thought to this. He just, well, did. There was another step. And another. Water splashing beneath his clogs. The boy didn't retaliate or acknowledge him, but now Chry was close enough to take a better look.

For a boy, he really wasn't small. He only seemed like this with how frail he was and how he sat. He was actually tall, taller than Chry if he stood. He was also strikingly scrawny—the Domum-kind of scrawny. Chry could see gaps between the bones of his forearms. Any stench he might and surely did have was weakened by the rain, and a cascade of long, drenched, and unkempt hair obscured a face sinking into a deep, dark pool.

Beyond anything else, he felt no signs of life from the boy, no reasons to live.

Now that he was here, Chry did not know what to do. *Was* there anything he could do? It wasn't like he had known what to do with Onvi, and he certainly didn't know what to do with the boy.

It's not like you're meant to do anything anywise. You were meant to live on a farm for the rest of your life. Now, look at you.

Mayhap but, he just…well, he couldn't just leave him here, right? The boy needed his help and Chry wasn't going to just ignore him and stroll into his bed and pretend he never saw anyone. What kind of person would he be if he did? Would Aimee do that? Would his father? No, neither would. And Chry, whether he was meant to meet the boy or not, wouldn't either.

Then, there came an idea.

Before dread and grief could deter him, Chry darted back down the alley with an almost eager gait and veered right toward the front of the inn. Someone, if they were watching, would have thought Chry was grinning.

The pile of rag did not stir. It stared absently at the drizzle.

A lifetime poured by before a body reemerged from around the corner of The Stone Basin and descended back into the joyless alley. It was Chry again. His steps were now tentative, but in his hands was half a loaf of bread.

For their trip to Cadaqu, the Runners provided him a meager sack of victuals and one of the pieces, alongside a handful of oats and a sandwich Onvi called a Salmon Misfortune, was a loaf of bread. In his hands was what remained of it. He clutched it tightly to his bosom, stopping strides before reaching the boy. He had not moved from where he sat. His features were that of a husk from the cornfield Chry had lost in the Wastelands.

There was a moment where Chry could have said something—anything at all would have been nice—that could have brought the boy out from his gloom. Yet the moment was fleeting. He stood around for too long in the drizzling rain, doing nothing but staring at the boy.

Oh Arbiter, I should've just stayed inside and never have gone to get this bread.

191

His tongue had retreated into his throat to tie into a knot, leaving an uncomfortable lump inside. The rain tapped his shoulders as if to ask when he would approach.

Look at the boy. He doesn't want your help. He doesn't care *about you. Leave, stay, stick a moxam up your rump, shrivel and die in Etherine, it's all the same to him.*

He gulped once and glanced again at the rags that had not acknowledged that another human was beside it. He then reckoned the bread in his hands but instead of white fluff, Chry kept seeing the face of Onvi, the skeletal mask that harbored the suffering of his past.

He never wanted to see his friend like that again.

Chry let out a long sigh, gazed at this half-eaten, half-soggy loaf of bread before bending to place it on the cobblestone.

"It's for you…" He mumbled.

The boy was unresponsive. The boy did not look. He did not want him. He did not want his food. But regardless, this felt…right. Chry couldn't say exactly how or why, but he could say that at least he had done something to improve the livelihood of another.

This, Aimee would have smiled at.

Chry hesitated again before his footsteps retreated into the alley, splashing in the puddles, and leading him out into the street again. Then he disappeared into The Stone Basin.

The pile of rags did not stir. It stared absently at the drizzle soaking the bread.

Soon thereafter, his stomach rumbled.

VII

Bar watched from above. He had had a conversation with Ambia. Thereafter, he could not sleep. So he watched, gazing long after Chry left.

That boy.

It was hard to distinguish his features through the glum of the alley, but his being was unforgettable. There was no doubt. He had seen that boy years heretofore in the wretched underground of the Pig Pen. Most of all, he reckoned again the tremendous suffering he must have experienced in those cells beneath Cadaqu. If Bar's assumptions were true, the boy should be as broken as Mesa. It was a testament to his resolve and perseverance that he was here this day.

Bar wished he could have adopted the boy like he did with Mesa, but he couldn't. The boy would have to wait until all the gems and the sword *Azrael* were retrieved.

That was his last thought before the voice and sleep vied for his attention.

The Council's Summons

I

They were late. Bar did not need a letter from a crow to inform him that the Council's patience was thinning. Under those hoods, he expected nothing less than agitation.

So be it, he thought.

They rode for two days.

The River Twins had converged to become the Great Coyous, and this was what the Runners followed through Southern Etherine. The route was well established and caravanned since the First War, so their travels were safe—as safe as a road in the wilderness could be. Marks into the morning of the third day, Bar's stallion became restless. Its walk had quickened despite attempts to steady it, and it neighed impatiently. This was not a new phenomenon. His stallion trotted because it sensed the undeniable promise for rest, a batch of hay, and a trough brimming with water.

It sensed civilization. It sensed Cadaqu.

Bar assessed their surroundings. The breeze carried the salt of the sea now, and the warm air, pleasant heretofore, had become sultry and clammy. Before them, the meadow lazed out forever as they trotted past fleecy sheep cropping grass. Afar, rising from the meadows, columned a broad cloud that looked like the hurricanes the city of Asunio would fortify themselves against. Not a hurricane, he knew, but the onset of a storm. Depending on the urgency of the Council's mission would be whether they'd have to set off into that storm the next day at dawn.

Oh you know what they want from you. You know you can't wait any longer if it isn't.

Bar wrinkled his nose and touched his throat where Chry had cut him, the wound sealed, scabbed, and now pink through a Sun-Fire's Embrace, cleansed by Goldendrake.

Horse hooves swished between a stripe of tall grass and crunched across a gritty road grooved to the years of caravan travel. Bar sat straight and stared forward expectantly at the horizon until a small black speck appeared. Discerning the end of their journey, his steed urged him to canter but Bar, knowing Ambia couldn't maintain a canter or trot whiles Chry rode double, leaned back and tugged at the reins. The formidable beast shook its mane, sneezed discontent, yet did not buck.

The speck grew steadily. Spikes broke through the grasslands like a crystal crown emerging from a green ocean. It grew and grew, and the scene soon overwhelmed their Discernments.

Cadaqu's sublimity became irrefutable.

Crystal edifices of serene blue pierced the skies above. Smooth walls reflected an abstraction of the firmament, impenetrable to any past marauder audacious enough to have reached the city. Its peaks were that of skinny mountains indiscernible from each other. Their heights lofty, they loomed over a muddle of hovels and huts. To Bar, the scene resembled shabby devotees genuflecting to a god.

The distant crashing of waves sounded clearer, and the strengthening smell of salt stroked his nostrils. Furlongs from the walls edged a precipice along the coastline. Beyond shimmered the Grey Sea. Islands, landmasses, and that supposed grey were nowhere in sight. Its blue mirrored the sky and waves spumed against the crags. The cloud column that promised a storm lurked over its waters, a dark tint manifesting from its wings. Along the precipice and below Cadaqu was a cavern for its wharves. Since the Lanke's triumph during the War for the Split, vessels rarely sailed through the River Twins, and caravans rarely rode on Courier's Road. Instead, commerce flourished here through the Grey Sea and periodically along Ainan's Trail. As such, Whitewall and Cadaqu became wealthier than they had ever been.

Their extortion of the suffering of innocents made Bar sick.

The breeze passed fingers across his cropped hair. As their horses neared, dilapidated and largely abandoned huts received them in between clusters of oak stumps. Bar reckoned there wasn't a living tree within five leagues of Cadaqu.

Soon, the solid dirt road trampled into mush, the traffic of too many bare feet. Moldy hovels infested every side and threatened to crumble against the sea breeze. There were neither donkeys nor horses. Women carried salt-stained buckets of water on their heads from a local tributary of the Great Coyous. In this community of the destitute, commotion was currency; children skipped around naked and screeching, their bellies sunken beneath their ribs.

The Runners kept their heads low.

After Onvi nearly trampled over a wayward child, his quip unnecessarily crass, the Runners arrived at the walls. The crystal dominated their view, and the land before them was clear half a furlong from the crystal. No hovels or refugees. To reach Cadaqu's only gate, their procession would have to travel through a tunnel smoothly carved into the crystal. It was about a furlong deep, intermittently arranged with wooden barricades felled from spruces.

From Ontinia, he thought.

To the right of the tunnel was the guardhouse, a chunk expanding from the crystal. It looked like a mole on the skin if it had exploded and, before it could disperse, froze to capture the picture. One guard lolled within its compact space. His legs were kicked up on a polished and extravagant stone table that could be sold to buy half of the refugees outside an adequate meal. The guard seemed to be picking at his fingernails but when he noticed them outside, he grumbled. Bar could've surmised what was said by the scorn he had assumed.

The tails of their steeds whisked as they waited. The guard was in no rush to stand, hitch up his trousers—chainmail rattling—and hobble to the entrance which was merely an open frame across the guardhouse. His appearance resembled his behavior; he gave the impression of a lazy drunkard who did not retain the paunch or stench. Rather, he was a skeleton, and the stare that looked out from his hollow and sleepless sockets told of a grumpy indifference. His grandmother could've been noosed and tossed over Cadaqu's precipice, and the guard would still be sleeping.

He yawned and rubbed at his eyes as if wakening.

"Hasten with yer words. Doesn't look like yer one of them, but that don't mean I want to talk to ye."

Bar retained control. The guard and those like him would be the first to go.

"We have business with the Council."

"And my mother has been fucking Eulgash. If that's your excuse, then go join er."

Bar didn't retaliate. Though his accusations expressed otherwise, the guard remained leaning against the frame. The horses stirred. Onvi, as had been seen otherwise, kept his mouth muzzled.

Bar stared hard at the guard who hitched an eyebrow up in asking, *well, what? You got a cock to show me?* Without waiting longer, he reached into his gambeson and drew out the letter the Runners received from the Council. He had opened it with the letter opener beside his stiletto but kept the Council's wax seal whole. When he revealed it to the guard, he only grumbled again and shrugged unimpressed.

"I suppose my mother *is* parting the sea with Eulgash. Reckon that." His bored expression didn't seem surprised.

Bar returned the letter to his gambeson as the guard hobbled towards the tunnel. Yawning, he entered between two wooden barricades, stopped, gave an incurious glance at one of them, then shoved it a knuckle to the side with a grunt. He looked over his shoulder.

"Well, what the plos ye waiting for? A courtesan to stroke yer fancy? On with ye."

Bar stared for another moment before kicking at the haunches of his stallion. His steed barely fit between the barricades, and his head cleared the tunnel's ceiling only by a hand. The others clomped behind.

The short trek through the tunnel shaded them from the gaining sun but not from the sea's oppression as Bar perspired through his gambeson. There were no torches or Illum stones inside the tunnel and the only light came from behind. Bar followed closely behind. Periodically, the guard would stop at a barricade, give it another look, shove it a knuckle to the side, and hobble on. There seemed to be no sense to the work. The horses could slip past most of the barricades.

As they neared, the gate appeared in the darkness. It was a hefty, iron door wedged into the crystal. Rivets edged along the steel plates which reflected warped images of the Runners. Bar noticed a new dent on its upper right side, and in its center chiseled the emblem of Etherine: three overlapping circles forming a triangle.

The guard approached the gate and rapped a fist against it three times. Flesh drummed and iron echoed down the tunnel. They might as well have entered into the belly of an Es'tal'mis giant.

"Open up, cocksucker, it's me." He cleared his throat and spat a glob of phlegm. "And I swear if you ask, 'who me is' again, I'll rip your balls off and feed them to ye."

There was silence before a thunderous *clunk* sounded approval. Then another which made the first sound pitifully puny. The gate squealed, and a chink of light broke through. It gaped open and through the piercing light, the city's gilded glory was revealed.

II

The crystal buildings were as impressive up close as they were from afar. The smudges and nicks that should've accumulated over time were polished to non-existence. Only above where no natural human could reach were scuff marks present. Doors of steel looked as heavy as if thirty men would have trouble opening them. Beside each one pegged a cast iron sconce containing a perfectly shaped Illum cube.

During the day its shutters were closed, and only shreds of white light seeped through their slits.

Every building at the entrance seemed as expansive as the walls. There were no wooden huts, stalls, or carts with merchandise for sale since most were cast out to the Slums, away from the prominent districts of Cadaqu. The smallest building housed the extensive living quarters of highly affluential citizens. It looked like an elongated carriage with its front open and supported by pillars, their heads carved into ornamental designs only the prosperous could love.

Bar detested the quarters as well as the guild leaders and governing officials who lived there. He knew, as most here knew at a deeper, more subconscious level, that these titles were mainly a front for their cruelties within the Pig Pen. Everyone who wasn't idealistic or lived in the Slums was part of the organization, and if it was left to Bar, he would've slit their throats one by one in front of the Council until their inevitable turn came.

With arms wrapped around Ambia's waist, Chry didn't lower his eyes from the towers when he mumbled, "I've never seen buildings like this." It was a half-hearted attempt at speech. The song of sleeplessness sagged beneath his eyes, limp body sunken into Ambia's. Bar tried to ignore this embrace.

Onvi rode beside them, eyes lively as torches.

"A benediction to Etherine's finest," he exclaimed, offering his arms to the city. "The finest trade, defense, infrastructure, and diplomacy aside from the abundance of corruption, but, more importantly," mischief stretched his lips from ear to ear. "Cadaqu has, undoubtedly, the finest brothels north of the Grey Sea."

Ambia amused a smile. "Onvi, you say that about every brothel."

Vion, who had notably kept his distance from Onvi, grunted and grumbled, "Don't get the thief talking. None of us want to hear—"

"Nonsense, my lovely friend," Onvi said, gesturing the accusation away. Underneath him, his dirty brown gelding neighed to his master's defense. "Houses like The Slippery Ship and Ainan's Chest are the pinnacle of what Eulgash imaged as a brothel. From—"

Then there came one of Onvi's ramblings. Bar hardly registered his speech, for most of it was balderdash. At its end, Onvi regarded Chry again.

"No, Chry my young friend, hear me now when I say there *are* no better brothels in Admah." He winked at the boy. Chry diverted his eyes but still paled beneath his grin. "And you must have thought Volumous was rough."

The wink silenced Ambia who only shook her head, a smile playing across her lips. Cavas rode forward unnoticing.

"And what was it that you said Vion? I couldn't quite hear you the last time," the thief asked, grinning over his shoulder.

Vion only grumbled to himself.

Bar hardly acknowledged their interaction.

Their hooves clomped across streets paved from bleached stone, maintained to the smoothness of a streambed and the order of humankind. The streets themselves permeated with a high-chinned silence. No one walked. Only carriages and litters were permitted between the crystal, and the Runners had to routinely guide their steeds around the slow-moving transportation.

Further into the city, the buildings hunched, and their roofs descended from the skies to become conceivable. From their shrinking, they could finally reckon the back of Cadaqu's walls where Aedilium monitored over the city.

What the capital lacked in height, it more than atoned for with sublimity. Resting on a plateau, Aedilium had a body that washed from the walls in waves, three cavernous combers about to crash onto turquoise tiles. The spume shimmered in white crystallized chunks. The coruscating underbellies shadowed onto itself. Freshwater lakes reflected their facades and cascaded down from the plateau in waterfalls. A blend of colors blazed from the mist, the waters both turbulent and placid. Cutting through the blue were a series of marble stairs leading up to an alabaster door—its height paralleling the waves. Descending, the stairs hugged one of the waterfalls whiles curving to pour onto the streets. This was where the Runners would meet the

Council.

And when the day comes, he thought. *I intend to keep Aedilium whole.*

Bar never broke his promises.

"Doesn't it look gorgeous Chry?" Ambia whispered, her head turned.

Chry, with those round, naïve, and muddled eyes, stared at Aedilium.

"I suppose so."

He might as well been reading from a record of how many potatoes the citizens of Cadaqu had eaten. A cloud of concern wafted over Ambia's expression, but it was just as quickly concealed by narrow contemplation. She regarded Aedilium again.

Her imperceptible reaction was enough reason for Bar to resent the boy; though Chry could wield the sword, his skills were grossly exaggerated compared to his own. Bar could cut him down before the flame of a candle clock had warmed.

Where Aedilium's marble stairs ended continued the stalwart road until its stone slabs succumbed to mud and dirt. From beneath them squelched horse hooves. Their eyes were stripped from the elegance of Aedilium forward to the destitution of the Slums.

From enchanting edifices to sullen shacks, the Slums clustered at the lower hip of Aedilium's plateau, the farthest away from the public eye. Their collapsing huts were a motley of rosewood, Depanen, oak, and Mas'Lem'Es panels, copper shingles, clay, or thatched straw. They were stacked on top of each other to climb the face of the plateau. At a certain point, a trench of Etherine guards lined the plateau and warded refugees away from the top. The rest of the huts were cramped into the convergence between the plateau and wall. They were like unkempt ant hills built in whatever space was available.

Residents, most of them refugees admitted into Cadaqu, reflected their living conditions with nails overgrown, bellies concave, and skulls moaning. The further the Runners walked, the more distinctive the medley between the refugees became: descendants from the Fall of

Pactus wore the reused attire of Cadaqu's aristocracy, expatriates of the Second and Third Immigration still had their Dua'Ron—a shorter cloak of unsewn sides—from Caris'ma, passed down from fathers to sons, and those from the recent War for the Split bore dirt-stained shirts and trousers from when the Lanke drove them off their farmlands in Western Etherine.

Regardless, everyone was caked in mud.

One child off the road, pallid and groggy with sunken eyes and motionless fingers, huddled beside a hanging rope used by children to climb the face of the hillock. As far as Bar could tell, none of the others noticed the child. It had not spread yet. No matter. Soon, Bar would release the child from his paralytic suffering.

They were a furlong from the horse stables when they passed a woman preaching along the side of the road. She was not a Devotee of Eulgash but of another, so the natural picture of what a preacher should look like did not apply here. Ragged and hunched, the woman had to stand on a rosewood box to oversee the roads. Its wood, about to crumble beneath her feet, was as old as her wrinkles were. A discolored shawl covered her head, and beneath it curved an aquiline nose that could've hooked and dragged them out of their saddles. Above her lip lumped a mole scraggly with strands of hair. As he recollected, the woman resembled the description of the Horror amongst the Hills his father told him about when they were children.

When your childhood wasn't ruined, torn apart…

Before he came…

"He saveded me!" The preacher hollered. The passersby—one naked with a shock of hair and a similar expression, another a mother swaddling her newborn—paid the woman no mind. Flies buzzed around her. Every time she spoke, spittle sprayed. "The Grey Death spilled me guts and near tooked me from this grand green Nomas. Nay! It wouldn't! He wouldn't allow it! Nostre me savior would not be stopped by the sniff of a Skinny and nay will he be snuffed out by Black Rings! No disease with the name of jewelry could break him! He'll find de cure. The cure will be founded! N' by Eulgash and his name…"

The apathetic Runners plodded by, save for Ambia who invested her attention fully after the Black Rings were mentioned. Bar knew exactly what she was thinking.

She's thinking about home again. She still thinks she can save them.

"A miracle I tell ye!" She gestured to the skies that had adopted a rumbling blue. Thunder warned of heavy rain, lightning beyond the city walls. "Miracle whose divine blessin's giveth life, giveth hope, *HOPE*. Oh giveth me the chance of life! God I say! God! The one true god that shall rid us of pestilence! A god swathed in the clothes of man, a god who—"

Onvi yawned. Cavas stared but was impassive. They distanced themselves from the sermons, steered towards the stables, and only when Ambia could not hear the preacher any more did she stop staring.

III

The sea-salted and cracked copper shingles of the stables were adequate for sheltering their steeds for the stormy night ahead. The Runners did not have the mox for the stables near the entrance. As civic courtesy dictated, Cadaqu's single stable of affluence was beside the gates to limit its streets of filth. Fortunately for the Runners, Bar was not bothered by civic courtesy. Since they were here on behalf of the Council of Crystal, residents had no other choice but to glare as they rode by. Bar found the sight gratifying.

After negotiating with the stable owner, paying a moxen upfront, another for thereafter, Bar gathered the Runners outside. Perspiration from being near the sea steeped their clothing and weighed on his gambeson. His skin was sticky like tree sap. The road here had widened, and a lad was yelling in hopes of selling a rosewood spindle. Usually, Hatchen would be selling his Skinny Reds near the preacher, but Bar had not seen Hatchen this day. Likely, then, he was at Dhymes,

Bachanos, or, perhaps, Viamous. A disappointment.

He looked upon the Runners.

"Ambia, Vion, you will come with me to Aedilium. Onvi, Chry, do as you please."

No one moved.

"Barloc, I wish to think over their offer," Ambia said. Her words were not of the shy girl he had saved in Samit; they were thoughtful and now accustomed to confrontation.

He scrutinized her. Her expression was gathered in accumulating a response as she subconsciously nibbled at her fist. He patiently waited.

She released her fist and said, "I hope you know that I'd follow you anywhere. Into any mission and any danger. Even into death if that's where the Runners are called to…Still," She paused. "I ask you now to please reconsider accepting the Council's offer. I understand your sentiments, but if the results are similar to that of Caris'ma and Lomano then I'd rather refuse them. We can find another mission in Cadaqu or Whitewall. I do not wish to witness the Runners suffer again as they had across the Grey Sea. To me, and I hope to everyone else, the mox is not worth the risk of losing one of our family."

"We won't," he intruded curtly. His tone denied further discussion. Ambia held back a wince.

"Ah yes, yes, just like there weren't any broken legs or living swamps or mossy creatures hoping to love on us heretofore." Onvi grinned. "Or Dinglers for that matter."

Bar throttled Onvi until he could not breathe and then snapped his neck. Instead of this, Bar gestured the excuse away.

"Our missions heretofore have no correlation with our mission with the Council."

"But mayhap they do." Ambia refuted. "When have we *ever* taken a mission from the Council that has been effortless? Goodness Barloc, you almost *died* in Caris'ma if not for Hearth. Think about what they'd have us do now."

"If we don't receive another mission like the Council can provide, we will starve." Bar said. "Our horses will be the first to die and you will—"

"That's an exaggeration," she said. "We've never run out of missions, nor are we desperate for mox."

Bar gave her a hard stare. Ambia, her disheveled brunette hair, her olive smooth skin, her hazel eyes and rebellious spirit, were so beautiful and frustrating to the point that he'd…

Fuck her. Fuck her now. *She's able. She's yours. Fuck her.*

No, not yet.

"I've heard enough," he said. "A decision will not be made until we hear what the Council desires. If you wish to come, then come."

Immediately, her defiance peeled away. She hesitated as if wanting to but unable and then looked back up the road to where the preacher stood. It seemed Ambia would stare forevermore until she whispered, "I…have other matters to attend to."

Bar knew what this was about. Just as she disliked the idea of meeting with the council, he disliked this one. Even so, he remembered the last time they talked about this issue and the harsh words he spoke.

If you wish to hope, you should have stayed home and groveled to Eulgash.

This time, he spoke softly.

"They are lost Ambia. There is no panacea for the Black Rings."

She wasn't listening to him. Chry was looking upon her with a pitiful attempt at concern.

"Well, you two love birds have fun yammering about where you wish to have your first date." Onvi again. "I think I'll pass on the invite to see our dark and gloomy friends at Aedilium and go fall into a lady's lap."

"No one wants your ekah rah," Vion muttered.

"Au contraire, my oafish friend. *My* ladies don't discriminate."

Bar did not think Onvi would be visiting any harlots on this trip to Cadaqu. There was another thief in Cadaqu by the name of Noctito Laguaio that was the more likely culprit. This concerned him. If this Noctito saw Bar and remembered where he had seen him from, what Bar had done in Noma Devolum years heretofore could be unraveled and revealed to Onvi. Unfortunately, Bar could not blatantly stop Onvi from meeting with Noctito if that was what Onvi wanted. If he did, there'd be two outcomes: the thief would ignore him and do as he pleased or he'd become suspicious as to why Bar was so invested in his affairs. Perhaps if the risk became too high, Bar could lease the help of assassins in the League to rid Noctito. They had branches in almost every city in Admah. For now, better to leave the past flailing in the water than to throw it a rope.

Vion grunted, glaring somewhere else besides Onvi. It was as if his insult toward the thief was instinctual, not deliberate.

Bar stared back at Ambia; she wasn't looking at him. Without taking his eyes off her, he said, "Do as you please, Ambia." He then looked upon the others. "Vion, you come with me. Everyone else, meet at the inn upon tomorrow's dawn. Do not be thereafter."

They did not need further instruction. Cavas left casually as if dispersing from a poorly-acted play. Even now, Bar was still reluctant in letting the mage go unattended. The others convinced him otherwise as much as he resisted.

Onvi shrugged his shoulders as to say, "We will see," and ambled towards the white stone pavement. Ambia and Chry were the last to leave them.

"Come with me," she said to Chry and strode toward the preacher without another word.

Chry first blinked out from a distracted gawk, looked at Ambia, glanced at Bar who bore no look of welcome and then to Vion. That must have settled it. He turned and scurried toward Ambia, tripping once to trail behind her.

The Slums bustled. Bar regarded Vion whose eyes of silver serpents offered no comfort. Even after four years of travelling together, these serpents never abated for him.

"Let's be on our way." Bar looked toward the shining brilliance of Aedilium and said, "The Council is waiting."

IV

The vestibule of Aedilium welcomed Bar and Vion to a refinement apt for a masked ball. Ornate chandeliers hung from crystal ceilings, casting gaudy light from Illum stones carved to mimic a candle's flame. The second, third, and fourth floor balustrades spanned across in mirrored symmetry. Its railings were obsidian glass bodies of ovoid shape, a shower of black tears. Behind these railings brooded the steel-plated doors of Cadaqu. At the backs of Bar and Vion towered the alabaster door they saw riding here. Across Aedilium's front façade on each side were smaller imitations of the door to the height of Vion. They had been escorted through one of those sally ports since the front door was used primarily for ostentation rather than practicality.

On the far end, another grand door of iron, steel, and inlaid silver dominated the scene. To emphasize uniformity, two wide spiral staircases revolved down from the ceiling and opened their mouths beside the door. They were like serpent sentries, here to protect the Council.

Door between the stairs, the guard had surly said to Bar, like he did not already know.

Their footfalls beckoned back from brilliance. The crystal flooring defied any scuff marks from feet or shoes and reflected the chandeliers' Illum light. Bar squinted to avoid blindness.

No one else was within the vestibule besides a diplomat Bar reckoned was from the main island of Voldev. For being the seat of the most powerful oligarchy in Admah and, perhaps, in the Four Nomases, Aedilium lacked an excess of guards.

Courage or hubris? he thought.

The man from Voldev was above them. He wore a tunic and mantle, both long and loose as if floating. The clothing was cinched by an alligator-skinned belt and from its silver buckle leered an imprinted fox-head. A dignified scowl pinched his features together to give a prudish pride. Grizzled, dour, with skin consumed by days of sun, the man was leaning on the second floor railings when he took his eyes off the parchments he was reading, accessed the two with a deadpan look, and then dismissed them for his readings.

Men and women such as these were no abnormality within the crystal walls. Aedilium housed Representatives and Consuls throughout Etherine cities, ambassadors from Ontinia and Noma Devolum, and diplomats across the Four Nomases. Consuls were the mediators between the Vassals and the Council since Representatives were, as the bare truth, prisoners in Cadaqu. None of the Etherine cities or officials would articulate these sentiments but Representatives lived in proximity to the Council in case they needed to subdue communities thinking to rebel or speak out against them. For more than two hundred years, the tradition was implemented, and throughout that time, there had been a number of fingers, toes, and phalluses returned to the cities. Obedience within Etherine was never a concern.

The grand door, as well as being an enormous spectacle, depicted the lands of Admah in precise detail and depth. The nations outlined their boundaries with inlaid silver. The mountains of Ontinia protruded, the Wastelands flattened, and the Arbiter's Gorge descended into the steel like a gash to Admah's skin. An octopus-like creature hunted ships within the Grey Sea. The map still depicted the Split as Western Etherine with homely hills waving across and the silver meeting along the border of Ontinia.

Bar stared long at Western Etherine.

Vion had little patience for their intricacy and, as they were instructed upon visits heretofore, knocked twice times, his fist slamming against the Forest of the Lost. Upon his command, the grand door made a grumble as if waking, a swish as with air rushing in, and then a crack dividing the map of Admah in half. Its yawning reverberated through the vestibule, yet no sound of unlocking, no scraping of the floor, nor the sight of anyone moving the door.

Behind them, the Voldevian read on.

Its hinges opened away from them, and its sleepy rumble wrenched Bar from his daydream. He made a face against the waning of a headsore, rubbed at his brow, took some breaths, and stared forward.

Focus. These next marks will not be so simple.

Within the opening stalked a darkness so absolute that light from the Illum stones shied away; it tried streaming in from the outside but could not pass an imaginary boundary where the door had stood. They stepped over this delineation of light and dark. Dark arms embraced them as the grand door murmured behind, sucked in air, and sealed.

The room was not pitch black. Four sconces of austere frames uplifted torches flushed with each other. Bar could not discern what they were attached to in so that the flames seemed to be suspended by the void. Shadows carved their features. Despite the fire, the room gave off an unforgiving coolness that stiffened the skin to leather. Cooler yet and he'd see his breath.

Below and between each of these sconces for a total of three appeared the Council of Crystal members. Stiff-backed and unmoving, they sat at a long, crystal trestle table of honed design. The tabletop was clear of distractions, veined in obsidian streams. A warrior or mercenary could've ripped a leg from the table and brandished it as a sword of exquisite make.

In appearance, as was similar to Aedilium, the Council members mirrored each other. Their cloud-white robes were made of pristine silk and draped low over their heads. The blackholes of their faces were like the hollows of a tree trunk but unending, lost within its inner folds. Their hands were tucked into their sleeves, and the hem of their robes puddled on the floor as to reveal no flesh or skin.

The torches guttered, and the Council's contorted shadows spilled across the table.

The two parties stared at each other. The amount of assassination attempts against the Council were beyond comprehensible. None had ever succeeded, and those involved with the League, assassins of no name and equally no complaint, now cease to claim the contracts. Poisons, arrows, daggers, suffocation: their mox was wasted. Only the crazed ones attempted now, and they were easy to detect. They approached the problem as they had selected their weapons, with blunt force. In so far as he knew, none of the assassins were ever seen from again, and soothsayers began reporting that the Council was impossible to kill.

Bar had his suspicions.

A silence as absolute as the darkness with only the flames to crackle. Even Vion knew not to make a sound. Then the Council spoke.

"Greetings Barloc, son of Mayontosh, erstwhile citizen of Templum Limous." The voice, solemn and toneless, seemed to arrive from the middle figure, but its words were all-encompassing as if the room were speaking down to them. "We welcome your humble return."

They're there. They're here. The time is nigh. Death is necessary.
Ignorant, ignorant.
End it. End their misery. End their terror.
  End their lives. End their misery. End their terror.
    End. End. End. End. End. End. End. End. End. End. End. End.
End. End. End. End.

"We are welcomed to be back," Bar said and then dipped low for a bow. Vion would not abide by the custom, merely glared. Indifferent to Vion, the members bowed their heads as one.

Bar lifted himself but found that he was breathless. His breathes were too heavy to control, and the anticipation that he had bottled for what seemed like lifetimes was now overflowing. His fingers were jittery. Bar licked his lips. He was beginning to be grateful that he did not bring Ambia along. Her defiance might've made the discussion more difficult than it already was.

"For what do I owe the pleasure, my lords?"

An absence of sound prevailed. The flames responded as guttural voices. The Council never stirred. They would not make any unnecessary gestures during their conversation.

"Before we proceed with the reason why you have been summoned," the middle member resumed. "We should inform you, albeit rather briefly, on Cadaqu's conflict with the Lanke in what is now known as the Split. By doing so, we expect to arrive at similar conclusions."

The Council bowed their heads. Bar and Vion waited.

"Five years heretofore, after the Lanke succeeded in splitting Etherine and Ontinia, the sundry clans of the Lanke continued the conflict against each other. The War for the Split and the continuing conflicts thereafter, as you Barloc know, have proved detrimental to the honest citizens of Western Etherine."

The two of them were all too familiar with this but did not elaborate. Vion grumbled to himself but bore no dispute. He had tried dissenting once heretofore, and that had not boded well for the erstwhile Lanke.

"For Cadaqu," the Council continued. "The Split left hundreds of refugees to abandon their homes in order to seek refuge in Whitewall, Bachanos, Viamous, and, as you have indisputably seen, in our city. Our hospitality has accepted them willingly. Outside our walls, the camps expanded. Within, the Slums became a haven as it has been for those heretofore."

Liars, Bar's mind thought. *There's no haven. Lies, all of it lies and more, more LIES*

"Be as it may, with the excess of refugees and our land routes to Ontinia severed, our capabilities and commerce has diminished. Refugees hunger. Trade has shifted from land to sea. Cadaqu and Whitewall survive and, at times thrive, but the consequences of the War have nevertheless strained our resources. Our wharfs are inundated, citizens and officials in Whitewall are harassed by Lanke at the border, Etherine cities inland are deprived of trade, and the refugees from Western Etherine are unable to return home."

"Why not kill them," Vion snarled.

The Council was supposed to interpret "them" as the Lanke, not the refugees. But from what Bar had seen from Vion heretofore, he could've meant either or.

They continued focusing on Bar. Their hoods never regarded Vion.

"We regret to say that despite the strength and prowess of our soldiery, we lack the forces necessary to reclaim Western Etherine. Our allies have departed since the War for the Split. Ontinia is compromised by the Black Rings, Voldev and Caris'ma, after witnessing our failure to remove the Lanke, are now unsympathetic to our domestic affairs, and thus this leaves Etherine alone." Their heads were downcast. "The odds are unsubstantial."

"And the Temple of Elemental?" Bar asked.

"They too impart reluctance in supplying pedagogues when the outcome is uncertain and, perhaps, unfavorable for Etherine. Guardian Peerage claims their protection of Whitewall is the extent to their support."

"Why not then bide your time? You yourself have said that the Lanke are engaged with each other. After their numbers have dwindled sufficiently, Etherine can reclaim the Split with little to no resistance."

Play the game Barloc. Sing their song Barloc.

"This is why we have summoned you this day."

The flames behind them dimmed. The Council's voice became whispery as how he reckoned a Kemal would speak.

Keep a smile

Keep a smile

Gouge and keep a—

His face was a mummer's mask.

"A new constraint has arisen that impedes our doing so, motivating us to seek further action within a timely manner. Urgency bounds the hands of Aedilium. As that may be, you should recognize that items of such confidentiality divulged here will not be divulged elsewhere. This is our verbal contract. Those beyond the Runners shall be ignorant of what will be discussed and any admission of what is discussed next means the termination of our association. Confidentiality means that certain steps, if need be, will be taken to keep these secrets contained. Abandoning your duties will end in—"

"Enough of your Katarc speak. Talk plainly," Vion snarled.

The white robes ossified, their words rotted, and the fires flared in an emulation of displeasure. Darkness bore down on them in extending beyond the physical domain. Suffocation, like a myriad of shadows enfolding onto their presence. Their sights tunneled, near to being overwhelmed by the abyss. The glow of fires hazed and hearts burst in palpitations. And those screams. Voices beyond voices of men and women, young and old, weak and strong. Screams of the dead that could not be put to rest, screams that felt like the billow of a forge blowing into his skull until the bone cracked and splintered.

Then it vanished.

There were audible gasps from both Bar and Vion even though the experience was merely an inkling of their time. Tension released their lungs still shuddering in memory.

The Council continued as if nothing had occurred.

Peering forward at the entrance, they rotated their heads to Bar. He waited until he could fully recover and then gave a nod. Their hoods remained on him as if judging his virtue and then returned forward.

This had never happened heretofore. Vion had interrupted at meetings heretofore but had never provoked such a response. Usually, it invoked indifference and disregard.

Then it must be, Bar anticipated. *They must be speaking of what I've been waiting for.*

His heart pounded.

"As you deem it," the members reverberated. "We shall cease these trivialities. Do you accept our stipulations?"

Bar did not hesitate, did not think to ask about the reward, did not think of prying, did not think about the harrowing experience they just had, did not think about Vion beside him attempting to restrain his anger, did not think of Ambia.

He expected so much more.

"Yea."

All three nodded once. The two members at the end then sunk their heads as the center stared forward. Its dark, hollow face subsumed all.

"We have been informed that one of the Lanke clans has discovered a gemstone of the Walker."

Bar's heart ceased a beat, his mouth dry and thirsty.

They've found it, he thought. *After all these years of biding time, of sacrifice and suffering, someone has finally found a gemstone.*

It took every knuckle of his being to keep from trembling. Images fleeted and left as the voice buzzed beyond recognizability. He could hear none of its suggestions. In his trousers, his manhood had stiffened. He loathed the lust it insinuated and the idea that what he had been preparing for hinted at this, but he could not contain himself.

"The gemstones have been disremembered by Admah since Guardian Simul's death two hundred years heretofore, yet the acquisition of one heralds disaster for Cadaqu."

They were not wrong; literature involving the Fall of Pactus, the Guardian, and, subsequently, the Walker was exceedingly rare. Admanites beyond the Wastelands knew about the gems but had grown to think of them largely as myth, folklore told by wetnurses to cease newborns from screaming throughout the night. The sword *Azrael* was just as obscure. More so, even. Many tales about the Walker left the sword out altogether.

This line of reckoning did not stun Bar. Those who lived during these times were now skeletons ten hands in the ground, and those who *had* witnessed the confrontation between the Walker and Simul counted less than what he could count on one hand. The populations of Pactus and the Temple had already evacuated before Simul had left, so his exploits during and after the Walker were merely told through his journal.

Bar stared flatly at the Council.

"Are the Lanke desperate then?"

"Whether they are or not is none of our concern." The voices boomed like the rumble of thunder. "Locating the sword and gemstones is Cadaqu's foremost priority."

"And our role?"

If it was not already obvious.

"The Runners shall attempt to retrieve the gemstones. Since we know naught if one or three gemstones are needed to unlock the puissance within *Azrael*, you and your Runners will need to trace and recover all three gemstones or, if able, *Azrael*. Either will be sufficient for the protection of Cadaqu."

You're playing the game Barloc. Now sing Barloc, sing

"And you wish not to retrieve them of your own accord? Through force or stealth?"

"As we have discussed, force is not applicable at this moment. And we do not have the requisite services to retrieve the gemstone from the Lanke."

Nay, they do but would not say the obvious; the Council could expend resources to try and retrieve the gem, but the outcome was precarious and perilous, as Ambia had warned. If the Runners failed, the Council could otherwise divert the blame. They would retain the mox they would have given to the Runners if they had succeeded and enough time would have passed for Etherine to have gathered their strength in retaliation against the Lanke, in whichever way that might look. The Runners could also be used as a diversion for further advancements in seizing the gem. As they were in Lomano, the Runners were both the fodder and the whipping boy.

Bar could not be more content.

"Very well. Which Lanke clan has discovered the gem?"

The Council lowered their voice.

"The clan call themselves the Derk."

The distant look in Vion's eyes erupted.

"*Verten!*" He spat, lurching forward as if the Council were Derk. "Those damned *Verten, I'll slaughter…*"

"Vion! Not *now!*"

Bar jerked his sword out of its sheath to block Vion. His chest of scars beneath his cloak bumped against its blade and this, fortunately, stopped him, albeit the Lanke seemed to be beyond his Sensation. His chest seethed and his nostrils flared like a predator during the hunt. He was clenching his battleaxe and would not release.

Raise it to his throat

It said.

Show them what you are

It said.

Perspiration popped across his forehead. A swell of heat descended over Bar: Vion's wrath, the Council's flames, the insatiable desire to

215

indulge.

And how easy it would be…

His arm began to shake despite the muscles straining to control it. The metal clicked.

"Calm yourself!" Bar snarled.

But don't you remember Barloc?

Remember what happened?

Remember what he *did?*

Vion wouldn't calm.

The Council asked in unison, "Do we need to take matters into our own hands, Barloc?"

Yea…

"Nay, my lords," he assured then tossed a scowl at Vion. A blaze of fury was burning through the moonlight silver of his eyes. Bar could hear his teeth grinding and the guttural rumble of a growl. This was what Bar associated with a Kil'mas Anthropophagus on the verge of starvation.

"Vion, I will say this once more. Release. The. Axe. *Now.*"

The threat in his 'now' seemed to fall through. It had no effect in calming Vion but after a long moment, Vion twitched his crooked nose, grumbled a growl, released his fingers, and retracted his stride. His eyes would not stray from the Council with neither the blaze nor the venom having left them. These states dangled from a thin string susceptible to snap.

The voice buzzed, buzzed, buzzed before Bar asked, "Should you leave?"

Vion glared at the Council more but then toward a point far from here. His fist squeezed as to break his fingers.

"No," he muttered.

Against a hesitation, Bar sheathed his sword. He sighed whiles rubbing at his brow. The headsores had returned, at his temple where the voice murmured, a readily steady throb.

He disregarded both in favor of the Council and put on a courteous smile.

"My deepest apologizes, my lords." Bar bowed his head. "As I shall disclose again, the Derk slaughtered my companion's original clan when he was a youth. Those who survived, as he did, were subject to the Derk, and I shall not remind you of the atrocities the Lanke can perpetuate. Needless to say, we apologize for our behavior. It will not be a further issue."

The hollow faces of the Council studied Bar. Vion grunted disdain. His Sensations could imagine the events that would transpire if Vion were to run amok once more. They were not encouraging.

"As we have discussed heretofore," their voice resumed in equanimity. "The Derk have possession of a gemstone of the Walker."

Bar took a fleeting glance at Vion.

Obedience…

"And you," Bar finished. "Have specified that the Runners will retrieve the gems and return them to you."

They nodded. They spoke.

"Or, if fortune favors you in travel and you discover *Azrael*, return the sword to Cadaqu immediately. The gems are meaningless without *Azrael*."

Meaningless…meaningless…meaningless…meaningless…

Every word was another throb to his temple. A jagged stone could've been swelling beneath there, cracking the bone, straining the skin.

"Do you know where *Azrael* is?"

"Nay."

Bar asked, "Where shall we find the gemstones then?"

The Council paused as if in thought and then said, "The Derk have discovered the first. They remain within the Split but have relocated North away from the remaining clans. Authorities in Bachanos speculate their bivouacs are between the River Twins, along River Overlook Road.

"Another is within Ontinia. Since the gem's withdrawal from Pulchrit after the reign of King Cantem the Second, its exact location has become unknown to us. Visit Queen Ashera in Pulchrit and inquire

217

about its whereabouts. She would know where King Ventem stored the gem. We shall send a raven to inform her of your impending arrival."

Bar waited for them to resume. They didn't. Vion grumbled to himself. Bar always had been patient but a nagging at his intuitions urged him to ask. That and his headsores.

"And where can we find the last gem?"

They remained quiet. The voice he heard seemed to whisper in his ear.

"The final gem is located within the Temple of Death, stored within the confines of Simul's study."

Vion made a contemptuous *humph* that sounded like a laugh and muttered under his breath. He at least had the restraint to keep his comments to himself. Otherwise, Bar thought the gems would be in places inconceivable or unknown. The Void was in the least conceivable, albeit arduous, treacherous, and largely thought of as untraversable. No one had returned from the Void since the days it was titled Pactus. Nevertheless, their locations made him grateful that none of the others had come. They would've vehemently protested, Ambia and Onvi, and Bar did not wish to risk giving the Council a reason to be doubtful. They were not here so they would not have a say. Those that were here had little to say. Vion feared naught of death. He would die hunting down those that have, in his eyes, betrayed him, and if the Derk planned to enter the Void, he would to, regardless of consequence.

And Bar…

He had already sacrificed himself for the alleviation of Admah. No price was too much to pay.

"What evidence do you have that this last gem is in the Void?"

"There is no evidence needed. The gem is there."

Cunts…

But he couldn't push further or they might question his commitment.

"And the reward?"

Games, games games, meaningless games…

Despite their indifference, he could sense the Council's growing impatience.

"After retrieving and returning the three gems or *Azrael*, Barloc and his Runners will be rewarded one hundred and fifty moxen each."

Bar stared, lips ajar. Vion glared suspiciously but then snorted. He tossed a hand and said, "You speak nonsense."

This was not truculence by Vion but genuine incredulity. The last contract the Runners received had been a modest bounty in the border town of Dhymes; the Sable Guild hired them to remove Vvuladevs disrupting their Sable Agave fields, creatures the size of wolves with sharp slender teeth and black, bristled fur. They usually roamed Etherine in hordes and dug pits with their blunt curved claws so to slumber during the night. After they dealt with the Vvuladevs and the repercussions of foolishness, the Runners claimed their reward— around three moxen total, or sixty mox, enough to feed the five Runners for about two turns of the Moon. When compared to what the Council offered now, the Dhymes contract was paltry. Not even Caris'ma or Lomano promised as much.

meaningless though…

Meaningless to the gems…

To the gems…

Meaningless to the gems Meaningless…

Meaningless…Meaningless…Meaningless…Meaningless…Meaningless…Meaningless…Meaningless…Meaningless…Meaningless…Mea ningless…Meaningless…Meaningless…Meaningless…Meaningless…

"—expect us to believe—"

It was Vion.

"Our word is true. Our offer is sound."

Echoes…

His head looked up. Stared

Meaningless…Meaningless…Meaningless…Meaningless…Meaningless…

"Upon delivery, each Runner will receive a hundred moxen," it said. He had to concentrate, the throbbing. "The other fifty will be given in pledge to compensate for your travels during the contract.

These shall be secured through Gonotes, to either be redeemed at Gontomal's Treasury in Cadaqu or trusts throughout Etherine and Ontinia, approved either by Queen Ashera or the Council of Crystal. If this does not satisfy you, Gonatonlos can arrange for full dispersal of the pledge into moxen, mox, or moxam. Any of these methods shall suffice."

Vion, he was glaring, Bar's thinking, but didn't retaliate or react or do anything of the like. Good. He did not know if he could control himself.

"Yea," Bar said, nodding, looking not at the Council but below at the hem of their robes where the light was not so bright. "I understand."

The words were difficult to say. Even if the headsore had not blotted thought and swelled blotchy and violent, Bar would not negotiate for more. No one negotiated with the Council. He had tried heretofore with the Caris'ma mission but had not gotten far.

Now, he could hardly speak.

The Council basked in excruciating silence. Every whisk of the flames were the pangs of a whip to Bar's skull.

Rest, he needed rest.

"It is as you wish. Presently, we must ask for your departure. Any other questions in regards to the contract or the mission shall be directed toward Amswa." The flames gathered strength as the door behind them opened its maw. It sounded as if the room were about to swallow them whole. The Council remained as the dead. Illum light peered at them from beyond the door. The walls of the room were indiscernible. "This meeting is thus adjourned. Barloc and the Runners will retrieve the three gemstones from the Void, the Lanke, and Ontinia, or obtain *Azrael* from whereabouts unknown. They will return the subsequent articles to the Council as they have found them in exchange for a fifty moxen pledge and a hundred moxen upon completion of said contract. Additional knowledge and items will be provided by Amswa. Thus the contract is sealed, the mission ordained. Barloc and the Runners. Be gone to your onus. Secure the gems and *Azrael* so Cadaqu may endure."

The Council then left them with a favor in the tongue of Elonamos. "Du ciso, nul zau. Du swa, lic zau. Du forta, ala zau."

Ambia's War

I

Chry felt uneasy.

Ambia had just asked the preacher where the doctor's home was (which was all well by him), but every time the preacher's bulging eye flicked toward him, he'd squirm inside his trousers. There was no time in that conversation when he could meet that eye. To him, it looked more like the eggshell of a spoiled egg.

He was fortunate, then, that Ambia had taken charge. The preacher, with a hooked finger and rambling description, directed them deeper into the Slums toward a litter of camps cowering beneath the high crystal walls. They looked to be built from torn canvases with frames subject to topple. Ambia thanked her, and they walked back through the Slums. The stables were to their left, their steeds neighing from within. Mid-day exposed the impoverished to the gloom of the storm. They sheltered beneath their shawls and foreign skirt-like garments, spread thin to avoid touch, and all bore breakable gaits.

The two traveled another furlong before Ambia asked, "How are you, Chry?"

His gaze was with his feet. Their clogs and sandals squelched through a skim of mud, mud too familiar to the roads of his home.

"Fine," he said without looking.

Ambia stared for a moment but did not respond.

Chry did not know where they were going. Ambia said to go with her, and so he obliged. He did not want to be with the other two. It felt like she was a mother, and he was the child; anywhere she went, he came along too. She probably didn't want to lose sight of him in fear that he'd act on an impulse to harm himself. She might be right. Right now, he felt as he had said: fine. Yet that did not need to stay. If he had one of those damn nightmares again, if he lay awake another night hearing Aimee and grandma call for him, he might just relent, say, "Damn the Arbiter," then begin tying the noose.

In this, he was at least thankful to have Ambia around.

The oppressive mumble of the Slums rolled by. The road widened and farther down, they could reckon clusters of folk bartering. Beside each were heaps of personal possessions: rags, towels, mugs, chairs, sheets of metal from a roof, bricks, moldy bread, the skeleton of a Redback. Many of the children slept naked next to their mothers and fathers, their clothing and shoes thrown into the clutter. Ambia looked on disheartened then refocused on Chry.

He heard a long sigh.

"I know the Runners don't always act like a family," she said. "We fight more often than we reconcile, and we bicker more often than we confer, but this means nothing to how much we care for each other. Or for you." She let that sit then said, "If you need anything, Chry, please ask. I'm here for you, to listen or to talk."

She said no more. Chry felt like he should have responded, but his tongue could not voice a response. Instead, he said nothing.

Boys, a shred of years younger than Chry, scurried before them, giggling. One slipped face-first into the mud but bolted back up to chase after his friends, a brown and soupy bib across his front. Thunder vibrated above.

What busied his thoughts was Onvi, when he was beside him in the Restless Ryders, when Chry had become too comfortable and asked Onvi what had happened to Maaria. Every detail screamed to him: the hollowing of Onvi's cheeks, sockets, and expression, his infamous grin shriveling into a coolness that burned, vengeful and mortal. This troubling picture of the thief had drawn out in Chry a lingering stench of apprehension. He secluded his only friend in Onvi, and worse, he felt like he failed the thief—sent him down a road where the thunder and clouds coalesced into a raging tempest that could not be calmed.

Chry wished not to experience that again.

They walked in silence before he asked in a mumble, "Where are we going," more in hopes of returning to the inn than of curiosity.

Ambia's hazel eyes turned smiles into bedrock. She gazed through the crystal walls of Cadaqu.

"The preacher we passed by…" A pause. "She preached of this physician, Nostre. As well as here, I also heard of him in Dhymes from a herbiest and a guardsman whose brother lives here in Cadaqu. The physician supposedly cured the Grey Death. Now it is mentioned that he would also find a cure for the Black Rings." Her voice didn't seem confident in this. She asked, "Do you know of the Black Rings?"

A puff of vertigo stirred Chry from his dazing. He heard that question heretofore. Ambia was like Aimee asking him that same question on the palisades of Domum before she left, before Chry rode back to a home of ashes.

"Um, barely. A little," he said.

Ambia nodded. "I do not blame you. The Vassal has no care for the knowledge and well-being of his citizens."

She breathed deeply. He gave her a sidelong glance that she did not notice. She was inside herself now.

"The Black Rings," she said with kind exactness. "Is a plague that has ravaged my home nation of Ontinia for over six years. Pulchrit, its capital and where I was born, has experienced the brunt of the Black Rings. Victims experience initial symptoms of pallid skin, grogginess, and sunken eyes that look like two black rings. Hence the title. Two days before they die—if it wasn't two days, it'd be shorter—the body will begin to denerve." She looked someplace else. "It starts with the fingers and toes, followed by the extremities. From there, the limbs become inert. In the past, when I was intimately involved with the Hypenian relief, those who still retained the function of their arms and legs were advised to stay home. There were too many at our doors for us to attend to, and these patients were denied care until further complications. Hundreds of thousands of men, women, and children, friends and family, lovers and owners, denied relief.

"From then on, the denerving exacerbated until the whole body was motionless. They'd have at most a day to survive in which the only consolation was to die peacefully during their slumber."

She paused again. This time, the silence stretched out long enough to leave Chry to a series of unwelcoming thoughts.

They were of Aimee; from beneath a grievous fog appeared her familiar face, her smile glowing gold alongside her hair. She said she would be traveling through the Wastelands to join the Hypenian in Ontinia...Right? He thought so. Back then, he was too distracted and distressed to think clearly and was too scared for her to face the Wastelands and the possible threat of the Lanke, but now that tiny, prick of fear blackened the pool of his soul.

The Black Rings.

He had not known Aimee was heading toward a plague this deadly. If he had known, how the plos could he have let her go? Only Eulgash knew how many folks she'd see that had this plague which made folk useless and limp. She might as well have said she was visiting a human slaughterhouse.

How likely then was he ever to see her again? Would he only see her as a corpse? Would she come back to Domum in a wagon with her dead, lifeless body sprawled in the back? Would some other person or man or brute find her alive but unable to move—a conscious body that could not fight back? What then? What would he do then?

Eventually, Ambia resumed.

"I can still remember when I was a child. My friend Lorna and I would dash through the streets of Pulchrit, passing its stone shops. Since we were in the mountains, the first snows would come early and stay late so we'd have to run through the muddy snow with our boots, stopping at times to dance to the shrill melodies of Mister Salamance's bagpipes. During festivals, there'd be other children and adults dancing with us.

225

"Afterward, I'd stop and converse with Mister Salamance, Lorna beside me but never talking. I enjoyed listening to him even though he talked as much as Onvi. He'd always preach that I, as a child, was the only sensible resident in Pulchrit and listed off the reasons why. It was a mystery to me as to why Mister Salamance made such a fuss about Pulchrit. Truly, I do not think my young mind could comprehend a world where my home bore a negative quality.

"In spite of his complaints, whenever I did have a spare moxam or two, which was not often, I'd give them to Mister Salamance. I suppose I felt sorry that he couldn't be as satisfied with the citizens of Pulchrit as I could. Or perhaps I merely adored his melodies. Either or."

Her smile died. She looked forward as to peer through the past.

"The Black Rings have taken more from me than I ever cared to relinquish."

This time, Chry gave his attention to Ambia, sharing in her grief. Somehow, it felt good to know it wasn't just him who suffered, even though this did not sound like something an honorable hero like Simul would say. Still, two marks heretofore, Chry would not have felt any reason to talk. Now, he felt obligated to say something. Anything.

"I, um, apologize for your loss," he mumbled.

That's it? He thought to himself. *Is that really all you can think of? "I'm so, so sorry that everyone you know and love died by this horrible disease that you have absolutely no control over and probably never will." Aye, beautiful Chry, just beautiful.*

Ambia didn't seem disturbed. Even so, he kept the remainder of his words to himself. She stared at her feet.

"I appreciate your sympathy. I only…"

Her walk slowed. Her stare was searching for a feeling that was not there. Lightning bolted over Cadaqu's walls with a rumble to follow. His head felt the first droplets of rain.

Finally, she said, "I suppose I can only hope."

They continued walking into the din of rain and thunder.

II

Compared to the canvas tents around them, the physician's home seemed steadier, newer, though far from perfect. Its stone foundation held the home erect. The garden in front was overgrown with weeds. Salt winds and rain had worn at its earthen walls enough to expose the Alderwood frame at the corners. It was like chocolate skin scraped to the bone. Above, the long, thatched roof defended well against the drizzle.

Nothing adorned the plain Rosewood door. Ambia ascended the last, stone step, hesitated a moment, then knocked with soft, light taps. They waited but no answer—not a peep nor footfall from within. As they waited, the sky violently wept. Children across the street blurred behind the showering curtain. Raindrops pelted the metal awning of the porch. They huddled beneath it, but its tongue protruded from the home only slightly. Chry's teeth chattered. His clothes were stained, wet, and cold. He rubbed his arms to stay warm.

Ambia gave him a look he almost missed. With a shaky fist, he knocked three times, then stepped back blowing hot breath into his hands. Ambia shivered beside him.

Nothing.

Chry rolled his hands over each other and shuffled his feet. Mayhap this Nostre person had somewhere else to be. Really, he probably was out tending to a patient in the Slums, and all they were doing here was standing like a pair of shivering ducklings waiting for an imaginary Kemal to open the door.

When he could no longer stand the strings of uneasiness vibrating between his ribs, he spoke.

"Ambia, I don't think he's—"

The door swung open, Ambia and Chry both flinching. From within the house spilled the light and fresh aroma of lavender, dispersing into the rain. Waiting within the door frame was a man whose essence embodied chivalry.

He was tall (about a head taller than Chry and Ambia) and lithe, but his muscles were condensed into every knuckle of his frame so there was no excess, only strength. His chestnut hair waved back in curls. Gold-rimmed spectacles hung low on his slender but handsome nose, the glass without a scratch or dust mote. His cheekbones and jaw were chiseled to complement his features. Buckled around his waist with a rawhide belt were three small pouches.

Aside from his allure, the man looked like he had been in the middle of work. Dark patches of sweat dampened the armpits of his cloth undergarment, and his breathing was faintly off centered.

The man greeted Ambia with an irresistible smile.

"Why, hello there, madam."

His accent was sly and elegant as would come from practice, and it had a touch of foreignness suggested further by his heavy tan. Even so, whatever accent he had heretofore seemed unlearned now and retrained to accommodate his audience. Chry could not guess where he was from.

Ambia gifted the man a civil smile and asked, "Are you the physician who cured the Grey Death?"

"I am," he responded. "And, may I ask, who am I sharing this exchange with?"

Ambia opened her mouth but then reconsidered what she was going to say. Instead, she gestured to herself.

"I am Ambia, and this is Chry."

"A fine name for a fine lady," he said. His eyes never touched Chry. They stayed with Ambia, shimmering behind his spectacles. "You may call me Nostre, and I do apologize to leave you waiting. I was involved with my studies."

Chry flicked his eyes at Nostre's sweat stains, back up, then to Ambia. Beneath the damp clumps of her hair, she was calm and gave an unreadable smile.

"I shall say," he said, his lips easing into persuasion. "You must be freezing. Come into my abode, pray."

Nostre offered his hand to Ambia. Her smile spread further as if amused. She shook her head, suppressing a small laugh, then accepted his hand. Nostre led her into his home and turned right into the first doorway. They disappeared, their shadows dragging through the lightless hall. The front door was left open for Chry but closed slowly with a maddening squeal. Nostre had left him.

Hand scratching the back of his head, Chry thought about leaving immediately. He could turn around and wade through the pouring rain until he made it somewhere other than here, perhaps to the inn, perhaps to the stalls. Bar did say he would purchase a new gelding for him. In the end, though, Chry did not go. Something was not right with Nostre or his home. The potency of the lavender scent was too much, nauseating even, and the physician seemed too cordial and gallant for a man living inside the Slums. Like the boy in Viamous, Chry didn't think it was right just to ignore Ambia and leave her alone with the man.

Arbiter, he thought. *Why can't anything ever be easy?*

He heaved a sigh, stepped in, and closed the door behind him.

III

With the storm's reign over the skies, the home had become as dark and depressing as the Gardens. The earthen hall he had entered breathed at his neck and ended at another smaller Rosewood door. Within, he could see the corner of a Depanen table and smell the lavender scent, so strong he could taste it on his tongue. He stared down the hall for what seemed like days but knew better than to walk down. He heard voices to his right and instead dawdled through the doorless frame.

Inside was a study, formal and built to discuss decisions with patients. The walls were suffocating, so any space available needed perfect organization. The mahogany desk in the center was sanded and coated in a fresh stain to conceal the scratch marks. There was no dirt, dust, or mess across its surface. Quills lined flush with the edge alongside a sheet of parchment. Its tan skin was cut into a seamless square, and tiny but impeccably neat handwriting made half the page.

With how large the desk was, the remaining space was limited. Nostre's seat called for ancient wood to be centered and lined with the desk from which across sat maroon chairs with cushions paled by the sun. They were open for seating but could barely be pulled out to sit. Cabinets sprouted from the walls but held its knowledge in tidy rows and columns.

Everything had a place, and nothing was out of place.

Before Chry entered, Nostre pulled a chair out as far as he could for Ambia and was now on the other side of the desk buttoning a leather jerkin. He left Chry's chair untouched.

Reckon that.

Before fastening his last button, Nostre said, "I do apologize for my appearance. You caught me at an inopportune time."

He finished and took his seat. His expression was silent satisfaction. After finding comfort, he leaned on his elbows and steepled his fingers. A clap of thunder frightened the flame on his desk, the jerkin concealed the sweat of his undergarment, and never did he look at Chry.

"I have not heard of you heretofore," Ambia said, ignoring what he had said. Her hands and satchel lay in her lap, and her posture was attentive. "And I have visited the city many times."

Thighs squeezing past the desk, Chry sidled into his seat.

"You have heard well then, madam Ambia. I have recently acquired a stay here in Cadaqu. However, my family bears its roots in Caris'ma."

"So, you're a Smar then?" Chry asked.

Nostre flicked his eyes to Chry as if to say, "know your place child," back to Ambia, and relished in a grin.

Rattle fucker, the thought was the voice of Aimee, but it was not too far from how he felt.

"During the Second Immigration," Nostre said. "My forebears expatriated to Etherine to escape from the Three Hundred Years War. But in their ignorance, they did not heed the rumors of Cadaqu expelling those like themselves West towards Western Etherine. They eventually reached Templum Limous where I was conceived under the title of Nostre Ren-Ras Light and raised on the works of Voradula Soulious and, eventually, Falmos Soulious."

"Unique med and surname," she said, adjusting her seat so she could lean forward.

Nostre offered a reminiscent smile.

"Unique indeed. If you are as intelligent as you are beautiful, then I assume you understand that expatriates are not proficient at giving their progeny Admanic titles." He gave a slight shrug. "I reckon the title is quite fitting for my work."

Ambia nodded.

Chry's knee bounced. He couldn't keep still. The lavender scent slung around his neck as a scarf tugged to throttle. His stomach kept flipping. No matter what he thought about, he did not feel comfortable here. The silence the physician maintained did not help. Chry watched Nostre watch Ambia as if waiting for her to speak. Only once did Nostre tear his gaze away from her to glance at the doorway.

Ambia breathed in. The rain pattered above. In front of her on the desk, Chry finally noticed, was a daisy inside a quaint, clay pot. The pot held neither cracks nor dents and was located precisely at the corner. The white petals of the daisy struggled to survive.

"I appreciate you divulging your origins. The lives of the Caris'ma people have been one that I take both a pity and pride in," Ambia said. She switched her legs, shifted in her seat. "In saying this, it…it is not why I am here."

"Then why are you?"

"The Black Rings." Her stare was slicing through Nostre. "What do you know of the plague?"

Another crack of thunder flashed through the window. When the light settled, Chry reckoned that Nostre's smugness and flirtation had dropped. The day's coldness stiffened his expression. The physician stared at Ambia before fixing his spectacles and leaning back in his chair.

"A better question is what do we not know, and a better introduction before discussing the Black Rings is what I have discovered of Heva Na Narth."

She regarded Nostre with a conviction that could kill.

"Explain."

Nostre gave a fleeting smirk.

"Gladly."

He rose from his chair, turned his back to them, and perused a pyramid of scrolls stacked on the lowest shelf. He slid a scroll off the top, peered long at the shelf, then set aside the scroll on his desk to rearrange the pyramid into three smaller pyramids. Now, the scrolls were perfectly aligned.

Chry paled.

He's obsessed. No, he's lost his rattles. That's it.

Nostre regarded them again before unfurling the scroll, perusing it first, then bearing a pleased expression. He moved the single sheet of parchment to the side and laid the scroll flat, securing the ends with teak woodblocks he retrieved from under his desk. To Chry, the intricate design of the blocks resembled the horrid faces from his nightmares.

Ambia ran her eyes over the writing as would a general over a map.

Nostre glanced at the door while she was preoccupied before saying, "Regrettably, I have not had the opportunity to treat a patient with Black Rings. Since we are situated in Cadaqu, the probability of encountering a patient is unlikely."

"Have you not visited Pulchrit?"

Nostre nodded as though he had predicted the question.

"The Black Rings are one of many diseases that I treat. As you have heard, I have recently discovered, after the many failures of my forebears, a remedy for the Grey Death. Those who live on the Southern coast of Admah will no longer have to fear starvation from an alien disease they know nothing of. This is, as I see it, advantageous and feasible.

232

"Now think what would happen if I visited Pulchrit during the height of its plague. Would it be prudent of me to risk my life and endanger the salvation of others in exchange for the chance to discover a remedy for a disease I might find elsewhere? Perhaps here? Nay, I think not."

"Some hopes are worth the risk," she said, her voice stern.

"Perhaps. However, I am not the Hypenian. You may call me a coward, that is understandable, but I need to consider Admah and the Four Nomases as a whole. And I simply cannot do that if I die. As I have stressed, there are other patients in need of my attention. In spite of this fault, I have managed to engage with the Black Rings and with diseases of similar like, such as Heva Na Narth."

Ambia stared broad and still at the scroll.

Nostre asked, "What do you know of Heva Na Narth?"

"Enough. Explain to me what you have."

Her words were almost as stoic as Bar's, only desperate. Nostre's smirk did not waver.

"I see we are sensitive of the matter. Very well. As you perhaps know, Heva Na Narth was a virulent disease twenty years heretofore that nearly decimated the Heva clan. Other Lanke clans were affected as well but bore minor outbreaks and did not see the same infectious spread. In its majority, the writings we have about the disease are unclear or differ drastically from scholar to scholar. The Nexlor and those within Admah ponder little about the internal complications of the Lanke. Thus their documentation of Heva Na Narth is, in the most optimistic terms, insubstantial. What you have in front of you is the most comprehensive account I have from a scholar in Odu, recently deceased.

"As for the Lanke, their documentation is practically non-existent. The Heva clan have no desire to write as is the same for most clans. What little I do have comes from a clan named the Derk. They seem to be the only ones that are literate and thus have documented the experiences they had with Heva Na Narth, however slight."

A wrinkle of confusion pressed her face inward. The look was that of unearthing a skeleton she recognized, buried and hidden from her for years. She did not interrupt Nostre as he spoke. She kept her eyes creased and focused.

"Even though the Derk have the capacity to speak in Nature's Tongue, they write in Jimraokah instead. In light of this, I requested the assistance of a late colleague in rendering the few Obolio parchments I retrieved in the Split and from others. What I found was disturbing. The Derk wrote about symptoms of pallor and extreme exhaustion leading to the fainting of men within the Wastelands. One of these accounts detailed a father's grief in having to kill his son after the boy was rendered immobile by Heva Na Narth. Sadly, there was little else to learn from it. The parchment is, as a whole, an expression of sorrow rather than of documentation."

"Do you think then that Heva Na Narth and the Black Rings are related?" Ambia asked. "Perhaps even the same?"

Nostre smiled.

"It would be disingenuous to assume otherwise."

Ambia read the rest of the scroll, and the farther she went, the more her creases smoothed away. Optimism was shining through.

Good for her, going off to find a cure and all that, Chry thought fiddling with his fingers. True, seeing Ambia calm somewhat eased him. Seeing Nostre calm did not. It wasn't necessarily because of what he said or how he said it, but because every time he spoke, every time he tried to coax Ambia, everything he promised, the unsympathetic way he discussed the tragedies of others, everything Nostre did compelled Chry to look behind him to see if a corpse—*grandma's* corpse—was slumped against the doorframe with a grin of death inviting him to sleep with her in a bed of burnt flesh. He didn't know why he felt this, but he sure as plos didn't like it.

"Do you have those writings in Nature's Tongue?" she asked Nostre, her words softening. "I would be in your debt if I could peruse them."

"Indeed I do," Nostre said. "They are in the cabinet over here. Allow me to retrieve them for you."

"Before you, ah, get too far," Chry interrupted. Nostre was gliding toward the cabinet. When he heard Chry, his smile melted away. "Where's the pisspot? I, uh, just haven't been since—"

Without looking at him, Nostre sighed. He bent, opened the wood cabinet, and rummaged through the scrolls and tomes within. Chry could reckon half of his expression. It was unamused. "If you must go, there are bushes outside. If you're bashful, go ask for a pot from someone else. Otherwise, you may leave us as we were."

Chry's jaw hung open like a broken hinge, words stolen and spent. He looked at Ambia for help and received a gentleness. It told him to best do what he says, she would be right out.

This, he could tell well enough, was a lie.

There was no more use in dallying. He licked his lips, adjusted himself, and stood there undecided. Nostre did not acknowledge his presence. Ambia laid concerned eyes on him as if wanting to say something.

You're just making them suspicious, Chry. Just leave already. Leave.

So he did.

Before exiting, he turned back and caught a glimpse of Ambia's stare. It was reluctantly returning to Nostre who had taken out a tome stuffed with parchment. He was now making his way to Ambia. He did not expend a sliver of attention on Chry.

That was good, he thought, because what he did next was move away from the entrance, out of sight. Nostre did not see this. Chry glanced back at the front door which promised a desolate but attractive trek back through the rain. He had the urge to leave again but thought otherwise.

There's just something…wrong here.

He shook his head.

It was the lavender that enticed him, and it was the lavender he followed.

IV

What am I even doing? he thought. *I don't even know what I'm looking for or why I'm looking for it or why I'm here.*

Despite this, his feet led him down the hall to the small Rosewood door. He slipped through its opening so it would not squeal. Immediately, the lavender was shoved into his nose. He gagged violently. He almost stumbled back and had to restrain himself from coughing or else alert Nostre of his whereabouts.

That wouldn't be good

Oh, I thank you. I had no idea.

He made the sound of a small animal disgusted with its scraps. Thereafter, blinking away the tears, he took in the space.

The first thing he noticed was there were no windows. This added to the list of behaviors that unnerved him about Nostre. He had a window in his study and in the hall but not in here? Chry guessed this room was at the end of the home, so why wouldn't there be a window open to the plateau and Aedilium. Wouldn't that be nice for sick people to look at? To take their minds off of whatever they were suffering from?

The other objects acted much like their owner: neat and organized. The sides of a long table were parallel to the walls. This was where Chry guessed the patients rested. Its Depanen wood was polished so excessively it winked at him. A pillow of brown feathers and no wrinkles headed the table. Beside it was a rosewood chair worn tan from age and use. Stocky bureaus and shelves upheld glass, porcelain, wood, and metal bowls. Chry could not name all the herbs within: There were pink ones, yellow and purple ones, Elos, shrubs, flowers, and too many others to list, each divided into a covered bowl.

Atop some of these bureaus stood sculptures of hand-carved creatures. They were, of course, at the exact corners and matched with a gem—a snake with a diamond, not a Dry-Mouth but a regular snake, a bird with sapphire, an Obolio on an opal box. Really, it just seemed like all of their twinkling, obsidian eyes were staring at him.

For decoration, a rounded rug displayed a cross-section of gold, black, and silver circles. He could tell by the depression of the wool that Nostre and many patients heretofore had crossed to reach the table. Even so, the edges were not tattered, and it had not a single stray string.

Everything had a place and nothing was out of place.

The tears of Eulgash thudded against the roof. A flash of lightning. Figures dimming.

Well, he thought. *It's not like I'm going anywhere else.*

First, he went to the smell of the lavender, but of course, right when he started, the floorboard he stepped on creaked like a crow. It nearly sent him running as his head jerked back to see…Well, nothing. Neither Nostre nor Ambia heard him.

Arbiter be damned, Chry, quiet yourself.

His tremulous leg took on the next board that did not speak, lowering his anxiousness from screaming to buzzing. He breathed again and remembered that, aye, the rain above was loud enough to mute his noise.

He at least had this to be thankful for.

The lavender flowers weren't too difficult to find. They were with the other scented flowers in the middle of a row of five apothecary jars. Nostre, Chry noticed, also liked to separate his herbs into distinct sections where scented flowers went with scented flowers and ingredients for potions went with ingredients for potions. But, like every other container, the jar was sealed shut. It seemed unlikely that the lavender could release a stench this potent through a sealed jar. He could try smelling where the lavender scent originated from, but right now his nose was too overwhelmed. This room was like the Pits where the sweat of men and piss of Dry-Mouths made children gag. Even a pack of Obolios wouldn't be able to sniff out the source.

That left him with a stone in his gut.

Aye, and a lavender scent that is much too strong for just pleasure.

Starting a mindless search, he eyed the herbs with their aromas diluted by lavender and jars. They all looked like herbs, nothing off besides the uncomfortable-looking sculptures he was beginning to wish weren't there. Aside from the door he entered, there were no others. He checked the tops of the bureaus that were dust-free and spotless. Behind them were just as clean. He opened some of the drawers—knives, scissors, tools he as a farmer had never stumbled across—but did not open all of them for fear of making too much noise. Really, he reckoned there were just more tools in the bureaus unless this was what Chry was supposed to think, and if that's the case, he really should look to prove or disprove if Nostre was guilty of…of…

Of what…?

What *exactly* was Nostre guilty of?

He stood before the bureau sawing his lip with his teeth.

What if, he thought. *Nostre is actually innocent? What if the lavender is just lavender, and I'm just convincing myself into thinking that the lavender is something more than it actually is? What if I'm convincing myself of Nostre's guilt just because I don't want to think about what happened in Domum or where Aimee is or where she could be or what would happen to her in the Wastelands with the Lanke or in the mountains with the wild things or in Pulchrit with the Black Rings?*

No. No, that can't be; there *has* to be something here.

Yet the more he looked, the more likely the conclusion became. He laid his eyes beneath the table and under the bureaus. He patted the pillow to feel if Nostre had stored an object in there but only felt a skim of feathers. Nostre would surely notice the ruffling of his pillow, Chry convinced himself, though desperation was surrounding him between four windowless walls. He had to find *something*. The room felt too *clean*; the corners swept of dusty clumps, surfaces wiped of stains, pieces arranged to a straight-lined perfection, the rug centralized and decorated with its circles of gold, black, and…

He stopped.

The rug.

He stared at it.

Well, have you checked beneath the rug?

The sudden revelation was like a shred of sunlight piercing through the clouds. His lips dared to hint at a smile.

At first, he avoided lifting the rug by edging around it, staring at it like some slumbering ox. His mind convinced himself of its taintedness. Down the hall, he heard a brief burst of laughter, light-hearted and friendly.

Ambia

He nearly forgot about her, but her laughter and presence now made the situation feel real and tangible.

They were laughing together—Ambia and that deranged man.

He wrung his hands, bent down, and hesitated for even his fingertips were trembling. He tried lifting the rug which slipped from his hands.

Arbiter, he thought, holding his hands together to tame their shaking, then took the rug again in a grip that blanched his fingers.

This time, the rug rolled onto the table's leg. He ceased to move. Gulped.

Where the rug was heretofore, there was a square. The bottom and top edges cut down from the rug as its side lined the slit in the floorboard. Across its bottom, another hand-sized gap depressed into the floor. A cast iron handle protruded from within.

Chry reined in his breathing. The simple existence of the cellar rattled him stiff. The lavender scent survived here, but the dread radiating from its slits smelled of a deathly rot. Nostre's guilt was no more of a fanciful possibility but the rising, raw stench of reality. There was no more hiding.

Gooseflesh prickled down his neck. He clamped his teeth together. His expression drained of color when his hand reached out to wrap around the iron handle. It was the frigidity of his heart. The knuckles of his grip were alabaster white.

Shit, shit, *shit*

It did not need to be this way. He could still turn back. He could erase this scene from his memory and return the rug where it was and leave, not so fast as to cause a ruckus but quickly, oh so quickly. Every step farther away would calm his trembling hands. That'd be good. He could take strides out of the room and into the hallway and down to where he could clearly hear Ambia's light and comforting voice. He could soon sit next to her and hopefully, neither Ambia nor Nostre would ask him why he had arrived from the opposite direction of where the front door was or why he was dry from the rain outside. They probably wouldn't anywise. They'd probably be too deep in conversation to worry about him.

Everything could be as it was, he thought, seeing himself enter Nostre's office. *Nothing would be wrong. Nothing would be out of place. Me and Ambia. Soon we'd be far, far away.*

It was decided. This was what he would do.

Chry opened the cellar door.

It wasn't locked which seemed odd considering everything he knew about Nostre; locking a cellar door seemed just as natural for the physician as holding a door open for a woman or rearranging scrolls into perfect pyramids.

The sweat stains. He was in a hurry.

Even so, Chry wished Nostre had been more attentive. He wished he had locked the cellar. He wished he didn't have to experience the ungodly stench that rushed up from below and assaulted his nostrils.

Death and decay. It eviscerated the lavender.

Chry whiffed and heaved, vomit shoving through his throat. He held it at the gate, mayhap by his will alone, but then it projected through his lips and hands anywise. It splattered forward onto wooden stairs. Nostre would not mind. The steps were far from maintained.

Someone can slip and break an ankle, his mind thought as he retched on his hands and knees. The cellar door leaned against the table. He was coughing and crying into the total darkness. The steps he could see slobbered with vomit. *They can hear me. They'll hear me and come barging in.*

At this point, he didn't care if Ralesh Sanal heard him and ate him alive. He could barely breathe.

Chry kept spitting and wiping his sleeve across his mouth and eyes. His panting reverberated back from the cellar. When he did regain a portion of his composure, he gave the cellar a proper scrutiny.

The space below was the darkness of an abandoned abattoir where the meat was left behind. The first steps, its wood as rough and splintered as Domum's walls, descended into a void. The stone wall had not aged well either: a desolate face of pock-marked nicks and branching cracks. Below, where he guessed the end of the stairs were, a weak white light streaked out from a wrought-iron lantern. It looked the same as the Illum stones throughout Cadaqu with its shutters closed and shut. It did little to illuminate the cellar. It barely even scratched the bottom stairstep.

Chry didn't realize that he was still holding his breath. He wiped his lips again before instructing himself to, from now on, breathe through his mouth. Then he listened. He tried focusing through his panting and heard a steady drip from below.

My vomit, he thought and shivered. But no. That wasn't it. It was more watery and thicker, distinct from any other noise in the house. It was all he could hear down below.

You don't have to go if you don't want to because you really don't want to, and if you don't want to you don't have to.

And what'll happen to Ambia if you don't? Will she die screaming, no doubt like your grandma did? Are you going to listen to Ambia scream?

Chry heard none of these thoughts. Instead, he kept listening to the innocent *plop* of that liquid, like the consequences of a storm where rain dripped from the roof and plopped into a puddle.

Plop

...

Plop

...

Plop

...

With an effort, he stood on sticklike legs. A faintness drifted over him. His sight blurred partly from standing too fast but mainly from inborn fear. He swayed and would've stayed safe on that landing if not for a crack of thunder. It startled him into taking that first step. This

241

was the hardest, the first step; old wood groaned beneath the pressure, blood rushed through and out of his head so fast he became lightheaded and dizzy in imagining himself tumbling down, down, down. It took too long for the next step but every time he took one, the shorter the time it was to take another.

His breath was husky in his throat. Avoiding his vomit on the steps, he descended but stopped often because the dizziness became too overwhelming. Its stench wormed in and out of his nostrils.

Another step, just take another step, don't think of anything else, just another step,

After the fourth and fifth step, his sapphire necklace felt heavy like a steel heart. His hands tried groping for a handhold, but he could only guide his hand across the wall. Its stone was as unforgivable as a gaol.

Halfway down, a headsore formed above and between his eyes. It throbbed to his steps like a cruel song and created another voice in the recesses of his mind that called out for a single name.

Aimee

Aimmmmmmmeeeeeeeee

At the edge of darkness, he could now reckon the outline of shapes that he wished to ignore. He kept his eyes downcast and planted on the wood. With quivery lips, he began whispering a silent prayer to Eulgash, repeating it over and over again.

After however many the fuck it was, he was about to fucking tumble *up* the stairs and roll and run and scream before his foot hit solid material. Stone. The stone floor. He recognized the light next to him that wasn't there heretofore. He could hardly remember half the steps he had taken.

Down here, decay was pregnant. Down here, there were…forms. Nothing made a noise besides that steady *plop*, and yet he had a feeling that at one point the things congealing from within the shadows had once made noises like he did now. It led to another realization Chry would not accept. He banished it from existence. It did not exist. He would not believe it as true.

But it is. Why don't you lift the lantern and find out.

He could. It was there. The Illum light clawed at his tan linen shirt, and one look at it caved in his ribs and tore up through his throat. He produced tiny wheezes.

It's like the cellar's handle, he thought, but it was only a reassurance. This was not like the handle of the cellar. This was far from it.

He placed an unruly hand on the lantern's cover. Apprehension condemned him to that position. The lantern kept rattling from how much he shook. He swallowed hard but could not contain the shiver he had contracted. He commanded his hand multiple times to move. It wouldn't. Panic was burying him alive. The only way to prevent it from inhaling him was to go, *go.*

Chry nearly screamed before lifting the lantern.

Iron scraped against iron. Imprisoned light shot free and vanquished the darkness. Chry flinched, blinded by a screen of white, and jerked his hand up to shade against the Illum. Lantern clanking into place, he stumbled back. His throat grunted and groaned. His heel knocked against a stiffness that almost sent him sprawling. He didn't, but when he tried regaining his footing, he heard the harmless splash of a foot stepping into a puddle. There was a wetness across his sole.

Oh fuck, that's my foot and that's a puddle, the *puddle.*

He had to stop himself before doing anything rash. His lungs inhaled the toxic air at such an alarming rate the room was force-feeding him, his lungs bursting.

It was too much.

Arbiter be damned, calm *yourself Chry, just take a moment and* calm *yourself.*

He did. Eventually. But his hands were still over his eyes, and a lump like a handful of nails prevented him from swallowing.

Against his fears, he could still hear that *plop* of the puddle. It was at his hip now.

I don't want to. I don't. I...

Timidly, Chry pried his hands from his face and opened his eyes. Within the omnipresent light, the scene opened to him. He wished it hadn't. His stomach dissolved, his eyes numbed, and his skin produced a buzzing that wished to break with reality.

Eulgash, I...I just...

Mortality filled the crevices of thought. Nostre, that good-natured physician, had painted the room grey and red. Any other color was impossible for Chry to interpret. There were shades of red, in jars on shelves but mostly piled neat and organized. The decay was set to the side. There were enough eyes on him to intercept thought, both within and without. They—*aren't real, they can't be, they aren't real, they can't be real*—could have once pled for salvation. Now they had obtained it. Tools were grey too. Some were grey and red. One dangled from a hook and dripped, fresh from use. That was the one Chry gazed at.

Everything had a place, and nothing was out of place.

Everything had a place, and nothing was out of place.

Everything *had a place...*

Nothing *was out of...*

The stench of death congested his lungs. His knees failed as he dropped and retched the liquid remains of his stomach. It added another color to the scene—a viscous dirty yellow.

His head bobbed. His stomach queased. Strings of spittle and bile swung from his lips. He forgot where he was and nearly gave a dumbfounded smile, but when he reckoned where he was again, he retched once more.

Beside him, the liquid plopped.

He raised a forearm to wipe the vomit from his lips. It happened in a sluggish pool. His arm trembled in keeping him upright. He spat but the taste of helplessness would not leave his mouth.

"Ambia..." He mumbled out loud. His lips glistened. Gradually, the present pieced together into the realization of who Ambia was with—who she was talking to. "She's...She's still..."

He twisted his head, and eyeing him were the hazel irises of a supine woman. Her cheeks were bloated, her skin was pale, and her thin brunette hair hung suspended from a table not too dissimilar from the one above.

Chry would not dare look at what was open below her neck.

A distant fit of thunder rumbled above.

His eyes welled and rattled. With a scream in his throat, he shot to his feet, raced forward, desperate, tripped, and fell into his own vomit. He did not process this. He tossed his limbs forward toward the light and up the stairs. He tripped and tumbled and bruised and splintered himself but did not and would not stop, the eyes behind him never leaving his back until he disappeared into the home.

V

Ambia and Nostre were absorbed in conversation when Chry careened around the door frame. He was panting. His eyes were of a man hunted in the Forest for three days, sweat drenched his hair, and his garment exuded a repulsive, slimy stench. His hand, still lumpy with vomit, had walloped the door frame, startling Ambia.

In contrast, Nostre was stone. He was leaning over Ambia with the tome he had brought over to her seat. Pieces of parchment were scattered across the desk, his impeccable longhand lined across. For a blink, sentiments whisked across his expression, warranting danger if it had risen fully. Instead, the physician gave him an indiscernible look.

"Ambia! Get-" Chry's panting hindered speech. He had to stop. He had to gather his breath. "Get the plos away from him!"

He lurched forward two strides before meeting Nostre's eyes. It stopped him still.

Nostre had the neutral stare of a physician listening to one of his patients. To Chry, it almost seemed like the stoic stare of Bar, flat and unworried. Moreover, there was a sense of knowing between them. They both understood the current circumstances, but the horror of knowing that Nostre was inured to his actions disturbed Chry into a slap of shock. How could a man be so tame, so calm and unresponsive to such gore and violence? It wasn't natural. Nostre wasn't natural.

He's an abomination. That's what he is. An unforgiveable abomination.

At the corner of the desk, the daisy wilted white. Ambia furrowed her brow.

"Chry, what's happening? What's wrong?"

Then the nonchalance of Nostre melted away beneath pleasantries. It was as if what happened in the cellar had never happened.

"Settle down, young man. There is nothing to be afraid—"

"There's *everything* to be afraid of because you killed them and-and butchered them you, you *abomination*!"

Ambia was out of her seat now, approaching. Nostre made no attempt to seize her.

She said, "Calm down, Chry, and speak plainly."

"Yea, I suggest we sit and converse as civilized—"

"Civilized! *Civilized!*" Chry's voice heightened, accusing Nostre with a finger. "How the *plos* can you say *civilized* after what *you* did to those folk down in your cellar. Civilized, fucking *civilized!*"

Ambia cupped his arm and touched his chest. Her hands were warm and gentle like a Mother's Touch. His chest seethed beneath her palm but receded a knuckle against a golden warmth. He reckoned that touch could feel the tremble of his skin.

"Chry. Please. Calm down."

The gritting of his teeth loosened. His panting was departing when he looked at her. Her image was watery and shaky. A cool liquid spilled over his eyelid and fell down his cheek. From below was the faint glow of a morning sunrise. Somehow, the dawning rage, resentment, and fear he felt at the start of their conversation was setting.

He sniffled, squeezed his eyes shut, head low, and wiped the tears with his knuckles.

"Aye, Ambia, I will. I just…" Chry directed an unfriendly look to Nostre. The "physician" did not interrupt. "I just can't even *look* at that…"

"Then you can look at me," Ambia soothed. She was rubbing her hand in circles along his chest and for the life of him, he wished she would never stop. Chry had not felt this cared for since the days of his mother and farmhouse. "May I ask who he killed?"

"The patients...Ambia I-I *saw* them." His eyes pleaded with her. "All of them...Dead."

Ambia gave a gentle nod, the warmth of her care radiant.

"Yea, I thank you Chry. Now, can you do something for me?"

He first threw his eyes to Nostre who only observed them. The man should be running, shouting, hunting them down with a knife to eliminate the witnesses. He did none of these things nor anything that would indicate he would. His behavior would've been the same if he had attended a meeting with Vassal Renega about the production of snake skins within the Rattle Trade.

Reluctantly, Chry said, "Aye."

She waited a moment, stopping her hand, and then asked, "May you please wait for me outside?"

His mind had to take a moment to process her request before telling his head to turn to her. His eyes were narrow as if trying to spot if she had misspoken but broadened when realizing she hadn't.

"And leave you with *him*," he said.

"Yea."

"I suggest you do as your partner has-"

"What the plos do you *mean*?" Chry had ignored what Nostre had said. His focus was on Ambia who clung to his arm until he stepped away from her. The warmth of her sun faded; a hundred more suns exploded within him. This idea, it was beyond preposterous, ridiculous, something he would have expected from Onvi or Bar but Ambia? *Ambia*?

"It's as I have asked," she said without bitterness. "I wish you to wait outside until I am done here."

"Until you're..." He could hardly believe what he was hearing. How could she think of this man as anything *besides* repulsive? His stance grew steadfast and defensive. "No. No, there's no *way* I'd *ever* let you stay in a room alone with a man like that."

"I will not be alone, Chry." Emotion rumbled inside her throat. "You will be right outside."

"And by the time I reach you, you'll already be—"

"I told you to *leave*," she barked. As if taking a blow, Chry flinched and felt his chest thumping again. So graceful and loving, Ambia was like a butterfly that had suddenly sprouted a maw and claws to bite and slash. "I was not *asking* you. I'm *telling* you. I do not need you here, and I do not want you here, so *leave*."

His ribcage had shrunk against his lungs so that the only action he could take was to gaze at her. Thereafter, Ambia looked at the hurt across his face, and the creases of strain across hers immediately lifted. There was a crack of regret in those hazel eyes that Chry hardly recognized. He lowered his head and licked his lips. He should have expected as much. A crazed man kills who knew how many folk and Chry still cannot convince the most trustworthy and caring of the Runners to listen. He was not wanted here.

After leaving his thoughts, Chry whispered, "Aye. Aye…" Trace tears popped at the corner of his eyes, but he quickly passed a forearm over them. He wouldn't give them the satisfaction of seeing him cry again. "Of course, I'll leave. What else would I be good for."

Her lips seemed about to respond before he turned to leave, slumping passed the handprint of vomit on the door frame and into the dreary drizzle.

VI

"It would seem you have the unfortunate task of traveling with a companion of less than favorable characteristics. I am truly apologetic for your misfortune."

Ambia would not give Nostre the satisfaction of a response. Instead, when Chry had gone, she closed her eyes until the winking stars from her use of magic faded. Her expression then worked through a series of premeditative thoughts. Her heart thrummed in three different places and each of her fingers inside her fist trembled.

Ambia tried using Amuias to calm Chry. The magic worked at first but only moderately. Unlike much of the hearsay Admanites uninvolved with the Temples tended to spread, magic was less potent than expected. In this case, Amuias, The Magic of Healing in Nature's Tongue, could not outright change the emotions of an individual, only lessen them like Amuias also did with pain. The magic, too, could only be implemented through touch.

Ambia wished she had not hurt Chry. He was a blameless and considerate boy, and though he now talked to the Runners more than when he first joined, Chry was obviously still suffering from the loss of his grandmother and farmhouse. Only time will heal his grief. She wished she and Chry could have left together without incident and saw to the arrest of Nostre until they or the authority of the Slums, a leader unrecognized by the Council named Sario Minatus, could investigate this and decide upon further actions or, if necessary, consequences.

But she would participate in neither; the voices of those who she had lost in Pulchrit were calling out to her. There were corpses in the cellar, this she believed Chry whole-heartedly, but the possibility remained that Nostre had not murdered them, that he merely used the individuals as subjects to research cures for the Black Rings and other diseases. It would not be the first time; there were plenty of cadavers—animal and human—inside the embalming chambers of the Nexlor used for Animelaronecy, Losonecy, and, as one would expect, Canomonecy, the study of diseases. As much as her body had rejected them, she too had partaken in the necropsies of these cadavers under the cover of night. Perhaps there was something here that she could use. If she could salvage *anything* from this man, she had to take the chance. To save her city. To save her people.

They are lost Ambia. There is no panacea for the Black Rings.

Ignoring Bar's words, Ambia regarded Nostre. Her stare reverted to the beginnings of their conversation: hard, unreadable, and clinging to hope. Nostre met her look without glee and without spite. The eyes beneath his gold-rimmed glasses were sober.

"Nostre...Be truthful when I ask you what exactly Chry was speaking of."

Nostre stared long enough for her to notice the dark furrows around his eyes, mouth, and brow. She reckoned they were from age and, more so, from tedious days bent over his patients and tomes. Just moments heretofore, he had seemed the pinnacle of health and charm. Now, his desperation was striking.

He spoke with the propriety of the Council of Crystal.

"I am many things, Ambia, but I am no liar. Honesty is a trait essential to our line of work. As such, I will give you nothing but the truth."

Nostre worked his way back to his chair. The room was compact, so he had to sidle past the corner of the desk and the cabinets. Everything he did was clear-headed and diligent. No action was wasted.

He sighed when sitting, stared at the roof, then leaned forward in his seat and rested his chin on his fingers. He did not take his eyes away from her.

"Throughout my years as a physician, I have encountered a myriad of diseases and symptoms. On rare occasion, I will come across a patient with fatal symptoms beyond the reaches of my medical capabilities. I loathe to say such since our primary duty as physicians is to foster these individuals back to good health. However, it is also prudent for us to distinguish when a patient is beyond relief or has otherwise arrived at a stage of needless suffering."

Ambia listened without word. Her eyes never stirred.

"For these few, there was no physician in all of Admah that could have saved them. Your friend speaks of tragedy. I say this is the true tragedy; patients who must be informed that they will never see another dawn. I did for them what I could. Then I allowed death to intervene. Some, I will admit, were relieved of life earlier than others, and that was due to my hand. I assure you they suffered no more than necessary, and afterward, their cadavers were utilized in helping the living."

"So you put them to death."

"If you wish to think of it as such. Or you could say they were heading toward death with or without my assistance. I would be negligent if I did not mention the hundreds of thousands of others who were saved by the death of one. In these terms, death is not an end but the origin of something greater."

Her eyes were focused on her feet.

"And those who died? Were they as you said? Were they truly about to die?"

"Most," he said, the word spearing through her chest. She clinched her teeth to stay herself. "Others were too far gone to decide for themselves whether they should live or die, and some asked for the suffering to end, those inflicted with Losa Ambusana in particular." He paused. This time, he could not look at her when he spoke. "I told you I would not lie to you, and I have not been inclined to do so until now. Honesty also means admitting to information you wish to withhold, and this…"

His voice was firm but his pauses for thought were evidence of struggle.

"There was a boy, a case in Odu. His eyes were sunken, and his movements were groggy which, in my eyes were obvious symptoms of Heva Na Narth. I was…desperate. Odu was a town that was supposed to give me insight into a disease that might have killed, at the time, the recent king of Ontinia. But there was nothing. The Lanke had already invaded Western Etherine in so that there was a dearth of Lanke to choose from. The worst I treated was Rotten Pig and accidental cuts. That is until the boy came along.

"He was with a branch of the Darkin clan who had come for food and rest. Upon noticing the boy's symptoms, I asked both the elder and boy if I could treat him, but they were opposed to an Admanite, foreign to the lands of Odu and the Wastelands, tending to one of their own. This was an opportunity to save their clan and progeny, but they were too inundated with bigotry to recognize it. I thus took it upon myself to gather the information needed and was nearly caught and reprimanded for it many times over. Threats were made to my life. Throughout these arguments and quarrels, the boy only deteriorated further. He would die soon, I reckoned, or would wish he had."

Nostre gestured an open palm to the parchment that Ambia originally read. "The account you have there. I was the one who wrote it, and the patient that died was under my custody."

Ambia glanced down at the parchment and reread the lines over and over again, reevaluating its knowledge. There was a hopeful light in her mind's eye. They were so close. *Nostre* was so close. She could feel it. Yet simultaneously, visions of Nostre's time in Odu painted the inside of her skull muddy. She could not wade through it to solely concentrate on the possibility of a cure.

With a set jaw, she said, "Tell me what happened."

There was a pause, a space to think. Then he continued.

"During the night, I suffocated the boy and took his body with me to Xey. I was gone before morning."

He said this dryly as if reciting what he had eaten this morning, but her expression hinted at discomfort.

"Would you like to sit?"

She did not answer him. She could not think clearly. For some reason, her mother's voice had invaded her thoughts again.

Ah doctor? Ha! My whore of a daughter thinks she can be a doctor. What the plos do you think you can do for them? Vomit?

She ignored it and made certain to glare into Nostre's eyes when she spoke next.

"Promise me that you will never do as you did with the boy. Promise me that you will never take another patient's life without their consent."

A somber string tugged at his lips. There was a sadness there that Ambia would not have expected from an emotionless and remorseless killer.

"I'd be forsaking patients who would otherwise die from diseases such as the Black Rings," he said. "I would be responsible for their deaths."

"That's callous and arrogant to think."

"It is but the truth."

"Are you refusing then?"

"As much as I wish I wasn't, yea. I cannot promise you this."

Whatever was left of his smile faded.

"The Black Rings have taken much from you, haven't they?"

Ambia bit back her tongue. Nostre was right. He was no liar.

The silence dragged into marks. A boom of thunder smote her ears. Rain pelted the roof. Ambia and Chry would have to walk through the storm to get to the inn where the Runners were staying. Imagining the cold, wet, and muddy trek back reminded her too much of her walks with Lorna through Pulchrit when the snow would begin to melt at the end of Swason, the Season of Death, with showers following in Swoson, the Season of Life. She wished she could return to those days, those innocent, innocuous days.

Nostre then said, "I grieve, you understand."

She lifted her hazels. They had become like Nostre's—exhausted, hollow, rounded with dark sockets of strain. He hid behind his collapsed hands and gilded glasses, his flat, devoid eyes peering through the desk.

He resumed.

"I still see his face when I sleep and think to what I have done and to what I will do to cure the suffering of my patients. When I think of it, the answers I manifest are terrifying if not accurate and acceptable. I do not shy away from them. I do not regret what I have done heretofore, not even with the boy, but eventually, I must sleep and as much as the boy there might think otherwise, I am still human, I still feel sorrow, and I still feel their pain."

He met Ambia's eyes again and behind those spectacles was a person she did not want to acknowledge. She wanted to forget meeting Nostre, become ignorant to his existence so he could continue on as he was. Perhaps then she would be free of guilt. Perhaps then he would find a cure to the Black Rings.

"We're more alike than you wish to admit," he said.

Cynicism furrowed her brow.

"And why in all of the Four Nomases do you think we're anything alike?"

"Because you'd do the same to save your people."

Ambia opened her mouth to retaliate but found there was nothing to retaliate with. Some part of her, some small, perhaps infinitesimal part, agreed with Nostre—that part would do *anything* to save Mister Salamance, Elon Halodepa, Mister Oppen, Miss Cartine, Miss Erindal…King Ventem. And that infinitesimal, almost inconsequential part, was enough for her to hesitate.

Nostre seized the opportunity.

"You engaging in this conversation with me is a testament to that notion."

"You are mistaken," she countered.

"Am I? Or am I mistaken that you should have called for Sario to have me seized before you even asked your first question? I could have the corpses of Slum children in my cellar or rather have been killing under the guise of a physician. As far as I see, you are ignorant of my conduct."

Ambia refused to respond.

Nostre leaned closer. "We are desperate, Ambia. We go to lengths that others do not because they do not have the courage to do what it takes to save the people they love. We are physicians. We are the saviors. If we do not care, then no one will."

Thunder cracked overhead. They remained there, still.

"The only difference between us is that I merely accept who I am and what I am willing to do to save the nation I love," he paused. "One day, you will accept this too."

Ambia digested this last statement—remembered the acts she had committed to find a cure, acts so similar to what he was doing now or claimed to be doing now—but finally shook her head. They weren't the same. They *couldn't* be the same.

"Nay. Never in my life," she said.

Ambia held Nostre's stare a moment longer. Then, without turning back, without retrieving Sario to seize Nostre, without speaking to

Chry, she left Nostre at his desk, never to return.

VII

Eighteen years heretofore

Mister Salamance, in a particularly swell mood—perhaps because King Ventem decided to return early from Etherine or simply because of the nighttime festivities—played his fingers across the chanter of his bagpipes. Skirls of merry frolicked from its drones. Its song embedded the residents—feet swayed, smiles beckoned, laughter rode across the winds. Their blissful ignorance knew no bounds. This night, the sun had promised them that it would sleep beneath the horizon forevermore.

Or so it did every night.

But this was only natural. Merriment was the blood of Pulchrit, the city fitting snugly between two mountain faces the townsfolk styled "Aius" and "Eius," named after the first and second King of Ontinia. At the foot of Eius slumbered antique homes of stone, glass, and a decision between fir or spruce. These gentle giants were built close enough to kiss each other but their two-story facades beckoned for hearth and home. This was where the hardy hearts of the townsfolk laid dormant beneath a night of spirits and ale.

At the foot of Aius buzzed the lively marketplace where Mister Salamance played. Partakers of the festival overflowed its flagged pathway as if giddy to be there but never shying away from each other. They were intimate, the jostling minimal, and anywhere they went, the rhythm of dance followed as would a shadow.

Aromas of abundance—from roasted venison and King Bass to leeks and onions—wafted from stone-block shops lining each side of the marketplace. Open counters welcomed familiar faces as well as foreign ones from as far as Etherine and Noma Devolum. Within their stony stomachs beamed merchants bartering for their wares, their cloaks clasped with renditions of mox.

255

In Pulchrit, each merchant laughed as they bartered.

But if an observer disregarded the mirth and instead followed Couriers' Road down from the mountains, cutting in-between the marketplace and residential district and then past the city, he'd see the road curve into the side of Eius like a fisherman's hook where its barbican bit into its face. From here, the High Castle protruded from the mountain, its stone weathered from centuries of vicious valley winds. The walls were bare and severe. There were no banners or flags on display, nor were they flaunted anywhere within the city. Any pretentiousness the kings and queens of Ontinia had remained within the mountain, a tradition upheld since King Cantem the First took the throne.

However, to seven-year-reckon Ambia, the traditions of kings and queens hardly mattered. What mattered to this girl of adventure was weaving through the marketplace with her friend, Lorna Maylord, and picturing that they were escaping from Mister Omna's terrifyingly realistic dolls. They were still innocent and giggled as innocents.

This night was, like most other nights, cold. The collective breath of the city created a mist of warmth within the marketplace, and no one strode out without a cloak and extra layer of garments. As foreign merchants or visitors would come to discover, the cold did not stop the festivities, and it surely would not stop Ambia and Lorna. They were engaged in childhood curiosities—skipping merrily when the throngs gave them a clear lane, waving a hand to Mister Salamance who winked in acknowledgment, engaging in a dance only children their age could perform, listening in on officials from the castle converse with the townsfolk, and goggling at the new wood sculptures Elon Halodepa had carved. For "their eyes only," he had promised.

This went on for two marks of a candle clock, peradventure four.

But then Ambia pivoted. Sharply. Behind her, Lorna almost slid and scraped her knee on the flagstone as Ambia hurled into the alleyway. After a couple of steps, she slowed and stopped. Ambia was breathing heavily. Her hands were coarse in their fists, and the disheveled hair of her upbringing had pasted to her forehead. Her eyes were alert and aroused by the night.

Behind her Pulchrit bustled, above her the stone walls cut the stars and night sky into a sliver, and before her was a new adventure. No one was within the alley, but she could reckon the backs of townsfolk further down. They were along Courier's Road and roared in drunken stupors, anxious for the arrival of King Ventem. There were too many for Ambia to discern where the road began and where it ended.

Lorna, beside her now with a gaze common to a baby doe, was frozen still. She had cupped her tiny hands against her blue and black silk dress. Its silver cuffs were not yet frayed. Beneath her fringe of raven hair shuddered a childish dread.

Ambia heard her gulp.

"I...Oh, please Ambia, I'm...I'm scared. I don't want to go...I don't..."

Already striding into the alley, Ambia glanced back at her with a look of questioning. Lorna seemed like she was about to melt into a puddle of syrupy fear, her knees quivering over her Ironskin boots.

Ambia rolled her eyes.

"Don't be a big ole baby," she teased, snatching Lorna's hand and tugging. It felt like dragging a plow without the help of a Shire. "We *haaave* to go. We'll miss King Ventem if we don't. Lorna, come *ooooon* already! Before it's too thereafter."

She wouldn't come. She dragged her feet, squirmed in her hold, and exchanged between pathetic whines and nonsensical words. Ambia ignored her. Lorna knew well enough that when she made a decision, Ambia would not stray from that path.

Stone dust puffed from their boots. The walls squeezed further inward as to give them no exit but forward. That perhaps did not ameliorate the fear Lorna was trying to overcome but thrilled Ambia. They were striving toward freedom, and freedom was exactly what spurred her forward. Ambia quickened her pace. For the first few strides, her legs had trouble hulling Lorna behind her but after a while, resistance subsided. They were in full sprint now. Behind her, Ambia could hear the giggles of excitement and anticipation.

They could not stop giggling. The eyes of the alley followed as they sped by. Gradually, the alley opened its mouth until they were behind the giddy townsfolk along Couriers' Road. Their backs were an impenetrable forest swaying in the wind, but instead of the wind swaying branches, their streams of ale and wine swayed arms. Instead of the caws of crows, there was the gabble of fat-bellied burps and bellows. Most everyone brandished fir-wood tankards but many were lucky enough to raise the curved horn of an Ironskin Goat. Thoughtful townsfolk whose homes lined along Courier's Road were propped at their windows. Their children stretched around them or across their laps, eager and star-blinded.

The two girls still could not discern the road or torches between the crowds. The bodily heat of the crowd warmed the air. Above, the constellations dazzled beneath the mountainous peak of Eius. The marketplace bustled behind them, distant.

Ambia clenched Lorna's hand tighter before her sense of adventure creased across her lips. She shoved forward. Lorna made a surprised, but excited, squeal and then said something like "Goodness, Ambia, I..."

Ambia wasn't listening.

She could not process any words, sounds, or thoughts outside of her need for adventure. Her vision narrowed, and her ears attuned to the creation of the night, as she turned her shoulders and slid into the crowd.

***

Entering the crowds, Pulchrit's natural scent of stone extinguished beneath the odor of ale and noxious breath. Their tiny bodies squeezed between hulking masses. Sweat slimed against their skin and greased their hair, and the elbows they passed were calm, shifting branches their short statures mostly avoided. They did not know where they were in the crowd for heads and shoulders had enveloped the skies, but Ambia could tell their shoving was nearing them to the road because the farther they went, the tighter the squeeze became. Nimble and evasive, Ambia felt the eagerness of the crowd's movement. It was practically buzzing.

Soon, though, their small bodies were overrun; those behind them that had arrived thereafter were not as intoxicated and wild as those farther in. The air became as thin as a leaf. Beneath a deafening canopy of laughter and shouts, Ambia heard the quiet wheeze of her breath. Threats of being jostled and struck by a hip or elbow roared alive. Ale rained from above and occasionally smacked Ambia in the face. She spat it out, and once, the lump hit the back of a hairy knee. Whoever it hit did not notice.

Behind and scrunched into herself, Lorna had one hand fastened to her chest and the other clamped in Ambia's hand. Their hold was like a ghastly manacle. Ambia heard Lorna mumbling something and was turning to address her before an elbow appeared and knocked Ambia right above the brow. Her skull rang like a belfry of tiny bells. Her jaw locked to withhold the pain as she merely staggered forward. A trail of blood and the inklings of a bruise rounded her socket.

Ambia could no longer hear anything from Lorna. The forest of giants around them had gathered close. Her shoulders now touched her ears, cheeks crushed. Her mouth dragged across the skin and sweat of others, and not once did she need to hold herself back from retching.

There was a push from elsewhere. A trunk jerked and pressed Ambia into another giant. Her lungs emptied and her throat contracted. There was a shard of time where she could not breathe, when the pressure was sinking her down into an inexorable dizziness, before the giant shot forward again. A space formed, and Ambia inhaled with greedy lungs. A tingling ran up her fingers. From above, the stars shone through as twinkles of hope. There was also a skim of roofs over the legion of heads. Exhilaration and exhaustion filled her lungs.

They were so, so *close.*

"Keep yar cock to yaself, Granis."

The slur of ale made the voice low-pitched. Otherwise, it sounded like a woman. When her dizziness and exhilaration wore down and her eyes reckoned who was before her, Ambia realized it *was* a woman—

Miss Cartine actually. Her brow had contorted into a drunken snarl, and her back faced them. In front was the man she was barking at.

Ambia heard a heckling voice respond.

"That's not wat ya said when ya were cleanin' me cock, me say."

"Not even ya mother would think to clean it."

"Oh suck ah cock ya Wild bich."

The next sound was the thump of a fist on bone.

Through a daze, the present flickered by as something separate and intangible. Holding onto Lorna's hand kept her grounded as the scene played before her, how Miss Cartine took another lunge forward before swinging. Tipsy, her lower body swayed, but her fists were precise. This was not her first drunken brawl.

Granis, an ignoramus asshole as Missus Veralesta was inclined to call him, took a jab in the gut and temple before recovering and raising his fists. Bruises and blood dressed him by the time the crowds had noticed. Some tried to create as much space as possible thinking they could simply see King Ventem up close and not be involved with Pulchrit custom. But the majority were keen about the fight and had chosen sides, yelling obscenities like "shove a foot up his ass" or "fuck her Wild cunt."

Ambia loved Pulchrit—really, she did—but she never understood the vulgarity of its citizens. Fortunately, the brawl acted as an excellent distraction. People were packed in like a forest of legs, but they were now shuffling away from Courier's Road to where the brawl was. The space they left gave them an opportunity through.

Ambia seized it. She yanked Lorna's arm forward. They dodged away from the backstep of Miss Cartine and took to a tight opening between two cross-eyed fellows. There were curses and shouts as they shoved past (whether directed toward them or the two fighting, Ambia did not know) but when they worked through a handful of bodies, the sounds subsided.

The two girls were near the road. They could not see it now, but Ambia could feel its presence tingling across her skin and remembered how close the stone buildings were when they were still beside Miss

Cartine. Still, the fighting between Miss Cartine and Granis did not eliminate the roughness of the throngs. It lived as one with the masses, and the girls' nimbleness could only help them so far. Townsfolk swayed as spruces, their arms stretched as outshoots, the gales of mirth and ale whipping at needle leaves.

"I…I don't think I can…" Another hip interrupted Lorna. There was a fragile cry and that cry sent spears of shock through Ambia. Yet, the only reasonable reaction was to push forward when another elbow connected with Ambia's cheek. More like a brushing kiss that would nonetheless leave another bruise.

This she could not care less about. What concerned her was her friend. In between blinks came a reoccurring picture of Lorna, with her innocent eyes and soft hands and unsullied dress, losing Ambia in the throngs and having to wade through them, frightened and alone.

Ambia would never let that happen.

"We're almost—" Ambia held a whine inside her throat as her tiny body nestled through a tight squeeze of hips. "Out Lorna. I'll get you out. Please, stay with me."

Lorna was breaking down into sniffles and squeezing her hand but offered no resistance and tried pushing forward, too. Ambia could barely feel her numb hand, yet the feeling was a comfort. They were together. Forever.

Then, farther up, between the legs and hips, came a fiery light. The shadows it threw out were as deep as the sea. It gave her exhausted limbs a second surge of energy. With all her might, Ambia tugged Lorna and shoved through, farther, farther, again and again, before her shoulder rammed into freedom. She let out a small squeal (so did Lorna) as they tumbled onto the packed dirt.

They nearly fell but caught their knees just before they could. Hunched over, Ambia and Lorna panted. Ambia's chin dripped with sweat and was watering the road.

The road.

The *road*!

Her grin blossomed. She was so excited she whipped her head up and around at where they were. There were no crowds here, but she had to squint against how bright it was. The difference was like opening the door to daylight.

The ground was smoothed dirt and did not bear the imprint of horseshoes or excrement. Torches burned behind glass boxes and on top of robust posts. These posts delineated the edges of the road, lining each side like soldiers. The road itself was deserted. Across from the two girls, the residents were clustered, the stone buildings had grown into the cousins of mountains, and the night sky gave birth to potential.

These two children, through determination and tears, had reached their destination: Courier's Road, the historic road where King Ventem would soon ride through.

This should've been a pause for celebration. Instead, they were greeted by a Knight of the King.

The Knight was about fourteen hands tall but the eyes of Lorna and Ambia saw it as a child born from Eius and donned in armor. That armor shimmered prowess, its vanadium metal polished enough to reflect the tendrils of flame. It concealed any skin the Knight may have had. There were no scars or scratches. The metal was flawless. Winglets sprouted from the temples of a curved helmet. It did not bear eyes. Instead, there was a clean slit where absence exuded from within.

In its left hand was a shield as tall as the Knight and which could be mistaken for a castle wall. Along its center protruded a gold-encrusted fowl against a forest green backdrop, scintillating curls radiating out. In its right hand was an oak spear the thickness of the bole it was hewed from. Its stone-breaker hands clenched the shaft which tapered into a slab of pointed steel. Its wood glistened. Its presence dominated.

The muscles of Ambia and Lorna petrified, their eyes staring in awe and fear. How could a being be so outstanding to gaze at but freeze their bones stiff? They could not know.

Its shield protected its front. A spell of shadows manipulated its armor into the screams of those it had punished. The thought was crushing. Lorna, every crevice and crack, every hollow bloated with terror, could not look elsewhere.

The Knight, one of twenty servants to King Ventem, legends to the lands of Ontinia, lowered its helmet.

"Back in the crowd."

Its words were a hammer to her chest. Ambia could not breathe. This was worse than the crowds. Much worse. The inhumanly deep timbre she heard reverberated between the inner walls of her skull— repeated, repeated. Her legs could not stop shaking. Her lips whimpered but could not articulate a sentence.

It said again, "Back in the crowd."

The strength of its command was the same as heretofore, but somehow Ambia heard the voice deforming into the creatures she imagined were in the Void. How they might have snarled, how they would've intimidated.

Lorna did not respond. The Knight stole her ability to think.

Ambia, however terrified she was (and she was as terrified as she had ever been), manifested the will to move her legs. She had released Lorna's hand when they had tumbled out of the throngs but now that was the first thing she grabbed for. She yelled something at Lorna before bolting down Courier's Road. Ambia was jerked back. The force between sprinting away and yanking an arm that went nowhere nearly took Ambia off her feet.

"Lorna wake up run run!"

Ambia could have smelt ore with how hard she was holding Lorna's hand. She jerked once more before her friend finally moved and scurried behind her. They passed the Knight's shield, a torch, another shield, another and another. The Knights were everywhere. The lump of apprehension throbbed at the center of her being. A headsore narrowed her vision. A sole idea was before her—escape. From the crowds, from the Knights, from *everyone*.

Desperately, they scampered away. Their lungs and hearts were about to burst. The stars above were falling as fangs to a maw, whiles the road kept shrinking, the stone closing in. Ambia couldn't parse out if this was her mind or the truth. So many people. Too many. All staring at her or at least she thought they were staring. It felt more like one of her dreams where she would wake in the center of Gabrien's Coliseum in which every person she knew in Pulchrit had taken a seat before a naked Ambia. Her hands would try to cover herself, but it would not be enough. There'd be no clothes. There'd be no shelter. She'd be small, she'd be powerless, and there'd be nothing she could do to redeem herself.

Having this dream linger with her for days, having it disturb her concentration at the library and her fun in the marketplace, unnerved her. Now that dream was birthing again, here, on Courier's Road, the Knights around and the ribcage of Pulchrit clutching.

Her little seven-year-reckon heart couldn't take it. She had to calm herself and calm herself quickly so she just said *to plos with everything and anything* and planted her foot and jerked a hard right. Lorna's body whipped to follow, and the feeling was like what Ambia had done in the marketplace. She made a decision, and now there was no turning back. Ambia was heading straight for the crowd, already determining that she'd shove, push, tear her way through to protect Lorna.

That was good enough for Ambia.

Lorna babbling behind, Ambia lowered her shoulder, careened forward and rammed into a solid mass of nothing. Surprised, she tumbled forward and landed face first in a pulp of dirt. It smeared her hair across her brow. She tasted its earthy clumps squishing through her lips and teeth. She could not feel a presence behind her. The hand was gone. An immediate threat blared inside her head: *Lorna, where's Lorna, I need to find Lorna.*

The fear propelled her up as she slipped again in the mud. Ambia did not register this. Her wild eyes jerked in search for her friend, this way and that until she looked up and found her.

Lorna was standing just before the mud pile. Her hair, once razor straight from days and weeks of brushing, had become just as disheveled as Ambia's, and her skin of nicks, smudges, and bruises was not so fair and clean as it was before they left the home of her parents, before the mountain Aius had swallowed the sun. Her eyes were as dazed as Illum lights. The sight of her friend like this sunk Ambia's heart (*I couldn't protect her...I told myself I'd protect her*) before that face dawned into a beam of elation and thrill, as bright as the Illum stones themselves. Lorna tossed her hands up to the skies and yelled to Pulchrit, "that was *amazing*!"

Ambia gave her a puzzled look that then smoothed when she looked around. The townsfolk had noticed the girls charging and promptly and politely stepped away from their path. They were not about to bear the brunt of her charge, and, as she scrutinized the nests of wrinkles and skin wizened from years of battling with the sun, Ambia was beginning to realize why.

Though they had not reckoned it until now, this side of Courier's Road was much tamer than the marketplace, for this was where the older generation gathered for festivals. These elders had long lost the desire to drink amply with their enjoyment now coming from attending the events Pulchrit hosted and watching the beaming grins of children like Ambia and Lorna. As Mister Marque would say from within his stone block, "We do not bear the hearts of lions like you do, young Miss. Not anymore, we don't."

Now, a scatter of creased eyes beamed at them, delighted to see the youthful exuberance of two children. The rest were patient in waiting.

Ambia couldn't stop panting. Slouched and dirtied beneath a disheveled appearance, she looked like an unruly child exhausted after throwing mud. Nonetheless, she was grinning a toothless grin. A clump of mud slopping off her forehead, Ambia flopped back into the mud, giggled, then laughed until the stars saw her tears.

***

The Knight did not chase after the girls. He rotated his helmet as they were leaving. He witnessed the one in front stumble and jerk her head to each of the Knights of the Kings edging the road. The one in the back pinned her gaze on him as her legs moved for her. The Knight was impassive at his post. The two entered the crowds on the opposite side of the road and did not exit again.

He wished he could have had their childhood.

"Whyda *PLOS* do dey go but 'e don't? Ya say blasshitemy! Dat's wha' de is!"

The Knight rotated his head to a sot with his mug aloof and eyes rolling. He had vomited over his tree-brush beard and was stumbling over the boundary the torches created. Everyone in Pulchrit knew not to cross that delineation.

Still, he swayed toward the Knight. He stumbled to his right, foot over unsteady foot, recovered to his left, tried to steady again but took another step too far forward. He was raising a finger and his frothy mouth was opening to protest again when the Knight's shield bashed the sot, every knuckle of him smacked with vanadium metal.

There was the immediate sound of bones crunching as his mug flew. The wheaty ale slewed toward the crowds. The pinewood landed with a softened clank.

The sot was flung backward with the force of a hundred gales. His feet hardly remained on the ground as two other drunkards had to drop their tankards to catch him. All three would've collapsed, but the crowd acted as a cushion for their fall.

The middle one with vomit on his beard sprawled into their embrace. From how hard he was hit, it was a wonder if he could remember where he was or where he was born. His nose could now be mapped as a constellation. Blood spat over his mouth and beard. A contusion exploded around the skin of his nose. His watery eyes were half-lidded but indicated no signs of consciousness. From the belly of his being sounded a long, grave moan as heard from a corpse. None of his limbs moved. They only twitched.

Unconcerned with the drunkards, the Knight returned to his post between the two torches. His shield and spear thudded down. His helmet scanned the masses as to ask if anyone else would dare to encroach on the delineation.

None responded. This piece of the crowd wound tight as the tension straightened their mirth. They could see what would happen to them if they became too loose again.

The Knight did not stir. It remained still and vigilant, waiting for his master's arrival.

***

"And did you see how *tall* the Knight was? Everyone said they were tall but *that* tall!"

Lorna's hands were blurring with gestures, and her toothless grin could have brightened the gloom of a Knight of the King. It was infectious. Ambia could not remember her as being the same friend who, not even a mark heretofore, was paralyzed and unmoving on Courier's Road. It made her heart swell.

Grinning until it hurt, Ambia said, "I'm glad you weren't hurt."

This was a lie. The not being hurt part. Both wore the wounds of their encounter—Ambia whose cheek and temple had become a sickly yellow and Lorna with dried blood trickling from her nose. Ambia could also feel how out of breath she was and the mud in her shoulder-length hair was only now beginning to dry.

"I know! But I didn't and, and you didn't and that Knight, it looked really scary but you, you just..." The wonder in Lorna's eyes now dimmed and dropped to her feet. The grin hid behind disappointment. She whispered, "You were so amazing, Ambia. You were brave and...and confident and, well..." Her fingers fiddled with her dress. The stony homes around them listened quietly. "When I saw that Knight...I was just so *scared*. I couldn't *do* anything. Not even think. But you, Ambia, you were just..."

Her grin was sinking, but Ambia did not let it drown. She slung an arm over Lorna's shoulder and pulled her tight. Though Lorna was taller by knuckles, she always slouched at the shoulders.

"What are you t*aaaa*lk*iiii*ng about, Lorna? You did wonderful! If you weren't with me, who else would I get in trouble with? Mister Omna? Why, I don't even think he could stumble out of the shop in his old age! And any*yyy*wiss*se*," she rose to her ear and whispered. "His dolls are funny lookin' and a tad bit scary, if you ask me."

This prompted a giggle from Lorna, and her self-deprecation

thawed.

Ambia and Lorna, after leaving the ruckus of Courier's Road, entered into the residential district of Pulchrit. The homes were quiet and empty, their stones cracked and weathered. The absence of candle clocks within perpetuated thought and solitude. They could not reflect the ecstasy the girls had after having conquered Courier's Road.

They skipped on clouds. They locked arms and bounced vigorously to the hum of a Mister Salamance song. Their giggles colored the mood. At one point, having exhausted themselves so, they had to slump against a wall of plaster stone to recover their breath. The girls were swimming between the constellations. Actually, more like darting through them. Not even the Bodil Mushrooms sold along the backside of the marketplace could have compared. They triumphed over evil. Their fears were vanquished.

With Gabrien's Colosseum rising beneath the mountain Eius, their bouts began to dwindle. They soon calmed. Their giggles remained. Traveling between alleyways, the pebble-paved roads were scattered as a web and would've been much like an unsolvable labyrinth if they had not been born here. Aius loomed behind as a protective father. The frosty air of Pulchrit rushed into their lungs and exited through toothless gapes.

With Courier's Road abreast to them, Ambia could still hear its commotion and see trails of firelight. Gradually, Lorna's smile shrank. Sweat plastering her black fringe to her brow, she regarded Ambia with a puzzled look.

"You…" Lorna couldn't retain her breath, so she had to stop, both speaking and moving. Ambia did the same and waited for her to recover. "You still haven't told me where we're going."

Resuming their stroll, Ambia kept her eyes forward as through the illusion of searching. She didn't have to. In having traveled there many times heretofore, she knew exactly where and how she was going to get there. Truthfully, Lorna could have blind-folded her, snuck her into the Crimson Crypts, left her there, and still Ambia would find her way back.

An invisible hook tugged at the corner of her smirk. Without looking at Lorna, she said, "You'll see."

She left it at that.

By the time they reached their destination, the first flecks of snow had fallen, and the chill valley winds whisked at their skin. Their hair clumped and tossed across their eyes like stalks of wheat. The windy shrills sliced across the throats of Eius and Aius and chafed against the building the two girls were staring at. They remained silent. Their breath puffed warm, visible clouds.

Beside the homes of Pulchrit, the library was impressive—twice the height of its stone neighbors and thrice the girth. Though its size could not match the esteemed Nexlor whose ebony entrance gave access to famous scholars such as Falmos Soulious and Valoma Bordeur, the library did claim the second tallest building in Pulchrit; the first honors were given to the four-story inn called the Sleeping Bear which beckoned for visitors over at the marketplace's Eastern end.

Across its front gazed circular glass eyes, three abreast. An arched ironwood door tripled the height of Ambia with steel rivets and a pair of pendulous handles. This was the newest addition to the building. The walls, having stood since the reign of King Aius, were further deteriorated than the stone around it and looked, to Ambia at least, like the wizened skin of Mister Omna. Inside, volumes and tomes—new and old, pristine and ragged—overwhelmed sight. Scrawny ladders slid back and forth between precipitous bookcases. The one-time Missus Veralesta allowed her to climb to the top rung, Ambia experienced a mingle of exhilaration and vertigo. She didn't know which one to trust but knew that one day she would try again and find out.

Nevertheless, heights and ladders did not stop her from exploring each word that inundated the hall. It was a pleasant sight to behold, a plethora of knowledge to absorb: extensive writings on healing and sealing, limited writings on destructive spells, Pidamos of Pulchrit and its former kings, tales from over the Grey Sea, within the Grey Sea, and along the Grey Sea (her favorite being from the writer Ye'Ming'Wah), troubadour songs about the throes of love that Ambia would often recite to Lorna at night. There were even personal accounts from the Temple of Health and Death Ambia had skimmed through once, twice, a billion times. Anything her eyes could inhale. The library gave her solace in times of distress. It was her sanctuary. Granted, she loved creating trouble inside the marketplace or exploring the city with Lorna, but she reserved these times for the onset of dusk. During the day, the library was where the townspeople would find her nose buried inside the satisfying musk of parchment.

Her hazels gleamed in the starlight. Her grin awoke as she remembered the readings she delved into that day—an extensive look at how Ontinia, during the reign of King Cantem the First, annexed the Silent Swamps.

Ambia could take it no longer.

Like an arrow released from a bow, she shot forward toward the side of the library where a ladder was.

"Ambia, wait, I…"

But Ambia was gone. Her objective was clear. She swung onto the first rung and before she could blink again, she had climbed halfway up. Her toothless smile was drunk with eagerness, and the times she glanced back down, Lorna was there, rubbing her hands together, glancing around with no one to greet her besides the howl of the wind.

With the ladders' twig-thin rungs squeaking in pain, Ambia ascended and was already approaching the top when she looked down again. Thankfully, Lorna reached the ladder with her hands firmly clasped together. Her eyes were ascending the ladder one rung at a time.

Ambia, under the drink of daring, hung off the ladder with one hand, wind combing through muddied clothes and hair, and waved to her friend.

This is what sailors feel like, Ambia thought for certain, even though she had never seen the sea with the nearest one being leagues away.

When Lorna's eyes touched her friend, Ambia could see her toy silhouette shudder.

"It's *wonderful* up here, Lorna!" Ambia shouted. From the way Lorna would not move or look away from her, Ambia did not think Lorna agreed. "Come on already. King Ventem won't be very happy if we're late!"

Another lie, but Ambia had to do *anything* to get Lorna up here; someone would have thought Ambia had picked the scariest ladder in all of Pulchrit.

Gingerly, Lorna regarded the ladder again. She reached out to touch one of its rungs and flinched. She stared at it as if staring at a blood-thirsty mountain lion, and then finally took to the first rung and began to climb, albeit as would a sloth approaching the jaws of said mountain lion.

Ambia gave in to an impish giggle and then finished her ascent.

***

Eventually, Lorna popped her head above the roof where metal clamps were the only structure holding the ladder to the library. A calmness curved the corner of Ambia's mouth as she turned back to behold Courier's Road.

She was dangling her legs off the roof's three-story ledge, rhythmically humming the same Mister Salamance tune they sang through the alleyways. Her head and shoulders swayed side to side, her legs to and fro. Before her was a sight only Pulchrit could have offered. Beneath her legs squatted one stone home though its roof hardly hindered their view of the road. Crowds were still rumbling but were becoming more and more restless. The marketplace had drained of customers. The alleyway they entered through was now thronged with onlookers. Together, they were one egg of anticipation that would crack and burst upon the arrival of their King. The Knights of the Kings bore their vigil sternly.

Above the marketplace judged the sheer precipice of Aius—an insignificant road carved as a wrinkle to its face—but even above Aius were the constellations, absurdly bright as they always were—the curves of Xeyes's Horns, the boat bow of Imes's Journey, the supposed face of Gargenexous.

Ambia's eyes were mapping these constellations when she heard Lorna from behind her.

"Do we...um..." Lorna was not even ten hands near the edge yet. Written over her face was the basic fear of a child hearing a snake in the grass. "Do we-we *have* to watch King Ventem from up-up here?"

Ambia scrunched her cheeks into an expression of discontent only an innocent child could manage without looking ridiculous.

"Of *course* we have to!" She said, throwing her arms awry. Having neither of her hands clutch the ledge to hold herself against the winds made her look like she was riding a loose wagon rolling down a hill. "Why *else* would we come up here!"

Ambia then shook her head, fostered an adventurous grin, and padded the spot next to her. Three soft taps, like everything was fine and nothing bad could happen.

It looked like King Ventem had told her to hop into a casket in the Crimson Crypts.

"Ambia...I...Please, I can't...I just can't..."

"Sure you can! You just don't *know* you can."

"But I..."

Ambia lifted a finger at her. "No butts Lorna! We see too many of those already!"

Despite her obvious fears, Lorna giggled. It couldn't be helped. Ambia had her now.

When the giggling subsided, Lorna cast another unwilling look at the ledge and then made her first shuffles toward it. Her eyes were downcast and squinted and were near to squeezing shut before Ambia leaned back to slip her hand into hers. The hand was a small clam of perspiration.

Lorna peered open her eyes the tiniest bit, reckoned their touch, and then loosened her stiffness so Ambia could guide her forward. Her steps were piece by piece. Reluctantly, Lorna took a seat next to her. She didn't hang her legs over; she scuttled her butt across the stone and peeked her toes over.

At least this time she came to me, Ambia thought and made another giggly and childish sound that rippled through her limbs.

King Ventem was belated in his arrival. The mood of the crowds reflected this. The marketplace was completely empty now—even of merchants—and every alleyway was so packed, they could not fit in another mouse. The scuffle between Miss Cartine and that Granis fellow disbanded in good cheer. However, this did not mean there weren't others. Pulchrit's anticipation for its King was swelling and so did their restlessness. Ambia and Lorna witnessed another three brawls break out and one disbanding when they had first arrived. Perhaps Miss Cartine and Granis were part of these, too, but the girls were too far away to tell.

In light of this, the Knights of the Kings had a harder time keeping order. Tumbles of fouls kept crossing over the boundary and many broken bones were sustained. Yet these physical punishments and warnings weren't enough. Along many stretches of Courier's Road, the Knights had taken on a defensive stance where their shields protected their massive bodies and their spears lowered as a threat. Their steel glinted, ready to pounce. The slits of their helmets gave access to the bottomlessness of their armor.

Beside her, Lorna's eyes were like unmoving, illuminous moons. She still griped her hand, wringing out the blood with how hard she was squeezing. Ambia didn't mind. Her fingers were now laced with Lorna's, her hold equally as firm.

Lorna gave Ambia a sidelong glance that ended in an uneasy smile. Ambia smiled back.

A sudden roar of exhilaration exploded to their left. This startled them, especially Lorna who Ambia feared would jump from her seat and fall into the alleyway below. When the girls recovered, they both gazed at where the throngs began on Courier's Road, where the noise was not abating but growing. The two could not see those in the very front because of a two-story home but those farther down were jostling and pushing and vying against the constant threat of the Knights. Regardless, the girls could very well *hear* them; hollers, calls for undying love, chanting in one pocket, shrieks that pierced eardrums, squeals like that of hungry pigs reverberated from the belly of Courier's Road.

Their exhilaration was contagious. It rode through the throngs in a waxing wave until nothing could be heard over the cacophony of voices.

It was King Ventem. Their King had arrived.

***

Ambia experienced that tingling again.

It resurfaced from her heart like a carriage emerging from the mountain's fog. Soon, her hands would tremble. Soon, her smile would strain. Soon, her eyes would beam from their sockets. Soon, she'd become so excited she'd jump off, forget she was sitting on a ledge, dash through the crowds and dash toward King Ventem and give him a hug thrice as big as her love. She'd do this. Somehow. In the realm of Ambia, it was all possible.

The crowds along Courier's Road were the combers of a relentless sea. Their bodies crashed together. The ale in their tankards spumed over residents uncaring for smell and appearance. Each time they surged forward, they were reared back by Knights and so on and so forth until they achieved the motion of an ocean.

Those in the windows above were tamer but not by much. Children fought for an opening on the sill, playful but bordering on a savage eagerness. Mothers were helpless in their control. The anticipation of children was too great. Across the homes, whistles shrilled. Flecks of snow drifted down.

When the head of the procession arrived, the crowds were positively vibrating. Men and women, groomed and shaven for the occasion, arrived first. There must have counted a hundred with mules to carry their possessions. Despite being part of King Ventem's entourage, their elegant doublets and dresses were dirtied from days of rough travel through the mountains, but their auras burned bright with the relief of being home.

They waved as they strolled past. The air rumbled not only with sound but also with tangible items. Mud pellets and pine needles were tossed to the procession in celebration and call for good fortune. From the windows came garlands, branches, and other mountainous plants. And, as it so happened, the procession did not shy away from returning the favor. From their pouches, they tossed back bits of bread and even moxam, the cheapest form of currency in Admah. The deadened Illum pebbles landed in the crowds and tipped them into a frenzy. Men and women scattered and leaped and stomped on the stones with feet that could break fingers. Most residents in the crowds were wealthy enough to sustain the basic necessities of life, but the prominence of having a moxam from the King was a treat sought by all.

The vanguard continued their act down Courier's Road followed by a horse-drawn carriage. The combers of the crowd settled as their gazes were rapt with wonder. The Knights never relaxed.

Though King Ventem was not a king known for how extravagant he was, his carriage was. It rode erect like a castle crossed with imposing battlements and detailed decoration. Watermill wheels rolled by with golden spokes, and dark velvet green curtains draped inside its glass windows. At each corner was a sconce structured like a merlon with a fist of Illum inside. The light's easy-to-the-eyes glow carried the carriage through the gutter of flames like an apparition rolling through a hearth. Burly twin stallions hulled the carriage from Ironwood harnesses. Caparisons were laid over their backs, the golden roaster of Ontinia sewn into a satin green background. The coachman—clad in Ontinia's decorous yet solemn hues, a man Ambia had never met but called "Lazy Eye" for obvious reasons—reined the stallions forward. His stare regarded no one besides the road, but the eye he was known for betrayed him by rolling around in the crowds. Across the top of the carriage was a headdress of snow.

If the carriage did not exude enough of a presence, the Knights around it more than compensated. There were five of them who had arrived with the King—one in the lead, two at the hip, and three rounding the rear. The Shire horses they rode on oversaw the crowd, their steel horseshoes able to easily crush a head by accident. Together with the Knights, they were moving mountains. Their spears were their peaks. Shields were the faces that eyed the residents. Their awe, both in fear and wonder, struck the crowds still. Despite their feral love for King Ventem, none were drunk or insane enough to impede on the Knights. They liked their heads rounded, not flat.

At the start, with the wind rising to whip her hair, Ambia could not clearly see the inside of the carriage. It was too far away from them. But once the carriage and horses became centered within their view, the insides of the carriage became clearer. Within, after a long night of anticipation, sat their beloved King.

Age lived with King Ventem, but its stay was amiable and cordial. His features were dashing. His hair of polished steel was combed and ruffled back in curls. A crown was nowhere to be seen, a circumstance common during his reign, and his lean physique bore a doublet whose cotton could have been bought at the marketplace. Ambia would have believed it. When his entourage was not traversing to another nation or when he was not invested with the dealings of Ontinia's Opinens, the King enjoyed walking through his streets and talking with his people and any authority or distinction between them was implied through his ancient azure gaze, dignified and gentle like a dream.

Wrinkles emphasized the wisdom of his age. King Ventem did not retain the glutton of King Salamance the Second, the sloth of King Halos, or the derangement of King Cantem the Second. He instead bore the smile of a friend, a lover, a common man if not for his title and presence. That smile made Ambia think she could achieve any ambition; the stars were but a hand away. If this was not convincing enough, the Pulchrit people, custom to their nature as residents of the capital, had given their king a title—Ventem, the Beloved King.

Ambia could not stop smiling.

Her whoops vociferated out from her caved hands into the uproar of clapping and screaming. Lorna was equally excited for King Ventem, Ambia could tell, but she only stuck to her voice muffled by the cacophony. Her hands were still cemented to the ledge perhaps griping tighter now against the onset of the winds.

Then, Ambia noticed something. Nothing detrimental or revolutionary but something that was just...different. She had experienced the arrival and departure of King Ventem several times heretofore and was accustomed to what should and should not be at these festivals. So far, much of what she had experienced was the same if not extraordinary a myriad times over.

But the boy...he was different.

He was sitting next to King Ventem in the carriage, and Ambia reckoned he was about four or five years older than she was. She squinted to distinguish him further but had little success in parsing his features. What she did find was not hopeful. His clothes were new, but she thought the roughness of his tanned skin did not match his apparel. It was like forcing a peg into a keyhole; it just did not fit. His shaggy fringe, long but clean, concealed his eyes and most of his face. His hands were on his knees, and his knees were in a position of waiting. The curtains on his side of the carriage, those opposite of Ambia, had been drawn close to seclude him from the mirth of the festival. He did not look. Pulchrit could have vanished with its sounds, sights, and smells, and it would have made no difference to the boy.

Throughout her childhood, Ambia had never seen anyone besides Queen Voluma in that carriage and that, too, was a rarity. Usually, when either the King or Queen left Pulchrit, the other stayed behind, a direct consequence to what happened to King Aius the Second and his family when they returned from Cotana.

Regardless, the boy intrigued Ambia. It was perhaps how he was not supposed to be here, in Pulchrit or in the carriage. It was perhaps his ambiguity, what she did not know about him and what she wanted to know. Perhaps, even, it was this foreign feeling of interest toward a boy older than she was. Attraction on the side of romance was not a feeling she often experienced. Her heart had taken root into the soil of Pulchrit, and no boy was enough to dig it out.

But him...this boy...just one look, just one, had struck that stalk hard.

For this reason, and many others she couldn't point at, she felt it necessary to comfort the boy as the trail of life approached, to tend to his wounds as his companion, to talk to him when his stoicism faltered, and to be there when he needed her most. It was all absurd. She had no basis for these feelings, and it startled her to feel this...intimate with anything besides Pulchrit's stone walls, marketplace, and citizens. It almost felt...well, wrong.

But the feelings were there. Butterfly wings fluttered in her stomach. Sweat became noticeable between her palms. If Lorna were to look at her now, she would be shocked to find her friend's cheeks baking bright and red.

Though after the embarrassment settled and her cheeks cooled, Ambia couldn't deny how interesting and incredible a future with the boy could be. It would be like finishing off the decorations to a house, impressive as it already was—her city Pulchrit, her friend Lorna, her new love, boy without name. It all pointed toward an optimistic future.

Possibilities swirled. Her smile became a daze and her eyes starry. Noises were in her ears.

It would be the three of them, she decided. They would caper through Pulchrit with the boy noticing small, unobtrusive details that Ambia and Lorna, in their seven years of living here, had become accustomed to over time and had thus—

A nudge startled her awake. She gasped, and it took her a moment for her eyes to adjust and her body to regain itself, but the first thing she reckoned was how strong the winds had become.

It whipped at the stone and stirred the dust, wailing between Pulchrit's fingers. Ambia had to squint during some of its bouts and push the heels of her palms against the ledge so not to be tossed off into the dark embrace below. She should've been scared, terrified, absolutely petrified.

She wasn't.

The screaming and hollering of the crowds had gone. There was only the backend of the entourage still in sight. The Knights had encircled behind its trickle to form a two-lined cavalcade at the rear. At the start of Courier's Road, the citizens were disbanding, spilling onto the road and becoming an unhurried stumble toward the residential district, like slow-minded ants ready to return home.

King Ventem's going had prompted the night's end. There were honorable citizens who were helping the worst of them get back to their feet. There'd still be bodies left on Courier's Road innocuously moaning until first light. Parents in homes along the road gathered their children, their small heads trying to pop out of the windows to catch the last glimpse of the entourage. The marketplace dimmed to the black of the sky. Torches guttered.

Ambia also noticed Lorna behind her. She had retreated many hands away from the ledge and shook in her boots. Her hands cupped opposite shoulders, and her expression crumbled back to fear. Her dress whipped like a flag. Ambia had not even realized she had let go of Lorna's hand.

"Ambia…The-the winds…I think it's time to…"

As if summoned, a gale roared. It whisked across her face and fed Ambia her brunette hair. She spat and made a disgusted sound. It tasted of muddied straw. Loose strands clung to her tongue so one by one she picked at them. After cleaning her mouth, Ambia squinted down into the alleyway, hmmed, and let out a long, low sigh with a shoulder slump.

"I guess you're right. Winds aren't too friendly this night, huh Lorna?"

Ambia didn't get an answer but did hear the muted chatter of teeth.

Even though the winds gushed across the valley, Ambia shoved herself up with minimal care. It must have scared Lorna to no end. She breasted the wind to near her friend and gave her a smile of love and warmth, one that, within the years to follow, when King Ventem would die of old age whiles the rest of Pulchrit—Mister Salamance, Mister Omna, Miss Cartine, Missus Veralesta, Mister Marque—were about to follow him to the grave, would become tainted by the hand of the Black Rings.

For now, she simply smiled.

"Let's go home, Lorna."

VIII

Whiles Chry and Ambia were gone to the physician and Onvi was unfounded until the following morning when the Runners stumbled upon him snoring inside one of the stable stalls, Bar remained at the Hungry Wolf Inn. They, both he and Vion, had returned after meeting with the Council of Crystal, breasting against the slashing rain and crackling thunder. The paunchy innkeeper glanced at them in friendly acknowledgment but then quickly returned to his patrons. This night, the storm was flushing the sailors out from the decks and streets to cluster beneath the closest roof.

Thus the commotion within the inn was as boisterous as the storm itself. Laughter bellowed from the belly. The sailor's sea shanties engulfed the singing of the inn's entertainment—a young, timid man whose hypnotic voice soothed the voice within Bar. Periodically, there'd be a hiatus between shanties for sailors to insult those from other ships. Intermittently, a brawl would erupt and the guards—twins of bald heads and brawny builds titled Kars and Yars—would interrupt the fists and throw out the ruffians. This did not deplete the night of foolishness. When two men were tossed out, three more sailors and a father from the Slums entered. By each mark of the candle, the common room became more and more vulgar, sweaty, and uncontrollable.

Bar had taken to a dusky, abandoned corner of the inn, a mug of mirky water beside him brought by the innkeeper's son. His finger could not stop tapping on the tabletop. His stare rarely left the entrance. He had meant to rest but couldn't, not yet.

Vion, having disregarded the innkeepers and unspoken to Bar since leaving Aedilium, shouldered down the hall to his room, unloaded his equipment, and exited from the back door. This did not happen often. When they normally stayed at an inn, Vion would seize a table and mug for the night or sit with Bar until the time came for slumber. Even then, words between them were by obligation rather than by leisure. This day was different. The Council of Crystal divulged much to the Runners, the most jarring being they'd encounter the Derk again on their journey for the gems.

Bar did not stop him or say a word. His troubles were of little consequence to his ambition. The irregularity was disregarded.

He sipped on his water. It was dirty and went down coarse, but it was the cleanest the inn had. The storm raged on. The hands of thunder clapped. Other than the door and those who went through it, Bar did not look elsewhere. Patrons entered and slipped from his vision, but his stare shuffled between each. He was in waiting for the others and was not greeted by a familiar face until the late stages of twilight.

Cavas was the first to return. He strode in as innocuous. His person and air should have been noticed like a bonfire in the night if it did not fill the space with emptiness. He avoided all physical contact, impressive in a room packed shoulder to shoulder, but his most obvious feature, if one were to pay him a glance, was that his robes were dry. The cloth of every other guest was dripping from the storm and creating pockets of puddles beneath them, but Cavas looked as if he had strolled through a garden on a bright and sunny day. This was not unusual. Bar took little notice.

Upon entering, Cavas stopped to turn his head toward Bar. He did this without searching as if knowing exactly where Bar would be. The mage stared and Bar did likewise. This was their exchange of information—Cavas had arrived safely and would now ascend the stairs to the room the innkeeper had set aside for him, a closet unused by the keepers. They preferred this. He'd rather have the mage stored away than to risk him being with sailors known to be precarious and violent. This way, there was more chance for stability and less chance for provocation.

Order was a necessity.

Ambia and Chry would be next but Bar had to wait for two marks before they showed. In that time, the inn roughened. He had finished his water in which the innkeeper's son replenished without him having to ask. How he tended to Bar so nimbly against these hordes of sailors was in of itself notable. Granted, Bar was well acquainted with both the innkeeper and his son. During his first visit to Cadaqu, Bar saved the son from the Pig Pen. Now, every time he visited the Hungry Wolf, the boy would shyly smile in bringing his water and both the innkeeper and son would make an effort to keep Bar satisfied. They were a hardworking family, friendly. Bar admired them and would remember their benevolence when the day came for Cadaqu to be cleansed.

The sailors were of a different ilk. They, with beautiful women sparse in the Slums and most so ugly not to be considered, would ogle at the pretty, young face of the man who had come to sing and even at the innkeeper's nine-year-reckon son. Bar imagined gouging their eyes and dismembering their fingers so they would not have the opportunity to satisfy their lusts. When the day came for judgment, Bar reckoned this fate would be much too benevolent and would assure their deaths were as excruciating as the suffering they inflicted.

This night, the sentiment exacerbated when a mangle of them thought they could intimidate Bar into relinquishing his table. The inn had depleted of seats and benches and now a disease had infected the minds of the patrons convincing them that they could take Bar's. It happened twice. His table was insignificant with two high chairs and a tabletop he could wrap his arms around. Nevertheless, the sailors were relentless. The first retreated after Bar fondled the hilt of his sword. The night was still young, and these sailors retained enough wit to forgo trading an arm for a seat. The second time was not as smooth. The supposed leader of the five, gabbling about his position as the quartermaster for *The Flying Maiden*, thought himself worthy enough to deny Bar his seat.

Once the quartermaster stood in front of where Bar sat, his doltish grin thinking he had conquered the table, Bar seized the lump of his head and smashed it against the wall's rotting oak. The act was so swift, the followers did not even gasp before Bar was ramming his knee into the man's stomach and *stabbing*

clawing his eyes

disemboweling his guts until he was

laying on the floor. Afterward, Bar took his seat and sipped on his dirty water. The others stared at him, blank and petrified. Kars and Yars chuckled at the door. From then on, none of the sailors bothered him.

Ambia and Chry arrived thereafter. They were both drenched from the storm, and their clothing stuck to them as if pasted with mortar. Ambia was the first real woman, slim but graceful, that caught the lust of the sailors. Though this was for naught. Upon the order of the innkeeper, she was under the protection of Kars and Yars whose jeers had become frigid glares as she passed through. All the same, the sailors were not warded off until they noticed Bar adding his stare as well. From then on, none batted an eye.

Chry followed behind Ambia but did not look up from his feet. His expression was pinched into petulant thought. Ambia first went to the innkeeper bustling between tables and waited for his services. Her hair was ruffled, and the wet tatters of her dress brushed at the floorboards. Here she stood beneath a circle of disquietude. They would have waited half the night with how busy the innkeeper was if he did not catch a glimpse of them.

Instead, the innkeeper tended to them as generously as he had with Bar. His smile was genuine, his plump lips moved, and his stubby fingers pointed upstairs. Both Ambia and Chry nodded, their eyes looking through thought, their lips motionless as they ascended the stairs to where they would spend the night. She did not look at Bar. Her eyes were absent.

Bar watched this from afar and was unsurprised by what he found. He warned her about hope, how flimsy it could be and had been. Her experiences with the Black Rings heretofore should have solidified his argument, but he reckoned her connection with Pulchrit was too hardy to break through the top soil. It would take time. Realization was a piecemeal process. He could uncover the truths and guide her toward her natural inclinations, but her determination was undeniable. It was one reason he had chosen her. For the time being, he would merely comfort and console her. Soon, she'd come to understand her duties as his love and then their mother.

Soon.

He continued sipping on his water until the mug was empty. As if sensing this, the son came around again with his boyish smile and their tin jug of water. Bar waved him off but not before thanking him with a mox. The son was beaming when he left.

Afterward, Bar regarded the inn. He reckoned the alleviation of suffering that could be achieved if merely the depraved were destroyed.

By fire, it said.

By fire, he thought.

Not long thereafter, he pushed his stool back, stood, dusted off his gambeson, and then ascended the stairs to Ambia, his intended love.

IX

The room was left for his Discernments to decorate. The closest object he could call a decoration was the candle cloak holder on the mud-stained floor, its iron rust coloring an otherwise compact and bleak room. Along the right wall, Ambia sat on a thin mattress of straw. She was staring out a window stained with grime as a cascade of rain struck its glass. There were no tears. Her eyes were distant and nonresponsive to Bar's entrance. He stood there at the door and admired her beauty.

He did not see Chry in here, leading him to believe Chry was in Cavas's room. If Chry was sleeping in Bar and Vion's room, it would be like a chicken slumbering inside a cage of Maroon Panthers. Even so, Bar did not approve of having him stay with Cavas either. Leaving Cavas to his own was not a written rule, but every Runner knew the circumstance was preferable—better to leave the spirits unperturbed than risk breaking the seal.

In regard to this day and every day thereafter, Bar thought Chry would stay with Ambia and Onvi as they were the Runners most interested in his well-being. But that, Bar could see, would not happen this night. Onvi was nowhere to be found, and Ambia was in no condition to comfort a broken soul. As uncommon as this was for Ambia, it allowed him the opportunity to console her. That, in the least, would be invaluable.

He bent down to rest next to her. Her stare did not find him. He stirred to make himself comfortable. Thereafter, he regarded her again, traced her still stare to the window, and mimicked her. They remained pensive like this as the storm raged on. Finally, he said with a steady voice, "If you do not wish to speak on the matter, then we do not have to. Your decision will be respected."

Silence. Strands of her brunette hair sagged over her hazels. They were deadened to the present like the nonresponsive eyes of a Black Rings victim. In a sense, she was a victim. Perhaps not literally, but her struggle against suffering was there and surely felt. The difference was she had the potential to shed its malignant coat and return to the moment as a stronger and healthier human being. He expected this to happen. Those who had contracted the Black Rings did not have the same potential. They were subject to insurmountable suffering before the grave. Relief was all Bar could offer them. This was what he had done. This was what he would do.

Searching for a cure was a child's folly.

Between their breaths drummed cracks of thunder. Below them was the muffled babbling of the inn, the sailors' shanties a distant hum. In the room next door, someone mumbled in their sleep. He could not hear what was said over the storm.

"Why did you not tell me about Heva Na Narth?"

What Ambia asked Bar was unprepared for. His response was reactionary.

"For?"

Her neck creaked to regard him. Within the bleakness of her stare was the decay of love.

"Do not play with me, Barloc. Not now. The Black Rings and

Heva Na Narth are too similar for you not to have noticed."

Bar looked at the far wall. The wood, rotten and mildewy as to exude a silent stench of must, was easier to cope with than to confront Ambia eye to eye. He could hardly stand it. He could hardly understand why this nest of worms had begun squirming inside his chest. Bar could not remember the last time he felt so undecided and disconcerted.

What was happening to him?

"Heva Na Narth happened before my involvement with the Derk. The details of the disease were inconsequential to my livelihood as a warrior."

Liar

"So you know nothing that would help me find a cure?"

"Nay."

Her nose twitched, but she nodded anywise and returned her stare to the opposite wall. Many questions and conversations could've taken place then, most of the roads leading to a gruesome tragedy.

His past was not a subject Bar liked to discuss.

Outside their room, the heavy stomps of a patron who had not stopped eating since birth hastened past the door. Their slurred, baritone voice commanded the hall, but Bar was too absorbed in her to have listened.

"I—" Ambia mumbled and dropped her hazels. Her dewy lips opened, hesitated, and then pressed close. Bar waited to listen. In a careworn murmur, she said, "Nostre...the physician, I mean...I was talking to Nostre whiles Chry was away and I...I..."

She paused. Her olive skin turned white like the petals of a daisy but flushed at her cheeks.

"I was in awe...Nostre...He possessed a scope of knowledge I had not seen since my time in the Nexlor. Goodness, Barloc, you should have met him. Hundreds of diseases, each one documented with precision and detail. A sea of patients and stories to tell. Pages and pages of manuscripts. He even possessed a personality that was easily accessible to where I felt free to express all my unbidden thoughts. I do not encounter people like him often."

A prick of jealousy. Bar stayed the image.

"Nostre had years and decades of conferring with and listening to patients," she said. "I value this experience as much as his documentation and knowledge. Perhaps more. However, this was not what I admired most about him. What I admired most was his passion...Barloc, I have not met a man so vehement in fighting against the Black Rings as I was during its first wave. Back then, I thought we could save everyone. I thought *I* could. I could still see the hope in their eyes, the same hope I saw in Nostre's even after all these years of frustration and failure. He was not outspoken of this passion, and yet he did not need to be. Each word he spoke in regard to the Black Rings or Heva Na Narth or any other disease held a promise that he intended to keep. He...He was everything I was and more..."

Whiles she related this, Ambia stared blankly at her lap. Her hands were limp and bore no signs of life.

"Then Chry returned and he..." She swallowed. "Told me about the cadavers in the cellar...I reckoned Nostre was using them as subjects in his search for the cure. This was not in doubt. What was in doubt was if he had killed them or not—if these patients had died naturally or if he had led them there himself."

Her jaw clenched as if the words she wished to speak had locked the bone. Eventually, she did continue, but her voice contracted an unbearable shake.

"I did not see what was in the cellar. I...I do not want to know."

She struggled to push forward. Her breasts, strangled by her kiwi bodice, fluttered. She kept swallowing but her breath would not be at ease.

Bar waited for an opportunity.

"Chry went on...He went on about how Nostre butchered the patients. I could see the hatred in his eyes and how he compared Nostre to the scum across his sole and the grotesque acts he had seen and what other acts would come if we did not stop him. All that became of his eyes were accusations and disdain. A physician that kills patients and uses their bodies as subjects. A physician that k— A physician that..."

Her throat worked, but nothing came. Finally, she broke. Her head trembled, her lips too, so intensely that every word from then on became an impediment. A tear escaped her.

"Chry could never understand…but I do. I'd sacrifice all of Admah if it meant saving Pulchrit…That…it…it would…"

She stopped herself because her breath was shuddering and what came next demanded much.

"I…Nostre…He said he could not promise me that he wouldn't kill again and I, goodness, I…"

Her chin would not release its stiffness. Ambia closed her eyes and tried not to lose hope.

"I let him go, Barloc. I left him there. I didn't try to stop him. I took Chry, and I left and…and all I could think about was if he'd have the cure by the time I saw him again. Nothing else, no, nothing else mattered."

She sniffed and then wiped a tear away with a finger, hesitated, wiped again and again, but each time there was more and more until she was sobbing openly. She concealed this with her palms. Bar listened to her repeat, "I'd sacrifice everyone, Barloc, everyone," with a motionless desire for vengeance.

He wanted to kill Nostre for making her cry.

He wanted to.

He would.

Her choppy gasps saturated the room.

"Who would allow such a thing? What kind of abomination would allow…What am I, Barloc? Who am I?" Her sobs were a river feeding into an ocean. She could not stop herself. "Am I like Nostre? Am-am I an abomination, too?"

This was when he responded. He leaned forward and took her into his embrace. She collapsed into his arms and stuffed her tears into his gambeson.

Her bodice and skirt were soaked from the storm and thus dampened his clothing. He nuzzled his nose into her hair which smelled of dank strawberries picked after a hard rain. He stroked her back. They were intertwined within a tender era, his heart beating smooth and steady for her to listen.

"Nay," he whispered. "You are nothing of the kind."

Her control had broken. The sobs were so immense, she could not speak and instead shuddered in his arms. This was fine with Bar. It was the moment he had wanted. A moment to console.

"You are only human," he said.

Then he held her as she cried herself to sleep.

Vion's Exhumation

I

Chry never saw the sea heretofore. Not once. They had imagined, he and Aimee, what it might look like, but he never truly believed it as true. To him, it was a fanciful legend more like a Kemal or those Es'Tal'Mis Giants. Now that he was riding beside the sea, now that he could see its never-ending surface, he could not stop gazing with baggy eyes. Before now, he never thought he'd see a blue so vibrant, Domum only offering blue in the form of dirty water and rusted pails. And those little birdies that soared and said *mine, mine* as if calling for the fish they were diving for under the water? What *were* those things? Compared to Dry-Mouths and that hound-vulture creature he had once seen when riding to Domum, they were the most innocent creatures he had ever encountered. He even saw, when first riding out from Cadaqu, one of those carriages called a "ship" riding on the sea's surface. Up until then, Chry did not think it possible for any man-made vessel to ride on the seas. How was it possible then for such a big, bulging block of wood to float like that?

Still, there was something missing from the picture, a part of him contained inside the sapphire necklace around his neck. Aimee. They had dreamed of this day together. Now it was here, and he wished she could've been here to experience it, too. Like they promised they would. In her room. On the Vassal's roof. Through the legs of Domum.

Now she's gone, he thought within a grogginess. *To a land far from here...with the Black Rings plague.*

Chry held in a shiver.

The sea, Aimee, and his sleepless nights made his heart heavy with a weird whirlpool of grandeur, disappointment, and grief. The feeling continued through their journey East toward a town Bar had named Neco. The storm from the night heretofore spilled over into this day but had become less violent. Skies were grey and drizzling as if too spent to pour. The coastal precipice had fallen off to their right. From its bowels sounded the ocean tugging at the crags of the coastline. Compared to the raging waves that had just ensued, its waters were calm with needles of rain pricking its face. Behind them ranged a flat and muddy field.

This stretch of the journey was dreary and silent. Their horses trudged through moist grass and shallow patches of mud while riding behind one another: Bar in front, Cavas in the rear, Onvi, Ambia, Chry, and Vion in between. The sumpter Chry rode upon Bar had received from a friend in the stables before leaving the Slums. This was also after Bar dealt with Onvi and his stay with the horses. Neither he nor the hostler was pleased. Bar thus settled the inconvenience by handsomely compensating the hostler, courtesy of his mox. Chry did not think to ask how he had received the mox when Bar had said, not too long heretofore, that he did not have enough to sustain Chry as a Runner. Mayhap he got it from his meeting with the Council. Mayhap he got it from somewhere else. Chry was too exhausted and timid to ask.

Ambia wasn't, but when she asked Bar why there were extra bags of coins rattling on his saddle, why their steeds had fresh bronze horseshoes with clean, groomed coats, or why they were heading to Neco when they were just there half a Son heretofore, their leader told her they would rest at his house in Neco and then discuss it the following dawn. She seared Bar with a suspicious scowl that she then tossed to Vion riding, at the time, beside Bar. He was glaring off ahead. She addressed him with a question but received only a grunt.

Unsatisfied, she rode next to Vion and redirected her questions to that Heva Na Narth disease. The conversation did not end well. Vion responded with his normal grunts and what pursued was a long, dragging argument. Ambia spat questions and then accusations. Vion ignored, gave one-off snarls, and grumbled a threat he would not deliver on but would have scared off any sane human being. It ended when Ambia, fuming, led her white gelding back behind Chry. Her expression was screwed into a frustrated scowl. Soon, she chilled and sooner still, she reverted to a face of brooding similar to when she was returning from Nostre's house.

After this clash, the Runners remained confined to themselves. Even Onvi, whose mouth could not stop moving, was absent of words. Instead, there was only a persistent moan. He did not speak to anyone. Yawning, Chry rode behind him with his hood protecting him from the drizzle. In truth, he was concerned for the thief. Onvi was swaying in his saddle, rubbing at his brow where there'd be a headsore, and mumbling to himself about "blood and ashes." The others did not seem to hear. Mayhap it was just one of those things that a Runner got used to, Onvi waking drunk and nauseous.

But if Onvi dealt with the passing of his sobriety, Chry dealt with the passing of his sleep. The Grey Sea could only capture his fascination for so long, yet it could not restore the nights he lost. He was still having those nightmares, as he had last night in the inn, but this time, it was not the farmhouse but Nostre's cellar, Aimee in the corner eating and slurping, tossing glances back at him and licking at her lips, Grandma on the table handling a hand, head back, moaning with pleasure. Like the nightmare with Vion, he was paralyzed and could not look away. Their lips never stirred, but their voices were just as clear.

And why would our courageous crow not want to join us? Much better to use that useless cock than to...

His sleeplessness added saggy bruises to his eyes, a buzzing sensitivity to his skin, and a sluggishness to his riding. He had nodded off in his saddle more than once, and once, he almost fell off his horse completely, but the stirrup caught his foot and woke him. Ambia saw this bumbling act and asked him if he needed to rest, that they could stop. He had said no, he was well enough to ride.

It almost seemed like these nights would never leave.

He bundled into his cloak to preserve the little warmth he had. Its wool was bloated with rain.

"Is that a necklace?"

Chry was startled into recognizing a foreign figure beside him. It was Vion, and those silver eyes, penetrating and unrelenting, were coiling around his neck.

Oh Arbiter have mercy, he thought. *Why didn't I see him sooner?*

Chry glanced down at his sapphire necklace dangling just above his bundled cloak and then back at Vion. He couldn't help from cowering into himself.

"Um, aye, I got it from…"

"You look like a pathetic boy."

A pang of hurt crossed Chry's expression. "But I got it from…"

"It is where your erok nak went," Vion grunted and turned. The conversation, as quickly as it began, ended. His attention was directed elsewhere, his mare driving forward to reach Bar at the vanguard.

Chry had his mouth ajar as to say something to defend himself but instead yawned. He couldn't help it. Vion, that beast, could petrify him with only a word.

He was speechless as the Runners rode on, his eyes weary and dragging.

II

Travel was laborious and longer than expected. They had to rest early on to dry beneath a copse of oaks and alders. They produced a fire with the tree branches and kindling by which Cavas snapped his fingers and ignited a flame. Much easier than flint and stone, Chry had thought, as his eyes drooped, closed, and jerked open again to an Ambia waking him to leave. A mark had passed by already, she had said, and Chry only nodded and stood.

Fortunately, after this brief rest of bread and warmth, the drizzle ceased. The grey clouds remained vigilant. The air was moist enough that their cotton cloth took five marks to dry. Their shivers died.

As they rode farther, the precipice alongside them flattened into a littoral of overgrown weeds and sand. Then the road turned away from the Grey Sea towards the grasslands. The waters washed away into the distance until the sea became yellow and green. Here the Runners did not encounter many other folk or hamlets. The road (a track of dirt cutting between wild grass as tall as their horses' hocks) was not well-traveled for the authorities of Etherine had neglected reinforcing and patrolling it since before the Fall of Pactus.

Hamlets they did encounter were a huddle of cottages off the dirt path, away from the prying eyes of strangers. The Runners could not see any indications of life from so far away. Once, a family of fawns— five of them with a buck at the lead—were cropping on moist grass. They seemed the only living animals for leagues. One fawn raised its head, its doe-eyes still with compassion and innocence. The buck gazed at the Runners from afar, its large, clawing rack threatening.

The riders trudged on. Thereafter, the clouds cleared for a sultry sun, the Runners perspired in place of a stormy morning, and after a day of monotony, they spotted the town of Neco on the horizon.

Neco, after experiencing the immensity of Cadaqu, was unimpressive. Its disrepair and isolation were much like the hamlets they had seen riding here. Thatched homes were erected with wood felled from what seemed like a hundred years heretofore. Most leaned one way or another, about to collapse. An Etherine Live Oak upheld one like a wizen elder pulling on a cart. The straw roofs had bleached white, and where there should be doors, there were open frames.

The Runners sauntered past residents and families huddled into their rags casting wary eyes to the newcomers. The road here was a slide of mud from the recent storm and cut straight through the town. Their horseshoes squelched through the mud. A mastiff of matted fur gnawed on a thigh bone beside an upturned plow. Somewhere beneath a dearth of shouting and laughter, Chry heard the random clacking of an anvil and the wooden chop of a cleaver. At the other end, they could perceive a thin strip of green across the horizon. This was the Forest of the Lost.

It took the Runners less than a moment to reach the end of the town. When they did, Bar stopped. Around Chry came a collective sigh. The sun was already sticking its toes into the Forest so to force the Runners to squint. It illuminated and darkened Bar's expression.

He said, "We will rest here for the night."

Chry creased his brow in puzzlement. He was squinting at Bar who was staring at the last of the cottages. He was still confused before realizing that the rest of the Runners were dismounting and leading their horses toward an overhang alongside the home. They had to enter through a white-picketed gate and fence, freshly painted but with some of the nails barely hanging onto its posts.

The cottage was Bar's house and a blessing to this tiring day of travel. Chry could hear the comfort of a bed and the warmth of a fireplace as his mouth watered and his bones ached and the cavities of his body broke open and the cellar hollowed his hopes.

He gazed at the cottage.

Differing from its kin, its basic structure was of stone and was raised two stories high instead of one. The stone blocks were cut clean and molded flush with each other. Within the picketed fence, the grass was trimmed to an idyllic dream save for under the overhang. Here the green had grown tall, yellow, and wild as if deliberately untouched for the horses to graze on. Onvi's horse had already taken advantage of the neglect.

Across the opposite face of the house was a garden raised in a crudely crafted bed with tomatoes, beets, lettuce, peas, a groundwork of sunflowers, leeks, and other plants withering in the face of the chiller Swason. Glass windows were cleaned and preserved against the salt winds but upon a closer look, its outside sills bore chipped edges while the ones inside were coated in dust.

They tethered their horses who were pleased to graze. No one spoke. Onvi moaned and rubbed at his brow again. Ambia's hazels were hard swells of concern.

At the door, its rosewood glossy as if polished daily, Bar fished out a keyring from his trouser pocket. There were four, each of varying rusts. He handled a severely plain bronze key, but before he could enter it, they heard a wood bar slew open from within, the iron lock thunk, and the door creak ajar. From within appeared an eye.

Unsettled, Chry could not make out any of its features, only that the eye was narrow with suspicion and that it hovered beneath the rusted links of a steel chain barring their entrance. Bar withdrew from the door but then displayed, surprisingly, a shadow of a smile. Up until then, Chry did not think this was physically possible for Bar.

When the eye recognized the visitor, there was a gasp. Its suspicions drifted. Hurriedly, the door closed, the chain slid across, and the door opened fully.

The grin that greeted them had half its teeth, each crooked and stained. It could've been mistaken for a Rattle's smile if it wasn't trying so hard to be welcoming and cordial. Chry almost felt sorry for the thing. It was not attractive to stare at. Thin hair had receded to a peak. Its hands were lazy claws, and its skin was spotted, caramel parchment crinkling around the bone. It wore scant sheepskin where otherwise Chry would've seen a bloated belly and rows of ribs. It looked like a withered Smar.

But the real tragedy was that any person could see how handsome the youth could've been if the days had been kinder and the nights shorter. His brown, soft eyes had a gentleness that hoped to please, crying out like a plead. His substantial height was cut short into a hunch as if shying away from the horrors of life. Beneath his sleeves and along his wrists were old but raw scars he kept scratching at. If he had not already drawn blood, the scars were scabbing over.

Instead of a nod, his head shook as if starved.

"Oh Barloc, yul, master Barloc, a wondrous sight. Mesa thought you gone, gone, but Mesa knew better than to doubt master Barloc. Knew better than to doubt, yul, yul."

He kept swallowing and licking at his lips as he spoke. His foreign accent would've been smooth and slick had it not been beaten, butchered, and dragged into a coarse rasp.

A sadness touched Bar's smile.

"Yea, Mesa. We are home."

Upon hearing his voice, Mesa's smile bubbled, but no matter how excited he was to see Bar, his eyes would not meet the Runners. They kept flicking to his feet, to the side.

"Mesa wasn't expecting, ni, not yet, but Mesa has—"

Onvi slipped by Mesa and Bar, his social smile forced against his exhaustion. Mesa's devout grin and eyes followed him.

"Eventide, Mesa," he sighed, hand over brow. "Too much last night. Bed calling."

Mesa fervently nodded as if admiring Eulgash.

"Yul, oh, yul. Onvi the Master knows best. Knows much. Is greatest of all, yul. Blankets clean, beds ma—"

Vion snorted before bulling through the doorframe. Luckily for Mesa, he already stepped away clearing a path for Onvi or else Vion's elbow would've broken his jaw.

"Supper," Vion spat. He said nothing else as he disappeared into the home. Cavas drifted behind him.

That same eager nod greeted Vion's demand. His expression beamed.

"Yul. Mesa shall retrieve Redback from Master Cutter. Mesa shall buy them. Caught them this day, yul he did. "

Mesa continued to nod and mumble to himself even though Vion was nowhere near. Ambia and Chry were next and as his presence neared and left Mesa, Chry felt a pinch of pity. He also felt a fleeting yet irresistible repulsion. Mesa did not belong here in Neco. True, he smelled of salt and wore the rags of other residents, but each was a mummer's farce. His accent, almost unrecognizable from whatever Eulgash had intended it to be, was not from Etherine. The scars across his wrists were tattoos of instability, and his many odd behaviors made the best of Chry stray away. Yet, these observations were second to that of following Ambia to the room he would be staying at. He did not know when he'd ever be able to truly sleep again, but the least he could do now was rest.

Mesa flashed a glance at Ambia and Chry, back at Bar, down, licking, scratching scars, then nodded and looked up again. Bar reassured him with a subtle smile. Mesa nodded again, grinning as to prevent himself from crumbling, glanced down again then turned and tottered off. His gait was stiff and weak. A cat's purr could've toppled him. Bar's smile disappeared. He stared long at the hunched back of the youth he had encountered in Cadaqu and thought about what could have been. He would not allow this to happen again.

Never.

Bar locked and barred the door behind him.

III

A collection of stars punctured the night, sometimes obscured by a shred of clouds. They twinkled beside the half-lidded eye of a Weary Moon and listened to the gentle breeze that arrived from the Grey Sea leagues away. Their light painted the stone of Bar's abode the pallor of a Black Rings victim. Houses slept but did not snore. Grasslands meditated. The Forest of the Lost bided its time furlongs from Neco, and beneath its shadowy overhang flickered a prick of fiery light.

Bar lay on top of his tiled and thatched roof. He could not sleep. Instead, he ascended to the roof to distract his thoughts. There was a tranquility within the constellations not yet achieved in Admah. It soothed him. And now with the Council tasking the Runners to retrieve the gems, the Nomas would soon be rid of a large portion of its suffering as to be similar to that tranquil existence. Bar would see to it. He would tell the other Runners of their mission at dawn and convince them of its importance. Bar would see to it.

For now, he kept glancing at that fiery light.

He was waiting. For what, he was not certain. The nights of his life had become predictable: The voice muttered about the erstwhile carnage of war and grief, and Bar would awake in the middle of the night. Sleep did not come easy since Caravan's Demise. He stopped resisting many years heretofore.

However, he could not sleep this night because of another feeling, separate from the voice but just as insistent. It tugged at his mind as would a shipmaster raising his sails during a tempest. It dragged him from slumber, prompting him to wait outside, to be patient, to be vigilant. He could not say why he had this feeling. The behavior was absent of reason—that on which he based the future—but throughout his years, he had found that listening to these feelings were advantageous even if nothing came of it.

That was to say, something was amiss.

He reckoned it had to do with that light flickering beneath the Forest of the Lost. This was a rare enough appearance to provoke suspicion. No traveler had reason to camp near the Forest with a hamlet so near. Nor should they want to. The whispers of the Forest burrowed inside the skull, maddening the mind. Its trails merely led travelers to the Void, a land thought to be untraversable by many, treacherous to all.

With arms as his pillow, he creased his eyes at the distant glow of that orange flame. A dog, the mastiff he supposed, barked once into the night. Insects hummed thereafter.

Whiles waiting, Bar reconsidered his preparations for their journey to the Void. The path would be

Bloody

Gory

pet them, Eat

perilous.

He planned for disaster.

One caution he attended to was navigating through the Forest and Void. The Council's Keeper of Accounts, Amswa, bestowed upon him ancient maps of Pactus to understand the general layout of the Void. It would not be exact. Two hundred years had passed and Bar was certain the Fall of Pactus altered its landscape.

Despite these changes, its lands were not expansive. If they made their respites brief, rode horseback, and stayed a night within the Void, they could reach the entrance of the Temple of Death within a day and a half. The way back would be shorter. If they pushed their steeds and sacrificed their breaks, the Runners would return to the Forest by the end of the day. Both situations were advantageous. The longer they remained in the Void, the higher the chance of catastrophe.

Even so, he could not rely solely on their compasses and maps. He retrieved two of the three Golden Dandelions from the chest in his room so to leave one inside the Forest of the Lost—just in case. If everything went as planned, they would not need it.

Bar inhaled deeply. He regarded the constellations again: Xeyes's Horns, The Boat, Alasaonoma, Imes's Journey, the Winking Moon. He reckoned this might be the last time for a whiles he could gaze at the stars in absolute solitude.

A low-pitched squeaking interrupted his thoughts. It came from below, and he immediately thought, *As to be expected.*

Bar adjusted himself to look over the roof's hanging.

The front door made noise as it opened and closed. No Illum or torches illuminated the hamlet, but the stars and moon were light enough to outline the cloak of massive shoulders emerging from the home. They could have rivaled a mountain. The giant wore a baggy hood to withhold his identity but was otherwise futile in his concealment. The Runner beneath the cloak was so massive that any attempt to be stealthy was compromised by a hefty stride and cumbersome stature like a bull sneaking through a home.

Vion

Slit his throat

If this was not obvious heretofore, the shade of his battle-ax clasped to his back confirmed his suspicions.

He would only need his weapon if he reckoned he might find danger.

Bar considered this as the erstwhile Lanke separated from the abode. He sidled beside the open gate of the picketed fence and spilled into the open field. He was heading toward the flame.

With whom he was meeting there, Bar had his surmises. Vion did not have many acquaintances, the least in Neco. So Bar recollected the days when he and Vion were members of the Derk and reckoned the person Vion was meeting was a Derk and, if his suspicions were right, the Derk that had raised them both. The possibility was likely and could account for why Vion had left the Hungry Wolf Inn after having just arrived from the Council of Crystal. Vion would not betray him—this was certain—but he could foresee Vion making a reckless decision that could threaten his ambition.

Even so, Bar kept his mind open to the number of others that could be at the flame. The Derk could be alone or with others or sent messengers to communicate for him, such as Nor and Narderk. He would need to approach from a distance.

He bided his time on the roof until Vion became a walking statuette on the fields. He had to squint to see the Runner. Even then, he could hardly recognize him beneath the starlight. It was time.

At the back of the house, he descended the roof by way of a bolted ladder. Near the bottom, his shin buckled. He nearly lost his balance but kept his grip tight on the rungs. The rest of his descent was an ache. Though his ambition was true, Bar could not escape mortality. His shin remembered the Silent Swamps. The scars across his chest throbbed. A headsore nagged at his temple.

Off the ladder, Bar dusted the straw and stone dust off his gambeson and then, limping at first but easing thereafter, followed Vion into the light.

IV

He did not need to see Vion to know where he would be. So Bar kept his distance. Mounds and hills were absent from the mind of whoever created these fields. Fortunately, Vion was too far to notice

Bar, but once the Lanke arrived at the flame and Bar neared, he would be as conspicuous as a galley unfurling its sails.

The risk was necessary.

The salty breeze brushed at his gambeson. He trod through the knee-high grass, Vion merging with the flames. At times, his stride faltered for his shin wavered between a pain he could tolerate to being as if Vion had struck it full force with a mallet. Bar condemned his body for its impotence but pushed forward.

For a breadth of time, the fire was too far away to discern between individuals. As he neared, the scene unfolded. Rosewoods stretched to claw at the stars. Flames stained their foliage and Vion's cloak with a fiery kiss. Vion was facing the fire with his back toward Bar. Across from him was a dark figure. Distance blurred its details, but it sat on an object protruding from the ground. As he approached, Bar reckoned that object as a hulking tree stump on the edge of the canopy, a rarity since most Admanites were reluctant to fell from the Forest.

Closer still, Bar strained to hear their distant mumbling. Vion unhooded himself to reveal a bald pate. It glinted off the firelight. Gestures from their conversation were curt as expected from a society that only knew conflict, struggle, and violence. Both their shadows yawned across the grass and bark.

Bar quieted his step.

The distant mumbles soon formed into words he recognized as the native tongue of the Lanke, Jimraokah. This confirmed his suspicions.

"Jarn fenhar ve," Vion grumbled. He asked this as if to uphold formalities rather than shove the words down its throat.

A lengthy silence made Bar think the strides to his approach could be heard. The pause stretched before a response from the other dissuaded him of this. Its voice was husky with age and experience.

"Velderk. Eirt leova galin eno. Parirt a—"

"Jarn fenhar ve," Vion repeated. The tone left no room for negotiation.

Noticing the violence vaulted within Vion's voice, Bar quickened his pace.

With each step closer, the figure peeled back another layer of obscurity: a grey wool cloak draped over two morning-stars hanging from its goatskin girdle. As for appearance and stature, it was disturbingly similar to Vion. They could have been father and son, but its cloak covered its bulk and brawn. Its raised hood obscured any trace of a face. From beneath the figure, the roots of the stump crawled away like the arteries of a dead heart. Over them splayed the willowy fingers of a rosewood.

Bar approached. Bar neared. The Forest gnawed away at the skies—rapacity. Leaves rustled. He heard them again.

"Vorna," the figure proposed, solemn.

Vion chuckled contemptuously. "Vorna. Vor—"

The figure turned its cowl toward the direction of Bar and then raised a hand to stay Vion. When the brute saw this gesture, his shoulders boiled with spite, and his hand jerked for his battle-ax. His knuckles gripped its shaft white with retaliation.

"Verten *har!* Sae kenor ehar—"

In precise Nature's Tongue with the only imperfection being a guttural accent, the figure said, "Someone else has come."

The breeze died. Bar did not hesitate. He strode into the light and unhooded himself. His gaze was a stoic mask that would not lift from the figure's face. He could discern some features now. The eyes he saw were listless and his senior, as old as kith and kin. The shielded nose could protect against a siege. If there was any doubt, it was eliminated by the undeniable gash across its hale chest.

This was what he had expected. The memories that poured in were poignant like an ulcer raw across the heel. He wished naught to remember those days.

So it's true then, Bar thought. *Vion wishes to—*

maim

—finish what he started all those years heretofore.

He did not regard Vion whose glare lurched from the figure to Bar and froze. His muscles and grip loosened, an unconscious reaction, more from bewilderment than from ease.

He heard Vion say, half surprised, half muttering, "Bar, what—"

Without a glance, Bar gestured him for silence. Immediately, Vion woke from his stupor vexed. His eyes hissed like serpents. Bar thought he could hear teeth grinding as a snarl defined his countenance. Bar still did not regard him, and despite his ire, Vion remained planted where he was. This was not without the threat of defiance.

Bar cast his stoicism toward the figure. He addressed it with caution.

"It has been many years, Rahderk. For better or for worse, whichever it may be."

The figure disinclined to respond but instead stared into the flame as if his fallen comrades were calling from within. A stare like that said it had not received a night of undisturbed rest since the days before the Split.

Soon it rose its hands and pulled back its hood.

At first glance, anyone could have seen how war and strife bereaved the leader. The deep trenches of his face were as if carved by a brittle dagger. The failures of his past weighed heavily within his pale, brown eyes. The sockets were pits. Battle had roughened his full lips. Sunspots and scars akin to the Lanke were tripled across his skin, even with the tip of his ear gone and scarred over. His broad jaw bristled with grizzled, unkempt hairs, untraditional for the Vex of the Derk, and a thinning hank tied his bedraggled hair into a ponytail. Its ends brushed at his hood, both dead and lifeless like a skeletal hand.

The man both Vion and Bar once thought of as mentor and father was now a hollow shell.

"It has, hasn't it?" Rahderk sighed deeply. His tone was a cross between an ax chopping down a rosewood and a diplomat conversing with the Council of Crystal. "I did not expect to see you here, Bellderk. I should know better. No secret is secret from you. Not as a Derk. Not as a freelancer."

"Address me as Barloc from now on," Bar's eyes were flat spears pinning Rahderk to the stump. Rahderk hardly noticed. "Bellderk has no meaning to neither me nor my comrades."

304

Rahderk gave a respectful but distant nod.

"I should know better than to assume. You are not Derk anymore. You do not bear a Cervexa." He regarded Vion with a paternal disapproval. "I assume Velderk has a new name. If he does, he has not shared. Be arrogance, folly, or both."

"Watch your tongue old man," Vion growled, jabbing a finger at Rahderk. "Or I'll gladly leave you without one."

"Coming from an erok, I am not shocked."

Silver ignited within his glare. He threw his foot forward about to leap through the fire and throttle Rahderk. He was not even clenching his battle-ax; his hands were balls of fiery.

"You're a dead man Rah—"

A blade hissed from its sheath and sliced through. Vion halted mid-stride when the skin of his throat met cold steel. A runnel of blood dribbled over the bulge of his Cor's Crux. Stamped across the blade was a line of circles, their insides intricated with spiderwebs. They gleamed from the campfire.

"Enough of this or I will not hesitate to *slit your—* your—"

Bar caught his words. He was about to say it, he was about to

slit his throat

He's going to

slit his throat

slit his throat

slit his throat

slit his throat

He wasn't. He won't. These simple—

Words

They're just words Bellderk

Words, words, dead Lanke and words

His composure relied on its stoic stare. That was about to break. Words, words, words cinched around his throat like a noose.

Do it before he betrays you like he did with Lanras

His sword shuddered in his hand. The moment stilled.

Do it before he discovers it was you

You, you, you

Nay.

Nay, I can't.

Not this day.

He will not die this day.

Fighting against the voice, Bar willed himself to steady his hand: not because he did not want to slide the blade across his throat—the voice was convincing, the voice was very convincing—but because the circumstances dictated that Vion live until his ambition was fulfilled. Temptations must be stayed.

"Vion."

His voice was unsteady, but it would mean little otherwise since Vion's unbridled glare bore no recognition of his name. The resentment boiling to the surface clouded his reason as would a Whorl Shark sniffing a wounded seal furlongs away.

Rahderk said nothing to either. His exhausted eyes remained with the fire.

And the sword, fuck, the sword kept *fucking SHAKING*. It wouldn't stop. Something tinked and tinked. A vivid streak of blood ran across its blade and dripped to water the grass below.

Barloc, control yourself before you become heedless. You cannot kill him yet, not before you retrieve the gems and cleanse Admah of its impurities. Stay *yourself or else lose everything you've dedicated these past six years to.*

There were breaths. He breathed before regaining the ability to concentrate. He tried speaking again. Clear. Concise.

"Vion. Enough. Stop this, *now.*"

Those broad shoulders heaved like mountains. A growl rolled from his throat, threatening. The blood down his neck touched and stained his cloak's wool clasped together. Yet, whatever Bar said must've broken through to Vion. How, he could not say, but the relief he felt when that truculent glare withdrew could have made a younger version of himself cry.

Vion stepped back from the blade.

"Kav," he grumbled.

Ignoring the scarlet lip drooling across his neck, Vion dropped opposite of Rahderk. The fire buffered them. Vion's body, with or without him recognizing, was leaning toward Rahderk as if the baleful desires he could not partake in influenced his unconscious.

Through the rest of the conversation, his glare never left Rahderk.

Albeit not preferable, this allowed for Bar to breathe. He lowered the blade weeping with blood. The inside of his mouth had become as dry as hay. When he swallowed or licked his lips, there was no spit to wet them. He tossed a sidelong glance to Rahderk. The Vex remained patient with the campfire, not giving his attention to their struggles. Bar rubbed his nose.

From the perspective of an outsider, preventing Vion from killing Rahderk seemed thoughtless. True, Rahderk and the Derk were the main culprits they faced in searching for the gems of the Walker, and perhaps eliminating their leader would make that search less arduous. Crossing the Void would be perilous enough as it was.

However, Bar had to consider every ramification. The rest were undeniable. Even after the Bloody Crusade, the Derk had enough forces to fend off other Lanke clans, and if Rahderk was killed within Etherine, the remnants of the Derk would have reason to invade. Etherine was in no state to enter another war (as the Council had declared), and once other Lanke clans realized how vulnerable Etherine was, they might consider invading as well. The aftermath would ultimately lead to the devastation of Etherine and the slaughter of hundreds of thousands of innocents. It would be another War for the Split.

Bar would not allow that to happen.

Never again.

From his trouser pocket, Bar slipped out a white and blue checkered cloth faded with old blood. He wiped off his blade.

He was thoughtful.

He would use Silver Oil.

It would be spotless.

It would shine.

There'd be no speck nor trace.

With a gaze burdened, Rahderk spoke, "I thank you, Barloc. I did not want this meeting to be violent, though your words might suggest different."

Without responding, Bar kept cleansing—*there's blood, everywhere, everywhere there's blood*—his sword. After he finished and the blade displayed a spotlessness that he would polish and shine thereafter, he sheathed the blade, folded the cloth, and returned it to his pocket.

"How did you find us," he asked.

Rahderk downcast his eyes again. His sockets fell deeper into their holes, and his speech continued as a sigh.

"Despite how Admah sees the Lanke, most clans are capable. They think we know only how to fight and fuck. That is not true. We survive in the Wastelands with more than brute strength. You should know this."

"You have been watching us then."

Bar's tone was impatient. Rahderk curled his lips into a wan smile.

"I see you still bear the fangs of the mind. Aye, since you first arrived in Ontinia. Everywhere you have went, we have watched. Cotana, Whitewall, Domum. You have visited Cadaqu, too, and have met with the Council of Crystal."

"I do not deny."

"And they talked about the Derk and what we found."

"Yea."

Despondence chipped away at Rahderk's countenance.

"Barloc. Know that if there was any other way to save the Derk, I would. It is not possible. We have little time left."

From the gullet of the distant Sea bellowed a gust of wind. The fire slewed toward the Forest and then guttered. Rahderk's ponytail whipped. A shower of Ainason leaves escaped from the Rosewood trees. Whispering. Whispering still.

"The Derk are dying," Rahderk said. "Ever since the Bloody

Crusade, the other clans see the Derk as traitors. They blame us for the mess in the Split. I've tried to speak with the clan leaders, but they would not give audience. My efforts as Vex have been useless. Not a day goes by when I do not expect an attack from a clan. I know if nothing is done, then the Derk will die like the Irnas clan did before we accepted you. I will not watch the men and women of my Orta be killed."

Bar had known about their depleted forces, but what Rahderk revealed was a new revelation.

Vion snuffed at Rahderk and crossed his arms which were too bulky and muscular to cross fully. Beneath his beard was a cruel smirk, the closest he would come to a smile. "You deserve nothing less."

Rahderk's dejection burned away for a zealous glare. It bore into Vion. He looked then as he had in the days heretofore—hardy, determined, unbreakable, and protective. But the threat lasted a wink. His youth fleeted. Composure and age returned to the Vex's withered face and dragged him back to reality.

Vion sharpened his smirk, stifled a hitching chuckle, but before he could taunt Rahderk again, Bar asked, "Do you truly believe the gems of the Walker and *Azrael* will help save your Orta?"

Without looking from Vion, Rahderk said, "Aye."

The brute was not intimidated but said nothing.

"And you know I would not take the risk if I did not have to. The Derk need a leader, Barloc. Not an erok. A leader." Rahderk paused and then shifted his eyes from Vion to Bar. His judgment bore into Bar. "The gems are a risk. I understand. I want peace between Lanke clans like we had. But that will not happen if the Derk are gone."

He wants them too

Kill him too

"This is why I have come," Rahderk continued. "I cannot have the Runners interfering. I want to make a truce between the Runners and the Derk."

He waited. Bar motioned for him to explain. Rahderk nodded imperceptibly.

"I want the Runners to forget about the Council of Crystal's request to track down the gems. In return, the Derk will give land to each of the Runners within the Split. We will give enough supplies to build you a home and enough food and resources to live the rest of your lives peacefully. Against what Nor and Narderk suggest, I would accept both of you back into the clan, too. If that is what you want."

Vion snorted contempt but then contended with a scathing glance from Bar. Instead of saying more, he made a grumbling sound. It was as if the cut Bar inflicted sliced his windpipe and Vion could only gurgle his discontent.

Across the wound, the blood congealed into a crusty black.

Bar regarded Rahderk again and asked, "How do you know of the Council's proposal?"

Rahderk displayed a timeworn smirk. "Not all Derk look like Lanke. Not all Derk live with the clan."

Bar assented with a mere nod.

"As intriguing as the offer sounds," Bar said. "We must respectfully decline. No condition nor pact can drive us from abandoning the duties the Council has bestowed upon us. I assume a Vex of your stature and loyalties can come to understand our position."

"I do. But I must try. Speak freely of what you want."

Bar looked hard at the Derk leader.

"Nothing?" Rahderk asked.

"Nothing."

Rahderk had a moment's hesitation before his mouth split into a rueful grin. Many of his teeth were missing or broken from the battles he waged, but the grin survived as if desperate to cling to life. He chuckled with the rasp of a dead man.

"I see things do not change."

Finally, Rahderk lumbered from the tree stump. His worn joints creaked and popped.

"I have nothing more to say. Next time we meet, there will be no talking. Only battle." He gave a formal nod to Bar. "Ver kanac Erktal, Barloc."

Bar returned the courtesy. "You as well."

With these parting words, Rahderk hooded himself, tugged the cloak over his grotesque chest scar, and passed by the fire and Bar. He did not look at Vion. Strides heavy and purposeful, Rahderk crossed into the meadows and drifted North toward Etherine's border. His silhouette retold the story of a Kemal sinking into the twinkling tomb of stars.

Thereafter, the fire dwindled, the night chilled, and Rahderk was no more.

V

When Rahderk was not around to see, Vion used the heel of his hand to wipe off his wound. Most of the blood smudged across his tawny skin or had already clotted into a brittle grin with dripping, dry saliva.

What blood did stain his hand he glared at. His crooked nose severed shadows from the firelight. His eyes, whose silver fangs were always bared, were now subdued. There were tragedies in that blood. Betrayals too. Those eyes waded through it expecting to avoid bereavement. They couldn't. It was a part of him now. No matter how far the Runners distanced themselves from the Derk, his rage and resentment would never forget.

Bar remained patient.

Vion wiped the excess blood onto his wool cloak. Finally, he lumbered up from the ground and strode to where his cobraskin boots straddled the farthest reaches of light. The fire clawed at his back and glinted off the steel of his battle-ax, the stars his twinkling tomb.

Bar listened to his resonant breathing.

Before long, Vion spoke. He did not turn his head. The voice Bar heard was a force that did not bark or bite but uttered the words as mere truth.

"Next time we see him, he will die. Stand in my way and you will, too."

A vision, lucid, sharp, Vion, sprawled on steps deteriorated from centuries of life, a fountain pouring from *slit his throat, slit his throat,* the blood, the blood, all the blood spilling across a scarred chest, silver *gouge his eyes* silver *gouge his* bursting into globs blinded by the screams, so many screams, screaming…

"Do as you please," Bar said. "So far as you do not compromise our retrieval of the gems."

Vion grunted as to say he did not need his permission, hooded himself, and conferred with the night. Once again, as to how the night had started, Bar was left alone with only the voice to comfort. The whispers from the Forest were there, too, far from instability but there.

He stared into the fire and did not move, his mind rearranging the chaos of introspection.

VI

Six years heretofore

The unclaimed hills of Katajin, or the Split as the Katarc called it, were thick with fog. He could not see anything beyond more than a furlong, and there would be no breeze to release its presence.

The day was ideal for battle.

Below, the river mumbled out from the valley floor to meander through glens. Once departed from the valley, it was near impossible to distinguish from the sparse beeches, the abandoned cottages, and that bloated fog. Yet, if the fog lifted, by Ornas's will or not, the Bolus mountains would appear to the West, close enough to smell, demarcating the border between Katajin and Ontinia. Residing at the mountain's foothills bustled one of the remaining Ontinian camps. From what they were told from the Vaz scouts, the defenses here were rushed and rickety, their equipment scavenged from the back of the armory, the soldiers gnawing on hard bread and cheese with morale dragging at their heels. They were resigned to a war they were uninvested in. Their families were back home in Ontinia. Their hearts, too.

As was custom before battle, Vion, current Vex of the Derk clan, sought seclusion from his clansmen. Rahderk and the clan leaders thought the act was too heedless for the Vex and made him vulnerable to the enemy—an unsuspecting arrow, an ambush. They had more reasons, but none convinced him otherwise. He needed a place to clear his thoughts. And here, sitting cross-legged at the ridge of a glen, would give him the peace to do so. To concentrate, Vion had taken a blunt steel dagger from Krederk who scavenged it from a scuffle at a cottage Northwest of here. Vion was now gliding it across a block of whetstone.

This too was custom.

During the day or before battle, Vion would hone one of his clansmen's daggers until the blade satisfied him. The steel he honed now would replace Krederk's bone dagger from the Wastelands, the bone having whittled down to the slenderness of a finger. This new dagger, in its current condition, could not pierce through leather. It might bruise the gut but would then slide off the hip like water over smooth stone. If it could not cut flesh or protect the wielder, then the clansmen were further risking their lives.

Vion would not have that.

He leaned into his work. His broad jaw was clear of facial hair as was tradition for the Vex, and the scars across his chest and back were negligible to what he carried in the present, like chicken scratches to haystacks. His battle-ax rested beside him on the velvety, valley grass. Its twin edges were newer and keener, bearing only a nick or two.

His hands labored. Conundrum screeched. Sparks flew. For how bulky his fingers were, they were not cumbersome in their maneuvers. They were gentle but firm, guiding rather than forcing.

He then raised the blade to his eye and thoroughly examined it. His obsidian ring gleamed dully, its silver lion growling.

No, not yet, Vion thought and resumed his labor.

In roughly fifteen Kverech Na, the serenity of the valley would be disrupted by the Lanke. The Western front had waited for a foggy day like this, as Katajin had occasionally given, to follow the river toward the Ontinian camp and claim the lands their descendants desperately needed. Archers from the Vaz clan, as they had during their watch, would be in positions overlooking the camp before the army's arrival. After waves of arrows confused and scattered the enemy, the clans would approach the camp. As Vex and temporary leader of the Lanke clans, Vion would lead them from the vanguard beside a hundred, manned horses spared by the Ras clan on the Eastern front. The remaining clans would spilt and strike the camp from opposite sides (Chechar from the South, Heva and the rest of the Derk from the North). As the Vaz reported, the camp was not built alongside any passage into the Bolus mountains, so the Ontinians had no opportunity to retreat.

If all went in Gintoka's favor, their surprise would bestow few casualties and a swift victory.

If…

Vion whetted Krederk's blade once more and then studied it. The dagger could now cut flesh with a lick. His thumb traced across its flat edge where it reflected the silver of his stare. The sun struggled to give illuminance to the valley. His skin donned the fog's cool coat. Birds sang. The river mumbled.

Peace.

The Council could have deterred this War, he thought. After another moment gazing at his reflection, Vion sheathed the dagger into Krederk's deer hide and tucked it into his wolf-pelt skirt. *King Ventem could have as well. Now the dead must—*

Vion whipped his head over his shoulder, unsheathed his Ironskin dagger from his boot, and glared through the fog. His blade simmered hungrily. Against the rumble of the river intruded footfalls, faint yet booming to his vigilance.

Rahderk's words of caution resurfaced but the blood of aggression and concentration silenced it. His battle-hardened scowl twisted. The serpents to his eyes hissed, muscles tense.

It was like preventing a thunderstorm with a brick wall.

From the inner bowels of the fog emerged a misty shadow. Its footfalls dominated peace until its blurry outline cleared and strode across the valley's ridge. It was the Derk's Orvex, Rahderk.

His demeanor spoke of a story in which hope drove him forward rather than desperation. The unkempt bristles of his chin had grown into a scruffy beard sprinkled with age, common to the Lanke. His straight back and stride were purposeful and proud. He still retained his ponytail, but the leather hank was pristine, and his hair was the black of youth, raked with grizzled grey. The dark circles of his sockets had regained their color, and the furrows of his skin from years of piecing together a broken clan were smooth and nowhere to be found. Most telling was that the grotesque scar slashed across his chest had disappeared. In its place revealed a barreled and scarred chest.

Rahderk was the pinnacle of what a Derk warrior should be.

He approached Vion and knelt paces away. He bowed his chest and head and thumped a fist over his heart.

"Vex," he claimed.

He did not move, and Vion did not loosen his dagger. An ancient force prevented him from unlatching his fingers from the leather. His knuckles were blood white. Blood rushed between his ears. His vision bled. On his feet, over Rahderk, expression heavy. Remembering the naïve Ontinian prisoner groveling before him, the splotch of wetness across his crotch, the senior Etherine veteran of emerald eyes who hawked and spat at his feet, the head rolling thereafter.

Rahderk was the statue of a giant overgrown with vines from centuries of neglect. He would kneel for a century more if Vion ordered him to.

Instead, Vion bore a genuine expression that, six years thereafter, scathed and scarred and unforgiving toward betrayal, he seemed unable to re-create.

Vion smiled.

"Kvenrahderk," he said in Jimraokah, sliding the dagger back into his cobraskin boot and offering a callused hand. "Eor zvenormo don varakerg dekar eirn ajin."

Rahderk lifted his head. Across his lips was a reflection of Vion's smile, still battle-hardened even in these times of triumph. He gripped Vion's forearm and rose.

"Formalities Velderk. I do not want our children to think they can ignore tradition," Rahderk said in Nature's Tongue.

Vion stifled a guffaw.

Nature's Tongue was not their natural tongue, but Vexes would not speak to individual Derk with any other tongue, forcing the clan to learn or become deaf to their leader. The reasons were simple and obvious when they were in the Wastelands where no other Lanke clan knew the difference between "charge" and "halt." But Nature's Tongue was not as important when fighting against Ontinia and Etherine whose first tongue *was* Nature's Tongue. Most Derk ceased speaking it when fighting in the Split but still retain the knowledge as another weapon to use thereafter. Some of the more hospitable Derk, like Landerk, would even teach other clans basic words and sentences.

In time, they will learn too, Vion had said. *If we are to live South of the Wastelands, then we are to learn how they speak in case we must interact.*

They released their forearms, and Vion opened his arm to the valley and fog.

"Our traditions are safe here. Our enemy has not learned how to soar like a crow and bear the smell of an Obolio. Or have you brought Nor and Narderk with you?" He chuckled lightly. "What a sight to see. Former Vex. Now a Vexa. Rahderk, you are getting too old. Soon you will die in battle and converse with Nartha."

Rahderk shook his head with light-hearted mirth.

"You have forgotten that you and Bellderk have never hit me in battle. How can you claim blows that have never landed? I expect more from my Vex."

His hand clapped Rahderk's shoulder with a smile that could not beam louder.

"Once this war is over and the Lanke are at peace, your

morningstars will meet my ax again. I will win. Thereafter, you can try again, but you will not succeed. Kren can promise you this."

"Aye. One day Velderk, we might see victory. Hopefully one day soon."

Their smiles lingered but gradually disappeared. A grim curtain fell over them as if the fog gained a physical presence in dragging down their shared consciousness. They both could feel what the day would promise.

Rahderk's steely eyes bore into Vion.

"That day will have to wait. This day will not be pleasant."

Vion gave a foreboding nod.

"Aye. It seems so."

He left no time to Rachma. He snatched his battle-ax and fastened it to the leather baldric across his back.

"Archers?"

Vion had switched his tongue back to Jimraokah, brushing past Rahderk. The Orvex did the same.

"They are in position," he responded.

Vion entered the fog down the valley slope. It was steep but flat enough to descend on foot, encouraging caution as patches of moist soil and pebbles threatened to break his ankle. He would not slow. Vion dug the heels of his boots into its sun-kissed face to control his impetus.

Rahderk followed close behind.

"Horses?"

"We're lucky that Darras could spare a hundred for our fight. The Eastern front has not made as much progress as we would've liked. From their accounts, the Etherine armies are stalling our forces at Cisario. After battle, if Erktal provides us with favor, I'd advise deploying the Tuk Southeast to recapture the town and bolster our Southern flank."

"They can manage."

Beneath the cover of fog, a motley of pebbles scurried down the face. The river grumbled louder with each gaining step, their hardened breaths huffing against the silence.

Rahderk thought over Vion's response then continued.

"I advise this because of other news. The King of Ontinia has not been seen out of his castle for Moons. We suspect he has died from the same plague spreading across Pulchrit and Ontinia. The forces of Ontinia are sure to weaken in the days to come."

"Tell those in Pulchrit to return home. I do not wish them to die from the same plague."

"Evederk won't leave. You know this."

"If she wishes to stay, so be it. But the others are not obliged. I will not force my Orta to stay against their wills."

Rahderk's chuckle was the rust of an aging blade. "What you say reminds me of your mother. She would've been proud to call you son."

Vion let there be silence. He had not thought about his father and mother for a very long time and would not think about them now. His concentration was needed elsewhere.

They trudged downward.

Strides thereafter, the slope dropped to a thirty-hand precipice. Its rock face was pockmarked with clumps of soil and dead vines. At the foot of the precipice was the river's berm, and if they squinted, vague images of the river arose. It was narrow but the frothy water roared through a gravelly bed. The sounds of fish leaped upstream and slapped when landing. Their movements masqueraded as hazy shades.

Vion turned East in striding across the head of the precipice. His steps sent pebbles raining down.

"The Derk?" he asked.

Vion could hear the pride in Rahderk's voice.

"The Derk stand ready. Always."

Vion nodded to himself. He had no more to ask. Preparations were complete. There was nothing left but to execute.

The two strode on. Sometime thereafter, Vion cast his silver stare to the berm where there lined a belt of jagged stones. On the berm, his memory crafted a vision from his time here in the Split, a grotesque scene. The corpses of the Derk who had died were draped over stone, mutilated by the realities of war. From their broken jaws poured fountains. Their guts spilled like fleshy Dry-Mouths escaping from their stomachs. Beside them, the grey was splattered with fresh scarlet rain. They were Orta he had known and loved, they were Orta he had known and disliked, but they were his Orta all the same.

One his mind could not subdue was a young boy named Ornderk who had just received his Cervexa—his name upon entering manhood—before dying at Caravan's Demise, a year heretofore. Here, a battle-ax, much like the one Vion carried across his back, hewed a chasm into his skull. The blade bit at his upper lip, split his shaggy fringe in two, and captured his fear. His back rested against a stone protruding from the berm like a sharp tooth. The familiar haft of the battle-ax was staked into the pebbled ground and kept the boy propped. His brown eye looked down in shock. A red rill trickled down steel and dripped onto his damp crotch.

Vion's expression was the stone of the river. Ornderk was not so different from him or Bellderk when Rahderk was raising them. The only difference was that they had survived and he had not.

His heart stirred. He delayed it.

Soon, Vion thought. *My Orta will not have to worry of such deaths. There will be peace. None will die of a lack of water or the bite of a Dry-Mouth or a Lanke axe or a Katarc sword. Shiderk and Ulajin will live on with the waters of Katajin as their legacy.*

They departed from the berm, and Vion did not speak another word.

***

The Vex and Orvex meandered upstream for a third of a league. The precipice had relinquished its height hand by hand until flattening into the river-banks. Here, the valley opened its arms to gentle slopes even if the fog remained vigilant in concealing its low summits. The roar of the water calmed to a murmur. The fish swam beneath the surface. Vion's boots were now brushing through knee-high grass. On his side, reeds sprouted high from the shallow waters. A misstep could lead him to plummet into a muck of twigs, water, and mud. As Rahderk and other Vexes have emphasized, a Vex's appearance outside of battle should reflect the righteousness of his spirit. Any blemish would be regarded as a smear to their name.

Vion stepped carefully.

Across the river was an expansive bank of flat stone and grass that would allow armies to pass. No living creature gave it life: no songs of a bird, no whine of an insect, no baa of a sheep. The grass swished beneath their feet.

They traveled another furlong before a faint rambling drifted down from the stream. It was weak and indistinguishable at first, enough for the trickles of the stream to overrule it, but it kept swelling with every step. It was as if the valley were gaining in its voice. Then, as they neared, the voice multiplied into a cacophony of voices, vying for his ear.

Vion curved alongside the stream, pressed forward until the haze peeled back its layers to reveal a vast and open dale.

Within were leagues and leagues of Lanke.

The stream, shallow and calm enough to ford, arrived at a copse of apple trees and, in passing, hugged the edge of its roots. Through the bloom of Swoson, the first apples were growing ripe. Many Lanke, the Derk especially, as Vion was pleased to see, had taken the opportunity to enjoy the fruit it bore. Other clans gathered around the trees, too, as to protect the life it birthed but were too many in magnitude to be as nearby. They were scattered in bivouacs, their war hammers, cleavers, and weapons of war set aside for the tools of conversation.

From one glance, Vion knew that even if they fought together and died together, the Lanke preferred to stay within their clans like they had in the Wastelands. The Chechar, three hundred strong, lolled opposite the stream, their weaponry a mix of the steel and leather of Southern Admah with the bone and rust of the Wastelands. The Derk, bearing the same number of men, either indulged in the sunset apples or tended to the horses drinking from the stream. To the far left, further isolated from the other clans, paced two hundred of the Heva—lips licking and eyes frantic for battle.

Smaller clans were amassed behind these three but were consumed by the fog. Not a single Vaz bow was found. Usually, they were out scouting for the clans, but this day had them close to the Ontinian camp preparing for when Vion blew the horn signaling them to draw their arrows.

The time for battle was near. But what the Vex encountered instead was the laziness of victory. Clansmen lounged in comfort as if the land was theirs to keep. Some rested against their weapons. Some created fires with the cedar trees littered across the dale and cooked the flesh of sheep or Cacusan, their fingers slippery with grease. Soft grass made beds for many whose snores were ignorant to the realities of death. Everyone else was guzzling ale they had retrieved from previous towns.

Those near Vion, a large circle of younger Derk with Nor and Narderk among them, two who *knew* better, were grinning at tales told by Uchraderk. He spoke with his small hands and big mouth about the adventures of Caravan's Demise, their defense at Katarcaval, and the glory to come. The naïve Derk roared with laughter. It was a wonder Vion did not hear them from where he was. Or that the Ontinians didn't.

They were branching off from the trunk of the story before they caught sight of Vion. One by one their chatter shriveled. Their grins were wiped. Each had to stare to convince himself the Vex and Orvex were actually there and not another dream.

When the two did not vanish, the Derk were stilled. With speechless lips, they capped their horns and grabbed for their weapons. Eyes downcast, Nor and Narderk would not regard them. Their soberness spread like the plague in Pulchrit. Even Uchraderk, last to notice, kept brandishing his hands to rein back their attention until he looked over his shoulder and nearly fell over cursing.

Vion's silence fumed.

For a Vex who desired the same pleasures as any mortal man, he could understand these warriors wanting to settle into the comfort they were promised. They felt the end of the war. In it was an escape from the hardships of the Wastelands and the mirth and the peace that would follow.

But the days were not yet won.

Every one of them could be slaughtered in the battle to come, followed by the women, the children, and Lanke like Bellderk, still encamped at Evana Ula. That was enough reason to be vigilant. Instead, Vion found them buttered and basted for the butchering.

These were not warriors.

They had forgotten their purpose.

They had forgotten Ornderk.

His teeth ground to the roots. Otherwise, his rage would have painted his vision red. An order swelled in his lungs that exhaled a seething breath. One look sent the Lanke before him scattering, hurrying.

Steady

It was a voice. From the past.

Steady yourself. They are doing as you wish. There is no need to anger.

The silver of his eyes vibrated. His hands carried the resolve to beat Nor and Narderk until their faces were too bloody to recognize.

The others would know then.

They would understand.

They would not disobey.

A callused hand gripped his shoulder. Vion threw his hand back. His eyes burned, and his fists were about to pummel the defiant Verten who thought they could *touch* the Vex after the laziness they had just showed. His lip twitched in suppressing emotion. Vion scowled at Rahderk. His face was steady. Steady. He was gazing out from where they had arrived.

His glare remained with the Orvex until Vion could return pieces of himself to the present. He then regarded the dale, his sight clearing.

From within the bellows of the hills where the stream lay like a blue tongue emerged a figure rushing toward them. There was an urgency in its jerking gait. As it approached, the fog unveiled it as a dark-skinned Lanke boy dashing alongside the stream. His strides were unsteady, stumbling every fourth or fifth step as if invisible roots were tripping him. As he neared, Vion recognized the frantic, desperate pumping of his arms and legs.

His passionate rage settled to a simmer as they watched the boy ford the stream and approach them. Although its ankle-high waters did not attempt to drown him, he had difficulty staying upright. He plodded and splashed and sometimes tumbled to his knees while throwing himself back up. Vion raised an eyebrow. Rahderk's expression remained flat as slat.

With his feet touching land, the boy finally reached them.

He was panting and had stopped to put his scrawny hands on his scrawnier knees. His eyes cried in desperation and exhaustion. And now that he was near, Vion could reckon the boy as what he was: weak. His scarless and heavy skin, glistening with sweat, was wrapped around bone. There was no muscle. He had a stubble of hair, a flat chest, and the hairless legs of a skinned chicken. His head seemed too large for his body in that it would sway during battle, a liability when death was the outcome.

Vion and Rahderk both waited longer than they would have liked. Rahderk grumbled something under his breath. Though he did not know what he said, Vion reckoned he felt the same.

Soon, the boy recovered enough of his breath to speak.

"Katarc…" He forced out between a gasp. "Lekatarc—"

Rahderk smacked the boy across the cheek so hard his body slew from the blow. Instead of tottering backward a step or two as would the strength of a Lanke warrior, he thumped against the valley floor. When his frame landed, it clattered like a skin of bones. The other Lanke gave sidelong glances but were too concerned with readying themselves to have gazed dumbfounded.

"You insult our alliance with your disgrace," Rahderk roared. "The Derk will have none of this. *Kneel* and give the Vex the respect and honor he deserves!"

The boy groveled on his hands and knees, rubbing at where Rahderk struck him. He was panting, and there was a trace of sniveling that was heard if one listened closely. His bones quivered uncontrollably.

Standing over him, Rahderk was thirteen hands of impenetrable morality. He took another step forward before Vion's hand rested on his shoulder.

"I appreciate your support, Rahderk," Vion said. "I can handle this from here."

Immediately, any fierceness Rahderk had fleeted. Vion felt his muscles loosen beneath his hand. In its place were self-possession and respect. He turned to face Vion, fist over his heart, and dropped his head.

"As you wish, my Vex."

There was no trace of anger when speaking his natural tongue of Jimraokah. All of it had dropped. Regardless, the Lanke clans had seen too much in-fighting in the Wastelands. Vion would not risk breeding the same loathing that led his father to death and above to Zarvena.

Vion left Rahderk, strode, and stood before the boy whose fear made the air he breathed tangible. On his back and elbows now, the boy looked up with the shame of bulging eyes. Vion cocked his head to glare down at him. Every look he made was a glare to an outsider, and he knew from his glare (persisting longer than was comfortable) that the boy's thoughts would scatter to each end of Admah in search for the possible punishments it suggested. It was what Rahderk did with Vion. Back then, waiting for Rahderk to look away felt like a fingernail scraping years away from his life.

There came movement. The boy flinched, slipped on an elbow, yet punishment did not follow. The swelling of his eye cautioned open to recognize an outstretched hand, the palm and fingers open. Vion gave him a faint smile.

"Stand, my Orta. Do not fear punishment."

The boy was speechless. Staring long and hard at Vion's hand, he hesitated before finally reaching for it. His fingers were dainty to Lanke standards and could be crushed by Vion's if he only squeezed. He didn't. Vion brought the boy to his feet. The boy swayed at first but soon breathed and stood steady. Still two hands taller than the boy, the Vex smiled down on him. Forgiveness was not a trait he was born with. Years with Rah and Shiderk taught him otherwise.

Rahderk looked on with a deadpan glare while the boy licked his lips and meekly wiped the blood from his bruised socket. He would not regard Rahderk.

"Ignorance comes from inexperience," Vion said. "You taught me this, Rahderk. I should not expect a youth from a different clan to know of our traditions." Vion glanced over his shoulder to Rahderk. "He will learn one day. When that day comes, if you are willing and the Vaz agree, you may teach him."

At first, the boy's downcast expression showed glimpses of relief, but Vion's last four words stole that hope. He shot a glance at Rahderk and what he saw was the glee of an overt smirk.

Vion swore his body was shaking.

"But war is among us, and the time for learning must be stayed," Vion said. "Your Cervexa, young Lanke. Speak quickly. In Jimraokah."

His stiff-stone eyes would not leave Rahderk.

"Cur...Curvaz. It's Curvaz."

"Curvaz. An honest Cervexa. What have you come to tell me."

He swallowed, but this could not relinquish him from the blade against his heart.

"I was scouting the Ontinian camp like I was told, and...and they...they're coming. They're coming toward us."

"Who? Be specific."

"Their armies. The camp is coming..."

Rahderk's glare was the fierce judgment of Gintoka. Consciously or not, the boy flinched and hung his head low, occasionally braving a glance.

"And why did we not know about this sooner?" Rahderk demanded. "Did you not see them preparing? Were you and the rest of the Vaz blind?"

Curvaz made faces that were conducive to an undecisive worm.

Before he could speak again, Rahderk waved the boy off.

"Of no importance. They know we're here," he shifted his attention to Vion. He thought he heard Curvaz sigh relief. "We need to act before they catch us swordless, my Vex."

Vion considered and asked, "Curvaz, how long before they arrive?"

"Hu…" He could not even regard Vion. His eyes were only for his fidgety fingers as he contended with the question. "How long…?"

He bent his head towards the skies. The fog obscured them. The whites of his eyes beamed brightly against his swarthy skin.

"It…the sun…it…"

"Take a hold of yourself!"

Curvaz was rattled from his daze but gaped not at Rahderk but Vion. Vion's voice had smote him like a hilt of steel. It was without patience, commanding. "We do *not* have the day to waste. The enemy is approaching. Say what is needed to be said and be finished with it."

"I-" Curvaz managed to swallow, blink, wipe away his sweat, and make a horde of other tics and gestures. His brown irises bounced between the Vex and Orvex before, slow as ice, he lowered his head. He did not speak for the moment as around them sounded the rustle and clang of warriors preparing for battle. Then he mumbled something, but when reckoning that neither could hear him, he spoke even louder. "Eight Kverech Na. I think…Most."

That was little more than a mark of a candle clock.

"How prepared are they?"

"Well, their steeds are armored and decorative, and they march in our exact direction. I…I have not heard talk of Ontinian scouts near or around camp."

"Neither have we," Rahderk added.

What they were implying fell over Vion. He grumbled discontent. It was not what he wanted to hear.

The actions of the Ontinians were more than an out-maneuvering. True, the Ontinian generals were strategic in battle, and even if they weren't, Vion would consider them so since the worst possible judgment was to underestimate your enemy and be wrong. But this was too much of a coincidence, too decisive to be reactionary. They knew where their camp was. They seemed, from what he had been told, unhurried in preparing their troops and had decided on a position of the sun that would best catch the Lanke swordless. This was a predetermined strike. The Lanke planned this advancement for more than two turns of the Moon, discussing, maneuvering, and waiting for a day of fog on which they would strike. That gave the Ontinians plenty of time to be notified, and it implied a possibility Vion loathed to think about—within the highest ranks of the Lanke clans was an Ontinian spy.

Unfortunately, he could not dwell on this now. The hunt and discovery of who betrayed them would be had but after the battle was won. They could not reckon who it was if they were all dead.

Vion rethought their approach.

"Rahderk."

"My Vex."

Vion nodded to the right side of the dale. Farther down, its summits climbed, cloaked by the day's fog.

"Take the Heva and smaller clans to where the valley rises above the fog. Ready bows to fire at my command. Thereafter, charge the enemy."

By Derk tradition, Rahderk thumped his fist against his chest and bowed his head.

"As you wish."

He was gone before Vion could address the boy.

"Curvaz."

The boy stiffened as if his Cervexa heralded lashes from a whip. The tendons down his neck strained from sparse muscle.

Vion gestured to the Derk gathering in front of the apple trees.

"Join the Derk. Quickly."

At first, he only gaped at Vion. When he reckoned the Vex did not stutter in his command, Curvaz blinked and hurriedly nodded. He scurried two steps past, stopped dead, and turned toward Vion. He straightened enough to hide how nervous he was, thumped a fist against his chest so hard Vion would not be surprised if it left a bruise, and then scurried back to the Derk under a gait that would humiliate the gods.

We should have stayed in the Wastelands, Vion mused.

He chuckled roughly at this, shook his head, and returned to his preparations as the Vex.

***

The deployment was smooth chaos.

Lanke were everywhere, scattered about as ants whose hill was disrupted by the passing of a wagon wheel. Even so, the common Lanke did not harbor the same confusion and indecision as an ant would. Their maneuvers were concentrated. Moving metal clanked together, but with no words floating in between them, eeriness deepened. Cackling and guffawing were absent. Fires extinguished with dirt and feet. They were like a rustic smithy, its metalworks abandoned and derelict but now opening its war-red forge to a pale, new day.

This battle was for the future of the Lanke.

Initially, Rahderk addressed the Heva clan by spitting orders, but the unstable and uncanny eyes he received told him that this time, the clan would not respond to simple commands. The Capar Weed and Narthema seeped into skin too restless to reside on flesh. So Rahderk resorted to the only dialect the Heva could comprehend—force.

Needless to say, one fist to the jaw of Hinheva convinced the lazy-eyed leader to quicken his step, and with the Heva on the move, the smaller clans were not far behind.

Vion addressed the Chechar and Derk. Kirgchar, leader of the Chechar, listened through the fierceness of his stare. He asked no questions, did not nod, did not acknowledge the orders Vion gave him before snapping at his clansmen to ascend the valley summit.

The Derk were as obedient and diligent, but what they struggled with were the horses the Ras clan offered them. Nearly half of them were restive to cross the shallow fords or even to clop forward. The smell of battle tainted the air. Most whinnied when being reined toward the valley. Some refused and reared. Although the Derk were well-versed in war strategy, intelligence, and general warfare, they were not horsemen. Ras horsehair twitches were foreign to the Derk, and any other knowledge of horses ended with proper riding and a few soft words. Force only made the horses more belligerent.

Considering most of the horses now as a liability, Vion ceased these attempts at coercion and ordered the riders of the disobedient stallions (over half of their horsemen) to ride East toward their smaller encampment at Caravan's Demise where they would await further orders. The riders were reluctant (their eyes said enough) but would not argue with their Vex.

With the remaining horses restraining their neighs, Vion hastened up the gentle slope behind the last of his forces. Expressions of the Lanke were stern as if the sun peeled away the skin until the threat of death stiffened. Across the stream, Rahderk, the Heva, and other clans were indistinct presences like the blurs of wanderers on the horizon under a brutal Wasteland sun.

They soon disappeared into the fog and were no more.

Their calves worked, and their grunts were oxen laboring corpses up a mountain. Cobraskin boots dripped wet like sweating snakes. Footfalls suggested sounds within the valley. The occasional neigh swelled against the silence.

Beneath his heavy breath, Vion grumbled. If the Ontinians were close enough to the valley, they would hear their army on the move despite striving for silence. He quickened their stride. The Derk around him felt his urgency and did the same.

After gaining on a flat ridge where the grass and soil ceded to patches of slate, Lanke could now look below at a stream blurred by the haze. They reached heights camouflaged by Ornas, and when Vion arrived at its top, the Chechar were already amassed—hundreds of clansmen clustered together as to resemble their motley of weaponry. Worn swords and war hammers, goatskin shields, thinned bone daggers, blunt iron maces, even the rare snakeskin whip. Riders, under quiet words and gentle tugs, led their forty or so mounts to the vanguard. Behind the herd formed the Derk, more orderly than the jumble of Chechar. In front of them, next to a Derk's black and white gelding, stood their Vex.

After the Derk and Chechar had settled, Vion listened to thumping feet across the expanse and the occasional hyena-yelp from a Heva clansman. Their footfalls soon trickled to an end, and the valley renounced its sound. The ridge they waited on could hardly be called a mountain or hilltop but instead one knob on the spine of a sleeping giant. Their descent would be a gradual decline. Any steeper and Vion would've reconsidered bringing any of the horses.

The stream bubbled below. A warhorse snorted. Ornas became wordless.

Unsheathing his battle-ax, Vion planted its shaft into the grass, rested his hands on top, and bowed his head.

He sealed his eyes and released himself into prayer.

Gods.

As you have listened to my ancestors heretofore, now, I ask, may you listen to me. May my steps be quick and nimble, my swings be strong and swift, both admirable beneath the presence of my forefathers. May this battle guide my Orta to salvation. May the blood of Lanke lost bring life to lands anew. May my Ajin thrive on the peace recovered from the sacrifices offered here. May my spirit give light through the bloodshed to come and be strong enough to save those that might otherwise return to you. Blesseth to you, Erktal and Nartha, others that may guide me, so you may bless my brethren before me.

"O ehar car yenetor," Vion whispered.

He remained like this for another breath before opening his eyes to the waiting valley below.

***

A Kverech Na went by. Another. A slew. But no hint of the Ontinians.

Their haste in the face of an ambush riled the Derk into restlessness. Their feet shuffled. Their grumbles muted. The bare chest of the behemoth beside him, Naranderk, bore a third nipple that twitched in anticipation. The panting Naranderk carried since birth became the wheezes of a man dying if he could not experience the thrill of action. Beneath the panting, he was muttering incoherent Jimraokah.

Another Kverech Na.

Finally, in the distance where he had honed Krederk's dagger, there glowed a will-o-wisp.

The fog suffocated its fiery form as it grew, bobbed, and swayed. Approaching, it elongated to imitate a lurid snake slithering through the valley floor. Sounds came next; a distant thud, like the valley's rhythmic heartbeat, beckoned from the earth.

Marching.

Then, if there was any doubt, the belly of the fog expelled the beginnings of the Ontinian army. Filed into four serried ranks, their soldiers curved around the valley bend and marched in hurried unison toward and along the bank where Vion was waiting above. Opposite of the stream were the reeds and mires forcing the army to this side of the bank. It was exactly what Vion had envisioned.

Sounds of war penetrated the air. Chainmail rattled and armor clanked, their treads thundered in a rushed heel beat. Round ironwood shields protected their scrawny shoulders and backs. Steel helmets were bent and deformed to the disfigurements of war. Each row had a torch, and spears infected with rust covered the army as if it were a porcupine enflamed.

Leading the cavalcade on a steed impossible for any normal human to mount rode a Knight of the Kings. Its winglet helmet scanned the stream and the banks, vigilant yet steady. A pristine, ironwood spear as lofty as its wielder sat across its back, freeing a gauntlet to rein the steed forward and the other to handle its shield. With no dents or scratches, the tower shield protected its left flank fully without opportunity for an arrow to break through. No skin was left open for a strike. The Knight almost seemed inhuman in its impenetrability.

Its steed snorted and ruffled a metal mane. It was clad in the same armor as its master—a dark-as-death metal revealing only the fetlocks—with a caparison of Ontinian dark green inlaid in gold stitching. In the center of its covering was a gold symbol that Vion could not reckon from this distance.

The Ras once mentioned a horse like this and named it a Shire. Some Ras myths, depending on who was asked, foretold these steeds were owned by the gods to haul mountains during the beginning of time. Aside from these stories, only a rare Ras had ever seen a Shire in the wild and none had ever tamed one.

But here was one now or at least Vion reckoned it as one, tamed and ridden by a man who could rival Naranderk in girth and height. Together, they rode as a roving castle, its walls impervious, its defense deadly, and its progress impenetrable.

That will be for Erktal to decide, Vion thought, scowling.

The Shire kept ruffling its mane and snorting as if unable to contain its excitement. The Knight took no notice. It surveyed the gentle slopes as would a sentry unfearful of death. Its army followed behind. Their flames reflected off the waters. As far as Vion could see, there was no end into that pale veil, but their footfalls were clearly heard, enough to overwhelm patience. Behind him, he felt the Derk restrain themselves to the movements of a mouse. Their limbs brushed against leather. Riders, with quiet words, hushed their steeds, somehow calming them so their nickers would not alert the Ontinians to their presence.

The Shire clopped forward beneath the Derk and Chechar to the valley's final bend, and when the Knight was directly beneath Vion, it turned its helmet—insidious as poison—to the valley summits. It knew. The slit where its eyes should be sliced through the fog and confronted the silver of Vion's eyes.

The Vex glared back. The Knight did not release him from its hold.

If the Knight discovers our position, our plan will fail, Vion thought. *Their sheer number of men will overwhelm us. My Orta will die. My clan will die. My family will scream. They will die. And who will be to blame?*

The Knight

That Katarc erok

His knuckles strangled the head of his battle-ax. They were as pale as the fog. A promise of grief resided within that black slit. Unforgivable. Vion had dedicated his life as Vex to protecting his Orta, and that was what he would do. At any cost.

Soon, the Knight lost interest in the summits. It traveled into the open valley where the Lanke had bivouacked and regarded its emptiness. Vion snarled through his breath. The Knight rode paces more before reining its steed and raising a fist. Behind him, the soldiers clanked their heels together. The sound was like an echoing thunderclap. It rippled down its back and through the ranks into the fog, the metal heels calling from within.

The Knight regarded the dale.

The stream gurgled by the body of trees. A blood-red apple fell from one and thumped near the water as if the Knight's slit had scythed the fruit from its stem.

From beyond the fog bleated a goat.

The Knight stared at the branches. Its steed was unappeasable, shying and nickering, stomping its iron horseshoes.

Now.

Without another Kverech Na wasted, Vion raised his hand, though the Lanke were oblivious to the gesture. It was an unbreakable habit.

"Elchre!" He roared.

His voice commanded the valley. Some of the Ontinians made a frightened yelp, but all began tossing bewildered glances above. From their legions rose an anxious mumble. Urgency now melding into its armor, the Knight whipped its Shire around to command. Yet the battle had already slipped from its control.

"Vira!"

Answering his call, the oakwood of a hundred bows creaked. It elicited in the Ontinians a memory familiar and lethal. Fear stole their hearts. Their actions became a sporadic welter: fumbling frantically with their shields, gawking above as if hearing a god, limbs and stares and feet rigid as ice. They were speechless.

But once the initial shock wore off, panic washed over them. They released their weapons and scattered. Terror screamed from their throats. They shoved through the throngs and, if they were near the front, scampered past the Shire toward salvation. The Knight tried steering them back to fight but was unsuccessful. The wildness in the eyes of both its steed and men was as untamable as the Heva.

The rest clambered up slopes slippery with scree or waded through knee-deep water. Many fell, but desperation threw them back onto their feet. Lagging behind were those few who had dropped their torches in favor of a frenzy. On the rocky banks, the flames burned helplessly, but closer to the dale where the banks had greened, the flames caught, spread, and guttered. Only the fog's mist prevented the fires from roaring ablaze. And still, there were those petrified and gaping as the realization dawned that this day would be their last day on Admah.

Vion's hand fell.

"Trag!"

Strings twanged. A salvo of arrows whistled and pierced through the haze. They cascaded onto the legions as arrowheads thumped against bone and punctured flesh. A thicket of bodies dropped. Men were thrown off their feet to roll down the slopes. Hundreds screamed. A cacophony of vicious sounds clattered like a grave where the dead cried. Gore splattered grass and rock. The stream drank blood.

The Knight whose shield and armor guarded against the fusillade brandished its spear toward the battlefield. Vion reckoned it was giving orders, but its men were deaf to its command.

Even before the Lanke descended, the Ontinian army succumbed to chaos. Bannermen tripped over limbs. Soldiers hugged their steel as their last companion, their eyes gaping at glazed eyes. Tears and sobs droned on. They rocked back and forth and not a single golden rooster on their jerkins, that proud emblem of Ontinia, was unsullied. If Vion had known about the Trench—that rut where the citizens of Pulchrit tossed the carcasses of Black Rings victims upon death—he would have seen the comparison. The sickness of war reeked within, and now it would be the task of the Lanke, Derk, and Vion to expunge that stench.

Vion raised his battle-ax aloft and bellowed his final command.

"Darg!"

The Lanke reacted vehemently.

Victorious cries were released. Across the valley, Vion could hear the distinct, ecstatic squalls of the Heva like the laughter of a rotting and mad wolf.

Geldings of black, brown, and grey brayed with stored restlessness then streaked forward in a blinding blaze. Riders stooped over flowing manes. Their speed spurred the air across Vion's skin, and their stampede drowned sound. When they met the Ontinians on the slope, their hooves crushed ribs and legs where the riders' stone and bone bludgeons caught the soldiers that were missed.

Their cries were unappeasable.

Behind Vion, the Derk and Chechar could no longer restrain themselves. The current rippled through Vion so to make his fingers tingle before they charged forward like a wave to the rivers they were fighting for. They barreled past Vion. He did not move. The disoriented Ontinians that weren't caught by the horses were caught by the hordes to follow. The heads of maces struck their skulls. The blades of axes guillotined. Chechar threw their spears, and soldiers were dead before hitting the ground.

From this, Vion watched until he, too, could not hold himself back. He had stood still long enough.

Without looking away from his enemy, Vion descended into the mayhem.

***

There were so many carcasses Vion had to weave between them to avoid tripping. The further he went, the more the will of Erktal entered him. His strides became second-natured. His breath tightened, his feet forgot themselves, and his battle-ax melded into flesh. There was an absence of hearing that created space for concentration.

He was living inside Erktal's domain.

Within its domain came vigilance, the ability to sift through the battlefield for details hidden to mortal men. He did not extract the information he saw into reason (more like a wealth of knowledge he dove through), but the tidings were indispensable.

These "soldiers" he passed were not the Ontinian soldiers they fought at Caravan's Demise. They were younger, their faces clean of scars and inflamed with pimples. Bristles of hair had started settling on their chins but none to what the Lanke would call beards. Vion could not reckon their manhoods bore any growth either. Many of the corpses had wet themselves.

They were also ill.

This condition was not realized until he inflicted his first kill. His silver glare met the milky hazel of the boy's eyes right before he swung his ax ten knuckles into his shoulder. It remained there as life drained from the boy. In death, his expression changed, but the face did not. The cheeks were still carved inward and so pale, they rivaled the reflection of the moon. The skin seemed clammy, and his grogginess made any movement muddled. He did not even try to dodge.

It was not unreasonable to think the King and his councilors were sending boys to fight in a man's war but, further, were sending boys already infected with the plague Rahderk and others had claimed was like Heva Na Narth. Their aim was desperate but simple—to win this war through infecting their enemies and hoping they would succumb as they had. It was beyond dishonorable. It was cruel and unforgivable. They claimed the Lanke were beasts when they themselves treated their citizens as expendable firewood to be burned through the furnace of war. And the Knight knew, it *knew*. It had thrown these *children* into battle as fodder.

A blister of bloody ravage strained against his skin. He growled when planting a foot on an Ontinian corpse, yanking his ax from its arm.

There was no stopping.

The Heva were first to reach the valley depths, even before their horses had. They threw their legs over the miry banks, frenzied when splashing, tripping, slashing, grinning mad when relishing in gore. Their flails whirled and connected. Bloodshot eyes, from the Narthema they inhaled before battle, foraged for Ontinian snacks. Rear to the Heva, the smaller clans surged behind the lead of Rahderk swatting aside a skull with the head of his morning star. Their horde flooded the human debris down into the stream. There was no one left behind.

The further the banks flattened, the further the bedlam bellowed.

Steeds and their riders dashed into the stream. Derk and Chechar screeched into waters darkened with the ichor of Erktal. Freshwater salmon bobbed to the surface, unblinking to the carnage. Axes cleaved. Swords flashed. Here, weeping tears pleaded for salvation, but pestilential blood bloated the throats. Ontinians who weren't dead, playing dead, or paralyzed by the dead tossed their arms at the Lanke. As a child, when Heva Na Narth snuck into the hearts of Derk, Vion experienced seasoned Vexa too ill to lift their swords, exchanging the strength of gods for the mortality of man. This was the state of the Ontinians. Any swing that reached the Lanke were deflected aside or effortlessly avoided, and the last expression these boys had before death was not stone faces of veterans or well-prepared soldiers but of terror. Childhood stories of beasts living in the Wastelands hollowed courage from their bones, but when faced with the living and breathing incarnation of insanity, their bowels could not hold. And the Heva were more than glad to relieve them.

This was no longer a battle. This was a massacre.

The Knight was a still night puncturing the mist. Beneath it, the Shire kept rustling its mane.

One boy whose leg was severed from the lower thigh down crawled toward the Knight. A string of tendons and muscles dragged behind as if his trousers had frayed beyond stitching. The trail of blood he left was soon unrecognizable among the droppings of bodies. Dazed, the boy kept reaching for the Shire but would always slip. The moans and grunts around Vion replaced what he could not hear.

The Knight's helmet did not waver from the boy even when he ceased to move. There was a silence to it that echoed death. For spans, one could even think its armor was absent of the flesh within. Empty.

Vion took all of this in as the focal point of his being.

He reached the banks where madness was greatest but heard nothing. Sounds had drained. Clarity redirected him to the Knight. There was no one else. Figures blurred around him. The Knight was before him. He planted a foot forward. The cobraskin of his boot sank into the mud.

Its children were pleading. It had killed them. It was *killing* them.

Vion bashed his battle-ax into a boy until the only movement left was the jerk of its limbs. His blade cascaded. The iron tinge of blood spoiled his tongue. It had tried attacking him. Vion had disposed of it.

The Knight was next.

It will not survive. It will be judged. It will die.

Regardless of any initial shock, the Knight rotated its helmet and considered a Heva from across the stream. The mad warrior was not as meticulous. With the hunched gait and predatory goggle of a starved hound, he dragged his cleaver across a skim of water and gained a gradual haste.

The Knight's demeanor was impenetrable. Instead of bashing the Lanke with its tower shield when he neared, it spurred the Shire. Immediately, the metal beast brayed and reared. Its hooves wheeled. It gained a height that could convince any Lanke this was the steed that had once moved mountains. It was a miracle the Knight was not tossed off, a testament to control.

By then, it was too late for the Heva. He tried to retreat, its predatory rictus never leaving even when the iron horseshoe smacked into his temple. Its head twisted like a top. The momentum of the strike dropped the Heva headfirst into the edge of the stream. His limbs plopped. Around its head, the current bloomed a pinkish flower and tickled at its disfigured rictus.

The Shire danced backward as if about to fall on its back but dropped on its forelegs instead. One of its hoary hooves landed hard on the arm of a dying Ontinian. There was a harsh crack like a tree bough breaking followed by a wrenching cry. The cry exploded when the steed stamped around to find footing.

Around the Knight, Lanke of Chechar and Derk stole a gasp and hesitated before the vengeful spirit of Gintoka swept them forward again. Ground combat distracted a fistful, but the rest expelled a roar for their fallen brethren, brandished their arms, and charged for rider and steed.

Unsheathing its spear, the Knight swept it across a Chechar's throat and skewered another. A Lanke Vion did not recognize thrust a halberd at the neck of the steed. It scratched across the black metal. With its spear and a faint struggle, the Knight heaved the Chechar from the ground. He was still squirming trying to push himself off the spear, the shaft lodged into his chest. The Lanke staggered back realizing the danger he was in, but before he could escape, the Knight swept its spear. The Chechar slewed off it and slammed into the Lanke. Mud squelched at their fall. A harsh crack ruptured the air. They squirmed together as worms unearthed. The spear had dug a tunnel beneath the Chechar's ribs, and the Lanke below spasmed. A gout of blood spewed from where its head slapped against a stone.

The Knight sat erect (*proud*) in its saddle. Its ironwood spear glistened as it flicked the steel tip aside. Around it, the strides of the Lanke were once again hesitant.

My Orta

Vion stepped on, over a corpse.

He's killing them

The next to try his sword, out of every warrior the Derk had, was Uchraderk. He was seventeen years reckon, and at his Kaicer Na, he had not stopped preaching to the Derk about his soon-to-be legend and was thus bitten by the Dry-Mouth he was supposed to eliminate. The boy acted on hubris. Since then, he had not changed; his mouth would not keep shut even when approaching the Knight from behind. Vion could not hear but saw his slim lips flapping about incoherent nonsense. The Knight's helmet shifted over its shoulder.

No

Urgency bashed against Vion's chest. He was sprinting before he could finish his thoughts, his hands wringing the neck of his battle-ax. Mud sucked at his boots. Raw tenacity clouded his silver.

Uchraderk was not aware of his Vex strides away calling his Cervexa. The spirit of Erktal had inhabited the youth. He raised his sword. His lips split into the same grin he had when attempting to kill his first Dry-Mouth.

The Knight squeezed its legs against the Shire. In response, the steed let out a raucous whinny and lowered its head.

A vice clamped over his blister of emotion. Vion knew that position.

That Chura, he thought. *Run. Run!*

If he was, he acted too late. The Knight hunched forward and kept steady as if welded to his mount. The Shire bucked its hind legs.

Uchraderk had no chance.

Its kick struck his chest dead center and threw him backward. The sword wrenched from his hand and whorled into the stream. Its steel, unhoned since birth, clattered against the streambed. Uchraderk landed and skipped hard as if Nartha had stolen his life and flung his body aside from a mountaintop. When he flopped to a stop, his back faced Vion, as still as the fog.

The Shire brayed for its master, but the sound drained from his hearing. The battlefield had blanked. The fighting around Vion ceased to exist. There was Uchraderk and only Uchraderk and Vion was trapped within the skin of his own mortality.

Despite his childhood with every scathing glance he had received, despite in his youth beating Haraderk until bloody bruises blinded his sight, the elders turning their eyes away from his unruly and unappeasable behavior as he woke every dawn and wished for every Derk to burn under the sun, despite this childhood, Vion had promised in the present, as their Vex, that he would sacrifice his sword hand for each and every one of them. To those who had wronged him. To those who had believed in him. There were no exceptions. He would sharpen each of their daggers, check each worn and weathered saddle, strangle any Dry-Mouth hissing at his children, upheave the Wastelands for the seeds of Narma, defy the threats of Nartha, sacrifice every life inside the Split to see his Orta laugh, cry, and live.

Not even Erktal could prevent the carnage he would cause. There was no return. His inner being evaporated any semblance of reason Rahderk might have taught.

He careened forward.

His throat bellowed.

He lodged his battle-ax into the flesh of those forgotten.

He swung, swung, swung, swung

Trails of corpses.

Screams

Kicking them from his path.

A plead.

Blood

Shire

mud

ax

roar

swing

bray

death

…

The rest he could not remember.

***

His swing brought with it the grievances of his forebearers. Its impetus rivaled that of horseback and was precise in its strike: the knee of the Shire.

The barding of the Shire exposed the knee as a vulnerability. Naked against the blade, the kneecap cracked back as if Vion had broken a thick bough over his knee. The horse brayed, horrified. The metal skin clanged together like tiny bolts of lightning as the knee buckled and the steed fell.

Unaware of Vion until now, the Knight swayed like the tower of a castle whose stone bulwark had crumpled. Instinctively, it tried holding them erect by staking its spear into a dry patch of grass. The effort was desperate but could not hold. The sheer mass of the Shire was too much for the ironwood. Its shaft bowed before splintering, sputtering, and snapping. The Knight and Shire toppled from their throne.

Lanke courageous or reckless enough to engage the Knight were now scampering away. Not all could escape. A Chechar whose legs were as unsteady as the bellies of Dry-Mouths slipped face-first into the mire. He was crawling away from the muddy banks when the hindquarters of the Shire landed on his leg. The noise from the Knight's fall muffled his screams and reverberated between the clashing of swords. Mud dabs shot out and splattered Vion's chest. The ground rumbled beneath their feet. There was a hesitation in the fighting—an unconscious understanding the battle knuckled closer to its end. The felling of a Depanen tree, their boles the girth of a small house, would have made a quieter descent.

A vicious silence followed before a Lanke hatchet gutted a pikeman.

Vion was numb. He seethed sweat, eyes uncoiling into silver serpents. The events heretofore happened through the keen vision of an eagle. Each action the Knight and Shire made screamed for gore. Everyone and everything else was grey.

The pair was flailing. Any preconceptions the Knight of the Kings inflicted onto the Lanke decayed into a soil of lies. Its prestige was as pathetic and weak as the troops it led. The Shire kicked its white hooves at an invisible enemy, the leg Vion struck jangling like a broken branch in the wind. Its barding and squeals clashed as a shatter of chimes. Vion feasted on its distress.

The Knight did no more to impress.

Its leg was trapped beneath its fallen mount. Like an owl whose claw had caught on a tangle of twigs, the Knight flapped its shield and half-broken spear. It hooted like an owl, too. Not until it had the wisdom to toss the spear aside and unbuckle its shield from its forearm could the Knight attempt to free itself. It couldn't. As it handled the saddle to shove the mount away, the Shire whinnied and walloped its bulk onto the Knight's leg. Frail wails soared above the chaos of the battlefield. Its voice sounded coarse and heavy, serrated with pain. To Vion, it was as sweet as water from a creek.

As the straggle of Lanke around the Knight recovered, a current moved through them to avenge their honor and Orta. Vion had exposed the Knight as human and thus vulnerable. The legends were untrue; no Lanke god would create a horse that could be felled by man. The Shire pretended to be divine. The Knight pretended to be invincible. And Lanke once intimidated were now emboldened—that was if they had not first felt the presence of Vion. Lanke confronted with the venom dripping from his glare stepped back. They read his warnings well and clear: do not step across his path, do not enter his line of sight, do not interfere with his retribution.

Around them, the Ontinian massacre was coming to a close. What seemed like a thousand tawny faces thronged across the slope, behind, across the stream, in the stream, and anywhere else was a cloudy blur. None were recognizable. The Knight lived. Vion could hear it scream. He could see it struggle. He was over them, unmoving.

The pair were worthless.

Skids of mud smeared across the Knight's dark armor. A winglet of its helmet was bent. The corner of its slit chewed on a dirt lump like the lips of the Ontinian king gorging on chunky pudding. Smudges and smears tainted the golden roaster along the Shire's caparison. It would not calm. It would not die. It floundered as would an Obolio in mud pinned by an arrow, approaching the gates of death. Vion would open those gates. Nartha would judge it.

His boot stomped on the horse's head. It dented the helmet. The Shire jerked in letting out a sound. He could not hear it. He stomped again and again. There were noises, thumping noises. Hooves kicked and slipped in failing to stand. A bright red spilled from its muzzle.

His boot could not land in the same place twice. There was a strain in his leg. He was yelling. He closed an eye smarted with sweat. He didn't need it. He persisted and cocked his battle-ax back and was about to execute before his glare caught a dark form outside the void that he took and regarded and understood as hard and drab skin.

It was armor. It was the Knight. He had forgotten about the Knight. His sight told him the Knight was still pinned beneath the weight of its mount. It was all he needed.

Pressure crossed his ribs. The spear. He could not remember how the Knight retained it. His hand gripped the glove that held the shaft. It would not budge. Vion punished the Knight by thrusting a foot into the fragile bend of its elbow.

Its impenetrable armor was a false strength; it snapped like a twig. Its groans blocked the agony. Its back arched. It tried to keep strong and not scream. It would. Vion would hear it scream.

It faltered in holding the spear. The ironwood was free in his hand. It would not do. The Knight could not die in peace. It had to die screaming, it would die screaming, it was screaming because his heel was digging into the crux of its elbow. Screams of agony. There it was. Ripping through its coarse maw. The crackle of bone arriving as gravel beneath his sole.

He went to kneel.

It did not surrender. It hurled a gauntlet at Vion. It struck his side then shoulder then his nose several times, but each strike came as a fist of mist. It dissipated before Vion could feel the blunt twist of his head. He had become numb. The battle would long end before he reckoned the bridge of his nose had fractured like a crack of lightning and would heal crooked despite the scolding he'd receive from Shiderk and the Vexi at Evana Ula.

This was not now. He was above it. He had somehow planted his knees onto its pauldrons so the bluntness would not land. He leaned his weight forward. Its sounds were a struggle in survival. Vion would not relent. His fists would not relent. They rained down on that helmet, a muffle of strikes. His glare dripped with the venom of disgust. The taste across his tongue was sweet.

Somehow, the next he could remember, Vion had the shattered half of the spear in his hand like a shepherd about to stake the heart of a lamb. His brow pulsated with an emotion that he could not distinguish as either fury or pain. It blotted the corner of his vision. His nose bore a second heartbeat. He could not recall how many times he punched the helmet but the back of his hands cried with red tears, and the edge of his consciousness located a discomfort lined along his knuckles.

The Knight was still pinned below him. The dark slit it peered from did not cut clean as it had when the Knight first arrived. Its opening was dented and jagged so to resemble the Orme Janak Gorge. From within the slit exuded a disquietude. The Knight no longer showed struggle, but the rasp of its breath was like the gales between mountains. Between Vion's knees, the peak of its chest rose and fell. This close, Vion noticed an engraving of Ontinia's emblem over the heart of its armor—a rooster pecking at its feet. Crusts of mud dried across its outline. A deep scratch decapitated the rooster.

Realizations formed around Vion. Within the area he could recognize, light carried a gloom. Night could not have broken so soon. Rahderk approached Vion on the valley summit during the first quarter of Rachma's Domain. The battle could not have lasted until the fall of the sun.

Mud, sweat, and another watery liquid coated his tawny skin. Droplets from his philtrum, red or clear, dripped onto the Knight's armor. From above, wet needles tapped across his bareback.

Rain

When had it started raining?

To the left of Vion and the Knight squirmed a pair of legs. But the narrowness of thought and vision was like an ethereal barrier, blurring any details. He could not even reckon the apparel it wore. Noise blunted against that barrier but could not actualize into sound. It was an unrelenting murmur. There were other things beyond it, other actions and movements, but Vion couldn't distinguish it even if he focused on them.

He didn't.

The Knight was his focus.

The Knight was his kill.

The Knight was his.

The Knight had stilled. The arm Vion crushed lay at an angle like the wishbone of a turkey. Where the ends of the wishbone joined, something sharp and solid jutted, covered by the stained rings of its hauberk. Its fingers were stiff. Rain rapped at its armor. The being beneath it bore the hollowness of a husk.

Vion could not think how long they remained like this until his ears caught a foreign sound.

"Please."

He had difficulty tracing the voice to the dark slit of its helmet. It was the Knight. The Knight had spoken. Its voice had the immensity of a volcano and the rumble of an eruption, but it spoke these words as if first learned and unsure of their pronunciation.

The most unexpected was how young it sounded.

Like the others, a voice said within his thoughts.

He ignored it. It spoke again. This time, it added a tearful sniffle.

"Please…Don't kill…"

The following was spent realizing that he could not bring down the spear. Its steel-end hungered for flesh, his blood burned for it, but neither pushed him to engage.

Vion was hesitating.

His muscles were about to force themselves through but stopped when the darkness inside the Knight's slit dispelled.

Its eyes…

Gintoka free me. They were like the pale emerald eyes of Ulajin.

"I'm too young to die…Please…T-too young."

His daughter's eyes were unique to the clan, as were Vion's. Shiderk, his wife, had the common but fierce brown most Derk had. They were like spiked whips. Ulajin's were like the meadows in Katajin. So when Vexi Calmaderk birthed Ulajin and walked Shiderk and her baby out of their tent, she regarded Vion with a furrowed look.

Ulajin's eyes had left space for doubt.

346

Jealousy might have tormented Shiderk and Vion. Incriminating thoughts of Krederk sneaking into their tent when Vion was beside Rahderk learning to be Vex lurked behind them like a shadow. Blame could have passed between them like Narthema throughout a Heva induction until accusations caught flame and burned their home to ashes. Neither occurred. Their life did not burn as most Derk thought. Instead, when Vion first caught a glimpse of those emerald eyes, he felt a vehement surge of emotion that he could not contain.

He felt love.

"I...I finish and return to mother and sister. Or they'll...Oh, praise the Masters, they'll—"

The more Vion glared, the more he could not stop thinking about how similar the Knight's eyes were to Ulajin's. The skin around its eyes had a tawny texture that the sun had forever imprinted. Its presence bore innocence. A veil of tears coated its eyes that once coated Ulajin's when she knocked her head against a Vanar's wagon. Every clan in the Wastelands could hear her wail. Vion was the first to tend to her and had put Ulajin on his knee to stroke her thin, growing hair and tell of the legends of Cahona and the old ways of the Rech clan. Eventually, after rocking her enough, she had stopped crying and fell asleep in his arms.

Vion glared at those emerald eyes.

The cuts across his bare chest cried. Bruises bloomed where the Knight had struck him. His clean-shaven mouth and chin bled a scarlet beard. And the Knight, he was sniffling like...like...

Vion balked again before hardening his features. Taken aback heretofore, his silver glare returned to hissing. He would not be deterred any longer.

A growl in his throat, Vion enclosed both hands around the spear, lifted, and thrust it into the slit. Steel screeched against metal. The slit gave a knuckle. The yelp he heard was cut short by a gasp. The Knight tried jerking back but couldn't. It would suffer as the Shire did. He had pinned it, he had conquered it, he would kill it.

Yet the spear was too thick to fit through the slit and had lodged

347

in-between. The edges of the slit were bent inward and held the spear back. Its steel point licked at the Knight's eyelashes.

The Knight gaped as its internal fear became external. Its eye shivered at the clawing spear. The jaw beneath the faceguard made its helmet shudder. There was a ticking of metal. Tension hurried his panting.

With one hand, Vion strangled the spear. He did not look pleased.

"Please, please."

The sounds shot through its lips. Vion's glare narrowed until there was only those emerald eyes.

"Please." It sputtered. Again. "Mother. I see m-mother and sister. Please. Only one year. *Year*! Many more before..." The Knight swallowed. Vion's silver glare vibrated with agitation and was how the Knight finally realized that he could not be saved. "If I die...Save Daaooni and Thadaata before...before the Masters- They-"

Vion listened enough.

His hands tightened their grip on the ironwood shaft, elbows out. Those emerald irises were sheened in tears. The white struggled not to burst from its skull.

"No..." Desperation cracked his voice. "No. No, no, NOO! *NOOO!*"

The violent spirit of Erktal apprehended the armor.

Its trunk lurched and pitched. Its leg floundered and kicked and dug its heel in and tried bucking but no maneuver was strong enough to throw Vion off its shoulders. Its arm waved like a bony flail. That strange, dark metal rattled together as if the Lanke gathered every weapon from every clan and threw them down into a gorge.

Vion kept the helmet fixed with its spear.

"I have to go back!" It wailed, no distinction between fear and pain. "Master Baghmir! He knows! He take mother and sister and leave them in yard for officers! You hear! YOU HEAR! THEY FUCK MOTHER AND SISTER AND LEAVE-"

The spear plummeted.

***

"Velderk! *Listen* to me!"

His silver eyes jerked open, wild as his breathing.

He couldn't see.

The pressure created a blank boundless sky. His sense of feeling sharpened instead and considered everything it touched. Restraints cocked back his arms which were like wings about to be clipped. His head could not turn. Even though he could not control himself, his knees ran as if they could. They kept slipping on a viscous substance like wading across solid water.

Rain pelted him, sluicing sweat off his skin. Not a knuckle of his body was dry beside the slab of his tongue. It made its presence known as limp and dead. A throb pounded between his sockets. What sounded like a tiny bell rung in his ear.

He heard that voice again.

"Tajin, *focus* on my voice."

Only one Derk could call him this without beratement.

His eyes fluttered to return to consciousness. An effigy against that white sky. Another Kverech Na hastened by before this tenebrous figure shaped into a human silhouette. The ethereal material of its skin began smoothing into real, tangible skin. It was tawny, and beneath it lined a simulacrum of muscles that deepened into the muscles of a hale warrior.

Rahderk

The enigmatic blotch of its face pieced together a description of his mentor—hard wrinkles and chicken scratches of age, a grizzled beard, the furrowed demand of his scowling mouth, and a silver-inlaid ponytail tied back with a leather hank.

Vion concentrated on that hank. He was remembering now, his mind clearing. Its leather was of supple sheepskin. He remembered where it came from. After the Derk, Vaz, and Heva successfully crossed the River Twins to initiate the War for the Split, Vion had sacrificed one of the sheep abandoned within its pen to skin, tan, and

349

craft that hank as a token of appreciation.

The reasons why were endless.

Rahderk did not need to adopt Vion as his Orvex. There was no good reason to as there were plenty of other Derk with honorable reputations and significant skill in battle to one day be called Vex. Since no Derk wished to be his Vexa, Vion would have fought as another naive warrior whose death in battle would be forgotten upon its ascent into Zarvena.

Vion was alone. The clan had abandoned him, so he abandoned the clan by lashing out at everything that breathed.

Rahderk changed that. He became the father he had lost. He provided him a Gods-Brother in Bellderk and guided him in winning the love of Shiderk, the water to his life. He taught him and beat him and shoved him down to points so low his frustrations and resentments were buried beneath the hardpan. Rahderk molded him into a Vex that did not demand respect but received it freely. There were no Derk clansmen who would not sacrifice their lives for Vion.

The hank was not enough. What it promised was.

Now that hank obliterated the blank sky. Vion blinked again. At once, the shapes of reality surfaced.

Rahderk was in front of him. He was stooped forward on a knee. His hair and cowhide skirt were drenched. The look he had would have dejected death.

The restraints behind him were two Lanke upturning Vion's wrists and elbows. A third had his arms wrapped around Vion's like a taut rucksack and fingers laced at the nape of his hulking neck. Vion could hear the exhaustion in their breaths and felt the third's tickling at his ear. Its beard raked at his shoulder.

The rest of the scene opened like the fangs of a Dry-Mouth.

The glen adopted the gloom of war. A horde of clouds oppressed the skies. Its cascade of rain extinguished the noisome fumes of rot and shit the War carried but did not eliminate its gore. The pits of the valley were an upturned graveyard. No survivor could maneuver without stumbling. Ontinians floated prone in the stream, the purple of blood billowing from their wounds. The rest of the enemy's corpses they would gather and burn. Any Lanke with further signs of Heva Na Narth would have to be sacrificed to the gods and be either left behind or burned.

Hands away were the Knight and its steed.

The armor did not move. The spear was tossed aside behind its body to where he could only reckon the shaft. This he could remember. The obliteration of its helmet he did not. The front, from what he could see, looked as if a mace had landed a hundred strikes. It created a rugged crater where the slit oozed with the mush beneath.

Vion wiggled his fingers. Three on his right and two on his left buzzed against a numbness. They were weak to respond. Across them, he could feel the thickness of blood and the threats of agony. The bones were broken.

The battles had long ceased. Heva were hunched knee-deep in the streams, their grating grins and giggles crawling across his skin. Hinheva and the wilder ones hollered as to receive him into their pack. Some of the Aacher clan carried the corpses of clansmen to lay them abreast on cleared land. Uchraderk was one. They would give the dead a ceremonious burning to hand their spirits back to Nartha.

But for now, most Lanke were moths gathering around the torch of Vion and Rahderk. Their glares were unmoving as they stood in silence clenching their welter of weaponry. Sheets of rain made them apparitions of the dead.

In between the rain, Vion reckoned faces of the Derk he had led. He could not look at them. Curvaz, the inexperienced and timid scout from the Vaz, had paled so that his swarthy skin became pasty. The older generation—Landerk thronged on the valley face and Krederk within its pits—held a hardened pallor. They knew what had happened. Ages of war in the Wastelands deterred the Lanke from peace and kindness, but the Vion they knew before he became the Orvex trampled over these inclinations.

The Derk judged him.

Their wariness returned.

"What…"

Vion attempted to wriggle from his constraints. He couldn't. Behind him, grunts and grumbles cursed his resistance. The mere act of denunciation would have received a fist from Rahderk or, in the least, a defensive remark from another Derk. Nothing happened. Rahderk only nodded at the Lanke. Vion could feel their hesitancy through the tightening of their grips. They did not want to unleash the rage they had just experienced.

"Release him," Rahderk said. His voice was flat and impassive.

There was that hesitancy again. Their throats rumbled with discontent before the restraints loosened, slipped across his flesh like the scales of a Dry-Mouth, and freed him.

Vion landed on his knees, mud splattering. His breath rasped through his teeth. He was tempted to rest his hands in the mud but instead regarded them. The broken fingers were bent at odd angles. The stabbing pains they induced, as if sticking his hands into a bed of needles, forced him to clamp down his jaw. This and the blunt swelling of his nose. It zagged like a shattered sword. Any time his upper lip snarled, he heard the grating of its shards.

The pain made his voice sound like a threat.

"Rahderk. What happened? Why-"

He was casting his silver serpents up when he stopped mid-sentence. The friction in his glare festered. The serpents of his eyes dipped back and hissed from within their hollow.

Overhead a storm threatened, the rainfall drained the Lanke from sight, and Rahderk did not say a word.

Lamentations of the Forest

I

"Chry is a member of the Runners now, Barloc. Whether you accept him or spurn him will *not* be discussed further. He will stay with us and listen to what you and the Council have discussed, as a member of the Runners should."

Bar took a stoic stare at Chry. In his mind, he repeated the scene of them first meeting inside the tent with Bar, instead of sparing the boy, ramming the dagger into his throat and allowing him to bleed to death on Ambia's Black Wool blanket.

Too late now.

"As you wish," he said.

Chry and Ambia—the shy-eyed boy mouthing a silent "I thank you" to Ambia who left him with a motherly smile—sat beside each other at the end of the dining table. Bar eyed the Runners: Vion to his left, Cavas to his right, Ambia across from him at the other head of the table with the boy and thief beside her. Spears of morning dawn intruded through windows of dusty glass. Behind him in the kitchen was the crackle of a fire and the clatter of Mesa preparing the morning meal. The scent of buttered leeks wafted through the doorframe, smelling of a homely treat they have not had in half a Son.

None of the Runners were prepared for the road yet, most in their slumbering attire aside for Cavas. He never took off his robes.

"On *that* note," Onvi spoke, the tassels of his nightcap waggling.

"Why don't you tell us what the Council told you. We're positively *dying* to hear about the mission they have for us."

A sourness scrunched Ambia's nose and lips together.

Bar ignored her and said, "Yea, so I will."

He relayed to them then about the meeting with the Council of Crystal. He kept his retelling as factual and inevitable, leaving aside unnecessary details such as the condition of Cadaqu and Vion's outbreak and instead focusing on the sword *Azrael*, the gems of the Walker, and their whereabouts. The brief was as the name suggested— brief. But as the candle clock they lit at the beginning of their meeting first started to melt, the expressions of the Runners adopted the somberness of their mission. The Void. The Lanke. Ontinia. By the end, no one was smiling, and everyone was listening.

With uncharacteristic thoughtfulness, Onvi ran his fingers through his disheveled hair. "Well, I guess *that's* why you didn't want to tell us about your meeting," he said. "Caris'ma and Lomano are puppy dogs compared to the Panther you just sicced on us."

This, Bar assessed, was not far from the truth; aside from the dangers of the Lanke and Ontinian mountains that searching for the gems required, the Void was and would be magnitudes harsher than what they had experienced in Caris'ma and Lomano. Even though the contents of the Void were unknown to the Four Nomases, its perils were undeniable. No one journeying into the Void had returned. The Forest devoured travelers by land and what ships tried from the sea returned as debris, its coasts now called Sam's Gulf in regards to how much flotsam Isaam and Cirva had received on their coastlines after the Fall of Pactus.

Needless to say, Ambia did not seem pleased.

"And you expect us," she began. Her voice was surprisingly calm. "To venture into the Void, a land uninhabited for two hundred and fifty years and which most think is untraversable to retrieve a gem that no one beside Simul has ever touched?"

"Yea."

"That's ludicrous, Barloc."

"We have experienced worse."

"Nay, we haven't," she retorted. "The Void is nothing like being forced to eat the intestines of a Falconfrog or escaping from a Maroon Panther."

Bar bit back his tongue. He had chosen Ambia since she had the characteristics of an effective mother—loving, empathetic, headstrong, assertive. Now, all those characteristics he was confronting head-on. Convincing her would not be simple.

Ambia rested her brow on her hand and asked in a voice more disappointed than contemptuous, "How are the Runners supposed to benefit? What are you trying to accomplish with this?"

Onvi's eyes popped into a realization. His grin played with an idea before his finger popped up to speak.

"No, no, you know what Ambia. I know what he wants. He wanted to wait until we were close to the Forest because he thinks now that we're near, we're more likely to enter it. He wanted us to smell the dung before he said, yup, we've stepped in it!"

Bar did not need to toss Onvi a scathing glance, for Ambia did. She, as did Bar, did not want nor need Onvi's foolery at this time.

Still, it was infuriating how exact Onvi was.

Everything that thief does is infuriating. Better without him. Go on without him. Bring him to the Gardens, Gardens, off to the Gardens.

Onvi threw his hands up.

"Fine, fine," he said. The thief crossed his arms, leaned back in his chair so two of its legs held him up, and propped his leather slippers on the table. The oakwood of the chair creaked. "I'll shut my flap."

The thief then glanced across at the boy who left him with a wan smile and a shrug that said, "oh well." This contributed to the thief's grin.

Bar ignored them for now and concentrated on the Runner who was of the biggest threat—Ambia. She had her sight on Bar again and would not relieve her gaze. It was demanding. It was enthralling. Sometimes, he thought he could not properly think beneath a gaze that penetrating and beautiful.

She shook her head. "Barloc, I won't have this. Entering the Forest and *then* the Void will only mean death for the Runners."

"That is not for certain," he said.

"Oh? And have you met another who had returned from the Void?"

"Nay."

"How 'certain' then will we be returning?"

Bar pivoted the conversation. "Each member knew the risks of joining the Runners. This is but another…"

"Enough of your pretentiousness, Barloc," she snapped. "These are *lives* we are discussing. *Human* lives."

Her voice had risen onto a current of frustration and her scowl could've castrated any other man, but she held back another emotion pressing against her eyes.

Bar listened, his face as hard as the bark of a Rosewood.

"You *knew* the dangers, and you *knew* I did not desire a mission like this, and yet you *still* accepted. I *asked* you to discuss the mission with us before accepting because I *told* you I was worried for the Runners' safety. But still, *still* you disregarded my pleads."

Her body had risen from her chair as if possessed by her words. Stakes of disbelief prodded her expression.

"How in the plos can I trust you if you won't even listen to me?"

"Because I have listened, consoled, and saved you times heretofore," he said as a matter-of-fact.

She stared hard at Bar, tears now veiling her eyes.

It was like a punch to the gut, just as mentioning the Falconfrog was to Bar. They had too much history. Bar could almost imagine those scenes he had mentioned of when Ambia needed him, one when he had hugged and held her at the Hungry Wolf Inn, the other when she was unconscious and violated near Samit.

Her eyes could not look at him any longer. She regarded Vion. "And what about you? You learned about the mission the same time as Barloc did."

"Rahderk is the one I want to see," Vion grumbled. "If he is searching for the gem, I will, too."

Ambia was taken aback, "You have to be as blind as a sick crow. Vion, *think* about what you are saying right now. Are you truly willing to sacrifice the lives and wellbeing of the Runners, those you have traveled with for nearly two years now, for the chance at pity revenge?"

"I will do what I must," his voice, although scathing whenever Bar mentioned Rahderk, was restrained when talking to Ambia. "Rahderk will die."

"And what if..." She stopped mid-sentence and merely stared at Vion. Bar traced her eyes to the cut across the brute's neck, above his Cor's Crux, the same one Bar had inflicted the night heretofore. Since then, it had congealed completely but was still untended to. For whatever reason, be it the early morning or her attention to the conversation, Ambia missed seeing that cut.

"Vion...How...?"

The grumbling of Vion's throat responded for him. Without having to speak to each other, both Vion and Bar knew not to mention how he had sustained the wound.

For a flutter of an eye, Ambia's expression twisted into something between disgust and nausea. Her features resisted this natural force before she swallowed it back. The struggle was gone, and in its wake was a stony determination.

She fished from her leather satchel, that which she always kept near, a clean batiste rag, a cloth swathe of wrapping, and a vial of what looked like Silver Oil before gliding over to Vion. Her mouth and brow were set. As she approached, Vion merely hitched his glare at her as an act of suspicion.

Beneath Bar's awareness, his shoulders relaxed. He was relieved of Ambia's defiance, at least for the moment.

"While she's busy repairing our buddy ole pal," Bar turned to the voice of Onvi who still had his feet lounged on the table. For some reason, his nonchalance irked the voice. "I wanted to discuss more of this adventure we've stumbled upon. There's just so much I want to discuss, and as much as I don't like to be the sour apple of the orchard,

Ambia does have a…"

Bar tossed a hefty pouch that clunked onto the table in front of Onvi. It was the faded, dirt-brown pouches that Bar would give to the Runners for when payments were received from missions. Bar had the rest of the pouches beside his foot beneath the table, three for the three other Runners, Vion having already received his and Bar sewing his Gonotes into the inner lining of his gambeson.

Onvi's eyes, in their broad grandeur, recognized the pouch immediately. He unwound from his lackadaisical posture as his hands did the rest of the work, loosening the leather lace and opening its mouth to a pile of coins, deadened Illum stones surrounded by rounds of gold with "Three Nations, One Nomas" inscribed along the edge of the coin. Moxen. The highest form of Admanic currency.

For a thief whose erstwhile life was of stealing coins and riches, Onvi's disbelief was slightly unexpected.

"How…"

"Fifty moxen pledge," Bar interrupted. "One hundred more for each Runner upon completion."

Onvi was oblivious to him. Any look of doubt or concern for the road ahead had washed away beneath his glistening, ocean eyes. His grin had become a bar of gold. Prostitutes and ale, Bar reckoned, were foremost to his primitive mind.

"Oh Bar my friend," Onvi said. "You know me so well."

Bar was not his friend.

"Buying us will not change the circumstances."

This was Ambia. She was leaning over a sitting Vion and wrapping the cloth around his tree-trunk neck. On the smooth table-top was a piece of the cloth torn and stained a blackish crust, her batiste rag, and the vial half filled. Her face was expressing the frigidness of a Withdraw hacking the head off a Dry-Mouth. Vion was that Dry-Mouth, and his glare could have poisoned an ocean.

"I did not think I was," Bar said.

Ambia finished wrapping Vion's neck and wiped her hands with the batiste rag. She did not respond to Bar, wanting him, he reckoned, to say more on why he had accepted the offer. He remained silent.

When finished, she stuffed the batiste rag and vial into her satchel but left the remains of the bloodied cloth on the table. Cross-armed and immovable, Vion grumbled something that Ambia seemed to ignore.

"Barloc, I am not going unless you give me a plausible reason *why* we have to," Ambia stated. "And do not tell me it is because of the moxen. That might be a valid excuse for Onvi but not for me."

"Hey, that's not very nice," Onvi said, but his grin implied he was less than offended.

They ignored him. Again. Bar caught of a glimpse of Cavas and Chry. They acted almost the same, their eyes bouncing back and forth between Ambia and Bar.

"The Council has asked us to receive the gems," Bar said. "We are a mercenary group whose role is to take such jobs, whether they are simple or complicated."

"This is far from complicated," she said, her throat grating. "This is the lives of the Runners that we…"

"Yea, and the lives of Admah and Western Etherine are of no importance?"

Hurt flashed across her face before it hardened to resentment.

"You *know* I…"

"Yea. I know. I know you care deeply for the Runners, I know you care deeply for Pulchrit, and I know you care deeply for people." Bar caught himself strangling the armrest and released his grip. "But the Runners have a mission: to search for the gems and, if possible, the sword, *Azrael*. To accomplish this mission, the Runners will be entering the Forest and the Void. *That* is the decision."

Resistance was what Bar saw in Ambia, yet his uncompromising resolve told her she would not be able to convince him alone.

A glint of desperation crept into her eyes when she regarded Cavas.

"Cavas," her voice was the soothing of when she and Cavas would meditate together. "What do you think of the situation?"

Bar held his tongue. They both knew that regarding Cavas in such a manner could mean further provoking the spirits within. However, he should not have worried. Cavas merely turned his head toward her, stared, and then turned it back forward. There was no further movement from the mage.

Chry asked, "Do I get a say in…"

"Nay," Bar barked. "You do not."

Chry opened his mouth to speak again but one look at the foreboding Bar shut his lips back tight.

Ambia was alone. She had no one else to support her, and this time, she would not win. The Runners were her family now, and both Bar and Ambia knew wherever the Runners went, she would, too.

Ambia regarded the Runners, but the only one who would look her in the eyes was Bar. He saw hurt and betrayal in those eyes and for the first time since leaving that cabin in Noma Devolum, a needle of regret pierced his heart. The pain was not enough to crease the line of his mouth, but it was there nonetheless.

What is this woman doing to me? He thought but just as quickly reverted the thought. He need not to be swayed. The gems of the Walker were what he sought. For four years he searched for an opportunity, and for four years he waited. He would not throw away the chance merely because the path forward was perilous or his emotions were aroused.

After this, Ambia did not stay. She nodded to herself, almost as if hiding the tears she was holding back, and whispered, "I hope, beyond hope, you know what you are doing, Barloc," before leaving them for her room upstairs.

II

A cushion of clouds yawned across the morning sky as the Runners traveled East toward the Forest of the Lost. Dawn streaked over the Rosewoods. The sun's radiance blinded the Runners who squinted and raised their hands to shade their eyes. As they approached, the Rosewoods grew giant and rounded with a hefty girth. It was like the crystal buildings of Cadaqu but now natural with branches and bark. Their lofty shadows brooded over the banks of the Forest. Evergreen needles persisted against the wintry warnings of Swason but lost their vibrant green for a lifeless grey. It was as if the Void, leagues beyond, was siphoning life from their roots. Behind them shrank the chimneys of Neco.

Riding alone on his sumpter, Chry raised a fist over his yawn. This was a common habit of his. Living in the Wastelands, Aimee would have the tendency, as a playful joke, to jab a finger down his throat whenever he yawned. He nearly bit her finger off countless times, but every time he did, she would only laugh merrily.

He missed that laugh. Fuck, he missed it so much.

His next yawn was that of half a sigh.

His hands felt loose on the reins, and the only reason the sumpter knew where to walk was because it followed Ambia's alabaster-white gelding. He resisted the droop of his eyes. The bags beneath them were like the eyes of the mutt that would bark outside of Jayce Rucker's home until Anesa Rucker tossed it a sliver of Dry-Mouth.

The following nights were rougher than normal.

There were not enough beds upstairs for him to sleep in unless he wanted to lay on the floorboards in a room with either Bar or Vion. So, for the two nights they stayed in Neco, Chry was forced to sleep in the servant quarters beside Mesa. He could hardly sleep. His bed was a toss of hay, and Mesa could not sleep without the light from a candle clock. Even then, Mesa would not stop tossing and murmuring to himself. Chry could recite his pleads of "me sir, yul, yul" and "no more food, no more" even though Mesa had no meat or muscle across his skeletal frame. There were many stretches when Chry's glazed eyes would gaze at the plastered ceiling as Mesa listed off the things he would do: Mesa will eat, Mesa will obey, Mesa will remain, Mesa will listen, Mesa will stay stiff, Mesa will never leave, Mesa will obey, Mesa will eat, Mesa will eat, and Mesa will love. He could not tell if the servant was awake to hear what he was saying or if this was leaking from the nightmares he had to endure.

Either way, the nights did not give him much peace.

At least the day of rest was more fulfilling. Mesa tended to their needs without the need to ask. Redbacks and the final harvest before Swason satisfied their bellies. During the day, Onvi and Ambia dragged him to the only mercantile shop in Neco, a two-roomed shack that seemed about to fall over if the sea breeze raised its voice. Bar left Chry's pouch of moxen on the table, so Ambia used one of his moxen to buy Chry turnshoes, a wool cloak, breeches, tunic, and deerskin gloves, all in shades of grey and brown. At the blacksmith, he even ordered new horseshoes and saddle for his sumpter that Onvi pressed him into buying.

All the same, as much as Chry found himself distracted from the tragedies of the last Moon and even, at times, enjoying himself, Ambia acted less than her usual self. She seemed…Well, distant like her thoughts were across the Grey Sea in another nation. Chry couldn't really blame her; he guessed she was still in the house, rehearsing in her mind the argument she had with Bar, disappointing herself over and over again.

I wonder if Ambia and Bar were ever together heretofore, he wondered, slipping in his saddle. *It sure seems like it some…*

Chry startled awake. Jerking, he nearly toppled off his saddle and threw Moon-round eyes around him but did not know where he was or why he was here and blinked away the haze of his vision and reckoned that, aye, he was only riding toward the Forest, that's where he was. The raucous sneeze of his sumpter awakened him. He had nodded off again.

It sneezed again. Its greying, upturned muzzle was no beauty to stare at, and its mottled fur right below Chry's thigh had pinched and twisted through the fingers of Eulgash. Its throat wheezed as it breathed. It sounded like an apple lodged in its throat. Regardless, its grizzled mane was smooth and soft, carefully washed and brushed this morning and the night heretofore. It gave Chry something to think about besides grandma, Aimee, or Nostre's cellar, even though he drifted off to sleep more than once when brushing.

Chry licked his chapped lips and swallowed. After his breathing settled, he slumped into his saddle. The morning air bore a gentle warmth that cradled him, the saddle clasps were tinking to a rhythmic melody, and the bumble of his steed was somnolent like the stories his mother would tell him before shut-eye.

Thinking about it more, Onvi mentioned something about sleeping on horses during their trek to Cadaqu—a brief saying, if anyone could believe anything the thief said was brief.

Doze on a horse, pose as a corpse.

At the time, like many things Onvi said, Chry did not understand what he meant. The boy from Domum rode with Ambia until Bar purchased his sumpter from a hostler in the Slums. It wasn't like he ever had an extended trip on a horse heretofore. He only rode his first steed, Simul, from his farmhouse to Domum and back, a trip lasting less than half of what the Runners traveled his first day.

Now he understood what Onvi meant—doze, fall off the steed, and its hooves will crush you.

His sumpter wheezed again. Chry yawned once more—placing his fist over his mouth—squeezed his eyes shut, rubbed the crust from his eye, and then tried opening them fully. They rose half-mast. He caught himself swaying again.

This was not enough. He'd drop and be swept by a Gardener before he reached a Rosewood.

Instead, he looked forward. Onvi and Ambia were in front of him, riding abreast. The thief, through his expressive speech and gestures, was blabbering about a misadventure during his time in Isadora's Guild, a tale he called "The Mission of Unexpected Excrements." On the other steed, Ambia showed every sign of listening, giggling lightly when Onvi cackled like a burning crow and could not finish his story. Together, they were like brother and sister. More than that, Ambia reminded Chry of his mother.

But she's dead. Like grandma. Like Aimee, too, I'm sure.

His smile waned.

Chry tried listening to the story but drifted off again. He didn't want to say anything either, to interrupt the story or to feel awkward in trying to insert himself into the conversation. Instead, he stared past them at the Runner's forefront. Of course, Bar and his stallion led them. Chry only saw his back, erect and unmoving. He never flicked his stoicism over his shoulder to check on his companions. Beneath him, his stallion maintained the same inconsolable air as its rider.

Chry planted his eyes on his saddle where the first shadows of the Forest cast their black, crackly claws. Around him wound a ring of loneliness squeezing his arms and chest together. There were many moments like this when traveling with the Runners, riding for many marks of the candle clock without a word or noise. In those silences, Chry could still hear them invading his thoughts.

We'd never *leave our lonely love-bird*, they would say. *Like he left grandma at home and Aimee for Domum.*

Oh no, never. Grandma and Aimee would never.

Sometimes, he would wonder if he and Aimee had met Bar in Domum like they had with Vion and Onvi, if they could have joined the Runners together. If so, Aimee would be riding beside him and laughing with him right now. Her sapphire eyes would sparkle when discussing Cadaqu, the Grey Sea, and what they'd find in the Forest. He would've fallen into them again and drown again in their mirth and beauty.

Don't lie to yourself, he thought. *You didn't want to leave Domum then. You were* forced *to leave. Aimee left on her own. She* left to go find a better life while *you* stayed in that pisspot.

He did not argue. He knew this was the truth. Rather, he felt at the sapphire necklace Aimee had gifted him before they separated. Its cold silver felt unforthcoming and unfeeling but was the only object left that connected him back to Aimee. He held it in his fist, squeezed it.

I hope one day I can see you again, one last time, he thought as the Runners rode between the first two Rosewoods of the Forest.

III

From what he knew about the Forest, Chry thought it would be devoid of life.

The stories the Rattles told him about the Forest depths, and the one time he visited the Gardens with his father, did not convince him that anything living could survive here. The Cages back at Domum—literal cages in the Forest the Rattle Trade would use as punishment—could drive the sanity of any Rattle into slush. No Domumite could have an intelligent conversation with Gunder Wood, the Proprietor who cared for those Cages, and none wanted to. Many Rattles tried fleeing into the Forest. Many did not return. Those who did, like Simon Hide, did not speak of their experiences. But other Withdraws could see it in his broken eyes. None who talked to him ever considered entering the Forest.

With these warnings imprinted into his childhood, Chry did not think he would survive. Mayhap that was why Ambia was so vehemently against entering.

But after the canopy passed over the Runners, after closing his eyes tight for the first mark of a candle clock until the arms of the Rosewoods lifted the voices of grandma and Aimee from his ears, after peeping his eyes open at nothing but Onvi's gelding and the greenery around, hearing the crunch of leaves and branches beneath their hooves, Chry was thrown. He could not quite believe it. He was in the Forest and not becoming as deranged as a Rattle in a cage. Actually, he felt somewhat *saner*. The voices in his skull were gone, his drowsy mind had cleared, the sweet scent of Alders and Rosewoods excreting their sap comforted him, and the whispers he heard in the Gardens he did not hear now. Instead, he heard the playful chirping of birds. Of *birds*!

Mayhap the Forest isn't that bad, Chry thought with an uneasy smile. *Mayhap all those tales were just tales told by the Gardeners and Proprietors as to scare Domumites into never fleeing into the Forest. Aye, I think that's what it was. And the Gardens? I guess it's just the dead haunting that resting place. The Void might not be so pleasant, but if the rest of our trip through the Forest is like this, then we'll have no trouble at all. Mayhap I can actually get some sleep this night, too.*

As he toyed with the possibility, his smile grew even more.

What a blessing that would be.

IV

Their first day in the Forest was uneventful. There was no discernible path they could follow since the undergrowth had invaded onto any trail that might have been here during the times of Pactus. Even so, the land was flat and easily traversable. The harshest obstacles they faced were roots and rocks jutting from the forest floor that threatened to roll and break a fetlock. Once, they were faced with a toppled Depanen tree whose bole ascended beyond the heights of rider and mount. Calmly, Bar worked his stallion around. The Runners followed, each staring at its loftiness.

During the first half of the day, Rosewoods brought a sweet, rose-like scent to their nostrils that Chry could not equate with the fear and terror he associated with the Forest. To a Runner, it could have been any other forest at the end of Ainason. Limbs barren of corncob seeds and needles tried hugging their caravan as they passed. Birds with vivid plumes he could not have named nested and regurgitated feed for their young. He watched worms nuzzle into the moist dirt. The sound of play soothed him. On more than one occasion, he caught himself smiling.

But the further they descended, the more the Depanen trees invaded. Branches ascended to the quiet skies above and blotted their view. The canopy was too distant for the birds to be seen, and Chry only knew them from their cries as if warning them from afar. The hollows of the Depanen were larger than his torso and were, to Chry, open mouths screaming into the void. Creatures that Onvi called squirrels were sometimes perched in these hollows and tossed beady eyes at the visitors. This, at least, gave Chry comfort.

They're kind of cute, he thought.

In the wake of the Depanens, Rosewoods and Alders struggled to survive. Many suffocated. Around the trunks of the Depanens were their sprawling corpses, tombstones to the dying. Beneath them were heaps of deadwood where not even a weed could thrive. They were like patches of dead skin on an otherwise healthy coat of fur. Chry, after riding around each, could not ignore how similar the grey bark was to withered bones.

Onvi made a joke about pissing on forest fires. None responded, but Chry could not cast away a feeling that something was off. The Forest of the Lost was not known for its fires and for as long as he lived in Domum, neither Chry nor any Domumite he knew had seen one burning across its canopy.

The thought was disconcerting. Domumites were well-aware of the abomination a fire could become if its deadwood did not burn off. Lightning from the one storm Domum experienced in its last ten years struck the Eduavel District where the Alderwood frame of an abandoned stable caught aflame. Domum's cracked and dry wood fed the fire, and a quarter of the district burned to the ground. None of its residents were prepared. Gladion told Chry of how he and Axel were awake throughout the night hauling children from burning homes, their mothers and fathers screaming inside. To this day, some areas were still leveled, most claimed by the Smars.

Considering what happened to Domum, Chry could not understand how the Forest was not under a torrent of flame. A spark should have burned the deadwood anew. That it hadn't, and instead piled in some places to the bulk of a Depanen, leant Chry to concern.

We could be burned alive this night, his fears manifested. *You wouldn't know it until the tendrils nibbled at your toes.*

Just keep your head down and try not to fall asleep, Chry thought. *Be thankful the Arbiter has blessed you with a clear mind.*

The Runners rested twice to let their steeds crop or feed from the feedbags. Bar warned only to allow minimum sustenance for both horses and Runners. The road ahead would be unforgiving. They would have no town nor tradesman to buy from until they returned to the Wastelands, and none could fathom the conditions they would encounter within the Void. Best to eat the nuts and quarry from the land and preserve their victuals for the Void.

The Runners heeded their leader.

On their first rest, one of those squirrel creatures scuttled down a Depanen and tilted its head at the Runners. Its bushy tail flicked like a whip. Its beady eyes asked who they were. "Vion, go catch the squirrel. We'll call it Vion Junior," Onvi teased. Vion did not look up from feeding his mare. Ambia giggled inwardly. With nimble claws, the squirrel scraped at its nose and then escaped up the tree.

Their second rest was longer to where the Runners could sit and eat the berries and nuts they had gathered alongside the hard bread from Cadaqu.

Chry was about to join but stopped to reckon Bar. He was tethering his stallion to a dead Alder but had then knelt over a burrow beneath the tree's roots. As far as Chry knew, only he noticed Bar hide a circular, gold-filmed object the size of his palm in the tree's mouth. He thought he saw a daisy imprinted on the front but could not have guessed what the thing was and sure as plos was not about to ask.

They ate and were off again shortly.

The humdrum of the day dragged on until dusk dripped from the leaves of the Depanen. Then the Runners established camp for the night. Their meal was the game Bar hunted while riding. He wielded Onvi's bow, struck three squirrels within the last two marks, and strung them across the haunches of his stallion. Their limp forms slapped against its hide and Chry could not think of anything other than the exposed, slender flesh of a Dry-Mouth thumping onto a Tanner's board.

His face tried to contain its disgust.

At camp, Cavas snapped his fingers to light the fire far from the deadwood, and the squirrels were roasted on skewers from Onvi's pack. Vion (still with the bloodless swath of cloth around his neck), Onvi, and Chry each had one to themselves. They ate as if starved. Bar told them he was leaving to hunt another but did not return before Chry retired. Ambia nibbled on her seeds. Cavas did not eat.

Thankfully, Chry still did not hear the whispers but feared setting his head down for slumber. When he did, droopy-eyed and exhausted, he fell asleep immediately and had no dreams or nightmares. He awoke the next dawn feeling rejuvenated and, dare he say, with another smile on his face.

It was the first night since the farmhouse fire that he had received a full night's rest.

V

Ambia could not sleep.

Usually after she meditated with Cavas, her blood relaxing with a sunrise glow between their hands, her internal candle clock would dim for slumber.

Not this day. This day, her blood simmered.

After their meditations, Cavas remained behind as Ambia entered into her tent, exited a mark thereafter, sat beside the dying fire where she prodded, and stared at its coruscating coals until, inevitably, her hazels latched onto the depths of the Forest. They wouldn't let go.

She would have glared if she knew what she was glaring at.

Everything she knew about the Forest heretofore was not matching with what the Runners were experiencing now. So far, it felt like another journey through the Bolus Mountains where the Spruces sang and the Ironskin Goats roamed free. But instead of Spruces, there were Depanens, and instead of Ironskin Goats, there were Toars.

Depanens and Toars.

Ambia tucked her knees beneath her arms. The air held a nightly warmth that could induce sleep, but she could not stop moving. After a moment, her finger started tapping her elbow.

She was the only Runner awake aside from Cavas who, for as long as Ambia was with the Runners, never slept. It was implied that their meditations were enough rest for the mage and was the reason why she engaged in them. Before Ambia joined, as Barloc had told her, Cavas would often detach himself from the sight of the Runners to mediate after dusk. This did not soothe Barloc's perturbations though he understood any decision Cavas made was as natural as a fawn searching for a field to crop in. Cavas did not need much. He wanted even less. And yet Ambia understood the circumstances he struggled with. The least she could do was mollify those circumstances with her Diamu.

When she initially offered to mediate with him, Cavas responded with black, lifeless eyes. They seemed to be born from an emotionless abyss and she, being naïve as a child (*how two years can change a person*), stumbled over her words. Barloc told her thereafter that she needed to lead the mediation rather than ask the mage, that Cavas would follow her if it did not mean compromising the seal, and that Barloc, despite how protective he had been of Cavas, trusted her.

Ambia appreciated him for this.

And now Cavas was here and eyeing her as he would if they were in the meadows of Etherine or over the waters of the Silent Swamps. It felt normal and made her worry that something sinister was snaking through the grass about to latch out with its fangs. If she did not recognize the threat quick enough, it would be too late.

She handled the iron skewer they cooked the squirrel on and prodded the fire. A char of wood collapsed. Flakes of ashes whirled above. Its smokey, wooden scent clung to her homespun dress. She squinted but did not smile. Their steeds, hobbled alongside their tents, nickered in their sleep.

Then there was Barloc.

He told them he'd return with another squirrel to eat. Though the task was simple enough, she did not like the idea of any Runner being alone within the Forest. Still, she was frustrated with him for deciding to accept a mission into the most perilous and enigmatic land within all of Admah without consulting the Runners. Resentment won her over. And now, he had not returned.

She reckoned he would've returned before she finished her meditations. Her ears would discern the crack of deadwood beneath his sole, the rustling of leaves, and the soft stir of the tent flap. They hadn't. When she opened her eyes expectant, convincing herself that Barloc snuck into the camp and settled next to the fire as he sometimes did, there was no trace of him. She checked for snapped branches and footprints, the tents, his and its interior.

Nothing.

The fear of losing Barloc sunk her deeper into a sinkhole of worry. Whether this was solely because he was a Runner or because she was feeling a close intimacy with him, Ambia still could not say.

Nevertheless, he was in trouble. Why? She could not say. So far, the Forest aired on the side of peace. The Runners had not experienced a single threat unless she counted the squirrel during their second rest nibbling at the hem of her dress. The prominent whispers along the tree line had vanished. That she did not truly believe but was merely what it seemed. Beings—or whatever those things were—did not vanish within the day. Her suspicions would not allow them to. At some point, she began to consider erecting the barrier to protect them from any outside threats the Forest had to offer.

Usually she had no reason to summon the barrier since the Runners could usually protect themselves. The Wastelands and Etherine had their own perils—Dry-Mouths and Vvuladevs included—but the Runners had Cavas within his vigil. Furthermore, Vion and Barloc lived within the Wastelands for years without a barrier. They knew how to handle a loose Dry-Mouth. Neither knew how to deal with these whispers.

However, she could not conjure the barrier without effort. It would take much of her energy, and thereafter, she would need to rest to stave off Over-Exertion. Another complication was that Barloc would need to be within the barrier so he could willingly pass back and forth. At this time, without him inside, he would not be able to enter. He would be secluded, left outside for the unknown to devour.

Ambia drummed her fingers. Not long thereafter, her foot played along.

The night between the Forest boles stole any opportunity for sight. The coals were her only light but were near death. Its glow scraped at the black eyes of Cavas. She sawed her lip with her bottom teeth. The Alders soughed in mourning. Any squirrel or Toar heretofore slept into a fiction.

The day the Runners rode through might as well have been a dream.

Noises from the woods were muted as if muffled by a muzzle. They were beyond the bubble of her awareness. The only sound she could hear clearly were her shallow breaths. Everything else sounded like a whisper.

Nay Ambia, stop convincing yourself of things that are not true. Those are not what the whispers sound like. You would know what they sound like.

The smoke changed directions and stung her eyes. Coughing, she knuckled away her tears. She calmed in her waiting. After what seemed like several marks of excruciating patience, there arose another sound. She tried not to be swayed by these random sounds of the night and listened for any hint of Barloc. Her eyes, tearful and smarting, were as useless as if they were closed. With the fire stubborn in changing its position, she actually did close them and was pleasantly surprised when that noise became louder and separated from the stillness of the forest.

She listened closer.

It made an unnatural sound, separated itself with a single crack which reoccurred like the crackling of a hearth.

Or like a foot stepping on branches.

She nearly gasped and shot her eyes open. The fire had led its smoke away. Hope swelled within her bosom.

Barloc. He's returned.

Relief nearly lifted Ambia to her feet. She repressed a smile as her heart fluttered.

That was her initial reaction.

Soon thereafter, a wave of frustration washed over her and

drowned her relief.

Now that her mind and body knew he was safe, she realized how infuriated she was at Barloc. He had given them a bushel of warnings about staying safe and preserving their strength for the journey to come that meant less to her now than Onvi promising he would not visit another brothel. The idea of abandoning the group for no other reason than to catch a stupid squirrel was reckless, doltish, and jeopardized the mission that *he* had accepted. She would not forgive him. He could not follow his own command and so Ambia would buck like a stallion.

Her glare searched for the leader to pin her accusations. Most of the woods feasted on a cocoon of shadows. Weaving the darkness together was the deadwood of an Alder, its branches contorting into the spindly legs of an Hour-Glass Spider. It was the only tree she could perceive against the dim glow of the coals.

Yet, she could only think of Barloc. In her mind, he would emerge from where that crackling was, reckon Ambia burning beside the fire, and, whiles holding a motionless squirrel by its bushy tail, apologize for his behavior with that stoic but somehow smug manner of his. She loved and admired Barloc, but this passion merely exacerbated her frustrations.

She decided she would not call for him. She would not give him the satisfaction. Instead, she fumed within a bed of coals.

If he does this again, he won't have to worry about the Void killing him, she thought.

But Barloc didn't appear.

The more she listened to those footsteps, the more her frustrations fizzled out. They were not even but unsteady. There'd be a crack of a branch then a splutter of them, as if tripping, then the crunch of an Alder's corncob before a long and burdensome silence. It was as if Barloc was struggling to stand.

The legs of the deadwood smothered her frustrations. Terror molted its skin. Ambia pushed herself up with unsteady legs about to fall.

Like Barloc's called a black voice ringing around her thoughts.

Instinctually and hurriedly, she dusted off her dress, but a mangle of nurture and passion thrust her forward. She unconsciously made the decision to meet Barloc and embrace him and tell him how grateful she was that he was alive.

She passed the campfire, but the Alder was all she could see. The snapping of branches was still there and gave her the courage to call out.

"Barloc, we've been worried about you. Where have you been?"

The crunching and crackling ceased. No response. The deadness of the Forest congealed. Behind her, the coals smoldered.

That's when she halted. Her determination had faltered, and her stance became numb as if bitten by an Hour-Glass Spider. Her hands twitched like a dragonfly caught in its web. Her steps led her closer to the Alder stooping over her as another hand to the woods. Its branches crepitated with the thought. The unseen expanses of its bark grinned. She felt eyes crawling on her.

Something's wrong, she thought.

A normal Barloc would have responded. Ambia would set him beside the coals and tend to any sustenance, wounds, or emotions that needed mending as she had in the Silent Swamps or after he had returned from the Dinglers, broken. The truth was not so ideal. The person out there acted as if caught sneaking into the camp to kiss a rusty blade to their throats. It stilled itself to refrain from alerting her, but its presence bloated the air with intention—slice each Runner down as would a scythe through harvest.

But what if it is Barloc?

The Forest might be birthing the creatures haunting her Sensations, but the only reason she reckoned it was Barloc was because she *wanted* it to be Barloc.

The Black Rings taught her reality did not listen to wishes.

Another moment without a breaking branch. The glow from the coals burned low. The Forest enveloped Cavas's black robes. The Alder receded behind a dappled mask.

Ambia was stranded. Alone with that…thing.

After her gelding started to whine, a light cry from an otherwise calm beast, she became desperate.

"Barloc, please, if you are there, come. I have a feeling we require the barrier. Something is not…"

Her words drifted off. It was a stench and sound that seized her. Before Ambia, from a depth unknown, pervaded the repugnance of a slaughtered beast. Within that stench bellowed the moans of the starved like that of the infected in Pulchrit.

Ambia tried swallowing, but her throat felt clotted with blood. She couldn't move. The dreadful manifestations of what could be impregnated her mind and paralyzed her limbs.

Stop this. You need to concentrate and protect the others. They need you.

She was right. She needed to clear her mind of worries and think. Whoever or whatever was out there would not be concerned with her wellbeing. She must prepare herself.

There was another crunch. The noise was near enough that she knew it as a heavy tread. The tingling beneath her skin told her how much closer the thing was then it was heretofore as if it had closed a furlong without her knowing it. The moaning swelled from that black, pregnant belly.

May the Wild be tamed. May my ancestors know me. May they aid me.

Her heart pounded in her throat as it shrunk to the size of a reed. No scream could shove through. All that came out was a harmless wheeze.

And why would you scream and make a fool out of yourself? If it's only Barloc, an innocent Barloc, and you wake everyone else, what will that make of you?

It would make her prudent. That was not Barloc out there. That was death.

She gave him one last chance.

"Barloc, speak to me, or else I'll wake the others," she said hoarsely.

It was a lousy threat that amounted to nothing. There was no response. Its tread hesitated before starting again, quickening. Its stamping cracked seeds as if crushing bones. The sound of malevolence hurled it forward. It was not stumbling. It was hunting.

She clenched her jaw. Her eyes sprung tears as she held back fear. Her hands manifested the golden glow of her meditations. She bore every urge to scream loud and hard and awake the whole damn Forest. But the fear she felt was not normal and would never *be* normal even if an horrendous creature sprung from those woods.

It didn't. It wasn't one of those creatures.

The thing outlined itself within the remaining light of the coals. It threw a disjointed shadow against the Alder. Its branching legs shriveled inward as would an Hour-Glass Spider in death. That thing staggered forward but only for a stride. Then it imperceptibly swayed.

Its outline was the caricature of a human. And the harder she looked, the more features she discerned—a gambeson, the sharp chin of a sword, a lean but strong face, hard cheekbones, coarse skin from years beneath the sun.

Barloc…It really is Barloc.

This should have relieved her. She would've gasped and thanked the Wild if not for what she had smelled. The stench of gore was overbearing, that which would flood out from opening the casket of a rotting corpse. She had to cover her nose with the lace of her forearm to stifle its potency.

It was not enough. The essence of her being was repulsed against what they had revealed. A pale shock inflated her eyes. Her stomach bloated as if stung by a consort of hornets. It took every knuckle of her concentration to hold it down. She hitched forward but did not release her guts, merely a spit of vomit over her bodice. Nauseous stars exploded across her vision.

She held the rest down whiles Barloc's shadowy silhouette emerged from the depths.

She wished it hadn't.

His fingers dripped with blood as if he had hunted down the

squirrel he had set out for and then ripped it open with his bare hands. If there was a squirrel, it was nowhere to be found. Instead, he took a liking to licking the blood off his fingers. There was a gleam to his eyes. It's where the moaning originated from. He'd suck one of his fingers, release a pleasureful moan as his eyes rolled, and then begin on the next. The blood at the corner of his lips sliced into a gluttonous grin. He did not reckon her. His collar was drenched and sticky with flicks of pinkish matter. The bearskin of his gambeson, once impervious and pristine without a tear or smudge, clung to his shoulders in shreds. The skin beneath could not be perceived since the cuts he sustained bled so profusely.

He was not the Bar she knew. This Bar was an abomination.

Disgust erupted from her stomach again. This time, her mind was elsewhere. She retched. A chunky slush of berries, nuts, and bread splatted onto the Forest floor. She could barely stand as if an iron mace had cracked her kneecaps. She reined herself back in to concentrate on Bar. The tears initially induced by fear spilled from her eyes.

Though her blood rejected the mere thought of being near Bar, Ambia forced herself forward. She could not see straight. The world tilted, and each stride felt like trudging through the Silent Swamps.

She had convinced herself that this was not Bar. Not her Bar anywise. The stoicism she adored and loathed had succumbed to an untamable ecstasy. His eyes flickered through its pleasures, a rosy drool lathered his chin, and his manhood was visible through his crotch. The last was not something she would have noticed if beside the Hungry Wolf Inn or within his abode in Neco, yet every Discernment she had responded to Bar.

Ambia saved her voice from falling into fear.

"Bar, I …" She was close enough to hear him slurping each time he finished a finger. Beneath his nails were the slivers of a Bloody Moon. Bar still would not reckon her. He was enthralled by his obsession.

Reluctantly, she reached out a hand. She was close enough to touch him, but he was too busy moaning and drooling to perceive her.

From below, she reckoned his crotch thrusting. Her hand hesitated. It could not get close enough to touch him. Streams of tears escaped her. His moans were excruciating.

"Goodness, please, *please* stop this madness. I beg of—"

The thing exclaimed a guttural sound before its arm knocked her away. It swung like a flail against her chin. Her jaws clacked together and radiated a cry. For the moment, she had a passing thought that some of her teeth had cracked.

Ambia staggered backward, cupping her mouth. Warmth spilled over her palm. Steadying herself again, she retracted her hand and reckoned a splat of blood. No teeth. She could taste copper dribbling down from her nose where it throbbed like thunder. Disbelief rounded her olive countenance.

"You *can't* have it," Bar barked. The austerity of his voice grated like rusty saws. He had hunched into himself, cupping his fingers to his heart, as if protecting the body of the squirrel he was hunting. His pearl-white teeth flashed within his snarl. "It's ours. *Ours!*"

Ambia merely gawked at the creature that wore his clothing.

It can't be. Nay, nay, please, it's just a dream. Just a dream.

The harp her mind strummed broke a string and repeated the same discordant note. It acknowledged the thing, its jerking, its whispering, oh, its whispers to itself.

A dream. A dream. My fault. All my fault.

Its lurching gait was undecided on where to go. It'd reach a few paces forward, stop, hunch over, violently scratch and tug on its hair as to claw out the indecisiveness, then engage in another ungodly behavior. It was as if a Carriona was devouring Bar from within.

Indifferent to her, Bar did a leap-lurch past Ambia, strayed away from the coals, realigned and swayed to a tumbling halt. Her gaze could not help but follow and catch a glimpse of ebony eyes.

There he is, her mind pointed. *Watching, like he always does.*

Bar made a piggish snort like a grown adult playing pretend. He was not pretending. He was voracious. He was gnawing on his thumb, and Ambia refused to believe in any religious affiliation and so had never prayed in her life, but now prayed to anything that would stop Bar from biting down. Her vision blurred with tears.

Pray. Not Bar. Not the Runners. They are all I have left.

He did not sever his thumb. He released and pressed his palms against his temples. His head shook wildly as if bucking. He made noises. Their steeds, hobbled next to the tents, were in a cacophony of deranged neighing. If they were close to a tree, their muzzles smashed against the trunks and bloodied the bark. One, she did not know which, worked free of its restraints, neighed victoriously, and galloped out of the clearing.

The Forest closed in on her.

She could not remember the expanse from when Bar was thrashing to when he became still. Presently, his head was bent to glare at his palm. She could assume the urges he had, that basic animal instinct, but he did nothing but look. He abided to the stillness. Something had happened. Pressure had lifted. The space between them abdicated sound. Under the last light of the coals, Ambia made out the loosening tension within his shoulders. Along his neck was a fine sheen of sweat. Any wild energy from heretofore had expelled. He almost seemed...sensible.

What's—

His head turned the slightest. His profile swam through a pond of darkness, but she swore she saw his volatile (*no, violent...there was violence in those*) eyes.

If there had been any sliver of humanity remaining, this was it.

"I—"

Its beastly growl departed. It was Bar's voice—definite and stony—but now there was a voiceless plead beneath it that told her he was in trouble and needed her help.

Tears wetted her cheeks. The air emptied from her lungs, and her jaw was clamped into place.

She wished it would stop. All of it. Even right now when Bar seemed like he was returning to himself. It was worse than if he had entered his tent crazed. It meant that what she experienced now *was* real and that this *was* Bar and that he *was* being tormented by a presence she could not contend with. It made the possibility of this being some dreadful dream distant and improbable. She could not hope anymore. She had felt, tasted, loved, cried, and shuddered. Together, it made this event more real than any reality could.

Ambia dropped to her knees and could not stop herself from bawling. He turned away so she could not recognize him. She heard his breath shudder.

"I'll…be in my tent," he whispered. It was the gentlest words she had ever heard from him.

All she could do was weep. If only she were with him. If only she had tended to his wounds when he had sustained them. If only she found him in the Forest and led him safely back into camp. If only she could have saved Elon and Edgar and Mister Omna from the Black Rings. If only she could save someone, anyone, from their suffering.

If only…

The last thing she heard before Bar retreated to his tent was the inkling of a whisper surfacing from the deadwood.

VI

It seemed Barloc had no recollection of the night heretofore. Ambia did not ask directly. That would have cued him into a line of questioning Ambia did not want to confront. Instead, she asked in a way that would not immediately reveal what she had seen. She was having difficulty convincing herself what she saw actually happened and was not one of those dreams where one of her fears—the death and dying of Barloc—became tangible.

She had startled awake within her tent not knowing where she was. Her skin, where the tears and vomit had stained, was smooth and clear. In spite of this, her initial reaction was to check on Barloc. She jolted up, rushed outside, and there he was, prodding at the smolders. Dawn sifted through the leaves to shed a light on him. He had no blood on his skin, and his gambeson was as pristine as it had been before dusk.

His responses now were just as unhelpful in assuring truth. He told her he was unable to catch another squirrel before the end of twilight and decided to return to camp instead and rest for the day to come. After his stoic stare would not reveal if this was a truth or a lie, Ambia retained her questions.

Cavas was no help either. He had not moved from where they had last meditated, so before leaving in the morning, she asked if he noticed anything unusual throughout his nightly vigil. As expected, he merely stared at Ambia until she hesitated to ask again. It was futile.

She would not outright tell either of them what she saw. She would tell none of the Runners. From what they knew about the whispers and how they could derange a person, Barloc and the group would have difficulty distinguishing her truth from madness. In addition, there was no plausible evidence that could convince her it wasn't just a horrible dream she had experienced.

She could mention again forgoing the Council's request, turning back, and returning to Neco, but this too seemed trivial. She might provoke Barloc, and that stopped her from asking. Presently, she did not want to see him as anything related to the creature she had seen him as. She just couldn't.

Saddled, the Runners were off before the sun reached its potential. Each rode singly. They did not speak. Only listened.

VII

The vessel named Cavas had watched the woman talk to herself. She had meditated with him that night. Thereafter, she entered her tent and exited. She had stared at the trees of the Forest, hitched her head and gagged, walked to the tree line, reached her hand out to nothing. She did not acknowledge him. She then staggered backward, held her cheek, and turned until she was looking at the leader's tent, gazed and then stumbled back to her tent. He watched. She did not exit her tent again until morning. The leader returned before dawn. The leader entered the clearing with his bow. His lips were red. He stared at the mage. He stared back. The leader nodded and entered his tent. He watched. Nothing happened the rest of the night.

VIII

The farther they traversed, the further the Forest relinquished its will to live. The dead bark of trees peeled and leaned over their path in trying to return them back from where they came. The graveyard of bare twigs, branches, and roots cried beneath their horseshoes. The only green was so far above within the canopy of the Depanens they could have mistaken it for a crimpled brown. Or they could be dead leaves. Chry did not really know.

Marks into their travel, the Runners dismounted and reined their horses by foot. The lands were becoming too woody and uneven. Sometimes, it would drop into a valley they had to cut through—their streams dried into a traversable bed of pebbles—or it would bowl into dells they could detour around and over. The woods crowded together in congregations too tight for their horses to ride through comfortably. Their course wound and weaved. None of the Runners wanted a false branch or stone to twist a hoof.

Whether this changing landscape was why the horses were now whining and balking, Chry could not say. Ever since they dismounted, their steeds were reluctant to stride forward as if knowing any path forward was one step closer to the Void.

Thus, the Runners rested several times to calm their beasts. Twice, Ambia went to each and laid a hand on their heads. Her eyes closed, and a golden glow like the sun radiated from her palm. She did this without Bar or any Runner asking her to. Gradually, their whines and restlessness receded like the retreat of a storm, but after calming the beasts for the second time, Ambia was out of breath and stumbling as if the pressure from her magic had liquified her bones. Bar forced her to sit down and rest. She did not argue. Chry did not think she had the energy to.

Only Bar ate during their rests.

Throughout the day, the Runners did not converse. Once, after their first rest, Chry tried speaking with Onvi—if anyone was bound to talk, it was the thief—but he was without words. He had the face of a skull, and his usual grin whittled away into a solemn stare.

What nudged Chry's anxiety even more was the silence behind the Forest. Pockets of nothingness replaced chirruping birds and scuttling squirrels. No streams with water were stumbled upon since the day heretofore. Chry, unknowing of living fish before experiencing the confluence of the River Twins at Viamous, had goggled at the little ones in those streams, no bigger than his pinky finger swimming together like a hive of horseflies.

Not here. Here, Chry did not hear the mumbling of a stream. Only the absence of life insisted as if Eulgash created this stretch of the Forest but neglected to finish. The winds refused to sing. The sparse deer trails had smoothed. He looked as they progressed and had wandered around searching during their third rest. Nothing. Even uplifting stones and rocks where insects would squirm within moist dirt did not leave a trace of their presence.

It was plain, unaerated dirt.

Chry could not find hope in this. He warded away the impending fears of where they were going and the hundreds of Pactus natives that had perished and how many of them had died here and were the Runners walking over corpses right now? Were these the grounds where the dead slept?

Chry shook his head. He did not want to think about this. He guided his sumpter over the body of a fallen Rosewood, the beast balking at first before relenting to him tugging on the reins. Afterward, Chry huddled into his wool cloak.

The day was getting chilly.

IX

Their horses were unappeasable.

Before Chry, Vion's mare stopped dead without warning and would not continue onward. She ruffled her mane, shaking its head "no" to Vion's prompts. He again barked a command through a foreign tongue and tugged, but the mare, unquestionably obedient to Vion heretofore, stamped its hooves and snorted. Chry was ready for the warhammer of ire to strike, but Vion only brushed the mare's mane and whispered in that same guttural tongue Chry did not know of. He guessed it was the language the Lanke used. To him, it sounded like the chopping of a rugged ax, but the mare listened without fault. Soon thereafter, Vion gave a firm tug and the mare moved forward.

His conciliation was an outliner. Progress did not last.

A mark thereafter, without pause, Onvi's gelding began whining a breathy, high-pitched whine. It was all the Runners could hear. Onvi did nothing to calm it. His lips moved, but what came out was not directed toward his steed. His teeth nibbled. His tongue licked. Behind Cavas, Ambia's horse nickered and nudged her shoulder for more feed. Bar's horse slowed tremendously, slowing the rest of the Runners as well. Whenever he would almost come to a complete stop, Chry's sumpter would stamp its hoof and make a noise between a neigh and a snort as if about to stampede. The line would quicken its pace thereafter. Each Runner was absent of these exchanges, lost within themselves.

Cavas's, a gelding blacker than the night, was the only horse not to be disobedient. Its long countenance bore the same blankness as its rider. They followed as one.

The Runners could not go on like this for much longer. They bound their patience until they were stopping and calming more than they were progressing. Rest did not help. Cropping did not help. Bar did not allow Ambia to calm the steeds with her magic. For good reason, Chry thought. Ambia was as ghastly as Chry was after discovering Nostre's cellar. He could not tell exactly what was causing this. He guessed it was her magic but would that mean all her behaviors were because of magic? Some? None? Did magic change a person's personality? Did it suck the life out of them until they became an empty husk that said nothing, heard nothing, and did nothing?

He refused to ask anyone in fear of what the answer would be.

Curiosity kille' da mule but ignorance slaughtere' da pac', Gladion had always preached.

Chry ignored the voice.

At one point, they could not convince their steeds to follow. Their hooves refused to move. Since the light around them had not dimmed, and the Depanens prevented the sun from peering through, they could not distinguish how late the day was. Regardless, they made camp between the hordes of deadwood spreading their arms like prosecuted men hanging from a cross. There was not enough space to erect their tents or gather as a group, and no clearing was in sight. Trees severed their interactions. This night, they'd sleep alone beneath the eyes of the Forest.

If it were not already obvious, things were not normal.

No one spoke. While hobbling and tethering their horses to deadwood, Bar stopped and tried jerking his food sack off his saddle but couldn't. He untied a knot and tried yakking the flap open but could only open it a knuckle. He grunted frustratingly and ripped it off the saddle to loosen the opening again and finally shoved his hand in and grabbed a chunk of hard bread. His stallion did not resist or make a noise. Along the soft edges of the bread was a mildewy fur. Bar breathed heavily.

He plopped down and tore it apart with his fingers and teeth. No one else seemed to notice, and Chry just looked on, petrified at the wildness of his behavior. This was not Bar. He was usually so...diligent with how he moved. And was, well, abstinent. The Bar he knew would take a modest bite, chew, and digest. This Bar did all three in a gulp.

Vion snapped Bar out of this. He snatched the bread from Bar's hands, glared for a moment, his nostrils flaring as if about to charge, and tossed the chunk into the wilderness. Bar gazed at his fingers where the bread had been but then blinked awake. It was as if he had risen from a daze. Recovering, he nodded slightly and said something to Vion. Stoicism returned to his expression thrice as hard as if to compensate for the madness that had leaked out. Vion went to hobble the horses the others left untethered starting with Onvi's and ending with Cavas's.

Bar was not the only one and Chry, sitting on coniferous needles with knees tucked into his arms, shivering, watched the others. He was too mortified to move. Though they were resting, the steeds were disinclined to silence. Each whinnied. One cropped weeds around a Depanen, but Onvi's munched on a tangle of deadwood. Chry diverted his eyes but could still hear the crunching of teeth.

Its owner was no saner. Onvi nuzzled himself into the roots of a Depanen to where the Runners could only see the tip of his head. But Chry could hear him. He glibbed on and on about Onvi and his little lambs, mumbling a song about how much Onvi loved his little lambs. He did not stop. Bar, finishing with his steed, yelled out "be fucking quiet." Onvi giggled to himself and sang even louder.

Cavas did as Chry did, sat and watched, but only looked at Ambia who was on a log two arms away from Chry, staring at the hands in her lap. He was waiting, Chry guessed, to do that golden glow thing with their hands again like they did every night. But he had a feeling Cavas would not get what he wanted. Not this night.

And then there was Chry.

His lungs were shuddering. He had on his wool cloak that did not help. He had the urge to bawl until his eyes dropped from their sockets but did not know why. He didn't know why *any* of this was happening. Leaves and branches would not rustle, the Forest refused to produce life, and he was forced to listen to the deterioration of the Runners.

Under his breath, he recited a tome Aimee had read at Eulgash's House of Worship named *The Consecrated Writings of the Devout*. When he had come to visit, she read one of its passages out loud so he could memorize it word for word.

Now he repeated it and repeated it for the rest of that day.

X

Light and warmth were dying, and Chry did not like what Ambia was doing. He didn't like what *any* of them were doing.

Onvi changed his tune and was crooning to himself. Chry heard whispers of it, paled and shivered beneath its damning words. It was the same passage Chry had been repeating to himself.

"Grant us the ability to be courageous in the face of Judgment," Onvi preached. "For our Deliverance will be total beneath the hand of the Arbiter."

Over the roots that concealed Onvi, Chry could sometimes see a crystal dagger raised in the air by both hands as if holding up a newborn.

Bar was nowhere to be found. Chry did not search for him.

And Vion seemed to be the only sane one. He hobbled the horses so they wouldn't escape from fright. Afterward, he gathered lodges, branches, and kindling near their bivouac to prepare for a fire. Cavas moved to light the fire and then returned to where he sat heretofore to stare at Ambia again. No one else helped Vion. Not even Chry because Chry would not approach Vion and confront him and be ridiculed by an insult or smacked aside like a whiny child because right now everyone was losing their rattles, and it's not like he knew exactly if Vion was losing them or not because he just *seemed* like he was stable. It wasn't enough.

Still, each behavior paled beneath Ambia's.

What she did was not grotesque or crude or absurd and that's what made her behavior disturbing. It was not what he expected. It was unassuming at a time when Onvi sang to his dagger and Bar ate like a boar. But Ambia was just…Well, standing there. She was in front of a Depanen, and her head had cocked back toward its canopy. That was it. Nothing else. She didn't move, speak, stir, shake, or do really anything.

Her actions were mute, her arms dangled as if broken, and her mouth and eyes were agape.

Cautiously curious, Chry scooted closer to Ambia and now noticed tears rolling down her cheeks. They rained from her chin. That was far from normal. Shit, *nothing* in the Forest of the Lost was normal. He couldn't hear the whispers like he had when he visited the Gardens with his father, but he could damn well *feel* them now, a million eyes crawling and digging into the skin. Aye, he could and, well, but, fuck. It really wasn't a sane thought. It couldn't be. None of it was. And each thought like this produced tiny, little insects of unease inside his belly that he could not vomit or stomach.

Despite this, he couldn't stand by anymore. Mayhap it was *because* of this uneasiness that he could move; the insects squirmed so much he could not sit still even if he was not thinking about helping Ambia. Or mayhap it was because Ambia's lips were beginning to move and murmur.

Like Onvi. Oh Eulgash, like Onvi's.

No. He couldn't let that happen. Chry couldn't lose his last friend to this…to these *things*.

He pushed himself up, but since his knees wobbled as if he were hundreds of hands from the ground, Chry dropped back onto his ass.

Come on Chry. Stop being a Smar and stand already.

He did, gradually, using the tree trunk of a dead Rosewood as support, but the same problem arose when he took a step forward. It was a baby's first step. His body was unwilling to confront the world before him.

But that's it, right? I must because Ambia's my friend and because she's my friend, I should make sure she's healthy and well and not going to bash her brains against a tree.

The image that came was harrowing. He regarded Ambia again. This time, her lips were clearly articulating words into sentences. What they said, he really, *really* did not want to know.

She needs you Chry. Grow your rattles and go to her already.

Shakily, he nodded to himself. He made his second step, easier but still awkward and cumbersome as if his foot had grown doubly instead of his rattles.

You know what they say about foot size, Onvi reminded.

Arbiter, too many voices. Too, too many.

Knees rattling, throat groaning, Chry tried another step and did not crumble this time or land in the mud or die an unfortunate death.

Progress.

And as Chry stumbled to Ambia's aid, slow and steady, off to quarrel with the unknown, Vion set down the twig he was about to feed the flame and glared at them, his eyes simmering beneath its silver.

XI

He was surprised Ambia didn't hear him approach. He was not very sneaky. His feet crunched on the needly, Depanen leaves that had fallen during Ainason, and the sounds were like the aftermath of thunder to his ears. But, as he thought about it some more, Chry didn't really *want* to be sneaky. He wanted to make sure his friend was herself and sane.

Her presence did little to reassure him. Her paleness deepened into a glow, and what he thought was a still, motionless picture was untrue. Her skin vibrated as if restraining a tremor within her bones. Her moon-wide eyes darted from branch to branch, frightened that they could not find the things they were looking for. They were the eyes of a mother who had lost their child.

Chry swallowed but concentrated on her lips. They kept moving in a murmur, the gibberish impossible to decipher. Then that gibberish cleared into discernible words. He stopped cold. She must have known he was approaching her because her words addressed him directly. What she said sent gooseflesh down his spine.

"…hear them? Do you hear them Chry? The children, Chry, the children…They're-they're out there and calling for us…Crying…So much crying…They…We need to…" Her voice could not keep still.

Her whispers slurred slightly. She did not turn to meet him. "You- you can hear them, right? Hear them...whispering. They...They're frightened...Goodness, all they need is a mother to love them. They need *me*. And...And they're pleading, Chry, they're *pleading* for us! For you!"

Limbs gangling, Ambia shuffled toward the Depanen, gazing above and placing a gentle hand on its bark. The roundness of the bole was three times her height. It was like they were within a surreal dream, he thought, or mayhap his anxiousness made it seem like none of this was real.

She dropped her concern down to where the endless leagues of Depanen retreated. She stopped murmuring and trembling. To Chry, she was hooked and tonged, paralyzed by apprehension.

Cavas sat behind them, cross-legged and staring.

Chry was near her now, but he was beginning to think he should have stayed far, far away, so Ambia would not be provoked into something absurd. He had enough of this Forest. He didn't know who these "children" were, but he sure as plos did not want to find out. All he wanted to do now was turn around and go back to shopping with Ambia and Onvi in Neco.

How he would convince Aimee to come with him...That he could not say.

Chry lifted his unsteady leg and pressed forward.

Upon hearing his patter, Ambia turned toward her friend. He could see the fullness in her eyes where her love was undeniable. Nevertheless, he shivered. There was something not quite right about that gaze. There was *too* much love in it. That's weird to say, he knew, but it was true. Her eyes said she'd massacre a village if they interrupted her flow of undying love. That, when she was talking about caring for imaginary whispers and pretend children, was not a comforting thought.

"Chry..."

Her hand slipped from the bark. As she stared at him, her hazels filled with a watery sheen, and her whole body pleaded for Chry to come, come with her. A tear rolled down her cheek. She sniffled. "Pray...The children...The boy...They're...They're just innocent little children that's all...Pray, they don't deserve this."

This was new—the word "pray." Behind a tomb of palpable fear, he recalled how often Ambia alluded to Eulgash or to any god in general. The answer was never. Through her speech and actions, she remained grounded. "Goodness" replaced "Eulgash," "I thank you" for "Thank the Arbiter," meditations for the Positions of Orison. The Arbiter had no play within her life. Her presence screamed desperation.

Chry could not stop shaking.

"They don't need to suffer like...like my home did. The boy. The others. Chry, they have no home. No mother to care for them." She stepped toward him, clasping her hands to her dainty breasts like a prayer. Her smile was a sickle of repentance.

How the fuck was he going to react to that? Arbiter, Chry didn't know what to do or how to do it or what he was doing right now and all that overwhelmed him and made him take the smallest step back.

She did not notice. She continued to plead. "Th-they have no home. Pray. Pray, Chry, pray. They have no mother...They...They..." She echoed "they" again and again to a murmur.

"They have no one."

Her wet stare looked through Chry and dawned with a realization.

"Besides me."

Immediately, her eyes dried. It was almost unnatural how quick the tears were gone. She nodded absently, and across her expression remained a solemn determination.

"That's what I need to do," she said. "That's what needs to happen. I need to go. I need to leave. I need to save them."

Leave, he thought. *Arbiter, what the fuck does she mean by that?*

The Arbiter did not respond, the Runners did not respond, but he knew exactly what she meant. It's Nostre's cellar again, it's the farmhouse, it's Domum's walls. He needed out. He needed to save Ambia and get the *fuck* out of here.

"Ambia, I just..."

He couldn't push the words out before she interrupted him again.

"That's right. Leave. I'll leave, bring them back to us. Pray, Chry, they're alive and well and I can see to their safety. Safety. That's what they need. I can give them safety this time. Not like last time. Not like Pulchrit."

It was as if she were blaming herself for the Black Rings.

Arbiter, does she really feel this ashamed?

Ambia whipped around. She faced the unknown and he had the jerking urge to reach out and grab her and stop her, but he heard them now. That's why he stopped. The whispers. They were looping lengths of rope around her limbs to manipulate her as the Forest puppet. The rope was tying off. They would begin pulling her in.

"Chry..."

He regarded her back. He could not see her expression, but her head was lowered and her fingers were fiddling with something concealed. But her voice...it did not sound deranged. This time, it almost sounded...normal, like it was actually the soothing, sweet voice of Ambia. He could be fooled. But if he was, then let him be fooled. Better that way.

Behind him were the rambles of Onvi and the breaking of branches. Unawares, Chry leaned forward and listened carefully.

"I know what's happening...Those children. They're just...afraid...They're afraid of death...They're afraid of the Kemals they have become."

He gazed at her back.

Kemals

Every Domumite knew of or heard about these myths, but knowledge of them was scarce. Interactions were nonexistent. The term Kemal, as Aimee had conveyed to him, was derived from the Lanke's native tongue, roughly meaning "Walking Men." But that did little to reveal what this term exactly meant. Eulgash's House of Worship preached the Kemals as Rumeramos, souls so corrupt in life that they were condemned to live again forevermore. Folk like Carp and Simon Harlequin insisted that armies of them lived within the Void. Oscar

Redback, the hostler outside of Domum's gates, took it a step further and claimed throngs of them roamed throughout the Wastelands.

Even Ambia, during their travel to Cadaqu, commented on what she thought they were: "From what I have read from the Temple of Death, Kemals are said to be spirits trapped within the physical realm. Furthermore, mages at the Temple of Death could employ these spirits to serve their biding, summoning their essences from the remains of corpses so to anchor them to our world. After the Fall, Lokemal, the magic used to manipulate Kemals, became scarce, and the Temple of Illusion salvaged the only known spell—Namolean. That's how Onvi knows it."

Now, Chry wished he had listened closer to that Ambia.

"Ambia, can we just…" he hesitated. "Just stop and think a little bit? I mean, we can help the children, aye. But, well…"

"You don't want to help."

"What…? No, I…"

"You're like the rest." She stopped fiddling with her fingers. The lullaby of her voice lost its tune with the pitch and tone becoming discordant like shattered chimes. Chry reckoned her head tremble as if storing a bundle of resentment. The figments of the Ambia he had known were succumbing.

No. Pray, help her. Arbiter be damned, HELP HER.

"You don't want to help the children. You want to see them scream. You don't care. You *never* cared. They could all stay as Kemals and you'd laugh. *Laugh.*"

Her voice was scathing. Chry was losing her. Her accusations, though he knew at some unconscious level that they were from a presence separate from Ambia, thumbed childish splinters into his heart.

She's getting in your head. She's going to—

Going to what darling? Bring you back to the farmhouse where all your hopes and dreams died? Grandma-ma is listening. Aimee-bear is—

mommy, mommy, please help us mommy, before—

He was losing focus. He was getting dizzy. He couldn't keep his feet. The maw of the Forest was growling at him. He could hear it. No, that wasn't right. It was Ambia growling. It was a discontented growl, hungry to sympathize.

She's a beast. You turned her into a beast, Chry. It was YOU. YOU DID THIS TO—

whispers, my lonely lovebird, they don't matter, none of it—

save us, mommy, please, save us from—

Fucking stop it! STOP IT!

Blood warmed his fingernails before Chry yanked his hands away from his temple, stumbling back. His belly felt like it was pumping air with how fast it was breathing. Swallowing hard, Chry regarded the red tips of his fingers and the moistness of his hair where those fingers had been. He was trying to scratch, no, *rip* those thoughts out.

Then, Ambia hunched down and lunged forward toward the Forest. Onvi laughed manically behind them. Without thought, Chry screamed, "*NO!*" with bulbous eyes. The scream expelled from his belly with enough force to hew an Alder, but his feet were planted and unmoving to the pleading of his will.

She didn't listen. Mayhap couldn't. Her sprint was a wild purpose as she hurtled around a bole, the Forest donning her with the first tatters of darkness.

Chry was about to cry out again since that was all he could do when a hand snatched her wrist. It clamped down like a heavy manacle and was so quick, Chry found himself stunned. Ambia jerked back from running and would have collapsed if the hand did not hold her up. The arm was a block of muscle. She had no chance of overpowering the restraint or slipping through. But she flailed as if she could.

The knots of tension in his belly, back, and shoulders were released, and an uneasy smile strained upon his lips. A Runner caught her. Ambia was saved. She would not succumb to the Forest and its fucking insanity. Yet one look at the Runner who had "saved" Ambia wrung Chry's skin too tight to breathe.

Vion, he thought, huffing. In an instant, every threat that the whispers could manifest Vion seized. The Lanke was not someone he wanted to interact with. In the Forest, he was someone Chry wanted to be ten leagues away from.

Being two hands taller than Ambia, Vion raised her wrist aloft. She writhed, cried out in constrictive pain. Her toes scraped at the forest floor. Every so often, her teeth would chomp at Vion, and Chry believed she would have chewed through his wrist if given the chance. Rashness exacerbated her desperation for freedom.

Vion regarded her as the menace he was.

"Let me go!" she shrieked. Like a Skinny on a fishhook, Ambia squirmed, but his grip was locked tight. *"They need me, you Esonio! Let me go! Let me go! Let me GOOO!"*

This isn't how it's supposed to be, Chry thought dreadfully. *We're supposed to bring her home and care for her and lie her in bed and be her family and...*

At one point, Ambia reckoned her teeth could not reach Vion but her fist could. Dangling, she walloped at his barrel chest, often missing because of how wild she swung her arms, hands, hips, and head. Swollen welts riddled his torso, but he and his body did little more than flinch. Dampness trickled down her leg beneath the frayed billow of her forest-green skirt. Water.

Chry forced himself to hold his stomach. *A Woman's Dew*, he thought.

Vion grunted in response, a noise that could be mistaken for a guttural chuckle, and then smirked. There was no grace in that smirk.

Behind Chry were sounds, a cacophony—horses whining and stamping, the popping of branches in the fire, the silence of Cavas who he knew was there and staring but couldn't turn and confirm, Onvi's mad call of "Little ones belong to him; They are weak, but Simul strong!"

Then he heard another yell. It was familiar and authoritative but unwelcomed and faltering.

"What is-"

A grunt of pain severed his speech. It was Bar. Chry did not regard him. His bones had twisted stiff. Sounds were flying around him from a distance. Colliding.

It was too much. The sounds were too much.

Rabid, Ambia must have recognized Bar's voice because daggers laced her screams and stabbed their eardrums.

"*NOOOOOOOO! NOT HIM! I'LL HANG AND LET THE EXECUTIONER FUCK MY CORPSE BEFORE I LET HIM LAY A FINGER ON MY CHIL-*"

Venom dripped from Vion's glare. He yanked Ambia closer.

"Another word," he snarled to her. "And I'll tear your throat out."

It was not an empty threat. Ambia's hand he held above him was darkening from how tight he was strangling it.

She did not stop, hesitate, or acknowledge Vion. She screamed many condemnations thereafter, not all coherent but all with spittle spewing. Vion was not one to go against his threat, not when he meant it.

And yet all Chry could do was stare. His flesh knew what to do, yet his nerves disobeyed. A crystal wall blocked his thinking. Beyond the crystal were the lessons he should have learned about being the courageous man his father wanted him to be. Its grimy crystal reflected the contortions of Ambia. Her...Its...Its contortions were...oh, Eulgash, it was a *thing* Chry couldn't even reason with. It had no right to exist, no reason to live within *his* reality. Yet it did. No matter what lies he told himself, Vion and that thing were *real*. All of it—the farm fire, Volumous, Cadaqu, Nostre's cellar, Mesa, the Forest, even almost clawing himself to death—was now part of his life. And the sooner he accepted these events, the sooner the crystal would melt away and he could stride forward.

Chry pried his mouth open. His jaw was chattering.

"V-v-v-v-v-v-"

Eulgash have mercy, I can't even say his name.

The little coward inside pleaded for him to stop, but Chry willed himself to resist. What stuttered out was a muddle of words desperately thrown together.

"V-Vion. Can you…Pray, put her…Or just settle down before…"

"Quiet, farm boy," Vion snapped. "We don't need help from an Ar Kah."

Discouragement crushed his throat.

Bar barked, "Release he-" but couldn't finish. He stifled a cry. Chry could not tell what Bar was struggling with. He was usually so direct and effective, but now, as he tried to control and tamper the hostilities, none of his commands broke through.

Chry's vision pulsated to the point he could barely see. The ground swayed beneath him. Tension built in his heart until it threatened to burst through his chest.

"But I…" He finally said. "But…we need, I mean the Runners need…"

Vion ignored him and clasped a hand around Ambia's neck. His fingers nearly reached around it, and he could crush her windpipe with a twitch. Still, she thrashed and croaked what could be obscenities if able to articulate. She was bashing Vion on his already crooked nose before thrusting a hand into her satchel and groping. Eyes wild with violence, skirt wet at her crotch, legs dripping and kicking, olive skin ill with suffocation. She seemed like a ravaged spirit, ready to drown in a crazed love.

Their voices clashed together.

"Release her Vi-"

"Die you Katarc bitch."

"P-pray, no-"

"*MY CHILDREN! MY CHILDREN!*"

"Simul loves me this I know-"

"Listen before I *gou-*"

XII

He sat. His legs were crossed. His hands were on his thighs. He was tranquil and wordless and still. His black orbs gazed from the slit of his hood. Night had claimed his robes. The fire his magic lit provided scarce light.

He watched the Runners. They argued about minor issues. He did not utter a word. He would not. His Temple teachings inculcated him into a silent life.

They would kill each other. He would do nothing unless commanded. It was not his purpose to act. His purpose was to remain vigilant. Every Runner could die. His emotions would remain null. The seal would stay sealed. The spirits would thus remain within. This vessel would continue on.

Vigilance came before companionship. It always would.

He blinked. He sat. He listened.

Another moment went by. Then another. Then another.

XIII

There was nothing she would not do for her children.

They were innocent of the Fall of Pactus yet imprisoned. That would not do. Ambia was here for them. She must be. The others. They would never understand. They wanted to tell her what to do and what to think and how to act, but that would not do. That would not do. She would not forsake them as Pulchrit had forsaken her. Never. She'd tear through them all.

Please mother. Protect us. We can't live without you. We need you here. Protect us from the bad man.

Yea, my children. I will protect you. The bad man is no longer here to hurt you. I am here. Shush now.

Save us from the old man, too, mommy. He won't let us leave. He's making *us stay. We're so scared. We want to go home.*

Take us home!

Please, please!

Mama. I can't feel toes, mama.

She could not resist their pleas. This was who Ambia was. When the Black Rings plagued Pulchrit, she and the Hypenian were the first to care for those infected, although the best they could accomplish was to set them at ease before the paralysis induced an eternal sleep. Her efforts and care never ceased, even when she had left for the Nexlor and eventually joined with the Runners. She could not forget her promise to restore Pulchrit to the city it once was.

She could not forget her promise to these children.

That selfish, cocksucker Bar didn't think she should. Of course he didn't. He'd see them on stakes. All of them. None understood. Chry was a coward. He cried at the sight of blood. Onvi wouldn't stop talking. He overwhelmed the little ones. They'd cover their ears. She'd rip out his tongue. Vion would kill. He slaughtered too many heretofore. He could not be trusted to stay his hand.

These were bad men. Very bad men. She could not have them influence her children.

Her children. She'd always protect her children.

Ambia resorted to drastic measures.

The sewing needle she groped for was snug along the bottom of her satchel, beneath a welter of vials, clothes, and instruments. She had never been one to organize her medical supplies. Thus, needles, surgical scissors, and glass broken from her persistence blocked her path. They scraped and punctured her hand like a pin cushion. It wept blood. Silvery liquid stung her cuts and punctured wounds.

Ambia was oblivious and raving obscenities. She kept shoving her hand in and around and held no recollection of the mutilation. Her vision became a tunnel toward her children. There was one aim. The rest succumbed to Oblivion.

She was conscious of her lack of breath but couldn't trace its source.

That Lanke. He's throttling my throat. He's trying to steal me away from my children, my *children. I'll kill him. He'll die.*

She finally seized the needle, held it between thumb and forefinger, and thrust its fine point into the side of her captor. It punctured above his hip. Her memory tried recalling when the Runners traveled to Lomano where, from a window, she watched Barloc and King Rocara the First fence in the courtyard. They doffed their equipment throughout their duel piece by piece until they were exposed to the edges of their sabers. She felt like that now—straddling death. Deadly, dangerous, and free.

But this memory and any other memory was cloudy and indiscernible. Her feelings knew only the thrusting of her hand. Flesh yielded to the needle. It was so *exhilarating*, more so in that her freedom meant joining her children.

Mommy's coming, she thought as her captor grunted. Around her was the force of yelling. She thrust harder. *Mommy will be there very, very soon. She will give you the loving you deserve.*

Her breath returned wheezing as if breathing through the collapsed well of her throat. It was not enough. Her arm was not yet free. That uncultured swine griped tighter as she heard a crackling across her wrist.

Not enough, not enough, not enough

Every one of these thoughts came with the strike of her needle until she was screaming, "Not enough! Not enough! Not enough!"

It became enough. She did not reckon how or why but she suddenly slipped from her shackles. The oil of tenacity and love had saved her.

Free at last. Free at last. Children, I'm free at last.

She collapsed but hastened to her feet before that *beast* could snatch her again. Her hands were unconstrained, but the one the beast had grasped she could not use. It bobbed at an unfamiliar angle like the limp head of a doll Mister Omna would stitch together. She listened to her harsh wheezing, unknowing to the contusions tattooed along her neck and wrist. Her children would heal her.

That's right. I'm coming. I'm free. No longer be afraid. Ambia is here.

She ducked beneath the club of an arm and hurtled between the boles. The hem of her skirt—once tattered but now torn to ribbons—

trailed behind her as did her hair, a mane tangled with twigs and mud. Tripping, she dropped to all fours, freeing herself from human conformity. Her broken wrist crunched behind her.

She left the cries behind her.

My children. My lovely, lovely children.

She could not stop herself from grinning.

XIV

How can this be happening? Chry thought, hearing Ambia echo from the Forest depths. "Where are you, my children? Come now. Mommy's here. Mommy's made it!" *This isn't supposed to be happening.*

He had watched petrified as Ambia stabbed Vion several times in the gut. It was gruesome and grotesque, but what else could he have done? There was nothing else he *could* do, unless he wished his head to be knocked clean off.

Shock from the initial strike forced Vion to loosen his grip on her neck, but nothing more. His hold of her wrist tightened as she had stabbed him. From the engaging sneer beneath his beard, it almost seemed like he enjoyed having a needle stuck in his flesh. Those pricks across his side were a scattering. The skin was dressed in blood. Though she was wheezing and could hardly breathe, Ambia would not stop calling for her children.

About then, Bar staggered beside him.

There were long moments when Chry could not stray his eyes away from the conflict, but he did so eventually and immediately regretted his decision.

Bar looked no better than Ambia.

Bent like the Hunchback, he was sweating and breathing heavily as if having breasted a storm. A frighting rictus contorted his brow. Wincing pains squinted his eyes. He fastened a hand to his brow to keep the pressure from bursting. If Chry did not know any better, he would have guessed that a nest of rats was nibbling Bar from within. It was the most emotion the Runners' leader had ever revealed, and this repulsed Chry enough for his unconscious body to step to the side. He hoped not to be corrupted by whatever distressed Bar.

Too late, my lonely love-bird. We're all so very fucked.

Bar ached a raspy curse.

"Ambia, get a hold of—"

He could not finish. He twisted further into himself, letting out a stabbing cry.

Bar was no help. Chry was no help.

Ambia wildly stabbed and spouted, "Not enough" with each swing. It seemed like forever to Chry when Vion tried to snatch her again yet caught her needle instead. It pierced his upper palm and poked its head out the opposite side. Whether this hurt any more or less was unimportant. It was unexpected. The hand holding her wrist opened slightly, so Ambia could slip through its hold. Her rictus was a triumphant glee like Ralesh Sanal's, the mad mage in the Well.

A snarl pressed against Vion's bared teeth, his silver serpents spitting. With little consideration of the needle, Vion swung his arm at Ambia like a club in battle.

Fortunately for Ambia, she retained the nimbleness of when she was lucid. The arm careened over her head as she lurched forward to where those whispers played. It was too late now. Chry could not stop her even if he had the courage. She tripped, she tumbled, she trod on each limb. The last he saw her she was like a gangly and rabid deer whose hoof was broken beyond repair. Soon, her calls were lost to the Forest.

She's gone, Chry thought. He could hardly feel his knees with how much they trembled. *She cared for me and now...Now she's...*

Vion did not chase her. Instead, he straightened erect then glared at his punctured palm. The needle was a glossy, scarlet post. The wounds he sustained across his side were like tiny tunnels from where worms had nuzzled in and out. The waist of his wolf-pelt skirt was bloated with blood. After an internal fuming, Vion yanked the needle out like a thorn and flicked it into the dead undergrowth. He glared at his palm. Those eyes could have burned through a village.

No one chased after Ambia. The tethered horses, though not tame, whined to themselves now, stamping like petulant children. Bar's hand covered an eye, but the one visible scanned Chry and Vion.

"Do either one of you want to tell me wh-" He flinched, growled to himself, and grumbled an exasperation. "Why the *plos* Ambia ran off."

It was asked as an accusation.

"She went to *looove* her children, didn'tcha hear?" Onvi cried out before expelling a splutter of maniac giggles. He was beyond sight, so his cries came like rain from above.

Chry held his eyes downcast, wishing he could retreat into the shell of his being. He caught Bar's reaction before then. Onvi's response did not please him—the steel stoicism of his expression suppressed a heated emotion that burned through his skin instead.

Without looking, Bar said, "Cavas, we're going."

His voice was level without emotion.

That was the only command Cavas needed. He stood from sitting and walked over. His strides barely made a sound. Next to Bar, he stopped and stared, the black orbs of his eyes impossible to read. He was stiffer than the branches he stared at.

As soon as Cavas was with him, Bar approached Vion. His strides were purposeful. Chry thought the leader was about to punish the Lanke, but he simply brushed past him. Bar was focused on saving Ambia.

The hunger in Vion's glare did not regard Bar nor Cavas.

Good. Keep him like that, Chry thought. *Let him stare for centuries thereafter.*

But then he started thinking that Vion was not likely to stay like this. He'd break free from his trance and notice Chry. That was terrifying. With Bar and Cavas leaving, it would mean that he was stuck tending to a blood-thirsty Vion and an Onvi of the same derangement as a Rattle imprisoned in the Cages for three turns of the Moon.

The future and fear of being alone with the two overwhelmed him. He felt a question tickling his throat before surfacing.

"But what about, well, us?"

He couldn't put his finger on why, but Chry knew right when the words left his mouth he should not have said anything. When Bar stopped mid-stride, he regretted every decision he had ever made. Bar's shoulders were still hunched, but his presence emitted whisks of ice. The Forest gave a warmer welcome.

Oh Eulgash, what have I done, what's happening...?

Bar whispered something,

The whispers, he's whispering.

And Chry swore, he *swore* Bar's head jerked to the side. Or did he just *think* it did? No, it did. Bar was losing his rattles, like Ambia and Onvi, and now he was going to chase Ambia and claw her pretty hazels out. Or was Chry just seeing things? Or, Eulgash take pity, was it *him* that was losing *his* rattles?

Bar turned around.

A log of anxiety squashed Chry's stomach. He clinched it. He had expected, as he always expected, an unforgiving sternness from Bar. But this was not what he saw. Judgment blazed through those eyes. His expression was elongated. Chry *swore* it was. It had the shape of a wolf's snout and the growling hunger of one too. Facial features once angular and precise were twisted and contorted into a snarl. Any details were unsalvageable because what he saw did not remain neat inside its box. He'd blink, and there Bar was—stern, of course, frustrated, understandably, but still human. And then he'd blink again and there were the silhouettes of the wolf-man snout, its maw yearning for the malicious, its saliva drooling desperate. And then, blinking again, there'd be a mixing and blending that disoriented his eyes. It was beyond human perception, almost like his face was melding with a mask.

His vision fought against a rising dizziness.

Take the mask off, oh pray, take it off.

Bar's face shifted.

"Us," he echoed.

It was his voice, aye, but pinned beneath it was a growl. Chry could hardly hear what was said. After glaring through him, Bar creaked his neck toward Vion. The Lanke still regarded his hand in vicious contempt, unawares of the man-thing behind him. A hunger rumbled from Bar's maw.

Chry's breath was now shuddering. Bar made his approach crouched. Against the dying fire, the two were more shadow than man.

What's he doing? What's he...?

At Vion's side, Bar rasped, "There is no *us*."

He lifted his foot and stamped it against the side of Vion's knee. It cracked askew. A noise spluttered from Vion as if violently serrating his guts. He toppled to one knee.

Bar did not stop.

On the ground beside him was a hefty piece of deadwood, greying but still whole. He snatched the branch, cocked back, and swung before Vion could regain his bearings. It smacked against his crooked nose, creating a cracking sound that came from either the branch or the skull, and threw the brute back. Bar flung the weapon aside.

"I should have let Rahderk kill you!" he said. Vion did not recover enough to defend against the kick to his abs. His teeth hissed. It was where Ambia had stabbed him, but Bar did not stop kicking. "I should have slit your throat at Caravan's Demise. Everything would have been so much *easier* without having to carry such a filthy piece of shit around. Your wife and child are dead, and yet you feel apologetic to yourself for not being able to save them. But, understand this, you Lanke *bastard*, they're dead because of *you*. *You* killed them. *You're* the reason. Not me. Not the Lanke. *You!* We *despise* you."

He stopped kicking. Sluggish, Vion writhed and groaned as a wounded bear disrupted from its sleep. Bar showed him his hands.

"And my hands, they're tainted because of *you*. *You! This is all because of YOU!*"

Vion could not listen. Pangs twisted his concentration, yet Chry thought, if Vion really wanted to, he could have fought back: grabbed

Bar's leg, yanked him from his feet, and retaliated with all the force his Lanke muscles could allow. But he didn't. All he did was glare at Bar, suppress his moans, and cough up blood that stained his bushy beard. Like blackberries, bruises bloomed across the wounds Ambia inflicted. The knee Bar kicked laid at an angle like the wishbone of a turkey.

The Lanke menace Chry'd always cowered from was now no more than an abused and obedient child.

Vion was human.

Cavas looked on from the darkness, calm as if listening to an exchange between strangers. Chry could not be calm. How could any rational person be calm at a time like this? The creature before him was not Bar; Bar was uninviting, sometimes unforgiving, but he was never cruel to *any* of the Runners, not even to Chry who he probably would have left in the Wastelands if not for Ambia.

Bar stomped once more on ribs that Chry *knew* were breaking—he heard them. Vion strangled a howl. Thereafter, Bar unsheathed his sword. The blade hissed like a hungry serpent.

"No more. I'll send you to Shiderk and Ulajin with a smile."

No, Chry thought. *You can't kill him. He's a Runner. He's—*

One of our family, Ambia had said.

A headsore blinded half his sight. His heart pounded between his ears as sweat made his skin clammy. His bladder sloshed. His knees shook or-or he *thought* they were but by simply *thinking* they shook they could shake and…and…He didn't know. How could he possibly know? There was only one thought, one penetrating scene of the Runners at the Gardens over the corpse of Vion and Ambia weeping and Onvi holding her and Cavas staring and Chry hanging his head with his eyes shying away from them all because he just couldn't fucking scream—

"*Enough!*"

A tremble flashed down his spine before he could reconvene with his body—a palm of throbbing against the back of his sockets, his teeth gritting. Afterward, he reckoned his eyes were clamped shut, and the sapphire teardrop of his necklace, its memory of Aimee reminding him of the first time they faced Vion on Domum's leg, clinched inside his fist. Though her memory was warm, the gem and its steel wings were a frigid chill.

Throughout it all, he forgot to breathe.

He still couldn't hear, see, or even imagine his surroundings. He swallowed, the clicking of his throat a deafening sentence. Then he opened his eyes.

Conflict ceased. The scene stilled. Bizarrely, Cavas rotated his head to regard Chry, but it was Bar, motionless, that gripped his gaze. The air around him was stagnant; a bird could fly past and die mid-flight. Knots were tight across his hunched shoulders. Images of a hyena would've been what those shoulders were like if Chry had visited the savannas of Cirva with Onvi.

He also heard growling. But Bar's face, that mask, that critical feature, had not turned to look at him.

Let Bar stay like this, Chry reckoned. Let him look away forever. Let him toss up his hands, say "Whatever may please the Arbiter," leave Vion, and enter the Forest depths with Cavas. If Chry didn't have to confront the thing that was acting as Bar then blessings to the Lord Arbiter and everyone who followed him.

A thread of his glossy hair drooped over his immobilized eyes. Darkness as suffocating as a night spent in the Wastelands encased them. He couldn't see. He could see no one. His eyes needed to adjust to this void of darkness but couldn't before he heard the dreadful crunch of a foot on leaves.

It was Bar. Bar was coming.

I shouldn't have said anything, he thought desperate. *I should have never...*

The footfalls quickened. Chry couldn't see a damn thing beyond his pale, clammy skin, and all he could do was take a meager step back while grasping his sapphire necklace as if he could squeeze Aimee out of the gem to come fucking protect him already from what was...

There was a stir from within the darkness. Fingers of terror crackled around his stomach and squeezed. His bladder loosened, and his crotch pooled with warmth. Any attempt to rationalize the thing within that darkness broke him even further.

The closest description he had was egregious.

Its head emerged as the slobbery muzzle of an ancient wolf so large it could fit Chry's head into its maw. Blood, old and new, crusty and dripping, matted its grizzled fur. It wouldn't stop growling with the voracious hunger of its black-stone glare. Within its rictus were blunt, yellow teeth, its canines dominant in flesh-rending.

If this was all Chry had to contend with, he would've been a joyful fool. It wasn't.

Wings, expansive wings that could hug Chry into nothingness, were made not from the bone of a bird but by a man through black feathers molded together with wax. Drifts of feathers fell from its bushel. The wax dripped. It was an impeccable contraption that would have been mistaken as true if given a passing glance.

On top of this, the body the wings were attached to was of a man, normal aside from the grotesque shambles of its clothing and skin. The gambeson it wore was more like tattered rags to where patches of cotton fell from the padding like snow. Chry reckoned the torso beneath. A voracious stomach was caved inward. Ribs were visible. The skin from where muscles once were flapped at its arms. Inside its forearms bled long, jagged scratches that Chry associated with a Smar named "Mi" when she would persistently scratch her arms until they were drenched bloody. And none of its movements suggested derangement—how it moved would have made the stone statue of Simul think it was lifelessly slow and fiercely meticulous.

The next second Chry regarded the thing, his eyes caught specific details he had overlooked heretofore—two sheathed swords in a leather girdle clinging to its waist, the bearskin of its torn gambeson, its rich, leathery skin, three vertical scars over its heart—that shocked him into a realization so obvious it should have been impossible to overlook.

The abomination he was staring at, that which petrified him, was Bar.

No, I won't accept that, he thought. *This can't be Bar. Not our*

408

leader. It's...It's the Forest. The Forest is doing this to him.

Its black-stone glare found Chry as its maw yawned and produced a snarl tearing into human ears.

Repulsed, his body retreated the slightest, but his feet only shuffled. Claws of calamity were hooked beneath his rib cages. His shuddery breath created a cell. His eyes were fixed. His blood ran cold.

Without warning, the thing jerked forward. It did not fly like a bird nor dash like a human but glided, *glided* like a human-bird thing escaping imprisonment. There was no escape. Chry's head was dizzy, his stomach flipping. He managed to stumble backward and near to a frantic scamper, but the thing was too swift.

Its jaws opened. The noise it made was butchered between a roar and a howl. It spread its wings as to defy the expectations of Eulgash, enough to blot out the sun. Talons. Its hands were talons or had they always been talons or were they now talons after he had recognized them? He could not reckon. They were before his eyes now. One talon was so close Chry could see his reflection within its glassy claw.

This is the end, his thoughts echoed. *This is where I die.*

The hand hitched back.

Chry gasped as if nearly drowning, but immediately thereafter, life returned to the clearing: the horses whining, Onvi barking with maniacal laughter, leaves falling from the Depanens. Cavas was a mere outline to the Forest, and Vion, shadowy beneath the dearth of light, had closed his eyes and rested his bald head on an arm of deadwood. His chest rose deathly slow.

This emergence into reality was so sudden, Chry at first could not distinguish between Bar and the abomination. The tips of Bar's fingers—fleshy, smooth, but most of all human—were fingers away from Chry's eye, tremulous as if *needing* to rip it out. The talons and wings were nowhere to be seen.

What did remain was the wolf. Half of his face was still snarled into its growling muzzle while the other half was the strained expression of Bar. The two expressions were melded together as one. The human side breathed through a hard rasp, had sweat lapping from his brow and cheeks, and bore an intensity within its common, brown eye that could fracture crystal.

With a struggle that resisted, Bar forced his hand away from Chry's eye so its palm could face him. Something akin to aggravation shook that palm. Chry blinked again, and the wolf was replaced with the normal and welcomed sight of Bar. Every crease was strained into a concentrated scowl. Chry was scared that, with how intense his expression was, Bar would end up reverting.

He didn't. Instead, his fingers were forced close, squeezed tightly so that the skin turned pale, then opened again. He repeated this again and again until his hand stopped trembling. Even so, he kept his hand balled. Across his expression, stoicism returned, and his emotions were placid.

Bar was back.

XV

Bar expelled a heaving sigh. After moments of recovering from his initial fatigue, he looked behind and gave Cavas a curt command with his chin. He was still sweating and breathing hard, a grimace breaking his angular features.

Cavas stared then eventually turned away and entered into the belly of the Forest. Hand gripping his brow, Bar grumbled from his throat. Though there was no more beast-creature thing, Chry still guessed their leader was struggling with another unseeable beast.

After a few breathes, Bar left to march after Cavas. He did not spare a glance for Vion.

Chry's brow scrunched under a dawning dread.

"Wait, Bar. Wait! You can't just-just leave us! You're not well and-and it's just too, well, dangerous, and...and..."

Bar stopped at the edge of perception. The arms of the Forest were greedy to accept him as they had his companion, but he just stood there. His sinewy shoulders had wound taut but were not hunched as they were heretofore. At least they were a feature Chry could relate to.

Bar tilted his head to the canopy and then looked over his shoulder. Through the obscure shadows was his jaw locked into its joints. He did not waver into a reality of fangs and talons and wings but was nonetheless intimidating. That was Bar. Unapproachable.

This should have relaxed his bones, knowing Bar was back to himself, but what he said next manifested a terror tantamount to what he experienced not a moment heretofore.

"Deal with Vion and Onvi," Bar whispered. "We will return soon."

Those were his last words before Bar faded from view.

Cavas's Emergence

I

Bad men are coming Mommy. Please, they're after you, Mommy...Please don't—

Die. Stab her to death whiles the others

You can't kill mommy!

Not mama

Please not—

We can do whatever the fuck we want. All we need to do is smile and—

Find her. Keep her safe. She will be integral to the plans we—

Run, mama, run before the bad men—

They'll find out, won't they, Barloc? Or, what should I call you? Nay, no, no, it's of no importance when *they find out. When they discover the truth, they'll witness the*

-wolf-

and that gilded mask you wear will crack beneath the strain of judgment and truth. The gems will be in your hands. The plagued and feeble will be released from suffering. The immoral will be slaughtered. The moral will retain their progeny.

Fool

The Lanke will go first. Throat sliced, eyes gouged,

Gone, gone, gone

Scary. He's scary. Stop it.

Tell bad man to go, mama. We don't want—

To maim him? To maim you*? Nay, the end is nigh. Know your—*

No more. Think. Shut the rest out and—

I'll always luv ye, Sivarses.

No more! No more talk! No more death! We don't like death!

Sivarses, is that you?

Mama, please.

Come close, my Sivarses, and know you are not releasing me from the life I live but from the plague I suffer.

Mama save—

Slit their throats

NO! MOMMY! MOMMY! MOMMY! MOMMY! MOMMY KILL THE BAD MEN BEFORE THEY—

Gouge their eyes

NO NO NO NO NO

Keep a smile

NO MORE SMILES NO MORE YOU'RE LYING THEY'RE ALL FAKE THEY AREN'T MOMMY'S THE ONLY SMILE IS-

SLIT THEIR THROATS BAR

SENDTHEMAWAY

GOUGE THEIR EYES BAR

MOMMYSTOPTHEM

KEEP A SMILE BAR

ILLKILLYOUILLKILLYOUILLKILLYOUYOUWONTTOUCHMO MMYYOUWILLDIEMOMMYWILLKILLYOU

II

The droplets of blood across crushed vegetation made Ambia's trial discernible, if not effortless to track, and Cavas, as if already knowing where to go, led Bar forward with a posture as stiff, erect, and lifeless as the tree trunks they passed. The constancy of his being was unfathomable compared to the stark changes of the Runners. He did not reveal a loss in momentum nor any signs of fatigue. He was mentally consistent in a place where a man knew naught his sanity.

Cavas might as well be strolling. The same could not be said for Bar.

Tracking was a skill he could rely on but was now beyond his capabilities. He could hardly walk. Roots and deadwood were hazardous hands groping for an ankle. He could not evade them. With every other step, he tripped on the undergrowth and sometimes could not save his footing and sprawled. A drunken Onvi with broken knees could have navigated better and would have laughed hysterically if the thief was, one, there next to Bar and, two, if the Runners' leader was not straddling the edge of death.

In this state, Bar was bridging into the land of Oblivion—unknowing of how he got here or where he was going. He was losing these perceptions quicker than he could piece them together. The only focus he had was on the concentration of keeping his mind whole and functional. Even this he had trouble achieving—the headsore that split his temple open had ruptured into a second jaw, severing his meticulous mind.

And none of this Cavas seemed to notice. Or perhaps he had, possibly when they had first departed, but would not act upon nor acknowledge the empathy that arose.

The latter was more likely.

The further they descended, the more remote the Forest became. Alders and Redwoods became non-existent to the massive bodies of the Depanens. Their girths spread for purchase and occupied the space of two stallions lined behind each other. Many times over, Cavas had to loop around the Depanens with Bar lurching and limping behind, hand supported against the bark. Any branches the Depanens had were too high to see. That was Bar's only grace: He did not need to worry about stumbling into low, hanging branches.

In soothe, he could not worry. When he started falling onto the dirt—once busting his nose on a root that looked like a bent elbow, another crashing into a tangled brush—he had long departed from the physical realm. Pain (which there was much of) he could not process. Recognition of himself was impossible—his second coat of sweat, a hand melted to his brow, bloodshot eyes aggravated and strained, a blind search for the next Depanen.

The whispers had drowned the excess. Bar was trapped.

At last, he collapsed onto his hands and knees: a position which, in normal circumstances, he would have resented as a position of servitude. Now, he had not the strength nor the lucidity to resist. He gasped and wheezed as if having sprinted the length of the Forest. Bloody perspiration dripped from his nostrils. His eyes swam through the undergrowth.

Through a croaking voice, Bar whispered, "Cavas, bring-"

He cried out, the scream raking his throat. Speaking was like juggling knives that he constantly missed: Every mistake made was an appendage stabbed.

Cavas had stopped. He was staring at Bar.

Bar's elbows shuddered like posts to a dilapidated scaffold. "Summon Hearth," he ordered, but the shakiness of the command bore no authority.

Cavas stared.

Merely two years heretofore, Bar would have scolded any Runner who even laid an *eye* on Cavas, let alone ask him to summon one of the spirits sealed inside.

Now look at you. Pathetic. Weak. Unworthy. You should be one of the immoral whom you kill. Slit your throat. Relinquish the world of failure.

Dazed, Bar groped for a support, placed his hand on a moss-covered log that broke inward beneath his weight. He collapsed. The entire Forest was conspiring against him. He knew it. They knew it. With all his strength focused on one arm, he threw himself supine. The blank canopy above him swirled. He closed his eyes but the darkness behind his lids swirled too.

He could not remain like this. Like this, he would die and be forgotten. The last circumstance he aimed for was to leave this world

415

without ameliorating it. His hand groped above but recalled that he needed to roll over and push himself up. It was as far as he could proceed—getting to his hands and knees again. It's as far as his mind could see.

Cavas stared.

The impotence of not being able to control his actions and thus future enflamed his blood.

"Summon the spirit," he growled.

When there was no answer, a wolfish snarl ruptured his mask.

"Do it *now* before I—"

He stopped, swallowed the order, and caught his snarl mid-fling.

This was not how he handled others.

The whispers…they were…

He eased his breath to a turtle's tread. He wetted his dry and cracking lips. The corner of his eye twitched.

After a moment to himself, he commanded each bodily function in conjunction. He bent his neck, raised his chin, lifted his eyes. They strained whiles regarding the pale orbs staring down from the shadows. The outline of his robes could vaguely be discerned.

It was a start.

But now, Bar took a risk he never thought he would resort to. He reached out with an unsteady hand and grabbed the cloth along Cavas's wrist. It felt like the soft warmth of a feather bed heated by a fireplace.

"Do not fear," Bar panted. "Hearth will save Ambia. I will detain it."

In his current state, this was a fallacious promise, yet it was of no importance. He had discerned a flash of *something* within those eyes, recognition, perhaps, if fleeting. Cavas still stared but he stared and *understood.*

Now he—

Slits their

A violent wince forced Bar to release Cavas's robe. The comfort of warmth abandoned him. He propped himself on an elbow.

Persistence.

He needed to persist.

Admah would not be saved without *persistence.*

Cavas stared for longer than Bar would have liked but eventually closed his eyes. It was a fluid motion. The blissful relief that flushed through Bar was like fresh water from days of trekking through the Wastelands.

Hearth could heal him. Would it was another question.

Persistence, persistence, persistence

His teeth chattered, his gambeson wet and heavy with perspiration.

The moment stretched on as eternity. Time was excruciating, and thus, Bar was unaware of when Cavas opened his eyes again. The only reason he knew they were open was because of the golden spangles of light his eyes produced. Its radiance eradicated the darkness like a divine door opening to a cell once too dark to see—the crushed undergrowth beneath him burst alive, dust motes frolicked within its golden shafts, and, to Bar's gratitude, its touch warmed his skin.

His vision became a field of flashing stars as he squinted against this new light and shaded his eyes with a hand. He nearly fell again, swaying on his elbow. Every function he had was crumbling. He could not command himself without another pillar of his mind faltering. The voices, whispers, everything, anything, shrieking.

Eventually, the light receded to become bearable. His vision adjusted so that he could release his hand and peer groggily above him. The blur was clearing, but Cavas, no, that was not the right name anymore. The body of Cavas was there—black robes and concealed face—but his presence shifted in totality. What remained of his black irises and pupils was replaced by a doublet of liquid gold. They glowed like small, yellow suns, brilliant and radiant and soothing to where Bar had the oddest urge to enter into those eyes, cuddle into a fetal ball, and rest forever in its cradle of intimacy.

In addition to its eyes, the irrevocable stiffness of Cavas had loosened. Its joints were not solidified into rigid angles and its posture did not cut through the world as a blunted broadsword. Both ebbed and flowed as the currents of wind and wave.

The spirit let the silence settle into a discomfort then it said, "Blessings to you, Barloc of Nowhere." The words were instruments harmonized together for a melodic tune. "It would seem you have not attuned to your circumstances."

The grotesquerie of Bar's face scrunched in further irritation. He muttered to himself but had the sensibilities not to provoke the being openly. He needed to persuade, not retaliate.

"B..." (Grunting, he struggled to articulate himself.) "Blessings to...to you, Hearth. Please listen as..."

Grimaces deformed a face once handsome. On the ground, both his hands clawed at the dirt and needle leaves. He felt his brow about to crack open like an egg held by a Heva.

Imperceptibly, Hearth lifted its chin and gazed down at him. The position was purposeful in establishing dominance. Bar was on his knees pleading. Hearth was here judging.

Everything it fucking did—

A fury of malicious desires flashed for Hearth. Bar shoved each aside and compartmentalized what thoughts he could, yet his headsore exacerbated. He was breaking. He couldn't last for much longer.

"I can surmise your desire, Barloc of Nowhere. Nevertheless, desire does not mean I shall bestow. I am no servant of man, I am no servant of yours, nor do I intend to be. So, if being restored is why you had Cavas summon me, then what you shall find will disappoint."

Bar resisted.

He resisted.

Resist. Resist. Resist. Resist. *Resist. RESIST.*

He clenched his stomach but vomited anywise. Raw chunks of half-digested meat—slimed in beast-brown fur—were strewn through the bile. He retched again before ending with violent shaking. He was powerless against this emergence of madness.

Hearth was unmoved.

"Your hardships are squabbles to me, Barloc of Nowhere. Two years heretofore in Caris'ma, your companions, too, asked Cavas to summon me so to mend you which I bestowed through the sacredness of my grace."

Throughout its speech, Bar coughed up logs of bloody phlegm. His entrails were strangling his gall, and the sounds his throat made were those of a moribund wolf choking on serrated bones.

Hearth gestured a perfunctory hand to the trees.

"But our realm is not of this world, where trees flourish such as men. You and others like yourself who walk through past, present, and future carry the skies of peril instead of walking on a bridge of prudence. Once the sky becomes too heavy for you to carry, you fall onto your knees and beg for salvation, as if bestowing a pith would lead to spiritual cleansing.

"Your folly precedes you.

"Nor is our realm any longer through the Scar, what you have learned to style the Unknown. Our realm settles within Cavas of Pactus where we shall reside until the vessel withers and deteriorates and the next presents itself, repeating the cycle anew."

The rattling inside his ears made Hearth's words shaky and chaotic. Hearth abandoned its melody for a divine resonance.

"But when those as yourself threaten to open the seal within the vessel and release the others, when it neglects the sanctity of a tranquility that has lived for centuries and will live on for centuries to come, then you not only jeopardize the stability of your companion but the preservation of Admah. For such a reason, I will not allow a mortal man of excess hubris to persist in rupturing our harmony. The action would be as riddled with folly as the initial demand."

He could no longer hold on. He dropped onto his shoulder, made one last effort to haul himself up but failed and landed on his back again. Though his chin reeked of vomit, Bar was not retching anymore. In the back of his thoughts, where corruption, even here, meant to destroy him, he could see the vomit welling through his throat, overfilling at the mouth, and, eventually, choking him to death.

Stoicism inside his sockets had shattered. His arms, legs, and other extremities were locked rigid. There was nothing he could do. Resistance left his muscles. He had no more strength against the beckoning of life. His wheezes were seething. The cuffs of his immaculate gambeson were frayed like a scarecrow.

He tried rolling his eyes to the glow brushing across his face but couldn't. Its gold was a distant and disdainful furnace. He could not feel its warmth. Death approached first as a harbinger of ice.

He would not give in.

"Am-Am-Am-"

He said, but his throat was lodged in place and made clicking sounds as if counting coins. Since he could not swallow, saliva puddled at the back of his tongue. Above was a sky of absolute darkness where the whispers hid.

Bar plowed through the syllables.

"Am-Am-Am-Amb-Am-"

Remember them. Remember their sacrifices. Remember.

"Ah-m-be-ah, she's…"

Dead, Slaughtered, Raped, Mangled, Mommy, Mommy, Mommy

"She's…"

Save her, brother.

"*She's dying, dying, dying, she's dying, dying…*"

His lips gurgled "dying" until inarticulation spluttered out and his ears could hear no more. A mute bubble blocked him from external activity. His internal state was chaos. Tears messed his cheeks. Spittle spat from his lips, sometimes falling back into his eyes. He didn't flinch. Disgust was not present. He had no control. Shivers so cold they could be regarded as Iceflesh infected the skin and shuddered the soul. His lids eclipsed his irises. Like guttural hunger, gurgling rumbled from his raw gullet.

Although he said nothing, his jaw trembled more and more. There came a point when it creaked open fully and clapped shut, creaked open and shut again until his teeth were chopping down relentlessly like a woodpecker against the bark of an oak. Within Hearth's glow, the pearl white of his teeth gleamed perfectly.

He leaped over the edge of painless Oblivion. The release was a blessing from Eulgash, for the following encounter would have castrated any conscious man. From the cave of his mouth lolled his tongue, but his jaw was still chopping. His teeth bit into the flesh. If Bar could have accessed his Discernments, that spurt of blood would have tasted of a coppery defeat. He kept chewing. It created a lapping noise within its bloody pools. Red runnels streamed down his cheeks as if extending his grin.

The third bite, the fourth, the fifth until there was a blunt clack of teeth-on-teeth. The severed head of his tongue swung from its body and dangled from the corner of his mouth. It was like a fleshy door hinge hanging by a bolt. His teeth locked close but were hardly discernible beneath the pooling of blood like the famed Fountain Heads in Lu'sa overfilling with the lives he promised to expunge.

Bar would not have known.

His bowels were letting loose. His crotch was dampening. His trousers reeked of liquid shit. His gurgles were drowning.

Faces flashed—a Western farmer without the strength to provide for his family, an honorable Derk who knows no better, a blind Ontinian scholar dying from the Black Rings, a callow princess of lustful intent, an enigmatic teacher with Spectral knowledge, an innocent servant whose name was now its servitude, a conniving bitch, an aroused Dingler bearing a grin, a fertile woman with a love that could preserve progeny.

Then they disappeared.

In the end, there was only one face he could see.

III

His irises rolled back so the veins could river through the whites of his eyes. The tremors he had did not necessarily abate but seemed to be restrained within a glass bottle, liable to shatter if tampered with. He bore no more sounds, just the jittering. The bulk of his tongue bobbled harmlessly.

The spirit regarded it as an ordinary occurrence without an inkling of interest. A roasted squirrel would have elicited more of a reaction. Regardless, it continued to watch as the tremors became near imperceptible. The sight, despite the spirit's unresponsiveness, was extraordinary for a mortal. It took another moment for consideration. The decision should not be a hasty one, if one at all, if the reasons were not attainable to a higher order.

Reasons were aligned.

The spirit knelt beside the human. As with the gentleness of a breeze, it placed its hand on Bar's forehead. The hand was null until a glow as golden and delicate as its eyes radiated from its fingers. Like a pulse, it grew bright, dimmed, and then grew bright again. The golden light from its eyes was still, and residue danced as dust in its wake. Beside them, a sprinkle of Depanen needles rained from the canopy.

After four or five pulses, the body's tremors ceased, not in death but in the quiet breath of life. Content, it flattened its glowing hand over its forehead. Nothing of its brow or eyes could be seen beneath the glow. Gradually, its hand passed over. The forehead revealed itself again, but instead of the tensed and dirtied wrinkles heretofore, it had become smooth with clear skin. It went farther past eyes closed as if within a serene sleep. Down over a bruiseless nose. Over a stern mouth; his lips relaxed, closed, and without blood. The tongue had returned to where it should belong. His beard of bloody spittle was wiped clean, the chiseled jaw sculpted anew.

It stopped after the chin. It lifted its hand and stared, waiting.

IV

Bar jerked forward, gasping.

Where was he? His eyes darted but recognized only darkness. Panic switched with his heart. Perspiration poured. For reasons unknown, his fingers scoured his face for deformities he did not remember having. His face had human eyes, nose, lips, chin, and was oddly clean as if recently washed. Nevertheless, he could have sworn that his being had changed. That irresistible hunger had evacuated from his stomach, and his vision was less keen than it once was like trading in a sculptor's chisel for a butcher's clever.

He could not slow his panting. Danger subsumed the air. Quiet. He needed out. Leave. But this was not how he was supposed to deal with unfamiliar situations.

Ease, calm, and assess

Ease and calm

He let his fears sink back into himself. He waited for his breath to settle and his sight to align before accessing himself and his surroundings.

The situation he found himself in was a catastrophe.

Piddle had spread wet across the front of his trousers. He could not recall the last time he wet himself. He should have felt embarrassed as any human would, but he did not. The only emotion he felt was spates of frustration.

He wanted to wring a neck.

Control, control

He did control himself—as he was proficient at—but his frustrations congealed into a bitterness across his tongue when he realized that his backside was mushy, sticky, and drying in some places with a stench that could slaughter game. It was as if he had sat in a tub of mud.

Instinctively, his teeth ground together to keep his stoicism. Not only had he piddled himself, he managed to shit himself, too. Hands clammy, he was shaking miserably like when he was trussed and hauled to that unforgiving cave in Lacoya Forest.

And still, this was nowhere near his nadir.

Externally, the world had not changed from what he had last remembered: beside a hulking Depanen within a pocket of land. He could feel the dominance of the Depanens around him, but the only one he could discern was within a golden glow that radiated from behind him. Still, its light only reached out a few hands.

Then, he connected the golden eyes with the spirit he was with, and the memories as to why he was with Hearth rallied back.

So I convinced it, he thought, nodding. *Hearth has saved me.*

Initially, Bar did not want to order Cavas to summon Hearth. It was more than scolding Ambia and Vion for summoning Hearth at Caris'ma and thus being a hypocrite for summoning it in the Forest. They would, if not initially, understand the predicament he was in when they realized every Runner would have died in the Forest if not for Hearth. Or Ambia would continue to resent him for entering the Forest in the first place. This response was always a possibility. But nay, going against his initial command was not the primary reason for not wanting to summon it. Just as Hearth had eloquently stated, if it were called upon too often, they'd reach a climax where the seal inside Cavas would leak or break, and the Spirits of the Unknown would be released. That could not happen. If Admah was to be ameliorated, the Spirits of the Unknown must be contained.

But after reckoning the state of his trousers and the harrowing future of Ambia if he could not save her, Bar felt the risk was warranted.

Behind him, Hearth rose from kneeling. His Discernments were too overwhelmed to interact with it clearly and rationally.

Nevertheless, he felt its contempt.

"I despise your haughtiness and that which you have to hide, Barloc of Nowhere." Hearth stood over him, staring him down. He did not retaliate. "If the circumstances were of another accord, you would have died drooling as a newborn to a pool of tar."

His fingers felt at his hands. Pinches of blood were drying across the palms from how hard his fingernails dug into his skin. He reckoned his face, too, clean aside from the blood he had smudged across it after Hearth had healed him, when his fingers and hands were searching for deformities.

The filth. He was so filthy. Bar pretended to listen but instead trembled with disgust.

"But my fondness for Ambia of Pulchrit is one I will not take for granted. Her heart is gold. Her honesty, solicitude, and love are

424

commodities that I wish not to deprive your sphere of in light of my enmities towards you. And since I cannot sense her presence beneath the torment of the forest, your skills as a tracker prove vital for recovery."

Filthy, filth, filthy, filthy

"Furthermore, as we have experienced heretofore, a vessel cannot be trusted alone. I desired naught that the vessel bore the urge to summon me, but that cannot be altered. In the least, you and I are of the same understanding when it comes to accompaniment."

Its golden eyes flared.

"As for you, Barloc of Nowhere, you should be grateful your words are not flooded with the transgressions of duplicity and connivance, that her spirit is nigh, and that what I have laid out as truth is to be heard and acknowledged. Despite your petulance, Ambia of Pulchrit bears a fondness for you and bears qualities that can mend your vices into a hammer of merit worthy of forging this sphere anew.

"Bear this opportunity with astuteness."

Bar clenched his fist until the palm nearly bled again. He did this beneath Hearth's sight so it would not think twice about its words. His guts were twisting as would a nest of caged vipers. He couldn't allow emotion to overrule him. He couldn't allow emotion to direct him.

After an inexorable silence, his stoicism returned. It burrowed into the deadwood with a revulsion that bore the same emotion he felt for the Pig Pen and Dinglers.

He scrunched his nose at the stench, wiped his lips with the heel of his hand—a little spittle blemishing his chin. He neglected to think too much about his trousers for they would have ruined his mind. Regardless, he could not search for Ambia like this. He could not think or track like this.

"My trousers," Bar said in a stable tone.

He did not look behind him, but he swore he heard a snort.

"As I've said heretofore, your comfort is of no concern to the preservation of Ambia of Pulchrit. Your inconveniences shall be dealt with otherwise."

It truly could not expect him to go on like this.

"Am I supposed to—"

"Quite so."

It expected him to go on like this.

Brutal images of his fingers thumbing into those golden eyes and popping them arose, yet Bar allowed them to pass through unabated. No use indulging in improbable fantasies.

Instead, Bar collected himself to stand. He groped for the Depanen next to him and used its trunk for support. His legs were pieces of straw. He tried relinquishing the support to stand but giddiness overwhelmed him. He slumped back onto the bark, his panting returning tenfold.

He had not ventured a single step and was already exhausted. He wiped his forearm across a drenched brow. He scrunched his nose against that stench again. He held back an exasperated snarl and continued cordially.

"I suppose I am indebted—"

"Allow me to reiterate, for your ears are as inept as your tongue: your courtesies and inconveniences are the insignificance of a beetle on its back. My concentration is on Ambia of Pulchrit and other solicitous souls who might seek guidance. Do not expect your frivolous comments to squander my time here."

His stoicism was steady on Hearth. It might have seen a different Bar, pale, weak, about to collapse onto his knees, but that would not have accounted for the tenacity within.

He said, "As you will."

That was it. The spirit waited for him to regain his vigor. Exhaustion ebbed away gradually. His stomach settled from its squirming, and his perspiration dried. He swallowed and finally stood. He swayed but regained his footing swiftly. He was returning to the Barloc that the Runners had known.

He adjusted his deerskin belt and trousers (though the discomfort and smell from his groin would not abate until he located a stream or returned to camp, changing into the extra apparel he had in his stallion's saddle) and dusted off his gambeson.

His speech did not squander its time. "From what I can recall, Ambia had resorted to an animalistic insensibility. Her mere desire was locating those things she called children. For the benefit of finding Ambia, if you have any further details on what these 'children' might be, please do not hesitate to share."

Hearth didn't share. If it knew more about these children or had any lingering suspicions, Hearth did not divulge the information. All it needed Bar for was to track. For Hearth, that was the extent of his usefulness.

He despised feeling like a puppet.

Bear it. This is how Ambia will be saved.

"Very well. We must then consider her state of mind. She is not sensible and her sole purpose is to reach these children. That means her trail will be erratic and neither will she be worried about covering her tracks. Both of these circumstances will make it easier for us to track her."

He hobbled past Hearth and knelt down beside a twig. A foot had snapped it, for there were no other animals around. Hearth turned toward him, too, so its light could illuminate the path forward. For others, the path beyond was ground similar to the Forest heretofore. For Bar, the undergrowth was a welter of knowledge. Even though its light merely reached the end of the Depanen, he could reckon the subtle signs of crushed vegetation and the long stretch of undergrowth where it looked as if someone had fallen and scrambled back up. The bloody trail they were following heretofore was now pin-pricks across the undergrowth and quickly receding. It was no matter. The blood could depart altogether and still he would have enough information to track her.

He held back a smirk.

Though the circumstances he found himself in were less than ideal, he had not lost Ambia.

He nodded toward the undergrowth. "We will follow her trail."

He refrained from pointing out the tracks and signs Ambia had left.

He did not need Hearth learning too much or else risk being discarded.

When he rose from his kneeling, his knees popped like wood in a fire. He grunted.

Aging, he thought but disregarded it. He could not become doddery before his purpose was achieved.

He faced Hearth's glow.

"I will need your light to guide us through the Forest, so I can see where her trail leads. Stay behind me to guide me forward."

Hearth crossed its arms. "Do not falter then, and know that I will not stop for the likes of your inconveniences. It would be a dishonor to the safety of Ambia of Pulchrit and for my time here. Of equal importance, know that I can sense the general presence of her being within the Forest. If you steer us away, I shall know."

"I won't," he said.

Hearth nodded knowingly as if to say it already knew this.

One day I'll wipe that smugness from existence.

Bar sniffed once, ignored his discomfort.

Concentrate, breathe. You will see Ambia again. You will feel her bosom against your chest in the creation of posterity. It will happen. It will be.

Without another word, he followed Ambia's trail into the gullet of the Forest.

A Child's Liberation

I

With Bar gone, Chry thought (just the smallest of thoughts) that his life could return to normal and that he could do normal things like, well, examine Vion. His injuries—the broken knee, the stabs across his belly and the one through his palm—did not encourage hope. And though nothing *seemed* detrimental, Chry had seen Domumites succumb to what Devout Payne called Corrupted Flesh and what Aimee called Sepsis. If Ambia didn't possess Goldendrake in her satchel, Vion might be staying in the Forest forever.

If she comes back, that is… Chry shook away the thought. *No, she'll come back. She always comes back…*

Chry had a hard time explaining why he was concerned about Vion. Aye, the Lanke had mocked him, tormented him, belittled him, threatened him, treated him as an outcast, and had intimidated him countless times into an insignificant speck. Aye, he understood this. These were reasons to hate him, to loathe him. They were reasons to walk away and forget Vion ever existed. They were all reasonable reasons he could point to as excuses.

But Chry couldn't just leave him there to die.

Bar could—he had a lethal side only tamed by his stoicism. Cavas might. He probably could snap his fingers and cease a person's breath. But most of all, Vion would. He would not hesitate to set his ax between Chry's skull. That was for sure.

But Chry's conscience, no matter how much he hated the man, could not leave him to die. He couldn't find the pride in it, only shame. It would feel like Chry was sliding the dagger across his throat. He had not the, what, mind for it? Sure, well, that's what it must be. The mind.

Even so, sometime after Bar and Cavas had gone, Chry collapsed on his bum and couldn't for the life of him stand back up. He squeezed his jaw shut so it would not shake and clack. His eyes were only for Vion who was shivering beyond his reach. The lower half of his Lanke body was bathed in the blood Ambia had inflicted. His knee laid askew at an uncommon angle. He still retained control of his eyelids, but they were low over his eyes which did not stray away from the shadows above. The glare he bore tried retaining a fierceness that could not be sustained. The silver of those eyes was weak, and his being was following them.

Chry had finally convinced himself he would do his best to save Vion when he heard a faint crooning. At first, he hitched an eyebrow up. He could not rightfully reckon what it was. Then his expression smoothed. It was a lullaby. Someone was humming, freely and deliberately. It came from behind him between the tree trunks. No words were said, and its high-pitched tune could have been played by a fiddle at any of the taverns he had been to so far on his journey. Chry also guessed who was humming.

Can't he see this is not *the time to be fooling around? Vion's about to die and, well, everyone else might as well be, too.*

It did not stop though, ignorant as the day it crawled out from its mother's womb. Now, the hum bobbed as if on the move. Its volume increased because he reckoned it was no longer obstructed. Chry could hear it approach. More than just the hum. He could hear sounds that an animal would make on the move: something scraping across bark, the scuttle of feet, a fall and the scurry back up, an uncoordinated rustle like broken paws pattering through Depanen leaves. It was as if it was trying to be sneaky but instead produced as much sound as possible.

Chry had a question in his throat but couldn't articulate it. There was something wrong here. Very wrong. This was not normal. None of it. His rattles shook. He tried standing from his sprawl but could not feel his legs. They were numb. A plague nuzzled into his joints and apprehended him beneath a thrall of fear.

And that constant hum. It sounded, fuck, it sounded like it was coming for *him*. It was quickening. Every passing moment, the sounds cleared further, but clearer did not mean more comfort. The beat slapped against the Forest floor like tossing around a long, lumpy sack from the Brew Beetle to Gladion's home.

A sack with a corpse in it that's going to the Gardens instead, bumpedy bumpedy all the way home.

He would not think about that. He did not want to think of the Forest as another Garden. That would slaughter any hope of the Runners reaching the end of the Forest unscathed, if there was any.

The hum gathered closer. The closer it came, the more ominous and frolicsome it became. At some point, he could not remember, the hum halted beneath lyrics of a song. The words were sinisterly slow, emphasizing the syllables with a guttural tongue. It sounded like a Tanner cutting the underbelly of a screaming Dry-Mouth.

"Ring-a-round da rosey

"Pocket full of posies

"Ring-a-round da rosey

"Pocket full of posies"

He wished he could plug his ears. His arms were propped beneath him but were more fragile than the tails of a rat. He wished it would stop. This was not a lullaby. This was something else. Beneath his breath, he repeated a real lullaby his mother would croon to him before bed, "the Feathers of a Peacock," but his lips could not form the words needed for song. He was forgetting what she sounded like. He was forgetting what came next. Arbiter be damned, he was even forgetting what his mother *looked* like. He couldn't remember. The melody—

"Ring, ring, a-round, a-round

"Pockets and pockets, full and full."

It was near. There was the crunch of undergrowth, each step telling of its direction: to him, to Chry. He couldn't escape. It was Bar all over

431

again.

Not again. Fuck, Fuck, FUCK, why is it always me? Why can't I just sleep and never have to worry about...

He could not finish the thought. Its humming rasped low. The soles of Chry's feet prickled precariously.

Eulgash, pray, if you are there, give me the strength to move. If you are there, give me the courage to face my enemy. If you are there, I hope you are—

It crouched over him. Its breath tickled the hairs of his ear, a purring snarl, and something like frizzled fur brushed against his head. He nearly gagged from the odious stench of days of meat rotting between its teeth. This was not who he was supposed to meet. He needed to leave. Now.

An object hovered over his right shoulder, but he could not look away from Vion. His heart bleated from his brow. His legs, arms, and Lirda would not budge.

If I don't reckon it, it cannot harm me. If I don't see it, it is not there.

"Liar, liar, cocks on fire," it whispered, jarring his eardrums. Then it snickered balefully. "In a field, a pocket full of posies."

The hovering thing touched his shoulder.

It's a hand, Chry thought. *It's just a stupid hand.*

But that hand had a playful way of walking its fingers across his shoulder and up his neck so to caress a thumb over his cheek. The remaining fingers hooked one-by-one beneath his jaw. It held his shaking head still with the slimy touch of a flesher unwashed from his handlings. A thick ooze slimed across his chin. How the thing held his face was how his mother—*oh mother, pray, don't come back, not anymore, I can't think of you now or ever again, no more, pray—* would take his head when she wanted to show him a creature or object along the Wastelands' horizon.

Now, the thing directed his head toward Vion as if he was not already looking at him. The Lanke's chest rose heavily and released quickly. He thought he could hear a wheeze through his throat. It promised Chry that if Ambia was not back soon, Vion would be permanently injured. Or worse.

"But you shouldn't be worried about either of them cookies, now should you?"

Chry could not distinguish whether this was part of his thoughts or if this was another whisper from the thing. Along the bottom of his periphery, he could make out a hand that could not be the hand of a human. Or was it? No, it was, but it was so disfigured with sores and scars that any reckoning of its skin as normal was ludicrous. Thereafter, he could not keep conscious enough to respond. His sight was blinking in and out.

"Oh you know the answer, Chry me boi."

An object like a scrawny stick prodded his temple three times.

"You know to stay away from dem posies, I supposies."

It expelled a cackle of crow-like laughter, and Chry heard the slapping of a hand on a thigh. He couldn't help it. Tears pooled where its fingers held his chin.

Pray mommy, save me

He escaped the hand by squeezing his eyes closed but could not escape that stench. It impregnated him with a dizziness that bloated his perceptions.

I need out. I need to run. I can't take this anymore. Get me out.

It got out. Its hand dropped from his chin and glided across the hard bump of his neck, leaving a trail of filthy gunk behind. He felt enough not to want to know what it was. He held his stomach stiff.

At his chest, it groped. Chry had a flat chest so there was not much to grasp, but somehow its hand felt for his nipple and circled a pair of fingers over the tip. Both his nipples were stone-hard from the chill of the Forest, and it took advantage of this, hiccupping a peal of laughter.

His manhood shriveled. He held his expression without reaction. If he reacted, if he resisted, it would—he was sure—be that much more inclined to punish him. Instead, he was separating from his body to watch from beyond, an innocence in mid-flight regarding the life of a farm boy.

"My bird, my bird, my lonely lovebird."

It stopped mid-swirl.

Startled, Chry whipped back into his body. A span stretched where he could not tell where he was or even who he was with but realized both by the movement to his left. Its hand slipped off his chest. Just as quickly as the thing had taken an interest in him, it had lost it. Its stench lifted. The thing left him.

He felt himself shudder with relief. Butterfly wings of darkness eclipsed from the sides, but he willed himself to open the wings again. His head bobbed. The pale clamminess of his skin thickened. It was tempting to stop fighting and let the wings envelop him, but for a reason he did not know why, he reckoned he needed to stay awake— that he could not leave this realm and awake afresh the next morning without disaster striking. Something would happen, and something else told him he needed to be here to ward it off.

Beside him, it entered into his view, stumbling forward and, fortunately, away from him. The paralysis of butterfly wings stiffened his head and eyes so he could not regard the thing, but after a brief moment, he shoved through the paralysis.

A boyish dread penetrated him.

This is a dream, he thought. *Must be. It's all a wild, unreasonable dream.*

But it wasn't.

It was dark for the fire was dimming, but the thing was still visible. It was unmistakably human—as was every other thing he had encountered here—but came from the dregs of mankind. Its skin was a crop field of sores, scars, pockmarks, and pustules. White pus leaked in-between and Chry realized that the slime he had felt across his cheek was that exact same pus.

This time, bile spilled over his lips, and his arms collapsed beneath him being too weak to keep him upright. His breath and sight were swimming as he scrambled back onto his elbows.

Leave me. Never come back. Leave me. Don't turn around.

It didn't. It kept scratching its skin as if an itch were beneath it—

from its cheek to the temple, chest, crotch, and back to its cheek. Its scratches were violent enough to pop the pustules and draw blood. That was why its hand felt like a flesher's hand. The blood dried there, but everywhere else it was bleeding or flaking. His throat withered to the dryness of a bone. The butterfly wings fluttered.

It would sometimes reach for its head where its crow's nest of hair became lanky like black strings. That's what brushed him. Its hair. Whenever it scratched its head with its sore-infested hand, patches of hair would scrape off and drift down. Across many of these bald spots were misshapen dents or dips as if a hammer was taken to its skull.

But these were things he could accept. They were horrifying and awful, but they were attributes that he had stumbled upon heretofore in some of the Well's remote alleyways. The things he could not accept were the ears hanging from its leather belt. Ears, the severed ends clotted black, dangling from homespun threads. And, of course, its crystal dagger.

His blood stopped cold.

Onvi?

No, he could not accept that. This *thing* was not Onvi. Not the Onvi that rambled on about pleasantries and nonsense. Not the Onvi that had taken Chry to the Restless Ryders to brighten his grief. Not the Onvi whose laughter painted the room with unwanted or regenerative mirth.

"Only Ryders can be so restless," it mumbled, jerking its head to the side to scratch it. "Now they can listen forever and ever."

No, Chry thought. *I won't accept that. I can't accept it. I'll never accept it.*

Whether he did or didn't would not matter. Whatever the plos it was, it was there, and despite having to encounter another abomination, Chry was thankful that it was looking someplace else. Let it stay away. He did not want to see its face. It would break him. Make him shrivel back into a child. Let him sit silent and be saved. That would be good. He didn't want to be anyone special anymore.

"Liar, liar, cocks on *fire!*"

The thing dug its nails down its temple. It left stretches of fleshy blood and peels of skin dangling from its cheekbones like long, skinny tongues. A clump of hair see-sawed down from its skull. It was almost like it *hoped* to scrape away all of its hair. Eventually, it tried snickering again but was hindered by a passage of snot. It hawked its phlegm and then swallowed. Chry thought he heard it say, "Tasty."

Thereafter, it set its sights on its next victim—Vion. Chry saw a smile rip through its decay.

"She never did love you," it said. This was said so low, it was difficult to hear. It shook its head and pointed a lanky finger at Vion. "You tried fucking a princess instead, oh yes you did, you can't lie to me, you lusty little fool you, all because you couldn't fuck your Lanke love anymore, no, no, no. She was gone with the wind! And let's just say that you killed her. Yes, *you* did that. All because of our hunky, bunky brute."

Vion responded only through a venomous groaning. His head was glaring above at the canopy, but his eyes were half-conscious. Through shadows, his bald pate gleamed.

"And to think!" The thing that was Onvi stumbled toward Vion, gesturing to the skies. "To think that she *ever* loved that hefty prick of yours. You'd probably rupture her spine with that thing. No, Vion, you just can't do these things anymore. She might die. Oops, I apologize for poking the sore. It's just that, well, you must know that your child was an accident, right? *You* weren't the, wait for it, father! Aye, aye, captain! Just look at the eyes, am I right, my Winnie the Whore? Shiderk, oh she was a good fuck and how she loved to fuck every other Lanke that strolled by your tent and how you knew it to be true, oh so true. She lured them in and made you watch their cocks and cunts. Oh you probably cried. I would—"

Instinctively, Vion swung his arm to knock Onvi off his feet. It dropped shoulder-first, hit the Forest floor hard, snapped two deadwood branches. But thereafter, it only cackled madly like a jester on fire. It made some rolling movements of enjoyment and then shoved itself onto an elbow. From behind, Chry could only guess at its grin.

436

More strikes would have come if Vion did not immediately cough up a gargle of blood. He rolled fully onto his back but still coughed bloody spates. Onvi was not so enfeebled. He scrambled onto his knees, swayed around until he was stable over Vion. It taunted with outstretched arms.

"She never loved you! That's the best part of the show! Oh you think she did when you were fucking her but she just pretended to moan while you were giving her your pathetic seed."

Vion couldn't fight back; he was violently coughing so that bloody droplets sprayed on its belt of ears. Chry didn't even know if Vion was conscious or if it was his natural tendencies that controlled him.

"Oh me no mind, your love was..."

It stopped, stared through Vion to a space beyond the physical, and then jerked its head once, twice, twice again until it became persistent and overwhelming. It was jerking out-of-control as if unable to comprehend the past. Its hands tried hard to hold onto its temples and keep it steady, but they were jerking too.

Then it stopped. It didn't release its head. It pressed its temples as to pop the pustule.

In a guttural but weepy voice, it said, "Life *fucked* her. Isadora fucked the life out of her. That's how it happened. I was useless. I couldn't help her. If you were Isadora and given the chance, you would have done the same. Worse, *worse*. So much *worse*. You would have had her tied and hoed around the clan. That's what you are—an untrustworthy, horny bastard. But they don't need to know that. You're with me now. We're together."

It bent over Vion and brushed its bony knuckles over his cheek, smudging the blood spilling from its mouth. From what Chry could see, the knobs down his back curved like hills. Some knobs, visible from the nakedness of its upper body, punctured the skin to reveal a smooth, white gloss. It was as if Onvi were decaying before his eyes.

I have to stop it, him, that thing. It's going to hurt Vion. He'll die if he's hurt anymore.

Chry did not move.

"You were so self-centered that you got your wife and daughter killed. But that's fine. Fine and dandy. They weren't the only ones you killed with your hands. Not through selfishness, oh no, that would be too easy, wouldn't it? Wouldn't it be, you hungry hound?"

Onvi was talking to Vion as if he were a sleeping baby in his cradle and it didn't want to wake him up. It touched Vion, too. Its fingers fondly slapped his cheek, and when Vion did not answer, gazing above unawares, its hand went back and forth across his cheeks while it asked if he was listening and why he wasn't listening and was this why he could never drink enough? It never got its answer and instead stopped and stared down at the brute. Chry couldn't see its eyes but felt the danger exuding from its pores.

Chry did not move.

"Nay, I know what you did," he whispered and then screamed. "You *killed* them. You killed *everyone*!"

It slammed its fist against Vion's chest. There was no time to react. Vion spat blood over its hand, but that did not stop it. It raised its fist again.

"They fell down, they fell down, they all fell—"

It wouldn't stop slamming its fist. Every time it completed a thought, its fist came down. Each time, Vion made helpless sounds from his throat. The force made his body jerk.

Chry was shaking now, and he was crying, and the tears were spilling in gulfs, and he didn't know what to do, but he couldn't just do nothing.

This is not your choice but your—

I know, I fucking know, so why can't you just leave me alone for once and just let me be here by my—

"Pathetic, why so *pathetic*!"

The thing was snarling and had reckoned that two balled fists were better than one. Raising up and throwing down its fists was like the sacrificial stabbings of the Novanian tribes.

Vion barely made a noise. His head rolled around in a trance.

"Pathetic. Die already you filthy animal. We should have ditched you in Raminus but *noooooooooooooo*, Bar didn't like that. Bar put his hands up and said no, no, no, not my lovely Lanke. He can't…"

Vion was going to die. The next time its fist came down, he heard a crack. The chest. The ribcage. The heart.

"But no matter. I'll just do it my—"

Chry slammed into Onvi. His impetus threw them over Vion as they slid and rolled through a patch of mud. Its slimy skin induced an instant disgust, but Chry would not release his grip.

Initially, the thing did not squirm or resist as they rolled. Its limbs were as loose as rope, for it did not expect a boyish coward to *actually* defend the brute. The shock did not last. When they came to a stop, dressed in the brown liquid of nature, it had the realization that the boy *had* acted and that its arms *were* restrained. Chry heard a gurgle of discontent then the thrash of resistance. It squealed incoherence. It tried to violently squirm out of his hold and Chry, on his back, had to continuously adjust his grip. Its skin was lubricated with the pus and blood of its pores. It was not the same as Ambia who bluntly threw her arms around like clubs but more like a slippery Dry-Mouth having bathed in a muddy pond.

Truly, Chry did not know why he was holding on. This was the beast, and its maw opened wide to swallow him. Fear shocked him like a shot of lightning. His ears were pulsating and moments hastened by as recollections. But that was it, wasn't it? He was acting, he was trying, he was doing *something*. He could not wallow in his own self-pity. He could not tell Ambia or Onvi or Bar tomorrow morning (if there was a tomorrow morning for the Runners) that Vion was dead. Despite their bickering, Chry knew Ambia loved the brute as she would an uncle. She forced him to sit while treating his wounds on more than one occasion, and no healer who hated a man would force them to sit and heal. Only passion could drive her actions. And no matter what he said now, Chry reckoned Onvi enjoyed having a bear to prod at. If there was no audience, there was no show, he had once said. And Bar thought of Vion like a brother. Within the Lanke, they were called (what had Onvi said?) Gods-Brothers. That had to mean *something*, right? And Chry guessed, somewhere inside him, too, that a Runners' life without Vion was a Runners' life not at all.

He was not thinking about this when he had tackled Onvi. He had simply tackled Onvi. And thus, he had ended on his back and held Onvi with his direness, adjusting and readjusting. His arms strained tightly as to pop the muscles like bands of a saddle strap, but Onvi kept slipping from him and yelling "Let me hug him. He needs a great, big HUG." Chry was already slimy with pus and blood and had to close an eye because one of its liquids stung his eye and had to hold his stomach again, so he wouldn't upheave onto Onvi and make it that much more disgusting and slippery. He did not make it an excuse for himself. He would hold on. Clouded through his mind was the sole objective of not allowing Onvi to kill Vion.

There was nothing else.

And remind me, how long can you stay like this before disaster hits?

The thought gave Chry pause. Within that pause was a hesitation, and with that hesitation came Onvi's squirming and success in slipping from his grip. At first, Chry had his arms beneath Onvi's armpits, but that hesitation allowed an arm to worm beneath his hold. The escape was instantaneous. Onvi shoved the grip away and threw his arms aside. The thing jolted to its feet, making a mad dash for Vion.

It was his body again that responded. Chry swiveled around on his rump and lurched out to snatch its ankle. Grasping and then pulling, his hand sliced down. There was a strained, watery rip like wet parchment tearing as the skin of its ankle jerked down, pilling at his hand like the wrinkled skin of a turkey. Chry made direct eye contact with the tendons and bone of its ankle, a vivid array of strings from a lute he would see Harlequin play at the Brew Beetle. But instead of beeswax, the strings were crafted from tissue and flesh.

The thing flopped onto the mud which splattered and caught Chry in the mouth. It wouldn't stop. With hands and a spare foot, it scraped at the mud and threw clots back into his face. He was nearly blinded, spitting out the mud as he tried catching the other leg with his free hand. Each time, it was kicked away. Once, its sole jammed into one of his fingers, feeling like a hammer slamming the bone through his knuckle. Biting back a howl, Chry still did not let go. Both his hands were around its ankle now, but its skin was slipping off like a sock.

I won't let you kill him, he thought. *Never. Never.*

He held tighter, tighter. Onvi was making ground by knuckles, dragging Chry behind it. In wild desperation, Chry would dig his knees under him to stop the advance only to slip, fall, and be dragged some more. Onvi was closing in on Vion, hands away.

His grip was so tight, his fingers became moon-white. Its ankle was weaker than a bundle of twigs when he heard and felt a crackling between his hands. At first, the thing was shrilling "Let me at 'im, let me at 'im" with spittle flying everywhere. As the crackling magnified, as the space between his hands narrowed, there came a strained spell of grunts before a soul-wrenching screech. It dropped onto its shoulder and kicked pathetically at his face.

The foot patted his brow, cheek, eye, but Chry held and held and squeezed until the tendons and muscles he held stiffened still. This was something new. He was about to fight and struggle with whatever possessed Onvi for Eulgash knew how long but now it had locked shut. It wouldn't move.

Lying prone, bearing a scratchy pant, Chry wiped his eyes and peered with one at an unresponsive Onvi. Its bones and muscles were stiffer than tree bark, and it laid there with its back toward Chry so he could not reckon its expression.

Then, from an act of stillness, its head jerked to the right so far it resembled a fisherman's hook. It would not release. It reached an angle that convinced Chry his neck would break. And words...

"Don't hurt me," it pleaded. "Don't hurt me. Don't hurt me. Don't hurt me."

Eulgash could Onvi ever tie his tongue and shut his mouth?

Immediately after its last call, all functions loosened. Its body rolled onto his back with a thump. There was no tension left, but Chry did not trust it to release his grip. He held his ankle where he could feel the shards of bone through the mangled skin and flesh. Nor did he believe that Onvi's mouth would not blunder again.

As if to confirm this, it let out a febrile cackle.

"Chry to save the day, again. Oh, again, again, again."

Its arms waved above in a grandiose gesture, not even regarding Chry.

"Part of the family now, Chry. Yes, yes, you are. You're with a buck and some does and will love the Runners til death do us part. Part of the family. Soon to be a death in the family. A Death in the Family. He he he."

Chry was so dumbfounded he almost let go of the ankle. Thankfully, Onvi did not try to attack Vion again.

What the plos is happening? he thought, blinking quickly, head spinning slowly.

He didn't get an answer. The performance Onvi was acting in had an audience of thousands perched on the branches above. He cackled and swooned, and Chry would have been intrigued if it came from an Onvi clear-skinned and clear-headed.

Mayhap Aimee knows, he thought groggily. *Or mayhap no one knows.*

But even thinking became strenuous. Exhaustion homed within Chry. He was huffing hard. The world began tilting from side to side beneath the crones of Onvi. Objects, trees, and people blurred together into blobs. His grip of the ankle loosened. The surge made him feel as if he could not go on.

But you have to, someone said from beyond, above. He thought it was Aimee. He made it sound like Aimee. He still wanted to see her again. *You have to keep going.*

Chry nodded but swayed precariously on an elbow and eventually dropped onto his chest. The coolness of the mud accepted his body as well as his mind. Noises were heard. Mayhap Onvi. He needed to stop Onvi. He had lost the ankle. He patted for it but couldn't keep control before his eyes and ears closed to a mad, unappeasable laughter.

II

Wild vegetation thrived, but Ambia's trail did not falter. Here, further into the Forest, the trail resembled more of a calm and steady stride. No longer was this Ambia erratic, desperate, or leaving a bloody trail. The step Bar followed was light and barely left an imprint on the leaves, contrary to her once lurching and ungraceful step that snapped twigs and crushed undergrowth. It made Bar more attentive to his search, increasing his stops to hunch down and survey the land. Nevertheless, he never lost her trail. Behind him, Hearth's golden glow brushed at the scarce undergrowth grabbing at their ankles.

It was enough.

But never could he stave off the thoughts of how filthy he was. His inner thighs and crotch chaffed to where every handful of steps he'd have to adjust himself. The watery shit that Hearth would not cleanse had smeared down the back of his thigh and dried there as a prickly crust. The piddle had dried too, but he reeked nonetheless. He could smell the virility departing from his loins. It repulsed him as a decaying offspring at the altar would repulse a god. Furthermore, there was no foreseeable future where he'd rid himself of this discomfort, not until they returned to camp. He had no Silver Oil or water to cleanse himself. He could have gone bare but when he had tried doffing his trousers, Hearth told him to forestall these unnecessary pleasantries and forge onward.

Normally, this would be a cause for argument, but the circumstances were fragile. He could not predict how much time Ambia had left. As such, her survival depended on their swiftness, and a potential dispute proceeded by an unpredictable conflict would compromise her chances of survival. He could not lose Ambia. Also, as much as he loathed to admit it, there was a strong possibility Hearth could revert him into that unconscious, mad corpse he had been when he had shat himself. Neither Admah nor Ambia would benefit from this.

Bar bore the filth. His fist shook with a bloody urge. Bar pressed forward. They did not speak a word.

With only Hearth's glow providing warmth, the night descended into an unforgiving chill. Bar had to bite back a shiver. Like her steps, Ambia's course straightened from its sinuous and unpredictable path. She had a destination, and she knew where it was. And although this was a forest (like the High Forest in Ontinia or the King's Forest in Lomano), their travels led into lifelessness—the vines that would sometimes crawl up the hulking trunks of the Depanens disappeared, the undergrowth wasted away into greying roots, and the already scattered trees distanced themselves even farther. They'd go for strides without revealing a bole, sometimes a furlong. Regardless, they could never reckon the stars nor the silver slit of the Moon above them. Only the smiles of shadows.

During their search, Bar nearly tripped into a small ravine, dainty to the gorges and dingles he experienced in Halomotas. A pebbly scree clattered down its slanted face, and Bar had a flash of a rolled ankle. Hearth ceased behind him. Its presence was the stillness of the earth, but he felt the impatience within its warm glow. This time, it would not heal him if he injured himself. It would not accept excuses. He wouldn't either.

Heart calm as a hawk, Bar hunkered on his haunches, a natural, perching posture for his surveying. Below, along the extent of Hearth's glow, he discerned a stream dried centuries heretofore. Down the slope slid a depression within the mishappen pebbles to where its scree spilled onto the rugged stone of its riverbed. Ambia slid down into the ravine (less gracefully, he assessed) but, nevertheless, they were on the right track.

Bar was just as ungraceful in descending the slope. In an effort to be cautious, he slid more than he trod, and the crust of filth across his rear rubbed naggingly against his trousers. Hearth flowed down like a gliding dove. Reaching the bed, sitting on his haunches, Bar appraised the stream. Ambia had not climbed the opposite slope for the face of pebbles was as flat as a tilted wall. He regarded the bed.

Archaic stones protruded from a rough sea of limestone like

wrecked flotsam. The occurrence was unique. Every rock was as jagged as extracted ore, for Bar assumed that water had not flowed through here since the days of Pactus over two hundred years heretofore. Nor could the wind slice through the Depanens to chisel the rock. The landscape remained undisturbed by nature and thus made Ambia's disturbances obvious.

Across the limestone and leading down the stream were the unnatural but faint abrasions of footsteps. They were little more than scuff marks to the stone. If they were in any other forest, he'd consider if the abrasions were left by an animal. Regardless, he would have disregarded the possibility. The abrasions bore a straight path down the stream to where any other animal would have wandered for sustenance and left smaller, inconsequential tracks. Farther downstream, he stopped to examine a vomit of excrement and dampness across the stone. This was not the droppings of a deer or the scat of a bear but the slop of human diarrhea. Within the cool air, it steamed afresh. Beside it, the damp patch smelled of how Bar smelled when Hearth first revived him: acidic and strong, a reek.

She recently relieved herself, he reasoned and rose from his crouching.

This was all he needed. Their pursuit bore promise.

Without a word, he trekked down the stream, leaving behind the ancient creation to its ruin. Hearth followed on, quiet as quietus.

III

The stone stream ended as a trickle back into the barren underwood. Just like so many other aspects of the Forest, the stream was depleted of life long heretofore. The pitch-black night pervaded. Their brushing footfalls rushed into the lifeless silence. The silence stared back.

Not long thereafter, Bar came to a whistling whisper followed by a distant sound of rustling leaves.

Not the whispers, he surmised. He had too much experience with the Forest whispers to forget how they sounded. He did not feel that bridge to insanity. These sounds were more natural: a gentle wind before the genesis of a storm.

More strides forward gave into a wind's kiss. It brushed against his skin to remind him of what her touch might feel like, how they would love when the day arrived. Bar clamped his teeth together. He needed to concentrate. They were nearing. He could feel her.

Then came the soothing voice of Hearth.

"We near. Her presence beckons."

Shut your whore mouth. We—

There was no logical reason for why there was a wind. From what he had seen at the stream, the Forest had not known the weathering of wind since the days of Pactus. In addition, the Runners had not felt any wind since first entering when they had traveled through the gentle zephyrs outside of Neco. But here, it was alive and singing, and the Forest gave no hints as to why.

Oh you know why. You're nearing Ambia. You're closing in.

Bar tucked the intuition away for thereafter. They pressed onward, and as they delved deeper, the wind grew to a loin's grumble then to a roar. Like the sudden snap of fingers, it came alive. The caresses condensed into shoving. Unseen boughs moaned above them. Bar squinted and lifted an arm against the oncoming gales. Somehow he knew they were directed against their progression with the full force of removing them.

Like the unpredictability of Novanian dancers, it uprooted the loose soil, needly leaves, twigs, and stones to bombard him. The leaves and twigs flicked off his stoic countenance, and chipped stones smote against his thigh, off his elbow, and beneath his left eye. He had a thought of the devastation to be if one of his eyes were lost.

He disregarded the threat and braced himself to stride forward. He knew that whichever way the wind was pushing him was where he would find his Ambia.

The screeching whistle of wind overwhelmed his hearing, and he could perceive nothing besides the cloud of dirt before him, twirling like an earthly night tinted in a golden glow. Behind him, Hearth strode true. It did not resist or stumble for it never swayed. It did not ward away the flying debris for it was never hit. Somehow, there seemed to be a protective field around it deterring debris away from its being. It did not change its demeanor. It could have instead been strolling through the peaceful streets of Odu.

Soon, trudging forward became a war in not being tossed away. Brawling with Vion would have been an easier endeavor. Scrapes of bark careened past his glare. Tears brimmed, ripped away from his eyes. Gusty talons clawed through his gambeson rippling like a flag.

It was the whispers doing, he knew.

Bar unsheathed one of his twin blades and stabbed it into the dirt, anchoring himself against its fusillade. With a white-knuckled grip, he'd haul himself to the sword, take a sturdy stance, then lift and stake the sword farther in front. His progress was unsatisfactorily slow like a stallion with a splintered hoof.

Even so, Hearth was ignorant of the struggle. Its hood never fluttered, and it did not need to anchor itself. Frankly, it seemed to be waiting for him to proceed rather than needing to resist. It was another aspect of Hearth's perfection that would have vexed him if not for his total concentration on his circumstances.

Further forward, the wind became a coil: the closer Bar got to that imaginary exit, the more pressure it bore to bounce him back. It utilized every tool and effort to protect, contain, and exclude him.

It would not contain him.

His skin pulled taut, his bones shaking with the pursuit of ambition, heart wailing, gritting teeth, expelling a roar from his stomach. The whispers would never win. They would never keep her. She was a Runner. She was *his*. *HIS*. Not theirs, *HIS*.

That truculent, little shit of a tempest bellowed rejection again and lashed out with a final effort. Blinded by tears, Bar jerked himself forward, yanking back on his sword. This time, he did not hit a wall. Instead, his shoulder shoved into a space of nothingness. The gales ceased completely as if he entered into the eye of the storm.

He hurtled forward, tumbling and crashing into a clearing of luscious…grass? He could not tell. The sharp contrast of light blinded him. His gambeson skidded across the greenery. There'd be more stains—green now. Green, fucking *green*. Somewhere, too, he realized he did not have control of his sword. He did not know where it was. Being filthy and tumbling and lacking control solidified the feeling of helplessness he bore. He was careening. His life was careening, and the ambition he pursued and sacrificed for was slipping from his reins.

It was their fault. *They* were to blame.

He rolled onto his back, his impetus halting. Though drained by traversing through an otherworldly tempest and unable to slow his breathing, he did not lay supine. That revealed weakness. Instead, he rolled onto his side and forced himself onto his knees. He attempted to stand but tumbled onto his hands and knees again.

Weak, weak

Exasperation flashed but faded.

Others are watching. They're always watching.

On his second attempt, he succeeded, swaying slightly as his hand groped for a support that was not there. After he calmed, his fingers assessed the tenderness of his cheek. No acute pain, but the points to where the stones smote him were aching. Perhaps the bruises were inconsequential. Nevertheless, Bar had enough of these improprieties.

He needed to find Ambia. Without her, the future was abandoned.

From behind him rose a melodic timbre.

"As to be expected."

He immediately knew that Hearth was addressing him and his stumble. Its words incited him. Twinges of gall boiled from within. It was too easy to give in. It was what he had in store for those who vomited their bale onto the innocent. Suffering must be alleviated. But as he had dealt with the voice, he resisted. As he had dealt with the tempest, he resisted. As he had dealt with the whispers, he resisted.

He resisted.

Yet he did not need to keep his temper tamed. He looked up from his toil, and what he saw flooded his temper beneath a wave of pure awe. From slits to round raptness, his eyes climbed to the sky as would a newcomer to the crystal edifices of Cadaqu. He was awestruck. All he could do was stare—stare at what could not be fathomed.

IV

They entered into a clearing shaped in a perfect circle to where a vigil of Depanens rounded its edges. The trees were close to each other now, standing strong amongst their watch, and bearing a height that would have impressed if not for the tornado before him. Its body was crafted from black smoke swirling slowly like the quiet stalking of a panther. It did not move away from the center of the glade, and contrary to what they experienced outside, there was no wind here. In actuality, the air adopted a strange stillness that lingered like dust. Above, its head could not be discerned. It punctured the night sky without end, obscuring any stars and clouds across its path. Along the ground and around the foot of the tornado circled a stripe of dirt like a ring to a black finger.

For the moment, Bar merely stared.

Questions beckoned him. How had this colossen managed to elude the Runners and everyone outside the Forest? Its height would be obvious from beyond and should have been a beacon for the people of Neco. That it wasn't gave prudence to another idea.

Those whispers must be concealing their presence from outsiders, he thought. *Perhaps with an illusion that not even the mages at the Temple of Illusion could match.*

It was possible. The peculiarity and marvel of this clearing could also be linked to Simul and his trek to what was then called the Forest of the Received. From what Bar heard from Domum, Neco, and Cadaqu, after Pactus fell and Simul departed from the Forest with the refugees of Pactus, trails to Pactus became untraversable. This, as relayed through their familial stories, was when Admah first experienced the madness of the Forest and did not dare travel more than a day's journey into its depths. Thus, Simul was the most logical explanation, but to be certain was impossible. What he heard from Admanites was folklore. The truth was left untranslated within Simul's journal. That he could not confirm his suspicions aggravated Bar.

If only he still had that journal.

However, these questions soon became numb to his objective. Ambia—

Ambia, yea, Ambia

Where's Ambia

We need Ambia

—was who he was here for. And she was here in the clearing. His gut told him so. But where was another question.

Upon closer examination, Bar reckoned the Forest itself was different here, too. The Depanens huddling around the tornado like pious Followers of Sospes retained a liveliness that died heretofore. The undergrowth and vines returned and were attempting to intrude into the clearing. Green and white lichen climbed bark. Bodil mushrooms rested on fallen Depanens. Bar thought he reckoned a large shadow between the tree trunks. When he looked again, he reckoned the shadow as a lone buck, its rack an ambitious endeavor, its snout uplifted and sniffing as if searching for someone or something. It gave Bar a scrupulous look and then returned into the brush.

Here, the Forest was alive and thriving...Everything besides the circle of dirt—no flowers, no undergrowth, no plants, no greenery. Lumps hid beneath its soil.

None of this, though, could hold Bar's attention. He couldn't find her. His eyes combed through every blade of grass, every whisk of the tornado, every branch of the Depanens, but could not find her. His palms began to sweat.

He slewed his eyes toward Hearth.

"Where's Ambia."

It was not a question. It was a demand.

Hearth did not respond. It liked tormenting him, he reckoned. It

450

liked the way he gritted his teeth and squirmed and shat and piddled himself, and it especially liked how he was suffering. It then gestured a perfunctory hand toward the tornado.

"Look for yourself."

He did but reckoned nothing. The immediate thought he had was that Hearth was lying to him. But he did not truly believe this. Despite the loathing he felt for Hearth, the spirit was not a deceiver.

Even so, his lungs were near to expelling vehemence when the tornado, at its base, blurred into thin shreds of opaqueness. These shreds were like faded, horizontal stripes branded across a black beast.

His aversion diminished.

Bar...No, he could not say he knew for certain but more like he had an intuition. His legs strode forward. Those opaque shreds—the tornado spinning calmly around them as black rivulets—waned so the weak strands of moonlight could penetrate its translucence. Within its center sprawled a limp and prostrate body.

There was no mistaking her.

He winced when first sighting her. The worst crossed his mind— death and the tainting of her elegance. Either or would have devastated him. But seeing through the tornado's translucence, Bar saw that Ambia was not only safe but cleaned and cosseted. Her skirt had cleared of smudges, tears, and retained a vibrant forest green that was once faded from her travels with the Runners. Her satchel hugged her. There was no blood. There was no dirt. Her frizzled, brunette hair she never brushed was now smooth and braided into one, long braid over her exposed shoulder. The skin along that shoulder was olive and dewy, and he immediately experienced an urge that told him to touch that shoulder, to kiss that shoulder, to embrace her. Only once in Cotana when the Runners were separated for a Son had he confronted this influence. He was always with her, and when she was always with him, he could control his attraction, the desire appeasable to ambition. However, the possibility of losing her exacerbated each.

She was the most beautiful thing he had ever seen.

He could hardly withstand it but contained his legs from sprinting.

He approached the tornado with an outstretched hand, his feet drifting over the circle of dirt, his fingers brushing at the translucence.

There was only one objective now. Only one was needed.

Ambia

We need Ambia

She's our hope

She's your—

"*Stay away!*"

Bar was blown away, hurtled off his feet and flung across the clearing as if the tornado had grown a voice of fierce gales. Like a frantic leaf, he tumbled across the grass, rolled, and then slowed knuckles before the trunk of a Depanen.

A bruise blurred his vision. He felt a metallic liquid trail down the corner of his mouth.

From beyond, he heard the petulance of the whispers screaming, "*She's safe! Safe with US! NO MORE BAD MEN! NEVER!*"

These whispers—which didn't seem accurate now that their voices were so deafening—sounded like they were approaching from every direction. From his throat rumbled a moan of disorientation. He should have expected, when approaching the tornado, a disturbance such as this but was too infatuated with Ambia to regard his circumstances clearly.

Even this was a distant thought. The most immediate feeling he had was annoyance. How *dare* these whispers think Ambia was theirs. Those irksome, whiny, petulant children exploiting her as a maternal figure. She was *his. HIS, ALL HIS!* Their selfishness would undermine the salvation of Admah all for the coddling and protection of a mother. She needed to be released. She needed to commit to her role through the judgment of Admah.

But the intentions are all the same, don't you see?

It was the voice again. Not the whispers. The voice from within.

You understand this, yea, aye. They want Ambia like you want Ambia—all to themselves. Her touch, her moans, the birth, the crying, the nurturing, the smiling. Yeah. The smiling. That'll be her only reason to live after who has left her?

You.

After you—

Recumbent, Bar heaved himself onto a knee and wiped a rill of blood from his chin. Small scrapes sullied his face, gambeson, and trousers. His close-cut hair that had grown to touch his ears since cropping in Viamous was disheveled. The aches covered over the disgust he felt from his crotch and rear, including a bump across the curve of his skull. It looked innocuous from the outside but made everything he perceived slightly off as if he were standing on an imperceptibly slanted incline.

Along his Discernments and beside him stood Hearth, staring at him with its irksome indifference. Somehow he had tumbled right next to it.

Excellent, he thought scathingly. *I am surrounded by those I despise.*

Breath seething, Bar shot baleful eyes at the tornado. It still billowed placidly around its focal point but, as if to conflict with this behavior, it expelled another outburst.

"*Mommy will* never *love you!*" It shrilled. As to annoy him further, the transparency of its tornado darkened into obscurity. Ambia, their "mommy," could no longer be seen. "*Never! Never! NEVER!*"

Bar spat aside scarlet defiance, wiped a forearm across his lips. He could *hear* the whispers now. They were not warring inside his head as it had been in the Forest but coming from the outside, from the tornado and trees as one childish voice, a shrill-pitched eight or nine-year reckon within a tantrum. That too made the whispers easier to interpret.

Hearth remained still, arms crossed, golden eyes observing. It knew how to appease these whispers but was holding back. No matter. Bar needed to think about his approach. He could not coerce the whispers in returning Ambia and would need to persuade them from a different vantage.

From his knee, Bar teetered to his feet before dizziness overcame him. He had risen too fast. White lily pads bloomed against his sight, partially blinding him. His balance distorted, a bundle of bricks shoved inside his skull. Then, the dizziness subsided, his sight cleared, and his head realigned.

He gave himself a breath before resuming.

"We have not come to hurt Mommy nor threaten your safety. We have simply come to converse."

Threaten, scream, bellow—

"*NO MORE VOICES! NO MORE THREATS!*"

Bar winced. No mortal man could withstand the shrillness of its scream. Deep within the recesses of his mind, a vile snickering implied this would not end. He would never escape. He'd never be free. Yet, Bar stayed calm. He needed to if he were to have any chance of recovering Ambia.

"Yea, I agree. There should be no threats between us since our goals are of the same ilk."

Their wordless mumbling heightened but did not madden his Sensations. He felt the whispers scrutinizing his every move and word.

"I hope, instead of violence, that this night, the Runners can show you how far we are from the entities you believe us to be. That we have not been sent to harm you but have, instead, arrived here to request the healing of Ambia for—"

"*MOMMY! MOMMY, MOMMY, MOMMY, MOMMY!*"

Their screeches, their excruciating pitch, ruptured his hearing and vibrated his sockets. He expelled a cry. He was forced to shove his hands into his ears. All he could perceive was that ringing.

"*SHE'S MOMMY! OUR MOMMY! NOT YOUR MOMMY, OUR MOMMY!*"

The screeching reached a peak where palms on eardrums could not mute them. He'd have to visit the Moon to be rid of its discordance.

For however long it took, the whispers did recede but left him in devastation. A colossal bell rang inside his skull, leaving him with its pestilent reverberation. His right ear bloodied his palm and numbly buzzed. After the screeching halted, Bar nearly dropped to his knees again since he could not balance himself. He could not control his swaying. He felt like his feet were hundreds of hands below him, and his upper body was a pendulous piece of cloth, susceptible to the faintest winds. He was suddenly thirsty and could not piece the tornado into a single, solid body. It separated and rejoined, separated and rejoined. His right ear was soundlessly buzzing.

This was not working. The compromising thought of asking Hearth for assistance manifested but was just as quickly tossed away. He would not ask. He would not stop. Not whiles Ambia was still within that damned tornado.

"Yea, she is your mother," Bar continued with a hoarse throat. "I do not doubt this nor try to say otherwise. If I have offended you, I thus express my sincerest apologies."

Bar chanced a step forward. The ground was unstable, but when he did not fall, and the whispers did not retaliate, Bar tilted his head into what he thought was a bow.

"Please accept my deepest sympathies."

He heard the whispers as muffled noises. Their words were beneath the realm of human awareness and sounded like Desert Beetles scuttling across the brain. Bar squeezed his teeth together and awaited a response.

"Where's-" The whispers hesitated and then said, *"Where's scary voice...What...What have you done with...with it..."*

Gingerly, Bar rose from his bow and curved a gentle smile. He was reaching them. The whispers were creaking the door open to trust and would, if he had more time, open fully.

This proved promising.

A chilly cloud plumed from Bar's lips before he took in the cool air to speak. He stopped mid-breath. His smile shriveled. His stoicism stoned. It was returning. The voice was returning from—

HERE, YOU LITTLE CUNTS

No, he thought but its reaction was abrupt.

"NO! NOT HIM! NOT THE SCARY VOICE! MAKE HIM STOP! MAKE HIM STOP! HE KILLING MOMMY! MAKE HIM STOP!"

The peals rang out again but were now a congregation of deafening tones. Bar cried out in agony. His palms were shoved into his temples so far, they felt like breaking inward. The pain would have been a relief. The noise inside his ears could not be silenced. Everywhere and anywhere his Discernments had gone awry.

There was no hiding, no escaping, no silence.

Mommy's going to scream, little ones.

Its rictus carved through his brow temple to temple. Whatever was happening outside of Bar was unattainable.

Beg for salvation. Beg for her cunt. Beg for her tits that will be sliced off and pinned for everyone to—

"NO! MOMMY WON'T DIE! SHE'S MOMMY! OUR MOMMY! AND MOMMYS DON'T DIE! NEVER DIE! WE'LL DIE FOR MOMMY! WE'LL DIE BEFORE-"

Before we slit her throat?

Before we gouge her eyes?

Before we give her a—

"NO! NO, NO, NO, NO!"

A gush of crimson seeped from his ears. He could not hear himself. The only way he knew he was screaming was through the vibration of his throat. He dropped to his knees, again, immobilized by the noises of the past: home, despair, savior, promises, espionage, assimilation, upbringing, war, Caravan's Demise—

Caravan's Demise

The caverns inside his skull quivered before that name, a name branded to his ambition. The clinging of steel on steel. The rumble of hoofbeat. Sweat. Sun. Hills. Screams. Faces. His face.

He could hear nothing besides his face and that name.

Caravan's Demise

Caravan's Demise

Caravan's Demise

Caravan's Demise

Tears stemmed from his grief, remembering forever.

V

The whispers flowed to this vessel, that which they called Cavas, as the concord of a small child whimpering for his mother's bosom. They did not know what to do, how they had come to be, or where to go next. In essence, the spirit would bestow the breath of life into its perpetual suffering.

At first, the spirit allowed the human to involve himself for the mere purpose of observing his failure. It would not go as far as to say his failure to retrieve his subordinate gave it satisfaction, but knowing the man was as impotent as it suspected reaffirmed its suspicions. He was no threat to this realm. Its otherworldly beings would absolve him of life soon enough.

Affirming this, it could proceed.

As it passed the aforementioned man hunched on the ground in a fetal ball, a whisk of its presence touched his shoulder. Tension had withered him into a feeble creature which amused the spirit, but after its aura wrapped around him like a warm, wool blanket, relief loosened his muscles and joints before he could flop onto his side. It was a pathetic display of feebleness. Clearly, he needed more than its presence was willing to give. The trail of blood from his eardrums insinuated as much.

The man gasped like a Toadfish on land. He shivered. It left him and regarded the tornado. The whispers were there, emerging as a call for help. Its golden illuminance limned the edge of the tornado. As it approached, the black smoke seemed to shy away from its embracive presence, but it knew of their true yearnings.

Everyone wishes for a Hearth.

Its whispers quivered with reluctance.

"*Wh-Who are you? Are you the man without the voice…You don't sound…We don't…W-who are you?*"

Radiating conviction, it felt the whispers flinch from the unknown, reorienting themselves when no suffering transpired. Around the being, its aura shoved aside the claws of darkness as it entered the ring of dirt.

Beneath each step, there was a soft crackling sound.

"You are safe, my children," it soothed. Its gentle words were the panacea of troubles. "The horrors which have plagued your innocence have long been removed from these lands. Safety is the climate for which you live in."

The spinning of the tornado did not yield from its gentle pace, the whispers did not hint at change, nor did they allow for Ambia of Pulchrit to be discerned.

All the same, its resolve was inevitable.

"I-I don't believe you..." The whispers reverted to a reserved withdrawal. *"You're with the bad man. He has scary voice...And...And scary voice is going to* hurt *mommy. We have to protect mommy. Mommy likes this place. We made it nice for mommy."*

It gazed into the smoke. It did not need to express any sentiments physically for, through its aura, the whispers could understand its intentions.

"As reproachful as it is, I must admit to being in his presence. I cannot and shall not deny this. Arrogance, vanity, and tenacity rule my associate if I should bestow him so high an honor. Nothing more in his life impels him otherwise and thus his vacuity is evident for all the realms to witness. As you are conscious of, he is a frightened and filthy man, conceited to his desires, damned to his ways. Certainly, I wish not to condone nor desire to condone any of his obdurate actions. The composition of the human race should not be based on a soul so crude in its virtues."

The whispers swirled. It resumed without resistance.

"That being said, I, despite my capabilities to do so, shall not prevent him from doing as he pleases, for it is, while I travel within this vessel, not the reason I have been created nor is it my obligation to manipulate what lies ahead."

"Then..." The voices stuttered. *"Then why* were *you created?"*

When it halted at the tornado's edge, the smoke at eyelevel billowed outward as if dropping a tiny pebble into a pond, its dark waters rippling outward. That was it. Soon, the smoke smoothed again.

The spirit regarded the tornado in full and then set its eyes forward. It was as if the whispers were in front of it as a two-legged mortal. The waves of smoke absorbed its glow.

It resumed.

"I have been created to alleviate hearts burdened by sorrow and woe. I remain within your realm to steer the innocent from disaster and to guide souls onto a new epoch. I am here for the vessel. I am here, my children, for you."

"*F-for us?*"

"Yes, for you. And for you, I shall give my utmost salvation."

They hesitated.

"*But…We…How can we trust you…?*"

It situated a reverent silence between them. When it felt the whispers nearing uncomfortability, it resumed as if not hearing what it had asked.

"I converse with those beyond. I have sought them as equals and have lulled their worries. I am cognizant of those who once resided in Pactus and could not alleviate themselves from the horrors that plagued its lands."

"*You…You mean…?*"

"Yes, I have seen to their company."

The whispers could have sniffled.

"*We…We want Mommy…And…And Daddy…*"

Hearth nodded once.

"Your wills are principled to the light of your souls. Thus, hear me. Know that, withal I am capable of, I alone cannot bring tranquility to their eternity. They are restless. They require remedies far from what I can readily bestow them—kith, kin, swains, Coyces. Mortals whose perturbed souls need those that were meant to carry their name onward but were stolen too soon from their posterity."

It tilted its glow above at faces that could not be seen.

"They await your arrival, my children. They harken during the day, weep during the night, to the kindred they have lost but have not forgotten."

The whispers uttered a long, undisturbed silence. Then a sniffling, a childlike sniffle from the boy that had encompassed the whispers so far. Now, its weeping was fragile like a porcelain vase. The spirit would carry it upon its bosom.

"We want to see daddy again. Want to-to see momma."

"You shall see them once more."

The single, boyish sniffle then separated into others with intonations from a range of children—boys and girls, tykes to adolescents, tones from soft-spoken to loquacious. They sniffled together but eventually swelled into a cacophony of uncontrollable weeping, vying for attention to bloat the clearing with their grief. They were like an orchestra of woe. The spirit remained quiet.

"It took our fadileda and left me alone and a-afraid and-"

"I want to see my mommy, I want to see my mom-"

"Fada said we'd be safe. Fada said me and Ellis if we go with old man to Forest we'd be-"

"Daddy...Where daddy? Where-"

"I wanna be hum with mamma and dadda and coyor and grandpapa and-"

"I'm scared...I'm scared, *Coyces. I...I don't want to be here anymore. Please, take me home. Take me to me hillie hill. I want to play on me hillie hill again with mommy and daddy and me fadileda. Take me home, Coyces..."*

It placed a hand flush with the tornado wall and sealed its golden eyes.

"As you wish, my children."

VI

Bloody trails dribbled down Bar's inner ears and around his lower jaw, now drying as a flaky crust. The sound in his right ear was a constant buzzing that barricaded noise from entering. His left ear heard sounds, but they were as if submerged in water. He did not hear what

Hearth or the whispers said but could faintly hear the cries for help.

Resting on the tornado, Hearth's palm manifested a golden glow as if coursing from its eyes—homely and pure, one correlated with Ambia and her Amuias, magic utilized in numbing the body before mending the broken bones of the Runners. Continuously, the hand brightened and waned as to search for the proper luminosity. Then it balanced. Afterward, the gold suffused into the smoke.

At first, the magic was like golden cracks crawling across obsidian stone, but the gold soon engulfed the blackness of the tornado's lower banks as would pouring a honey poultice into a tankard. No smoke was left undisturbed. It scaled the tornado leaving behind a coruscating curtain. From what little he could hear, the farther the gold ascended, the more the weeping faded until nothing could be discerned besides that incessant buzzing. The tornado was becoming a pillar of mid-afternoon sun, tapering to a sharp point that pierced the clouds. Bar, on his knees now, had to squint as more succumbed to Hearth's will. Where the shadows once hid none could. No presence was left in the dark.

The sublimity of what he saw before him consumed any bodily aches or feelings of isolation he had. Sparkling dust danced across the skin of the tornado, awaiting further instruction. Hearth released its hand and took an indifferent step backward, its eyes cast above. Bar could not hear the whispers wailing anymore, but there was a mumbling of some sound that seemed contained within an enclosed space. Through the buzzing of his ears, he concentrated on discerning what they were saying but couldn't.

As he was concentrating, something soft and warm landed on his ear. Coolly, he touched it but whatever it was had melted into a tingle of warmth. He bent his head back and regarded the flicks of golden snow falling from above. Or that's what its texture and appearance seemed like. Its touch, as was with the first, was not cold but instead a brick's blaze. Then he saw another fall, then another, and another, until they came in a shower like shining snow during a calm Swason. Depanens edging the clearing held the flakes in its canopy as tiny stars.

461

The first that landed endured but eventually dissipated. Yet, more were dropping into the clearing than could depart and made the landscape a field of dandelions, the Weary Moon eclipsed by its luminosity.

He continued to peer at the skies, these flakes touching his cheek, warming his skin, and evanescing. Initially, the tornado looked the same as it did heretofore, but after two cycles of new snow replacing the old, he discerned the head of the tornado dispersing as a glorious fountain. That's what was creating the snow. The flakes were springing down from its center.

Any mumbles or whispers were gone now. He waited for the fountain to descend below the canopy, gushing out founts of warmth, and as the remains of the tornado dipped below his person, he saw her—sprawled, inert, and innocent, the same as he had seen her before the whispers had stolen his view. The only difference was that between him and her was a sparkling sea of gold. He could not see nor feel his feet. Hearth was standing off to the side, but he did not recognize it. He could only recognize her.

It almost did not feel real. He thought it had to be a lie, another illusion conjured by the whispers to deceive and deprive him of her wellbeing and of their future—the passion to be had during their inevitable night together initiating the arrival of a posterity who will live on after them. Forever upholding his name. But there was also his body, his loins stirring. That never happened heretofore. Sex and lust did not appeal to him as did other men, but now his body was reacting to her as if it did.

What was this feeling?

It was no time to think. Impulse lurched him forward, but his mind struggled to register. He might have been calling for her, lips mouthing her name. He might have tripped and fell. He might have felt the rush of snow dragging him back to days of comfort and rest. He might have felt warm.

There was but a fierce focus on his blessing. He was there. She was in his arms, his cradling the delicate attentiveness of a king to his queen. Strands of clean, brunette hair stuck to her lips. A transcendent paleness glowed across her olive skin, yet, as he had first seen, any scrapes, cuts, and bruises she had were cleared. He placed his blood-stained ear on her bosom. He heard what he wanted to hear.

Buh-bump

...

...

...

Buh-bump

...

...

...

Buh-bump

...

...

Alive

Barely...but alive.

Relief hugged his lungs, releasing the strain building for so long it had become thorny to his throat. His hands brushed the hair off her lips, threaded fingers into the base of her braid, and lifted her head tenderly. He closed his eyes and laid his forehead on hers, his lips so close they ached for release.

She's alive, he thought.

Bar huddled beneath the warmth of a golden sea to conceal a joy that could not be contained. This and the wetness streaming down his cheeks.

She's alive.

VII

The man dropped to his knees to embrace her. It was of no consequence to the spirit. Suspicion took precedence.

It turned away from them and bent down to the patch of dirt beneath the sparkling sea. As its golden surface dissipated, the spirit again discerned the lumps protruding from beneath the dirt. It could feel his presence on those lumps, from a time heretofore, as well with the whispers. It dusted off the thin layer of soil to reveal sullied white objects—curved, connected, but separated into multiple rows of slender rods and gapes. Some of the rods were cracked with hollow insides. Some intact. Its suspicion proved precise.

They were ribs, the small ribs of a child.

VIII

"Those bones. They were children?"

"Quite so."

Bar was following Hearth back to camp. After they departed from the clearing, it had strode forward without the need for conversation. It knew where to go. Now, cradled in Bar's arms was Ambia, a warm comfort. At times, she'd nestle closer into him and rest her head on his shoulder, making what seemed like the innocent mumbles of slumber. Her respirations were shallow and serene. Her leather satchel thumped against his thigh after every other stride.

Hearth did not slow. It did not need to; it lacked the need for rest. In contrast, Bar's bones had grown heavy. Energy used whiles searching for Ambia forced his fatigue back, but without the excitement of rescue and with the monotony of a long journey back, exhaustion returned to drag at his eyelids. His body wanted him to drop, to sleep within the undergrowth and hold Ambia in his arms forever. He would do neither. He needed to pry information from Hearth. He needed to bring Ambia home. He needed to absolve himself of filth. Thereafter, he could rest.

Silent, Bar waited for Hearth to explain further of what it knew about the children and the bones. It almost seemed like it wouldn't.

Finally, the spirit said, "The bones and the whispers are the same—weary souls from the time of the Fall of Pactus, when the Forest was of the title The Forest of the Received and when Pactus was escaping from the Scar."

"Who summoned them?"

"Simul of Pactus."

"How do you know?"

"I know."

Bar held in a retort. *They could have been there*, he reckoned to himself but did not continue along this line of thought.

"So Simul summoned the souls of these children from their bones. Could they possibly be Kemals?"

"They were Kemals. That is of no doubt," Hearth answered. "He, Simul of Pactus, would have the prowess as the Guardian of the Temple of Death to employ their bones to summon them."

I could have used my swords then, Bar thought. *The Spectral magic Lorka taught me.*

A lost opportunity. No matter. The knowledge could be utilized for another day.

For a time, Bar allowed the conversation to peter out and regarded the canopy of the Forest above. Its differences were striking. After the last of the golden sea had vanished, the clearing became as it should be—still and empty without a tornado or whispers. When they left, the illusive boundary separating the clearing and the Forest was absent. No tempestuous winds. No resisting. This he had expected. What he did not expect was the transformation of the Forest.

It was as if the three of them were entering the Forest through Etherine again. The deadwood, if there was any, was overcome by a thriving understory—huckleberry, Elos, ferns, sorrels, mushrooms, a spread of Depanen needles, and a diversity of shrubs and plants he could not reckon. This made the Forest more pungent than it was heretofore, pervading with the odor of duff, decay, and vegetation. No wind was felt. The Depanens were still spread thin, bearing less than a furlong between each. However, unlike heretofore, they had opened to the night sky. Animals appeared, too. The squirrels had returned. Finches, too. Yet, he could only perceive the shadows of them since light from the Weary Moon hardly reached the Forest floor and

Hearth's glow could only carve a slim path forward. He did see signs of their presence—piles of mixed nuts within the large hollows of Depanens, pellets of dung, nests of straw, needle leaves falling from above. There was also a deer which, he reckoned, was the same buck he had seen in the clearing with its full, clutching rack like amorphous claws. Now, there was a smaller doe beside it. They were along the outskirts of his vision, grazing for nuts on the Forest floor.

However, he could hear none of these living beings—the buzzing in his ears had overwhelmed his Discernments, making hearing impractical. During their trek, he had sneezed and found he could distinctively hear air blowing out from his left ear. He assumed the other ear would have been the same if it was not clotted with numbness. The best he could reckon of this was that there were tears within his ears, but he had not experienced an injury such as this heretofore so could not assess it further. Ambia would know more. Either or, his circumstances did not bode a fortuitous future.

That doesn't matter. Nope, never. That pretty little thing in your arms, she's yours. She'll let you do anything to her. You've saved her. You're her prince. Her crotch will be gushing. More than the fountain we saw.

Fuck her Bar Fuck her

Bar ignored the voice and asked a question arising from his Sensations.

"How did Simul obtain these bones? Did he kill the children? Did he bring the bones to the Forest from Pactus and then bury them?"

"That is a question for those who no longer walk with us."

You do not know then, he thought and pressed.

"Why then? If you cannot tell me what happened to the children, divulge to me why he did it. Why would he create a Forest which drives mortals mad?"

On this, Hearth remained silent and did not speak again on the matter. Yet they both knew this was the question lingering. Neither his readings of Simul's journal or Hearth were of use, and the uncertainty upon the topic rankled Bar. Perhaps it was to keep travelers from

466

wandering through the Forest and into the Void. Perhaps it was to keep the Void from wandering into the Forest and into Admah. Perhaps it was an act of desperation to flee from the Void and the Scar. Simul's journal would have revealed the answer if he had finished its translation; Bar was certain. The journal would have told him.

Just then, Ambia curled closer into him and pawed tenderly at his chest where the three scars were. Her soft touch did not provoke the recollections associated with these scars, and this eased him from his initial tension. He did not prevent her from touching the scars.

Quietly, he strode through the night.

Bar's Revelation

I

Bar reckoned the obvious—Onvi had gone mad as they all had but, surprisingly, Chry had prevented Onvi from killing Vion. Courage was not a natural attribute to the boy and was not what Bar expected from him. As such, his presence within the Runners might further complicate his plans to retrieve the gems.

They reached camp to where Hearth and Bar tended to their own pursuits. The spirit drifted to Vion to tend to his wounds. The leader made a circuitous path around the sprawled bodies of the boy and thief, cautious of Ambia in his arms. They did not stir from their slumber, Onvi snoring like the rumble of an Asunio earthquake. Both were coated in mud from their tussle. Onvi's ankle was injured, but the sparse moonlight and dim coals did not give enough light to reckon the mishap. Even so, any injury to Onvi was inconsequential. They could always acquire another thief. Perhaps not one as skillful as Onvi and one not as emotionally integrated, but a thief nonetheless.

Bar lay Ambia in her tent and then cleaned himself outside with the Silver Oil from his stallion's saddle pouch, thereafter donning an extra outfit acquired a year and a half heretofore at Whitewall. Before leaving Ambia, he had removed a Sun-Fire's Embrace from her satchel. This would help his ears recover. He was certain he would also need to consume a Goldendrake to prevent the spread of Sepsis. But since the concoction was rare, expensive, and hard to concoct, he stayed himself in favor of Ambia's decision when she eventually awoke.

After cleaning, Bar returned to a campfire of smoldering coals and found that Hearth was no more. The pitch-black eyes of Cavas returned to its owner as he sat cross-legged along the outskirts of camp. Gazing directly at Ambia's tent, the mage did not interact with Bar nor any other Runner. He acted like he always had—apathetic and distant with cavernous eyes, a husk acting as though nothing of the previous night occurred.

Bar tossed a quick eye to the thief and boy. Their wounds were still neglected and unattended. In a growling sleep, Vion rested not far from Cavas. His knee was straightened and recovered from its shattered remains whiles tanned and clear skin replaced the stab wounds across his abdomen. There was no blood. Both injuries Vion had looked as if they never happened.

Why Hearth would only heal one Runner and not all three was beyond Bar. He would have asked if he reckoned the response would have granted him an answer. A blank stare was what he would receive if he asked Cavas now. Hearth was no longer present. It returned into the seal.

Perhaps I will never know, he thought and reckoned the last words Hearth spoke to him before they entered camp: "Never have the vessel summon me again or risk withering the seal further and unleashing spirits far more catastrophic than I."

As far as Bar was concerned, he would never be speaking with Hearth again.

Bar crouched near the coals, stirred them with the prod beside the ashes, stopped and stared at her tent, the woman who lay within. He planned to place Ambia in his tent, as to give off the impression of a protective partner, as he had protected her outside of Samit from those touching her. But when he tried carrying her to his tent, his stride shortened the closer he approached until he could not force himself to take another step. The voice was in there, cackling for him, compelling him to take her, to have his way with her. Bar merely stood there, outside his tent, stuck trembling as his legs resisted him. In the end, they drew him to her tent as if he were a horse being reined in. It felt like weakness. It felt like submission.

He did not stay in that tent. He couldn't—he could not be the man she wished him to be. The future was set. He would retrieve the gems, and after he rid Admah of those who were morally depraved, he would die. His plan for Ambia was to have her be his link to the future. Bar would leave and die, his child would be born, and Ambia would live on to care for his progeny. That was what would happen.

But staying in that tent now, with her, where his ambition was as still as water…Nay, he had to leave. The future of Admah, the alleviation of its suffering, was what he needed to concentrate on. Not the realization of a relationship.

Near the coals, Bar slumped into the hollow roots of a Depanen and hoped for rest. His body was heavy with exhaustion. The night sapped enough energy from him to turn any man old with deprivation. The mere thought of breasting the rest of the Forest and the Void did nothing to alleviate his fatigue.

What could was a restful night.

However, no amount of reasoning or forethought could alleviate the restlessness of his body. His elbow and forearm itched. He could not prevent himself from scratching and nearly breaking the skin. His tongue lapped in saliva. His heart, so unperturbed and steady throughout the years, now thrummed inside his ears. Those reins drawing him to her tent tugged gently but continually.

He could not fathom what was happening. It was not the whispers. It was not the voice. Something else was wrong. It was a feeling, an unconscious feeling arising that wished to do everything he could to protect Ambia after nearly losing her, one that wished to live with Ambia in Western Etherine on a house not so dissimilar to the home he had as a child whiles he sat on the porch chuckling at his children's laughter and play. He had almost forgotten what this…closeness felt like, would not have known if it weren't for the days before Caravan's Demise, having been alone and secluded with his thoughts for seven long years.

Bar shook the feeling away. This would not do. He could not give into idealistic wants. Children now were suffering in Cadaqu or needlessly dying in the Split. They would still die after Bar retrieved the gems, either from age or another unknown consequence, but in the least, they would not perish or suffer to the likes of the Pig Pen or Lanke.

He attempted to sleep within the hollow but couldn't. The feeling would not leave him for his thoughts. He tossed and turned but could not lay still. He was attentive to every branch and bark that prodded, rubbed, and dug into him. His eyes eventually squinted open to his tent, but what should have come the promise of rest whispered the disquietude of the voice.

Come closer, Bar. The children are gone, Ambia is tucked away, and now we can have you all to ourselves, the only children you ever need.

Bar, head nodding off in an untreatable doze, remained where he was.

The path forward was clear—beguile Ambia into loving him, lay with her days before retrieving the gems, assure the survival of her and their child—yet his body was rejecting him. Reason could not suppress emotion. Where had he heard this heretofore? Obina Mas? Yea, all those years heretofore next to the Ironskin Goat. He who pulsated over his chest now as one of three scars, one of three reasons why he would kill those whose immorality harmed the wellbeing of Admah—the Pig Pen, Dinglers, Lanke, Queen Ashera, pedagogues of the Temple of Elemental, Isadora. None of them deserved to live. It's why he lived. It's why he was here. It's why he had assembled the Runners. It's why he needed the gems. It's why he would leave Ambia. It's why he could not enter her tent and lose everything he had prepared so long for.

But you will, the voice snickered. *You will not be able to resist her.*

Sleep stalked the outskirts of his mind but never entered. Eventually, Bar closed his eyes. The deprivation of sleep did not stop his mind from wandering.

What would our lives look like? Together? What will our child look like? Will they have her hazel eyes or my brown ones? How about their skin? Olive, tawny, or mixed? Their countenance? The slimness of Ambia's or the stark angles of mine? Will my stark countenance suit a girl? How will she take being raised without a father? Will that prove detrimental to their development? Will they become as mangled inside as I have become? Will they become empathetic like their mother? Will a son become overly empathetic in that they will become meek and submissive? Will my son retain the assertiveness of a father in light of my absence? Will they—

Will they—

His chest jerked up. His eyes whipped around. He heard something. He thought he was about to nod off but before he could descend, he heard a whisper. It came from somewhere. Someplace. Or was it the voice again? He looked around, but the scene was the same as it was heretofore. He had trouble calming his breath. Although the voice regularly hindered him from sleep, a state he had grown accustomed to, this night proved challenging.

Sweating, Bar rubbed the bags beneath his eyes with the back of his hand and reckoned that he could faintly perceive the tiny hairs across his palm, the curvature of his nails, and the green of the Forest floor. It was no longer pitch-black.

Dawn was approaching.

And yet, he would order the Runners not to travel this day. He expected no resistance. The lack of progress would be detrimental to their supplies and victuals, but the Runners' need for rest was vital. They would not make it another day unless they recouped and recovered—unless Ambia alleviated them.

Ambia

Alleviating

Admah is too close to being alleviated to think like this, he thought. *I'm—*

Not close enough. No, no, no. Never close. Not close.

Sleep. Sleep before you can't—

You're scared, Bar. You're scared of the possibility of losing control. Oh we already know this. Scaredy scared of losing years of concentration and planning. You'd never admit it. You'd never want to admit it. But you're just as scared as Chry. Yea, Bar, you're terrified. You're afraid you might not obtain the redemption you seek for them. You're afraid you might like being a father and raising children and being joyful with the life you have.

But do you know what you fear most?

Your greatest fear is exposing your true intentions to the one you love. You can't bear to let her know. If she knows, her disgust will rot your insides until the suffering is a sore to bursting. For you, Bar of the Fanciful Ambition, this will be a punishment tantamount to the suffering of Admah.

His breath boomed eons. Behind the tents, a horse blew its lips. Thereafter, the remains of daybreak settled as the graveyard silence of a city before waking. Smoldering smoke carried its scent to the canopy. Through sagging eyelids, he peered through it to her tent.

Whatever the outcome might be—of this night or the end of his time—the least Bar reckoned he could do was to steer posterity away from the same suffering he had endured. If this was all he accomplished in his life, he'd deem his endeavors successful.

Whichever path that might be.

Beneath a slumberous and laborious breath, he mumbled, "I am sorry, brother." On his chest, the three scars sung a myriad of sorrows as he stood and staggered toward her tent. That night, the voice did not wake him, and he slept deep and innocent as if a child once more.

II

The Runners took the day to rest and recover.

Outside, Vion awakened marks after Bar entered the tent. Being miraculously healed when he had so clearly remembered bleeding to death on the Forest floor had startled him awake but left him just as quickly. Death would not arrive this time. He would not reconvene with her this day. As such, he reverted to his instincts as a past Lanke—survival. Since they must preserve their victuals for the journey to come, he started with water—searching for a nearby stream with his and Bar's water sacks in hand—then with food—squirrel or deer. He was gone for the rest of that day.

Cavas did not stop staring at Ambia's tent.

As for Chry, he was still unconscious when Onvi awoke within a blaze of agony, the pain exacerbating since he had not anticipated the opposite of pleasure after dreaming of the Restless Ryders. This was what stirred Ambia awake like a nudge, even though she was not aware of who or what it was.

At this present moment, she was pure feeling. What she first internalized were two kinds of warmth—the warmth of light on her skin and a warm, solid embrace she had curled into. She could not articulate what this second feeling was. It was…unique. She had felt warmth heretofore—the warmth of Pulchrit inside her bosom during its festivals or of the Nightwell's hearth when the fire roared, but rarely the warmth of human touch, of a man and his—

Disgust splattered the realization. It was immediate, a boil bursting open with defiling pus. It threw her into a state of danger. Frantic, she jerked away but was seized. Again. Arms imprisoned her. Hands groped, fingers wet. A nose shoving into the sheaf of her brunette hair.

She couldn't stop. The flesh under her skin shuddered. She was a weather vane inside a tempest, her bones juddering together. A breath inhaled her scent only to be heard as panting. She struggled to rip herself free before realizing that no one was touching her and no one was penetrating her. She was perspiring and trembling and thought she had screamed and her arm had nearly walloped against the tent and her eyes were wide and insistent on spotting their hands or their bodies or *anything*.

There was no one. No one was touching her. She was safe in her tent.

More than safe, in actuality. She felt…clean. There was a span where she had to calm herself from that horrible recollection before she could recognize that her hair was in a perfect braid and her forest green skirt, that which she kept dear to her from Pulchrit, was untattered and unspoiled. It was as if she were living in Pulchrit before the Black Rings.

How...?

With an unbelieving hand, she touched her bosom where her heart throbbed, her cheek. The last she could remember was the whining of her horse and the trek forward into the Forest. At some point, she awakened here without a clue as to how.

Questions swelled when she rolled over onto her side and saw that she was not alone. Her joints stiffened at first sight of the intruder, her mind tricking her into thinking it was them, *them,* but relaxed when she recognized that familiar gambeson next to her, albeit tattered and spoiled.

Bar, she thought.

He was laying with his back to her, curled away and into slumber. He made no sound with his shoulder rising and falling as a serene wave. It was the most tranquil she had ever seen him.

After her initial revulsion and within the puddle of her unconscious mind arose the faintest of desires.

About time he reached my tent, she thought, but her rational reaction was one of both confusion and empathy. Why was he here? Did something happen outside? Was he hurt? What happened to the rest of the...?

"Oh for the bloody bitch almighty, get me a—"

Her heart skipped. Ambia jolted up without realizing it.

Onvi, her mind recognized as she flew to the flap of the tent before hesitating. Ambia glanced behind her at the slumber of a man so far for so long and now so close for so short.

So many times had he felt so distant from her that she could not know if he was with them at all. Sometimes, his stoicism made it seem like he was on another Nomas entirely. Sometimes, he was the man she had dreamed of as a young woman—assertive, valiant, consoling her at the Hungry Wolf Inn. Now, he was here and—

Along her skin she felt their grips again, the bruises she had on her wrists, their moist tongues licking. A clenching of disgust inside her gut. She wreathed in helpless constraint, snickers an echo imprinted to her ears.

She couldn't. She thought she could be with someone again, but those men, how they had…

It was too much. She ran, Onvi's screams pulling her away.

Acknowledgements

Thank you to PJ Hoover and Patti Smith for editing my manuscript into a novel readers would enjoy reading.

Thank you to Lisa Markle, Mike Sheely, and Sheila Linton for reading the manuscript before it was edited (bless your souls, I do not know how you made it past the first page).

Thank you to the friends who took the time to read the manuscript before its publication.

Thank you to my family for being supportive of my wildest dream.

And thank you, Reader, who decided to give this book a chance.

An Important Note on Reviews

Dear Reader, I hope you enjoyed my book, and if you didn't, I am genuinely surprised you gritted your teeth and slugged through until the end. Good for you! Regardless, being an indie author, I am quickly discovering that reviews are essential to the publicity of self-published novels. Books of this nature soar or sink in large part because of the amount of reviews they receive, either on Amazon or Goodreads. The Runners Revelation is no different. If the structure of the book is the skeleton, the content the flesh, and the cover the skin, reviews are the words to express that you do exist as a human being and do have a story worth telling.

So, if you can, please leave a review on Amazon or Goodreads. I, as an inspiring author, would be greatly in your debt.

Sincerely yours,

Matthew Normand

Made in the USA
Middletown, DE
19 June 2023

32356841R30275